THE WOODSTOCK PARADOX

By Edward DeVito

ISBN 978-0-9910791-0-0

V4.7.2 – June 1, 2020

First Edition printed by Odin Prints
Portland State University Bookstore
Portland, Oregon, USA

Cover by HuangDau Nguyen

THE WOODSTOCK PARADOX, is fiction with a touch of fantasy/sci-fi. It is however, well-researched, and contains many historically accurate details. Most of the characters are based on real people and many of the scenes are recalled from actual events.

I Very Much Wish to Thank

Wayne Chadburn – for rolling with the project and paying bills while I finished it.

Mary Ellen McArthur – for financing the road trip.

Sally Reno, Denver – for her Woodstock stories, mentorship, and advice.

Bruce Spainhower and Eadi Popick, – for technical assistance and encouragement.

Rob Beckman – for his company on the road and belief in the project.

Cullen Howe & Jason Benton – for inspiring the story.

Tina Priest, Berkeley, c. 1969 – for a brief but beautiful moment.

The Brothers & Sisters at Dole Street, Oahu, c. 1970 - 1971

The Angels of Light, San Francisco, c. 1969 - 1972

Peter Sun, and Andre Illias, c. 1969 - 70 – mentorship and good connections.

Sea of Grace Circle, Key West, 1978 - 1981 and Tucson, 1981- 1989 – for providing a receptacle of magic

Marty Galean, at Cross-Cultural Studies Program, Tucson, c. 1984 – for introducing me to the Tohono O'Odham, and Cypriano Manuel, Tohono Elder – for sharing his Way.

A Nurse at Herrick Hospital, Berkeley, CA (Name lost to time) – for remembering.

Frank Brownell, Monticello, NY – maps and Woodstock stories, and Duke Devlin – historical assistance at Bethel, NY.

The Good People of Salamanca, NY – for their enthusiasm, friendship and historical assistance, especially, Carson Waterman – help with Seneca names, stories, and his enthusiasm and support, former Mayor, Ron Yehl, and Melissa Shaw at the Salamanca Historical Society, April Vecchiarella – for a wonderful essay of her memories.And, the Railroad Museum of Salamanca – historical assistance.

New York State Police – for historical assistance.

The Staff People at the Library of Congress and the USDA – historical assistance.

Staff People at Oregon Department of Transportation – maps.

The Historical Museum at Prineville, OR. – historical assistance.

And these References:
Woodstock, Three Days that Rocked the World, Edited by Mike Evans & Paul Kingsbury – in association with the Museum at Bethel Woods. C. 2009.
The Road to Woodstock, By Michael Lang, with Holly George-Warren. C. 2009.

"I want to be free!" he said with a rising voice. "No one will tell me where to go, ever again! No police! No judge! No PO! No foster folks! And if I'm anywhere where I think I am, I'm going to Woodstock!"

"Far out, man," Jeff praised in a drowsy voice. He sat up and rubbed an eye.

"Yeah!" Tina seconded with a clap of her hands. And then, puzzled, "Where's Woodstock?"

1 — Andrew

Arien Danner was all set to run. After nearly three weeks at Youth Promise House the very idea sent a shudder through his body, and as the days passed it was turning into a thrill. He was close – Oh! It was so close! The stupid rules and indignities crawled down his back. His nerdy roommate got under his skin so quickly it bit. It would be a piece of cake. He could use the simplest ruse, or he would just go; he would walk out the door and that was that.

Now the TV was on and this stupid news was coming out. What a drag! Just because Darvy, the Assistant Resident Supervisor, liked that shit – the fat-assed dick head – Oh God, he hated that blimp! (The kids all called him Larvy. Ha!) A smirk crept across his face. Larvy!

Dan, his roommate, stood in the door to the living room. Oh God! This guy was too much! All day, practically nonstop, Dan ran on with stuff like, "Hey, Arien, what's the duffel for? Practice isn't until tomorrow. You dropped out, didn't you? Three days and you dropped out. That's going to cost you, you know. You get no brownies that way, jerkin'it. And we know you're not getting a weekend pass. You haven't been here three months yet. There's nowhere for you to go anyway, right? So, c'mon, Arien, that bag's packed! Where you taking us? Don't I get to go, too? Are you sure you have enough T-shirts? And the ski jacket, did you pack that, too? That should have been my ski jacket, by the way. If Bert hadn't sent me on that errand I would have had it and I need one. Did you pack that, too? ..."

It was relentless. Arien decided whatever he was doing he'd have to keep it real simple.

"Oh what a larvelous program! I can't watch this!" Dan turned on his heel and disappeared up the stairs.

Arien couldn't resist the smile. Maybe Dan was so irritating because he could be cool, sometimes. Why couldn't he always be like that?

The front door opened. Arien could see from his chair in the living room that it was Bert, the Resident Supervisor, and some other guy he had never seen before. Who's this now? His smile turned glum. More "Staff" probably. Always more people he couldn't give a hoot about were shoved in his face. All these damn people! Oh, they knew everything; every little thing, but they were all strangers; strangers with all the power, who turn on you for the stupidest reason and then put you on detention. No phone calls. No free time. No nothing. It really sucks. At least in the lockup they didn't tell you one thing and then do another. At least there you knew what was what; you were in until you got out. But this. This damn place!

The stranger shot Arien a startled glance, how curious.

Youth Promise House was touted as an "independent living facility" but there was nothing independent about it. "Save your money," they said, so you couldn't buy anything *you* wanted. "Take your GED" – at their convenience, so you couldn't get a job with decent hours. You could hardly listen to your own music, wear the clothes you liked, let your hair be, and forget the piercings. Everybody had to go to Drug Treatment, too. Yuck. Bury me in mega borage.

"Hello," said Bert. The black man was jolly as he welcomed this guy into the room. Darvy looked up from the TV and gave a perfunctory nod. "This is Andrew," Bert announced. "Andrew is our new weekend Assistant Resident Supervisor."

Darvy moved his hands to his chest, entwining the thick fingers as he nodded again, but Andrew reached out to shake his hand and Darvy reluctantly untangled himself to reach from the chair.

Andrew shook vigorously, and, in spite of himself, Arien smiled again. Darvy had been caught off guard. Ha! He was such a jerk.

The man was youthful middle-aged, athletic looking, medium height and weight. But who was this new toon?

To Arien's surprise Andrew extended a hand to him also. It was irresistible. It felt good. Their eyes met. "And you are —"

"Arien."

"Oh. Neat name, fella."

Yeah right. But Arien felt sheepish. He'd been taken off guard, too. But then this Andrew dude looked back at him as if he'd been punched by a ghost.

"Come on," said Bert. "Let's see who else is here." And the new presence was maneuvered out of the room.

There was a let down. Darvy resumed his hypnotic attention to the television and the room sank into a cathode glowing emptiness.

The way Arien shook his head would have launched a fly into the air. There were thoughts that began to crowd him. He didn't want to grant any of them an audience. They might hurt him and his soul already throbbed like a festering wound. "I'm going out for a cigarette."

Darvy waved a pudgy finger.

Outside Arien took a breath of the chill evening air and fished in his pocket for his last cigarette. Then the idea fell into his head. His heart leaped. He gasped. *Now!*

Oh, he was so close. All he had to do was walk down the street into the night. He would melt away in the darkness and lose himself in the city. He knew the streets so well. The streets had been his teacher; all the people, the hustles, the excitement of the lights and the action. He longed to get high, to roll some sticky bud and suck down the delicious smoke; a thick wave of delight.

There was still another cigarette left! It was hidden bent into a corner of the box. *Not yet.* The thought itself was pleasure enough for now. It was his power to exercise whenever he wished. But it would be soon. He knew that. *Soon.*

Back inside the TV was turned off and the living room was dark. There was a light on in the kitchen. Arien could tell it was Darvy rummaging in the refrigerator again. That's my food! It was outrageous. Arien, when he was hungry, might be told, "No!" No explanation was required. But Darvy – Larvy – he could dip into the box whenever he wanted. But Larvy was Staff and Staff was All Powerful. The damn pig! How Arien wished he could just slap that fat face until it spun in circles.

"Bed time, Arien." It was not what he wanted to hear, but the voice was kindly. It was Andrew, this new Staff dude.

"Where's Bert?" Arien answered.

"Gone to his room."

"Can I have a glass of milk before I go up?"

"Yeah. Then bed."

That was easy. Is this guy a push-over?

In the kitchen Larvy was stuffing a sandwich into his face. Arien, with a stern look, dared him to say something as he opened the refrigerator door, but Darvy said nothing. He must have heard Andrew say yes. I can play them off, he thought as he poured the milk. Ha! It might prove to be fun. But then, he wouldn't have time for that. Soon enough, he would be history.

In the morning Arien was awakened by an unfamiliar voice. It had more of a melody than a bark. It crept into the depth of his sleep and coaxed him out like a thin beam of sunshine in a deep, dark place.

He sat up groggily and frowned when once again his awareness met the reality: Youth Promise House! Oh God! Another day in stupid Hell.

But not for long. Maybe today he would make his break for it.

The thought dispelled Arien's gloom. He listened to hear the morning's greeting repeated down the hall; first in one place and then another. It was the new Staff dude. Larvy was not there. The schedule must have been changed again.

Arien was on breakfast detail. It was a fluke. He got right out of bed. *Lucky!* He was first in the bathroom upstairs. Today would probably be the day he sacked this place for good! He felt an exultation of rising excitement as he stepped into the tub, pulling the shower curtain around him. It even aroused him. He looked down at himself, firm, wet, glistening, his eyes resting on the small birthmark on his pelvis (It was barely an inch from his penis). How he loved that thing! If anything fortunate had ever happened to him in his life it must have been this mark that immediately conjured a butterfly's silhouette. He was certain it set him off special in some way, and he had already found, to his delight, the babes loved to see it. It was so much fun to show it off! What a conversation piece. *Ha!*

He laughed aloud and did a tight little dance in the tub that ended with erotic thrusts at the jets of water. Oh today – tonight – I'll run so far away they'll never find me again.

Arien dried off, dressed, and then headed down to the kitchen. Mike, who was to do breakfast with him today, soon joined him.

Saturday mornings were devoted to major house cleaning chores. The whole place had to vacuumed, windows washed, floors mopped, bathrooms cleaned and sanitized, rugs shaken, even the outside porch area had to be swept and the yard policed for litter, so breakfast was not as much of a production as it was on Sunday. There were eggs to scramble, cheese to grate and toast to make. Mike was an easy person to work with and there weren't any delays or contentions.

Soon everyone was seated around the table in the small kitchen; seven in all - six residents - and Andrew, the new "Staff".

Andrew unnerved Arien. He seemed to look at him a lot.

"I don't want any eggs," Dan proclaimed.

"Who gives a shit?" Arien countered. Hands and food were moving over the table.

"Stifle it, Arien. We don't need to start the day like that," Andrew said.

"I want some cereal," Dan insisted.

"There isn't any. It's on the shopping list today," Mike said.

"Larvy probably ate it." Rob said.

The phone rang and Andrew got up to answer it in the front room.

Dan said, "Damn!" He shoved his chair back. It hit the wall behind him. "I hate eggs, especially scrambled!"

"What don't you hate?" Arien spat.

Gary was spreading jam on his toast and a large glob of it rolled out of the jar and fell - splat - on the table. He swore under his breath but the action broke the rising tension and laughter went all around.

Everybody knew the routine, so after breakfast the six young men at YPH's Salmon Street facility dug into their chores. Mike and Arien remained in the kitchen to clean up after breakfast, put things away, and scrub counter tops and the floor in there. They worked hard to get finished. Andrew told them he had authorization to use the van. He would take them up the Gorge for the day where they could get out and hike around a bit. As soon as chores were over they could go. That was incentive enough.

Soon Mike and Dan were sent out for snacks. Rob, Jerry and Peter were up in their rooms getting ready, and Arien lingered in the kitchen by the door to the office where he was suddenly startled. He caught a real hard stare from inside. It was Andrew, who was seated at the desk. His expression was intense.

There was an awkward moment.

"You look so familiar, Arien," Andrew said at last to the handsome, sandy haired kid with cat-green eyes. "You are so familiar!"

Arien tilted his head, raising eyebrows.

"Why, if I didn't know better," Andrew continued, "I'd say I knew you once."

"I - I don't think so." The boy hesitated. He was sure he had not seen this man before and his penetrating scan was uncomfortable.

"Well of course. It's impossible," Andrew admitted with a note of distress. "But it's a fantastic coincidence, I must say."

Arien shrugged. He was about to move away.

"It's really incredible. The way you hold yourself, your tone of voice, mannerisms, expressions, figures of speech – even your name..." Andrew's voice trailed off. He was visibly shaken.

Arien began to feel uneasy. He'd been though a lot in his seventeen years and he'd come to some definition of "strange". Now this was beginning to be like that. What's the game here? Yet, there was something about this new Staff dude... Arien couldn't put his finger on it.

The front door burst open and Mike and Dan stumbled in laughing. They both swept into the kitchen carrying paper sacks with bags of chips, fruit, candy and soda pop. Now the others were thumping down the stairs and soon everyone was there, pouring over the goodies.

Rob was already fussing because Gummy Bears were nowhere to be found, while Jerry and Peter grabbed the same chocolate bar and started a tug-of-war with it.

"Enough!" Andrew barked, coming out of the office. "Not now. Put it back. That stuff comes with us."

All along the Scenic Highway flaming trees glowed red and golden between folds of tall Douglas fir to be reflected like strewn embers on dark, green fields and rocks in turbulent, cliff-side streams. This, and the shocking sky of sharpest blue and boiling white puffs, the magnificent expanse of the glittering river between its great bluffs and the swooping birds combined in Arien an image of freedom with such an emotional intensity, and with such suddenness, he actually cried out! If anyone had been listening it would have sounded squeaky as he choked it, blushing, down. It stabbed him square in the chest. He was so glad he sat by a window. Surely nobody saw the tear he pretended to scratch on the side of his face.

Then there was a tug on his sleeve. He ignored it as long as he could, but with its persistence he turned to see the open bag of taco chips being offered by - of all people - Dan!

"No! I don't want any chips!"

Dan recoiled the bag with lavish disgust, as if from the clutches of a greasy, slimy creature.

"I'll have some," said Andrew. His eyes were firmly on the twisting road. Then he reached around. His glance met Arien's. "Beautiful! Isn't it?" Andrew exclaimed, as he took the bag of chips from Dan and turned back in one efficient motion.

Arien's heart tumbled. He said nothing but set his jaw and looked again, intensely out the window. He could hear Andrew say, "This is one of the finest views in the world and one of the finest moments to see it. I wish I had my camera! The light's perfect. It's Magnificent!

Dan said, "Andrew?"

"Yes?"

"Shut up!"

There was laughter and snickers from some of the others.

The thunder of the falls folded young voices in a misty blanket that sounded like distant barks and chirps. Arien was perched on a damp, mossy log, where he pondered a Frito between his fingers. He wondered how long it would take the mist to steal the crispy crunch away, until the Frito would lay limp in his hand like one of the glossy-wet autumn leaves all around his feet. His reverie broke when Dan sat down beside him.

"What do you think of Andrew?" he asked unexpectedly.

"Strange." He tossed the chip in the water and watched it spin away.

"He's cool Staff."

"He says he knows me."

"Oh - everybody says that."

"No," Arien said, "it's like he does or maybe, wants to."

"Maybe he does – know you, I mean."

There was a sudden lumph and splash where a rock was pitched into the water from the other side of the stream.

"Cool it, Pig Shit!" Dan screamed out. It was so loud it hurt Arien's ears. He winced. It was doubtful anyone on the other side of the stream could have heard anything more than a squeak though; the tumult was so powerful here.

Arien mused on what happened on the trail up to this place. His heart quickened its pace. Andrew was beside him and asked, "Didn't you find a Swiss Army Knife here once?"

"No, I didn't! You must be bonko! I've never been here before!" he'd answered. True, Andrew didn't seem like the others, but he was still Staff and Staff always pretended to know all this crap that just wasn't so.

Later he went up off the trail to take a leak. He opened the zipper and soon was following the arc of yellow stream down to broad ferns where it finally splattered on moss and some small rocks and dead leaves and – he simply could not believe his eyes – Awesome! – A Swiss Army Knife!

"Maybe he does, but he couldn't possibly."

"Couldn't what?" Dan asked.

"Nothing." Arien didn't want to tell anyone he had found the knife, least of all, Dan. The residents weren't supposed to have any weapons and if it got out he had a Swiss Army Knife – well, first of all, nobody would believe him. They'd surely say he'd been hiding it, or worse, he'd stolen it! But now, how the heck?

Arien felt chilled. He got up and stepped carefully back toward the trail. He worked his way around a very large, old rotten tree stump with some exceedingly slippery roots exposed. Dan followed closely behind and almost took Arien with him when his feet skidded out from under and he fell down hard on his rump.

Dan fought back tears, and swore a few choice words.

Andrew seemed to materialize out of nowhere. He brushed by Arien to kneel over the boy on the wet ground.

Dan started to pick himself up.

"Are you ready for that?" Andrew asked. He gently supported the boy's arm.

"Ow ow yeah, Dude." He struggled to his feet.

"Get on the other side of him, Arien, in case he slips again."

Arien didn't want to hold onto Dan but stood by as ordered. "Is your ass broke?" He inquired of the victim, cracking a smile.

Dan was not amused but he already stepped more strongly on his own and Andrew let go of him. He let Dan move out in front.

"You know," he said to Arien beside him, "I guess I'm glad you never were here before."

"Oh yeah?" Arien sucked his breath in and unconsciously slipped a hand in his pocket to grasp the knife he had there.

"Right, because this is all too crazy anyhow. I realize that the boy I knew who looked like you was a friend of mine a long time ago. It couldn't have been you. I haven't seen him forever. He'd be nearly my age now."

"When was that?" Arien was almost afraid to ask, but he began to feel some relief and even a bit of giddiness at the strange coincidence that happened earlier.

"It had to be in the late '60's sometime," he answered. "'68, '69. It was '69. I should know that, because... but, you know Arien, that was his name, too; Arien. It's so remarkable. Maybe he was your father, and you look just like your dad!" Andrew seemed to smile at the possibility.

Arien, on the contrary, grew dark at this mention of his father. His hand hurt. He realized he had been clutching that Swiss Army Knife very tightly in his pocket.

"Did your dad have a very cool birthmark anywhere near here?" Andrew pointed almost to his pubic area at the front of his pants.

Arien was quite unable to stop his jaw from its sudden, precipitous drop. He froze, flushing, able to hear the heartbeat in his ears. His eyes grew wild in their sockets. He felt like a trapped animal – but trapped with what he had no inkling.

"Did I say something wrong?" he heard Andrew say.

Dan, just up ahead, was watching now. Had he heard some of this? Arien ruled it out when Dan said something inaudible. The thundering falls and rushing water overwhelmed all but the nearest voice.

Arien, speechless, shook his head from side to side as if to ward off the improbability. Who is this staff dude? What's his game now?

"What is it, Arien?" Andrew asked. "Tell me."

Arien laughed nervously. "You wouldn't believe it," he said. He didn't believe it. Why should anybody else?

"OK." Andrew turned and slowly picked his way further down the trail. He moved Dan on before him. Arien watched with an uncomfortable combination of relief, amazement, curiosity, and a dawning desire to risk more openness. Maybe there was no game afoot. Maybe between them there would be an answer to all of this.

But no. The moment passed. It was better not to trust Staff, any Staff. Maybe it was a trick of some kind. He had been tricked before by adults he trusted. One of them was the pig that busted him and told him with a straight face it was for his own good. Then there was the creep who suddenly went off and beat him within an inch of his life when he was a little boy. He shuddered. What was the point anyhow? After today he would be history!

They took the freeway back to the city. There wasn't much conversation in the van. The boys had all worn themselves out on the trail and anyway, they had the music turned up too loud to talk. Arien admitted to himself this was another cool thing about Andrew. He seemed to like, not only tolerate any kind of music. Though the boys bickered over what played, Andrew merely acted as referee and never seemed to mind what was finally decided. Then Andrew pulled off impulsively at the exit for the giant Bonneville Dam. He turned the radio down. A strong staccato rap by a black group that Arien liked was playing. *"Colors. Colors..."*

"We have an hour yet before we have to go back," Andrew announced. "Let's stop and check this place out. I've never seen it, have any of you?"

Both Peter and Jerry said they had, but there were no objections. This was their first day out of town for a while and no one was in a hurry to get back.

"I'm staying," said Dan. My butt hurts and I don't feel like walking any more."

"OK," Andrew agreed.

The music on the radio stopped when everyone got out.

"Turn it on!" Dan said. "Turn the radio back on!"

"Sorry, Dan. I've got to take the keys with me."

Well, leave them here!" Dan pleaded. "I'm not going to steal the car!"

Arien laughed. "Yes he will, Andrew. Ha! That's what got you in trouble to begin with, isn't it, Dan?"

"Don't do it Andrew!" Mike added.

"Shut up, guys!"

Dan was getting pissed. This was too easy! "He stole cars," Arien warned, with a wide grin on his face.

"Yeah, and you got a sissy tattoo!"

To everyone's surprise Andrew reached through the open window and stuck the keys back in the ignition. The music returned.

"Let's keep this under our hats, boys," he said.

"Cool. Thanks." Dan was visibly pleased.

The others moved away up the black top towards the looming installation. Arien stepped alongside of his Staff. He opened the conversation that followed: "What was your friend, Arien, like?"

"Like you."

"Did he have any folks?"

"I think his family was from Berkeley, California..."

The others walked faster and were almost to the visitor entrance. Arien gazed intently at the limber but graying man beside him. It seemed his every revelation was a shock. Besides that, he had proven to be quite unpredictable; willing to bend rules. He actually seemed to like the kids, and was, no doubt, crazy or psychic, too. Perhaps he was more than that. Arien determined to get at the bottom of the mystery now. He was intrigued. There was no denying it. Maybe this man really was different.

"He was a cool guy," Andrew recalled. "At first we didn't believe his story. Then, I'd say, we all eventually did. Then, as if that were not enough, he became something new in the world, at least to me – or, maybe, it was really very old. He was so – far out."

"Far out." This was going over his head. Arien repeated the words with a grin.

"God!" Andrew exclaimed.

"Yeah, what?"

"Say that again."

"Far out?"

"Yeah."

"Far out!" Arien's grin broadened. And then it was checked, and evaporated when Andrew suddenly covered his eyes with his hands.

"God!" He heard again, but it was more of a sob than a word. "My beautiful brother!" And, after an awkward pause, "Oh, Arien, I'm sorry. You're so like him I can't bear it! That was over twenty years ago and I am not the boy I was – as you are now. How could you –? I mean –"

"Were you hippies?"

Andrew seemed to collect himself some. "I guess you could say that."

"Oh, cool! Jesus! Andrew, I'd give anything to have lived in the '60's."

"Ah!" Andrew croaked, and he began to walk quickly away.

The others had spread out and disappeared all over the complex, but Andrew sat in a heap on a low concrete wall down from the visitor entrance. He made no effort to keep tabs on his group. Only Arien followed, to linger by him.

"Hey, Dude, you okay?" Arien asked after a very long silence.

"Though I should know better, my friend, I want to believe that it's actually you here with me again."

Arien huffed. This was exasperating, yet, in spite of himself, he couldn't go away. Not yet. He searched for some way to move this along. "Can you keep a secret?"

"Sure."

"Promise?"

He nodded.

Arien took the bright red knife out of his pocket. He offered it up for Staff to see.

Andrew looked at it and said nothing. He just took it and turned it over in his fingers.

"I found it today, honest."

A cool breeze came up off the broad river. The day was turning inevitably towards evening. Some of the other boys had drifted back to the parking lot. Andrew followed them with his gaze, his eyes, however, were focused off to some unseen place. "I believe him all over again. Oh God! I believe him," he whispered. He gave the knife back to the boy. "You should scratch your name on it, Arien."

"I'll do that. Thanks."

"One more thing."

"Yeah?"

"Are you planning to run?"

"Shit." It was all Arien could bring himself to say.

Andrew didn't press. He looked at his watch instead and then back to the parking lot.

His eyes widened. "Whoa!"

Arien followed Andrew's gaze. "There!" He pointed at the other side of the lot where the van had been moved. "Ha!"

He lay in his bed staring up into patterns on the ceiling cast from the light in the hall. Contradictions held Arien now like chains of iron. Though the house was silent and sleeping his effort to rise up and go through with his plan could not overcome the enigma around this man, Andrew.

The boy cursed in a long, hissing whisper, slamming clenched fists beside him - thump - on the mattress. *GO! GO! GO! Damn it!* He churned his sweaty head from side to side and with a lurch threw the suffocating covers from his clothed body and, making a slight effort to be quiet; he got up and went down the stairs.

Instead of proceeding on out the door, as intended, Arien turned into the living room to throw himself on the tired sofa. He would gather himself. From there, he saw the light in the office.

He held his breath.

Papers shuffled.

Arien got up and followed the sound. Sure enough, it was Andrew, slumped glassy eyed over some folders.

The young man crept up until he got so close he could easily see these folders contained his own files! His name, Arien Danner, was right on top.

Andrew ran his fingers through graying temples. He turned, with a start, to see the boy watching him.

Arien felt a momentary tinge of fear. Maybe this man was obsessed. He braced himself for what might happen next.

Andrew's dark-ringed eyes regarded him. His chest rose and fell heavily. There was perspiration on his forehead. "I don't know how you did it," he said. When the boy didn't answer, he added, "I think, maybe, you are reincarnated. That must be it! You know, Arien, a long time ago I read a book by great Yogi who taught about wonders like this." He laughed softly. "And to think even your last name is the same!"

"Oh, Dude," Arien implored, "Stop it! Please?" He was growing afraid.

"I'm sorry, Danner, or is it Grove?" Andrew spoke softly; matter-of-fact. "I wish I could have said nothing at all." Then, he stood up from the little swivel desk chair and, reaching out, took hold of the boy in a strong, sobbing embrace.

Arien began to resist but was presently filled with a rush of pity for this poor, suffering man. The sobs were genuine. He melted into the embrace. It felt so good. Oh God!

"Hey. Hey now, Dude. Be cool. It's okay." He looked earnestly into Andrew's bleary eyes and slowly, gently pushed him back. Real tears were in those eyes, real tears. He couldn't remember a time that somebody cried over him. It was a new feeling; detaching, exhilarating even. He felt all of himself to be totally present: Here. Now.

"It was in the '60's you knew him?" The boy grasped for anything.

Andrew began to compose himself. "Yes."

"Say, did you go to Woodstock?"

The man nodded. "Damn! You don't know how many times I've been asked that. But yes, to answer your question, we did."

"Awesome!" Arien was genuinely impressed. "I'd give anything to be able to go to Woodstock." He sighed.

"Why?"

"Because it was so cool, Dude. It was really awesome. And a guy could be free there, live happy; be high." The boy's eyes sparkled. He glowed.

"It was a special time, indeed," Andrew agreed. "But it was not all sex and drugs and rock and roll. There was pain and struggle; hungry times - injustice."

"So this dude, you know – who looked like me, where did he come from?"

Andrew smiled wistfully. "The future."

"Yeah." Arien exhaled. He put his hands up on Andrew's shoulders and pushed him down into the chair. Then he turned on his heel and headed out through the kitchen, down the hall to the foyer, where he reached for his ski jacket from the stand by the front door.

He didn't hurry as he pulled the dead bolt and turned the inside lock. A cold breeze off the street pushed the door open.

"Wait!" Andrew called from back in the house, his face drawn and anxious. "Wait up! Let me tell you what happened at least."

Arien turned to Andrew as he came nearer. "Please," he said. "Let me find out for myself."

"Ok, Brother. You always were your own man. Namasté," he added tenderly.

Arien stood for a frozen moment. He was touched by the unfamiliar equality of this exchange, crazy as it was. For this still and silent space of time the strange man, the staff dude he had never known before was his brother.

"I never had a brother!" Arien's reply was choked with a rush of emotion. It was that old feeling again. It hurt so much. He fought it, swallowed it down, turned on his heel and walked out on the porch, down the steps, out to the sidewalk and away.

The evening was cold. He zipped his jacket up tight. There was an icy mist freezing to the sidewalk. Arien had to step carefully, flat on his soles without pushing forward, to keep balance. Spectral shapes loomed in the glow of the streetlights.

Everything changed in a moment.

The roar of a vehicle going much too fast for this neighborhood came up around the corner ahead. A car, weaving madly banged - CRASH - into a parked car, knocking out a headlamp, lurching like a drunken Cyclops to smack - BAM - into a power pole, ejecting a fantail-spray of glittering nuggets. The incredible wrenching sound of tortured metal, shattering glass and screeching tires split the night air with explosive resonance. Arien, frozen, terrified; watched the pole sway. There were sounds of falling-crackling-rushing-snapping above him as wood, branches, wildly exploding sparks and wire cascaded down all about in a spectral radiance of flying ice crystals. He tried to dash away – too late, sliding headlong to fall utterly trapped in a crackling ozone flash!

Silence. Distance. Gray nowhere. Drifting. Drifting. A far off light.

2 – Beyond any previous experience

He focused on the assembling image in his fuzzy head. A young man, about 20 years old, with long, flowing, brown hair was looking down at him like he was some kind of object. "Wow!" he said. "Freak me out!"

Arien looked dully back at him; up from the crazy angle he was at. It didn't make any sense. He tried to sit up. This fellow helped him.

"What happened, Brother?"

"I - I don't know." He struggled to remember.

"Maybe you better come with me, Man."

Arien stood unsteadily. He felt very dizzy. He smelled a burn odor. It was strong and acrid, like melted plastic.

"Wow!" the young fellow said. "You must have been in some heavy trip, Man!"

With difficulty Arien looked down at himself. Through blurred vision he could make out burn holes in his jacket. *Oh no!* His new Columbia ski jacket! He said, "Shit!" It sounded distant. The speech - his speech - was slurred. His stomach heaved.

"Eee-yeechh." The longhaired fellow barely stepped out of the way as stuff inside splattered on the sidewalk.

"Hey, Brother, you're in a bad way. Are the pigs looking for you? Anyway, we gotta get you off the street. My pad's down this way. You better come with me. okay?"

Arien didn't object. They started off, one supporting the other.

He tried to make sense out of what happened as they shuffled along. Something just wasn't right. For one thing this fellow who befriended him looked odd, even in the dim light of the street lamp. Arien took him for a punk slammer at first. He wore an open pea coat. You didn't see those too often. But it was the pants that really threw him. They were bellbottoms! The pants were covered with a colorful assortment of crudely sewn patches. Arien could see a pair of rainbow suspenders inside the open coat that held the pants up. The fellow wore beads, too. Lots of them. Arien thought he looked pretty cool - but those pants!

Then, there was something else. A light mist was falling. It was cool enough, but not cold. The branches on the trees along the street had something on them: BUDS and LEAVES!

Arien swooned. The partner who gripped him by the arm, quickly adjusted his balance to better support him. Arien was all mixed up. "No," he said aloud. "I'm good. It's okay."

"You probably are, man. "Are you high?"

"I don't think so." Arien shook his head.

A car drove by. It was an old car in really good shape. Arien watched it as it turned the corner ahead.

"Hey!" The young man exclaimed. "Those sneakers are far out!" He was looking at Arien's Nike High Tops in the circle of a streetlight.

"Far out." Arien repeated the words matter-of-factly. He chuckled to himself.

"Where did you get them, Man?"

"Look, Dude, are you bozo or what? Haven't you seen a pair of High Tops before?" He was growing irritated and stopped to stand when the incongruity of everything took hold again. Meekly, he relaxed, swaying a little like he'd been popping downers.

"Can't say I have. What's your name, Bro?"

"Arien."

"Cool. Mine's Blue Star. A lot of my friends just call me Blue."

Arien took this in. He guessed it was a street name. "Are you from around here?"

"I've been here a couple of months. I used to live in Arizona. Then I spent some time down in Frisco."

Another car wound its way down the street in the opposite direction. It was old but it looked really good, too. Arien followed its progress past some parked cars. They all had unusual silhouettes - low, long. He was feeling dizzy again.

The two young fellows came up before a big, old house that looked familiar to Arien.

"Come on in, Bro. You don't look so good." Blue Star helped Arien to move up the wooden steps and they went inside. Arien wondered what it was about this house that made it seem like he had been here before.

They entered a hallway and now went up a set of stairs. Blue Star opened the door and ushered Arien into the apartment there. Things inside glowed brightly in the velvety darkness of a room with a stuffy smell of incense. It was rather strong. There was mismatched "salvage" furniture on a worn rug. There were posters. The Beatles. Jim Morrison. Hendrix.

"Wow! Bitchin posters, Dude! Where'd you get these old posters?"

"Old? Say, Man, not that old." The young man in bells took off his pea coat and dropped it in the shadows of a chair, then went over to a record player and took out an album from what seemed to Arien like a vast row of them just beneath the player in some wooden crates. There was a faint hissing sound as Blue Star set the needle down, and Hendrix crooned out from the speakers.

Arien sat on the floor with his back against a worn-out couch. He was fascinated by this series of unfamiliar images, scents and sounds. Had his waking awareness ever held such fascination? He felt caught up on a wild ride. And then he let out a little "whoop" when his host took a shallow bowl off a cluttered shelf and began to roll some flakes in paper between his fingers.

Blue Star smiled. "It's real good. Just in from Nam."

"Nam?"

"Yeah, Man. Got it from a sailor on leave." His smile broadened. "Right place at the right time."

"Nam," Arien said to himself, wiggling out of his ruined ski jacket. "Shit!"

He stood up dizzily. "Bathroom?"

"That way."

He stepped carefully down a hall to where a door stood open. He switched on the light and saw himself suddenly in the mirror over the sink. "Bitchin!" The image before him was a genuine surprise. A handsome youth in wasted clothes, ragged and burnt, returned a green-eyed stare. His face was smudged but he was apparently unharmed. It was arguable that his new jeans were better than ever. They had holes in the knees now, and appeared to be well broken in. He would definitely need a new T-shirt. Arien thought the holes at the nipples of his chest looked pretty stupid. But -thank God! - His Nike High Tops were undamaged.

He chuckled at the small tabloid by the toilet. It had an exotic, swirly design on the cover, ***Rolling Stone, San Francisco, California***. "Hmmmm." Real collector's item. Eyebrows were up. His host was a most unusual dude. He washed his face and rinsed his mouth out before returning to the living room.

"So - a - Arien, are you okay, Man? Like, do you need to see a doctor?"

"I think I'll be alright. Thanks."

Blue Star lit his small, hand rolled cigarette. He raised it in supplication over his forehead and then inhaled deeply, and holding his breath, he passed it to his guest.

"Rad." Arien hesitated. Would he be picked up and turned over to Juvenile Detention? They would surely give him a UA. No way. That wouldn't happen if he could help it. And then, damn if it came to that! This was his night. He was free. What might happen tomorrow wasn't going to spoil it.

He coughed out a boiling little cloud of aromatic smoke. "Bitchin! This is good, Blue Star. Nam. You got to be bonkers. Ha! Nam. You mean, Viet Nam?

"Yeah Man. Honest." He took it as Arien passed it back and held it up in his fingers as if to demonstrate the fact. He inhaled again. "You talk funny," he said.

Arien burst out in a torrent of laughter. This was so absurd. Blue Star joined in. It seemed so funny. They both laughed to tears.

Footsteps and creaking on the stairs outside stifled Arien's outburst with a tinge of fear. He tensed when the door opened, but Blue Star barely raised an eye when two guys and a girl came in to sit down on the floor. Blue Star passed the joint to the new comers. It was as if they had been there all along. A fellow with a dark, dense, close-cut youthful beard and mustache, and long dark hair that grew out abundantly on either side of his head, not quite reaching his shoulders, took it first. He wore a plain white T-shirt, a fringed leather jacket with matching knee-high moccasins and jeans. The other boy looked almost normal. His fine hair, which was such a light blonde it was almost white, was close cut. His eyes were a deep blue. He wore black canvass tennis shoes, jeans, and a dark blue T-shirt. He also had a sweater tied by the arms around his waist.

Arien carefully observed the girl. She wore no make up or eye shadow, but she was very pretty. Her long, blonde hair flowed out over a heavy turtleneck sweater. Her denim skirt was cut short. It had a peace sign embroidered in yellow thread on it, down near the hem. He admired her boots. They looked real good on her.

Blue Star introduced. "I found Arien, here, on the side of the street, people. He was smoking! Like, man, he was really smoking, like he'd been on fire! Look at him!"

"That's cool," said the dude with the short beard. "I'm Otter. This is Tina, and that's Jeff." Everyone nodded.

"Were you on fire?" the guy who had been introduced as Jeff asked. He spoke with a soft Southern accent.

"I don't know what happened," Arien said apologetically. "I - I remember walking down the street. There was an accident, some speeding car. Damn. That's all. I just can't remember. I - then I saw Blue Star."

"Can you say where you were before that?" Blue Star inquired.

"Right - right down the street - I think."

"Where'd you find him? Was it near here?" Otter asked Blue Star.

"Down the block, he was lying near the curb and there was smoke coming off of him. It was out-a-sight! I didn't see any accident, either."

"Maybe somebody ditched you," Otter offered.

"Where you from?" Tina asked.

"I've been living in a group home," Arien admitted. "Right down on Salmon Street.

"Groovy," said Tina. "Like a commune?"

Arien smiled to himself. 'Groovy.' He shook his head in disbelief. He wondered why such a cool babe would talk so hokey. "Huh? Uh - no." His expression displayed his befuddlement.

The roach was passed to him. He took it carefully.

Blue Star put on another album. Arien didn't recognize the singer. He liked the song, something about a hurdy gurdy man. It wove engaging lyrics with a catchy melody and some cool guitar riffs

Good Energy.

Conversation dropped off as they smoked. Blue Star rolled another joint. Time slipped past. The singer on the record had the gentlest voice.

It began to dawn upon Arien that something wasn't right. For one thing, these people - with it, beautiful, real, were never-the-less into something that he could not relate to; it was beyond any previous experience, and Arien had always considered himself up to what all was going on. It wasn't that he had to be still to reason about it all, he only had to begin to recall the recent sequence of circumstances. He fiddled with a roach clip that restricted the flow of smoke. There. That was better. Too much now. He coughed.

His mind raced. The sweet smoke in his lungs had already taken him deep inside himself. Now the feeling in this room was so warm. It was very peculiar. He was so comfortable it was almost as if he were sitting in a room full of his "other" selves. He said this. He looked around at the people who were equally deep into the music, or their own thoughts, and said, "You are myselves - and I must be dreaming all this."

Tina laughed approvingly. "Shit."

Arien thought the way she said that sounded so cute. She was so hot.

"It's all Maya, brother," Blue Star added. It is a dream."

"Whose dream?" Jeff asked. "It can't just be Arien's."

"Brahma's," said Blue Star.

"So then, this Brahma dude, did he drop me in the same town I was in today?" Arien asked. It was about as philosophical as he had ever been. He trembled; enough, he thought, someone would see.

"No, that was probably Krishna," Otter interjected with a wry grin.

"Brahma dude." Tina said, and she laughed again.

Arien liked her laugh. *God!* He couldn't believe it. "Your such a totally rad babe," he told her. He blushed because he really meant it.

She delighted him with her smile. It was just half a smile. It was personal. There was only enough smile for him. Her eyes twinkled that smile, too. "Totally rad babe?" she said, cocking her head. It was like she was hearing this for the first time. How could that be? She was rad! He smiled back.

When the music stopped Otter started thumbing through the albums. He picked out a record and put it on the turntable. Again, it was something Arien had never heard - lots of tinkly strings, sweet voices, it reminded him of Irish music. As stoned as he was, he liked it. "That's radical," he said, scratching his face. "You people are into some cool tunes. Is it all old '60's music?"

Everyone looked at him. They seemed puzzled.

It was Tina who spoke. "What do you mean?"

Arien shrugged. "I mean, I like it. I like the sound. The records are cool, too. They don't sound like CD's, do they? You have so many records. I had a friend once whose dad had a collection like this. Beatles. Stones. You know. And lots of stuff - like this - I'd never heard before. These must be worth a lot of money. Where did you get them all, Dude?"

"At the uh... record store." Blue Star blurted, grinning. There were chuckles all around, and some perplexed expressions, also.

"Where? Downtown? That place down by Powell's that sells used records? Django. That's it. I've been there a couple of times."

"Django? Powell's? What town did you say you're from?" Blue Star looked at the others. He got blank stares from Otter and Jeff. Tina shrugged. "No, man. These are *my* records. I've been buying them since before I was in high school." Blue Star patiently explained. "I rarely buy a record used. I buy them when they come out, like everybody else."

"Wait a minute. Wait a minute!" Arien was getting pretty worked up. "Do you - you mean to tell me you don't know Powell's?!"

"What's Powell's?" Tina asked innocently enough.

"The big mother bookstore on Burnside, Babe! Powell's! Powell's Books!"

The silence was deafening.

Arien thought he'd pass it up. It was so outrageous it bordered on insanity. Surely they were messing with his head! But what was so unsettling was the perfection of the act. "So, you bought this one - the one that's playing now, for instance, new?" The veins in his neck were popping out.

"Yeah, so what's your point, Arien?"

"Can I see that?" Arien pointed at the album jacket on the floor beside Otter, who passed it over to him. *Incredible String Band. The Big Huge.* As if to prove Blue Star's point the jacket was in prime condition. The young people on the cover looked to Arien like a band of hippies if he had ever seen hippies. "Mega radical, Dude!" Arien exclaimed wide-eyed. "Are you pulling my leg or what? This is hippy shit from the '60's, right?"

"Well, where are you from, Dude?" Jeff intoned. He emphasized the word *dude*.

Arien's mouth opened in the universal gesture of incredulous people. He looked from face to face, straining for some acknowledgment of what he expected. Everyone was too serious.

"Okay. okay then. Somebody say what year it is. It's 1990, right?" Arien was making his point. His tone was intended to be sarcastic. It seemed ridiculous that it came to this, but it did. Now he waited, folding his arms, defying anyone to cope with the facts.

"Right. And I'm Rod Serling," said Jeff. He began to mimic the weird theme to The Twilight Zone: "Do do do do - do do do..."

"If you really believe that then it is probably true," Otter said.

Arien had an attack of paranoia. These people were playing with his head! His complexion whitened. He folded his arms tightly around himself and sat very still.

Tina shot a concerned glance at Blue Star.

"Be cool, man," Blue Star said. "You're with friends. Everything's gonna be okay."

Tina got up and went over to the visibly shaken newcomer. She smiled into his troubled eyes. She put her hands on his folded arms and gently untangled them, and took his cold, moist hands in hers.

He sighed. Now some old, painful thoughts invaded to add to his anxiety. Somehow he had messed up. He didn't know how, but he must have really scrambled it.

"Heavy trip," said Otter. "You should take more acid," he advised, grinning.

Blue Star nodded knowingly. He got up and interrupted the music to put another record on the turntable.

Arien recognized this, alright. It was Dylan. He'd heard Dylan before. He never could understand what the old hippies ever saw in him.

He relaxed some, though he still trembled.

There was something startling about the singer's voice now, as he tried to return Tina's smile. It was clear and melodic; haunting. Maybe it was just that he had never heard Dylan stoned.

Tina massaged his shoulders and the back of his neck. His tension began to loosen. He allowed his head to roll with the motion. God! She was touching him! It felt so good.

"Do you think I'm a geek?" He said softly to her.

"Geek? No. I think you're spooky but cute." The warmth of her voice rang true. It lifted Arien's spirits immeasurably. If he were a balloon he would have slipped through her grasp and shot to the ceiling.

"You got another doobie?" Otter asked Blue Star.

The group was silent as Blue Star rolled. He lit it and passed it to Otter, who seemed to caress the little thing. He inhaled with a beatific expression of reverence and pleasure.

Jeff passed. He took it and passed it to Tina, who passed it to Arien. She massaged his back now.

Arien stared at the joint he held. Moments passed.

"Bogart," Otter called.

Arien took a deep draw, held his breath; suppressed the cough as long as possible.

Now, Bob Dylan was wailing through Tamborine Man.

Arien said, "Wow. This is awesome. Totally rad." He gestured with all sincerity but appeared comical to the others. There were chuckles.

"Totally rad," Tina repeated, obviously delighted. That sounds so groovy."

"Original," Blue Star agreed. "This man may look kind-a straight, but he's hip."

Arien let these comments pass. He allowed himself to be amused by them, and he wasn't going to stick his neck out again so soon.

"Are you an Aries, Arien?" Tina asked.

He smiled; nodded. "You?"

"Gemini."

"Ahhhh. That feels good, Babe." He thought about asking how old she was. "When were you born?" he phrased it.

"March 10th, '52. You?"

He shuddered under her hands. Slowly removing his wallet from a back pocket, he took out a laminated ID card and offered it up to her. She let go of him, took the card and read, "March 22nd, 1973. Nineteen seventy-three!?" She squealed, "Out-a sight! Where'd you get this?"

Jeff got up and came over to have a look. He laughed. Shook his head.

Otter, also. "Well. I've heard of getting false ID to prove you're 18, or 21, but never zero! But then, now you have reason to believe yourself."

Blue Star didn't bother to move. "That's minus four, Otter. So Arien's from the future," he said generally. "And I'm from Jupiter."

Jeff sang, "do do do do - do do do do..."

There was laughter. This time it was Arien. Stoned. He had come from Hell to the Kingdom of the Absurd. Though absolutely nothing had been solved, his breakthrough was cathartic. He leaned back into Tina, who put her arms around him. Her hands covered the bare nipples protruding through his T-shirt. She teased them with her fingertips. They hardened as he expanded his breast with a careful, exaggerated intake of breath. He sighed, blushed, closed his eyes and melted into the sensations of pleasure that seemed to fill his entire being.

3 — What did you eat in the future?

"I saw the old cars!" he said. "This is awesome!"

"Totally rad!" Tina said with a dreamy smile. She still held Arien. Her soft cheek rested on his shoulder. Jeff leaned into some battered cushions against the wall by the record albums. He had fallen asleep. Otter and Blue Star were rummaging in the kitchen. Appealing odors of cooking food drifted in.

"I want to go outside before this dream is over. Or - is there a TV?"

Tina crossed her index fingers in front of him in a mock remonstrance to ward off evil.

"You don't understand," he said, stirring. "I think I may be crazy. But, maybe I'm not, you know?"

"No TV. But that's a radio." Tina slowly released her arms as Arien stood. He turned and smiled gratefully to her. She was so warm, so kind. It hurt. It was like he didn't deserve it and if he liked it too much it would be taken away. It was those thoughts again, the thoughts that ate him. By the second day at Youth Promise he had seen a counselor. Arien had been in no mood to see anyone at the time. It hadn't helped in any way, yet, to his chagrin, this shrink dude went right to the core with his searching questions like a hound on the chase. All it accomplished was to make Arien remember things he'd struggled so hard for so long to forget.

He found a function switch on the tuner. The light of the tubes inside shone out through vents behind it making visible patterns dapple the wall.

The radio came on. Rock music was playing. Some oldie. "Awesome! Even the radio's in on this!"

Tina watched him turn the channels - Classical, a car lot commercial, the news. The announcer said, "...that had been going on since Thursday. A student spokesman said that if their demands were not met they were prepared to occupy the buildings indefinitely. It was not known what action, if any, was planned by the trustees at Harvard. In other news, National Security Adviser, Henry Kissinger, told reporters today the planned four billion reduction in the budget was not likely to affect the war. He did not say if French overtures on behalf of the United States in Hanoi were being taken seriously by the Administration. President Nixon met with members of Congress in the Rose Garden for an offi - "

Arien turned the radio off. "In this dream I have no past," he mused aloud.

"I like that," Tina agreed. "You can do your own thing, Arien; be whoever you want to be."

"I want to be free!" he said with a rising voice. "No one will tell me where to go, ever again! No police! No judge! No PO! No foster folks! And, if I'm anywhere where I think I am I'm going to Woodstock!"

"Far out, man," Jeff praised in a drowsy voice. He sat up and rubbed an eye.

"Yeah!" Tina seconded with a clap of her hands. And then, puzzled, "Where's Woodstock?"

Gust-driven rain began to pelt the two living room windows facing over the street.

"Some things in Portland never change," Arien observed.

Blue Star stood in the entrance to the kitchen. "There's veggies in the wok," he announced. He sat down cross-legged on the floor with a bowl in one hand and a pair of chopsticks in the other. Soon Otter was there, too, sitting beside him.

"Thanks," Arien said.

"Oh boy!" Tina chimed.

Jeff followed them into the kitchen.

Though Arien was hungry he could not be sure it was food he saw here. The other two went right ahead. They filled bowls with clumps of half raw vegetables, sprinkled sesame seeds on it and poured soy sauce.

Jeff, observing Arien's reluctance asked, "What did you eat in the future? Did you press a button and it pops out?"

Tina burst out laughing.

Arien couldn't hold back his smile.

If there was any lingering doubt in Arien's mind it was dispelled in the morning. He awoke alone on the lumpy old couch covered with an army blanket, shirtless, still wearing his pants, and with his shoes and socks off. The couch smelled musty. Arien sat up surveying the room with sleepy eyes and recalled the events of the evening before. He'd fallen asleep with Tina beside him. She had him so turned on when she took his shirt off he could have burst a nut. She laid quiet with her head on his chest and teased him with a finger in his belly button. But he was tired, so tired it eventually got the upper hand. Oh, how sweet she was, though! He could not believe how pretty she was. "Righteous babe."

Sunlight was angling in through the two windows over the street. It shone on the bare floor by the wall and seemed to glow in a halo around the dust balls in the corner. There was a damp chill in the room. Arien got up, hugging himself, and strode over to the window to stand in the sunshine. "Rad!" He praised, peering down to the street below. He watched a Falcon drive by, then a Volkswagen Beetle. There was a big Buick Electra parked across the street and on this side was a classic '60's Mustang and a VW Bus.

Perhaps more astounding to him was the time of year. It was obviously springtime. The fresh, golden-green little leaves and oversized buds were everywhere on the trees and shrubs. Steam rose off the wet, glistening pavement. Grass on the tiny front yards glowed bright green.

Arien pinched himself. "Ow!" Then, on a sudden impulse he was out the door, down the steps, and on to the street, mindless of the early morning chill. The sun felt warm on his bare skin. The air smelled fresh. The sidewalk under his feet was still cold and wet.

The Mustang had a new look to it. There was a little pack of Lucky Strike cigarettes on the passenger seat. Details like this were such a thrill. Arien looked at everything, turning in wonder at every direction, and though his surroundings in this old residential area of the city looked so much the same as it had the previous day it was yet so different. It was truly like another version of reality. With excruciating anticipation, Arien scooped up a soggy newspaper that lay folded in a driveway a few blocks down from where he'd spent the night. Aloud he read the date: "April 14th, nineteen sixty-nine! Oh shit! Awesome!" he cried. He whooped and shrieked like a young buck monkey.

With his heart soaring in his breast, Arien ran, like Mary Poppins in the living hills. Every car on the street was an "old" car. There wasn't a Toyota, a Mitsubishi, or a Nissan in sight. He ran back to Salmon Street and came huffing to stand before the house where he lived "yesterday." It had a crisp, well-tended look. There were daffodils in the yard and petunias in a flower box on the front porch. Lace curtains hung in the front room window.

"Ha ha! Arien hooted. "Good-bye, Bert! So long, Larvey! See you later... Brother." I suppose now... I'll find out who Andrew is. "Oh God!" The questions that raced through his mind hollered and clamored. How long would this last? Would he ever go back to 1990? Might he ever go to other times? Has anyone ever had an experience like this? He began to feel dizzy.

About three hours later when Arien returned to the house of his new friends he found everyone but Jeff sitting in the living room. Tina looked like she was just waking up – Arien vaguely wondered where she was when he awakened – Otter smoked a joint and Blue Star was holding up one of Arien's High Tops for a close examination.

Arien's feet were cold and sore. He was not used to going barefoot but the lure of the world outside had been immediate and irresistible. He had covered a considerable distance. Most of the differences he saw in the old district were subtle, aside from the traffic of another generation, but some things stood out so blatantly Arien would stop in wonder and fascination. He noted one corner lot where he recalled a low wall and an open area where a house used to be. Today he saw the house! People lived there, oblivious of a future that would take their home. There were some empty lots, too, where houses should have been. These were covered with lawns, or landscaped, or even stands of trees!

Blue Star tossed the shoe over, followed by the other. His expression was quizzical but he didn't say anything. He watched Arien reject the dirty socks inside and put the shoes on over his bare feet.

"It's cool - that you don't believe me," Arien said generally as he tied the laces loosely, only halfway up to the top of the shoe. "That would be asking a lot of anybody."

"I'd like to believe you," Tina said.

"Maybe, eventually, you'll prove it," Otter said..

"Damn!" was Arien's exclamation. They looked at him. "I wish I hadn't hated the news so much!"

"You hated News?" asked Blue Star. Good for you, Man. It's all propaganda, anyway.

Arien soberly responded, "You don't get it. I have nothing here. Nobody - but you. I don't even know what's happening. Oh - I know about the '60's, and Woodstock. Everybody knows about that, but, I'm a stranger, you see?" It's like, I have no home. Not that I did anyway… But, geeze, I could be rich someday if I could remember, remember something." The implications weighed upon him.

"When do we get out of Nam?" Blue Star casually asked.

"Oh I know that one," Arien groaned. "Right after I was born." Arien could barely contain a rising sense of desperation. Why had it already come to this?

"That's in 1973?"

"Yeah, and I guess we lost."

"Ah!" Tina cried, smiling broadly. "Righteous!"

"That's cool," Otter agreed, looking bested. He chuckled. And then he asked, "When do they legalize grass?"

"Forget it." Arien shook his head. "Won't happen."

"No? Oh c'mon, man! That's no future I see. They're gonna legalize. Just you wait."

"That's bogus!" Arien cried. "You don't know shit!"

Otter bit his lip. He remained silent. Blue Star picked it up. "How about the folks at your - what did you say? - group home?"

Arien looked up in helplessness.

Tina was watching him closely. "You can't go back there," she said.

"Hey! Right!" Arien rallied. "I stood right there just a little while ago, and, and, I'm buggin', Babe, totally! Some little ol' lady lives there now. Everybody I know hasn't happened yet!"

"Well you can stay here, Brother," Blue Star offered, "And get your shit together."

"Righteous," Tina approved. Her eyes seemed to dance.

Otter's joint had gone out. He was holding it pinched between his fingers the whole time. Now he pulled the last match in a matchbook out. It fizzled. The air smelled like sulfur. He looked around for help.

Arien reached in a pocket for his Bic. He tossed it.

Otter fumbled with it; flicked it a few times.

"Hold it down."

"Ah." Otter scrutinized the lighter. He shook it and turned it over. "Where do you put it in?"

Arien was laughing. "You don't put anything in it. It's disposable."

"What else do you have?" Blue Star asked.

"That's it, I guess." Arien went through his pockets to be sure. "Oh bogus!" He frowned. Along with his knife and lighter he had a quarter and a couple of pennies. The date on the quarter was 1965.

Tina and Blue Star came over and looked at it from either side. "Well, how about the pennies?" Blue Star asked.

"Oh my God!" Arien couldn't believe it. The first date was 1967, the other, 1969.

Otter came over to look also. He smirked.

Arien was devastated.

"Well," Blue Star offered, "This '69 penny does look pretty worn."

Otter guffawed.

Footfalls on the stairs ended with Jeff's entry. He nodded to everyone and flashed the peace sign at Arien. *How bozo*, Arien thought, but he liked Jeff. Jeff seemed closer to his age than the other two dudes, but it wasn't only that. There seemed to be an understanding with him that was easy and natural.

"You know what, y'all?" Jeff announced.

Eyes were on him.

"I heard it from Sarah Moon, just up from Frisco. She got it from Nicky Hopkins, who told her the Airplane got it straight from the promoters in New York City: There's going to be a rock festival to beat 'em all this summer. She didn't know where yet, but it's back East someplace. Everybody's going to be there! It'll be out-a sight!" He looked at Arien who grinned broadly.

"It's Woodstock, Dude!" Arien affirmed. "One bitchin' time! All these cool old bands: Jimi Hendrix, Janis Joplin, and everybody gets high, naked and all, and, oh damn - I can't believe this - but I'm goin' for sure!" He paused for breath. "But first, I want to say thanks, for your invitation, Blue Star, but I think there's something I got-a do first."

His voice changed so abruptly it caught everyone's attention as much as his previous excitement. He reached down by his clump of socks for the T-shirt with holes in the nipples. "Killer!" he cried, eyes sparkling, he turned to Tina. "I'll trade you something for this." He held the shirt up.

A burst of laughter went around.

"I've got something you can wear," Blue Star offered.

"Yeah, and I've got something to trade," Tina said, winking.

Arien chuckled to himself. "Promise me you'll wear it for me sometime."

"Like this?" She put it over her head and looked at Arien through the holes.

"Oh, it's you, Tina," Otter said.

Arien grew more serious. "I don't want to leave you people," he confided. "I don't remember when I've felt more comfortable with - strangers." The word sounded out of place. These friends didn't seem like strangers at all.

"Then maybe we'll go to this festival together," Jeff said. "You called it Woodstock. Where's Woodstock?"

"Oh, it's in New York State, Dude. And the festival wasn't right at Woodstock, if I remember it right. But it had something to do with it." And after a short pause he said, "Sure. We'll go together. We'll all go!"

Blue Star smiled. "We'll take your bus, Jeff."

"You have a bus?"

"A VW bus," he told Arien. "It doesn't go very fast. I don't know if it will -"

29

"We'll get us that *Idiot's Guide* we've been talking about," Blue Star broke in.

"Yeah," Otter agreed. "It'll make it."

"I've never been to New York, y'all. I've never even been to Idaho!" Jeff admitted.

"But you came up here from Texas, right?"

"Yeah, but my momma did the drivin'."

"It'll be awesome! But we don't need to leave today. Anyway, I have to go to Berkeley first. Arien finally said what was on his mind. "Have you ever been there, Jeff?"

"Oh yeah, man. We were all there last fall to Frisco, Haight-Ashbury, and we went to see the Dead at the Fillmore."

"I go there a lot, Brother," Otter said. I've got friends there, and the Mary Jane's always fine."

"You got that right," Blue Star chimed.

Tina asked him what he wanted to do in Berkeley. There was a long silence. Everyone waited. Arien struggled with words that tried to be spoken. "I - I want to see my Dad. I never knew my Dad."

Arien Danner stood before the house on Derby Street still disbelieving, still wondering at the impossible twist of destiny that in effect had transported him to another life. And yet this visit to Berkeley in 1969 was not only possible, it was actually happening right now!

The springtime sun shone brightly on the white stucco house. It was warm here, too - a lot warmer than in the city just across the bay. It was quiet. A car or two worked along the street towards Telegraph Avenue. Arien deliberated. His heart was beating rapidly. Arien hadn't been to this house since he was so very young he could hardly remember it; but find it he had. It must have been instinct, he thought (though he used the phone book, too). He could hardly remember the dear old lady who used to live in this house - who lived here now! For that matter, he could barely recall his mother, either. He could hear the heartbeat in his ears. He drew his breath quickly. He felt a little dizzy, exhilarated, and afraid all at once.

He removed the big Army greatcoat with the brass buttons that Blue Star had given him, and for a moment he felt vaguely self-conscious about the "PEACE NOW!" T-shirt that used to be Jeff's. He didn't know these people he came to see. Would they appreciate the political slogan? He didn't feel one way or the other about all of it himself. Yet, the novelty of his feelings for those who had so selflessly befriended him in Portland still warmed his heart and soothed his troubled soul. Arien was proud to wear their clothes!

He smiled. Jeff, Tina and Otter were across the bay now. It was Otter who decided they could all "kill two words with one phone" if they went down to the Bay Area together. They took Jeff's little bus. Otter said he could work his little hustle to ensure enough "stash n' cash" for the trip, and Tina decided she wanted to get to know her handsome stranger better. Of course, Arien had no objections to that. Blue Star stayed behind to settle affairs and work on some of the other preparations for their trip to New York. The plan was to return to pick him up, cross the country, and get there before the crowds. An ample duration would be available around the parts of their plan for what Otter called "hippie time," which was roughly defined as "doing your thing." Arien swore he knew where they were going. He didn't remember all the words, but he did recall the lines "Yasger's Farm" from a song he'd heard once by some lady folk singer. This wasn't the kind of music Arien usually listened to. If it hadn't been a ballad about Woodstock he wouldn't have remembered it at all. The refrain would have taken him back to the Garden itself.

Arien didn't know what to do now. Should he wait for somebody to come out? Should he go up and knock? Who should he say he was and why was he there? Though he'd had all the time in the world on the ride down to the Bay Area in that under-powered VW bus, and though he'd thought of nothing else (short of the intense visual assault the vast changes two decades made in the City of Portland - To have ridden on a freeway where the Riverside Park should have been! And the skyline! What a buggin view it was! The lay of the land was so plain to see: the West Hills, views of the Willamette and Mt. Hood that were totally obstructed just days ago. Such Marvels! He remembered pointing things out to Tina the other day. She bore with him. She even seemed to appreciate his predictions, like a kid listening to the prophecies of a wizened great uncle. "And here - Right here," he said on Broadway that day, "Is where Pioneer Square is going to be! Oh awesome!). Now that he was actually here in front of this house in Berkeley he was unable to think at all.

A youth brushed by and startled Arien out of his musings. He bristled at the way it happened. There was plenty of room to go by and yet this fellow obnoxiously brushed him as he went past. He went briskly on up to the porch of the house and turned to stand in the shadow of the Spanish tile roof.

"What do you want, Hippie Shit?" the young man demanded.

Arien didn't know what to say. The recognition was immediate. This fellow could have been his twin. Even his voice was almost an echo!

"I want to know your name, Dude," Arien heard himself say, ignoring the insult. He looked at the teenager who moved now to sit on the low stucco wall surrounding the porch on either side of the front steps. The wall. This was familiar. Oh. Oh, Jesus! There was a rush of memory. His mother: She was calling him. "Arien! Arien! Get off that wall! Get down now, Baby! Get down before you..." She screamed. It was too much. Arien swooned. He recalled how he slipped off just as she was about to grab him. He remembered that scream, and Grandma came out of the house to see what happened.

"What's it to you, anyway?" The dude on the wall said. There was a lot of bravado in the voice, but Arien could tell he was getting nervous. He slid onto the grass and slowly walked up to face Arien just a few feet away.

"Tell me, please, are you Alex?"

The stance was tough and threatening, arms akimbo, with an arc to the spine and tilt of the head. Now it subtly changed. Though the figure before him scarcely moved a muscle, tough became curious and threatening melted.

"Uh, yeah, that's right. Who are you? Do I know you?"

Arien peered into the deep green eyes. They were the same eyes he had. The hair was lighter, but not much. The face was more angular, but not much more. And the voice! By the time Arien spoke again Alex seemed to hear it, too. His eyes blinked as if to clear the view.

"I - I got to talk to you, Alex. Oh man! Arien said that as Otter would have if he were *really* stoned. Something he saw blew him away. He fought back tears. It was too much! Oh God! Feelings threatening to overwhelm him sprang up inside. He was dizzy; intoxicated.

He sighed. It was awkward but genuine.

Alex, silently, did an unexpected thing. He sat down on the short cut grass of the little front yard, folding his legs beneath him. Arien followed, sitting to face him. He put the irrelevant greatcoat down in a bundle alongside.

"You know," Alex said, squinting in the brightness, "there's something about you, like I know you. But where?"

"Well, Alex, you don't know me from anywhere - at least not in this world." Arien shaded his eyes with his hand.

"Is it deja vu?"

"No. I don't think so. But we - I guess you could say we're related." He allowed the words to dangle like bright objects in the air. "Look at me, Dude." Look how much alike we are!" He spread his arms out as if to reveal more of himself.

Alex fidgeted. It was absurd, but Arien could tell he was hooked. Intently, he asked, "Are we cousins?"

"Nah." Arien shook his head.

"What's your name?"

"Arien."

"Funny name."

"Ha!"

"It is! I've never heard a name like that. It's – it's a hippie name."

"Well, I was born on March twenty-second," Arien explained. "The sun was in Aries, you know."

"Oh. I should have known. You hippies are into that astrology shit." He wrinkled his face.

"I'm not really a hippie, Alex. At least – I wasn't before –"

"Yeah?"

"Before I came here."

"Yeah." Alex looked down at the grass.

"Wait. You got-a give me a chance. I don't know how to explain this. I guess I probably shouldn't. I shouldn't have come at all." He looked up at the blue sky for some answer. Alex said nothing.

"Nanna," Arien said. "Nanna. That's Grandma Bessie."

"Bessie!" Alex exclaimed. "I've got some cousins that call my mom Aunt Bessie. Her name is Elizabeth."

"Yeah, that's Grandma."

"Right." Alex would have winked if someone else had been there. But it was just the two of them. He began to fidget again and look around.

Arien struggled with the apparent impasse. "I know so little about you," he tried. "I used to have some pictures, when you were a baby and stuff; when you were in the Marines. But I don't have them anymore. I wish I did."

"I was in the Marines?" Alex looked incredulous.

"Yes," Arien said quickly, to hold his attention, "and I had one of you and Nanna at Disneyland and you held a Donald Duck balloon in your hand and - and you had a - a, crown or something on your head!"

Alex flinched. "When was that?" He was obviously stunned.

"You were just a kid."

Without speaking Alex jumped up and ran into the house.

Arien waited. Some minutes went by. He anxiously wondered if this guy would stay in there when the front door opened and Alex came out again with a large book – a photo album. Alex was about to hand it to him but Arien said, "No! Wait." On the first page is your dad. He died of polio, right?"

"Wow! How did you know that?" Alex asked, clearly astonished.

"Like I said, Dude, we're related."

"Anything else?"

"It's been a long time since I've seen that. Let me think. There's some wedding pictures. Grandpa and Nanna. They were young. And they vacationed in the mountains somewhere. There's some pictures - maybe honeymoon - in the mountains. A canoe. There's one with a canoe and Nanna's got a fish on her line."

"Wow, man o man! That's right! But, but when did you see these?" Alex grew so excited he stood up again. Some photographs fluttered out of the album onto the grass.

They both picked them up.

"And there's a picture I remember with you on a new bicycle in front of a Christmas tree," Arien went on. You got that silly hat on from Disneyland! And, and graduation pictures. You're on the baseball team at school, right? I remember a picture of that. Your whole team." Arien was glowing. Memories he had thought lost forever flooded back to him now. He couldn't help himself. He sighed. It was a deep sigh ending so mournfully. Mom was showing him the pictures. It was before she was killed; she and Nanna in that stupid accident. Tears he couldn't stop suddenly slid down his cheeks. They dripped on the grass. Damn. It felt good though. He cried. He made no effort to cover the tears. He sat on the lawn again, leaning back, supported by his arms out behind him. He felt the grass between his fingers and under the palms of his hands. Sunlight was impossibly bright in his liquid lenses. His nose got all stuffed. But, it hurt so good to cry.

Alex watched his improbable visitor dumbly, in wonder, in some kind of awe. He reached out to grasp Arien's shoulder. "Hey. Hey. It's alright. It's alright." He looked deeply into Arien's face. "Oh, man. Who are you? Just tell me who ... No! Oh wow... You - you could be - my brother?" His eyes grew wild; uncomprehending.

"And where have I been?" Arien dully asked, realizing the impossible riddle he presented. A cool tingle crept up his back. He knew he mirrored the other, and the energy between them - it was like something that kick ass weed from Viet Nam could do to people. But these boys inhaled the legal air. "Let's get out of here. We've got to talk," he said, wiping his eyes. They set the album and the greatcoat on the porch and walked away from the house.

The two boys strode slowly up Telegraph. A steady procession of bicycles moved up and down. They wove in and out of traffic, crossing to opposite sides, going every which way. There were many young faces, some with books, dark beards, army fatigues and pin on buttons.

The street didn't look right to Arien. It was changed somehow from the memory of his childhood. He had yet to become used to this. There were so many things to call his attention this way or that, yet rarely did it offer any explanation. Telegraph Avenue was much narrower in his memory. The landscaped sidewalk of planters and greenery and trendy shops were not there at all! Instead of two crowded lanes there were four. There were head shops, coffee houses and bars; a bookstore with magazines spilling out into the way. Posters were plastered everywhere. Along with all these sights and images were the interruptions of glances stolen from each other. Alex seemed to loose his balance in every assurance he sought from his companion.

The two of them were now reflected in the great, black, impenetrable window of the Bank of America. They lingered there spontaneously, slowing their steps until halting altogether near a workman who cleaned splatters of blood red paint off the glass. For a moment, a dripping crimson smear of it divided their twin reflections.

Arien turned away from the bank. The image lingered in his mind's eye.

Then, at last! His gaze took in the beckoning plaza of the University of California that capped the head of the Avenue.

"Awesome!"

A hoarse voice rasped out a tune over a strumming guitar. Lots of people milled about and went everywhere. Bits of paper blew between passing feet. Sandals. Arien saw a lot of sandals. And bell-bottoms. And army boots! And there were some tables with garlands of brightly colored cloth where people took signatures, handed out fliers, sold pin buttons, and there were portrait posters here and there of strange looking men. One of these was a smiling china man with a red star on his yellow-green cap and collars. The other, Arien recognized was some Russian guy with a goatee.

It was all so cool! Arien missed this somehow on his way into town. Now, although all the buildings were in the right place, the Plaza of his memory didn't look like this. "Do you ever come here?" He asked the young man by his side.

"No. I hate it. It's full of communists." Alex scrunched up his face in disgust.

"But it's awesome," Arien protested. "And anyway, it's a great place to disappear."

They sat on a low stone bench facing the action and for a while neither of them spoke. They watched the passing little multitude; to Arien a sensational panoply of sights and sounds that revealed its own ironies. The backdrop of stately campus halls contrasted with chaotic rhythm where the energy ranged from an aimless drift, on one end, to a Vaudeville show at the other, with all else between that the tawdry Avenue could serve up like a great, belching serpent.

The sweet smell of grass was in the air. There was an intellectual-looking fellow with delicate round spectacles who smoked a pipe. Perhaps it came from there. Or, maybe it came from a foxy-looking babe who sat on another stone bench nearby. She *seemed* to be smoking a cigarette.

Arien offered Alex a smoke. Alex was staring uncomfortably at the people. He shook his head, no. Arien lit one for himself. "I still can't believe how cheap these are," he said, turning the pack over in his hand. "And there's no Surgeon General's warning. You can just smoke and not have to think about it. Tell me – How can you live so close to a place like this and never come here?"

"It's infiltrated. It's crawling with communists." Alex's answer was direct with no hint of apology in his voice.

"That's a load of crap. You've got nothing to worry about. The Russians aren't going to take us over."

"How can you be so sure?"

"Because, Pop, in 1989 the Wall will come down. Even I couldn't miss that." Arien marveled. Maybe he would be able to remember more! But he'd also called Alex, Pop. Did he really know what he was doing?

Alex stared at him. "You do drugs, huh?"

"You don't?"

"Hell no!"

"Hmmm. That's funny. I thought everybody in the '60's did drugs."

"That's probably what the communists want you to believe."

This guy is so sure of himself, Arien thought. He looked so young. Did he look that young, himself? He recalled their reflection in the window at that Bank. The resemblance really was striking. He realized it was the magic of this phenomenon that held them together now. There seemed to be little else these boys had in common. He wished for a moment that he was older. He struggled to think of what an authority might say. But, what kind of authority? Were there any authorities on time travel?

"So how did we become separated? How come I never heard about you?" Alex demanded.

"About your brother?"

"Yeah."

"Well that's what you said – this brother bit. It's much more complicated than that, Al. But I don't understand it at all, and you won't believe it anyhow."

"Tell me."

"There's a Beatles song. I really like it. It's called "A Day In The Life." It's about everything, I guess. Everything's so dumb; everything people do is so stupid. And you know?" Arien smiled as he formed the words, "It's right on. The only way you can see it all is to step outside yourself to see that other things are true, too; things that you would never have thought possible otherwise."

"I'm not doing any drugs."

Arien forged ahead. "I did some acid with some friends I met in Portland. It was just before we came down here. I-I never thought I would ever love anybody, Dude. But. I did cid before, in the Portland I came from. That's where I got into trouble. But it wasn't anything like this. Oh Jesus! It was awesome! We all melted together! We were so beautiful inside! And - and we played outside - it was so much fun! Like, we made love together. My God! We were in heaven, Dude. I didn't know it could be like that."

"You made love together?"

"Yeah. It was like that. I don't know if it could ever happen again. I like girls, and I think I like them better one at a time, but I know I can feel love. I never knew that before. We had no secrets. I could have screwed the whole world that night, and, in a way, I did."

"Wow," Alex marveled. "I never even..."

"Well - you will, Dude! You will!" The irony put a big grin on Arien's face. How lucky I am, he thought to himself, to be able to talk with my old man like this!

For a while they were silent. They watched the procession of students and impromptu happenings. The raspy voice with the guitar was singing an antiwar rag to the top of his lungs. Arien liked it. The tune was catchy, the words sounded original, and the singer provided free theater.

"I can't stand it here!" Alex said. He stood. "Let's go!"

Arien frowned. Reluctantly he followed. Alex was already walking away.

They headed back down the Avenue. Alex walked with his hands in his pockets. He kicked fitfully at a pebble on the sidewalk in front of him. And he almost blundered into a girl in his way.

Arien, too, had been thinking, and moving steadily to keep up. But he saw the girl before his companion.

"Oh Alex!" She exclaimed. She looked at him with a great big smile that got stuck when she saw the teenager next to him. She looked back and forth to the two of them.

"Oh, hi, Sarah."

"Well, Alex., I didn't know you had a brother!"

Arien's heart started racing when a thought struck him like an electric shock. No, he remembered, collecting himself. Her name wasn't Sarah, it was Maggie.

"Oh yeah, Sarah, but, ah – I didn't know it either," Alex stumbled. "That is, I never saw him before today." Then, "Arien, this is Sarah."

"Hi." He reached out smoothly with his hand, dimly cognizant of how much he'd changed in just a few days.

Sarah took it and smiled. "Alex has a double! You are new in town?"

"I'm new in the world," Arien said. He grinned.

Sarah seemed to like that.

Alex shuffled.

"Well, I'd best be going. Will you call me tonight?"

Alex nodded an affirmation. She looked at them both, smiled, and continued on her way up the Avenue.

"I'm really confused," Alex said. "I've got some questions to ask Mom." They were walking again, more slowly this time.

"She's not going to be able to help you much. She doesn't know anything about me, Al. Look! –" He took Alex by the arm. "I just had to see you. You've got to try to understand, Dude, even though I can't explain how I got here."

"Who did you call her? Nanna? Alex looked like he was going to faint. The color drained from his face. "Let's go and see her, Arien!"

"No. Not yet. I can't see her yet. I've got to think. I blundered in here without even thinking about it. I just came. I never knew what I would tell you, Pop." The words slipped out again but with more resonance this time.

They faced each other on the sidewalk. Occasionally someone passing would have to go out of the way to get by. The world itself seemed to revolve around them now. It swirled away from the still center that hung suspended in their locked gaze.

Arien spoke first, but ahead of his voice were signals from a very subtle level. He was only dimly aware of them himself. It seemed such a simple thing to just trust his own nature.

"I left my coat at your house."

"Well come back and get it."

They were silent all the way to Derby Street. In front of the house Alex waited, as if expecting some other shoe to drop.

"Later, Dude."

"Yeah."

5 — Zadkiel

Arien wasn't familiar with San Francisco but he found his way back to the Haight without much difficulty. He'd hitched a ride from Berkeley, at a place along the road just out of town where throngs of people thumbed rides for several blocks at a stretch. Many of these travelers held handmade signs declaring destinations to points all over the Bay Area, up and down the State of California and beyond; Vegas, Tacoma, Portland, Tucson. One bedraggled fellow had a sign that stated simply, NYC. He got a ride before Arien! It was a thrill to see.

Otter sat on the steps of the large apartment house on Page Street, breaking sections of an orange as Arien drew up.

"Well, how was Bezerkely?" Otter said. He spit seeds into the curb.

"Rad town, Dude; partly the way I remember it and partly not." He sat down beside his friend.

"Did you find your - ah - old man?"

Arien swore he saw a grin appear on Otter's face, though lips were still.

"I saw him."

"You should have brought him back for us to meet."

"That would have been cool. But Alex is – totally square. He hates Sproul Plaza. He's down on hippies. The Haight would seem like Hell to him." Arien hung his head.

"Then I guess you don't take after him much, huh?"

"Oh, but I do, I think. I look just like him, Dude." Now Arien smiled. "And it's – it's like he recognized me somehow, though he couldn't –"

"Cop to it?"

"Yeah, I guess."

"Out-a sight. So, you going to see him again?"

"Yeah. His head's buggin' now. He doesn't know what to – I'm thinking he might be hard on Nanna."

"Nanna?"

"My - uh, his mom."

"Oh yeah, Man, Nanna." Otter's lips did move this time. They formed into an unmistakable smile.

It dawned on Arien that there wasn't any harm in Otter's irrepressible skepticism, either that, or he really had changed – grown, as Tina observed, in the days he had been among them. This time he kept the lid on. He smiled back. Otter had never been afraid of him, but he had deferred to him, several times. Otter was stronger than he let on, Arien mused.

"Go for a walk?"

Arien nodded. He stood and wrapped himself in the maxi coat he'd hauled over his shoulder all the way from Berkeley. It was definitely cooler in the city. A haze blocked the sun. Gusts of breezes blew.

They headed to the corner of Schrader and walked up to Height Street.

"It was really groovy here in '67." Otter said. "I don't know any more. Still a lot happenin' but you get all this smack around now; people burnin' each other, cops all up tight. It wasn't like that then."

Arien looked down the street for any evidence of the smack. He was finding it difficult to imagine any time being much better than this! There were a lot of people in the street; a lot of smiles and nods and a pervasive costume of outlandishness. There would be nothing quite like this in 1990. People wore buckskins, like Otter, or were draped in tie-dyed smocks, they wore copious beads and bells on shoes and feathers and headbands in the hair, paisley shirts with billowy sleeves, a lot were barefoot; even cars were richly painted in swirls of color in suns, moons and rainbows. Lots of color: in windows, on doors and signs, on posters of nearly illegible letters in swirly designs proclaiming this event, or that concert of legendary ghosts, all risen from the graying headed graves of Arien's former present. Here he was: a youth in the bawdy time of his parents! Though he clearly accepted his predicament Arien never ceased to marvel.

They worked their way down the crowded sidewalk. A black dude with a large Afro sauntered by them. He was saying, "Key-lows" softly, in a baritone voice, varying his pitch with the syllables. Arien grinned at him, but waved no when the fellow raised an eyebrow. Arien had never seen so many longhaired young people - some, really young people - in one place. Not even a Guns and Roses concert could compare with it. It just went on and on down the street. So many cool lookin' dudes; rad babes –

I wonder what she's doing now. Arien thought, seeing Tina in his mind's eye. Rad babes always had him thinking of her lately. He didn't mind that either.

A thing that stopped Arien short was a large bus plying down the street. It looked for all the world like a tour bus. Old, buttoned-down people inside were staring at the folks on the street. Some were taking pictures!

Arien's hoot caught Otter's eye. He grinned and winked. "Since that started they've got an old school bus that takes the flower power to the suburbs! It's out-a sight, man."

"Awesome. I'll bet that's fun."

Otter halted before a storefront with large plate glass windows on either side of the entrance. The sign over it announced the unlikely name, *The Hungry I*. He opened the door and walked in, motioning for Arien to follow him inside. It was a big space. The hardwood floor creaked under their feet. The air was slightly musty. There was dark wooden wainscot all around walls adorned with various posters. There were some mattresses along the wall on one side with Indian bedspreads on them and a girl of about fifteen with long, blonde hair, in a simple dress and bare feet sat on one of these. She was embroidering something.

"Hi." She looked up and surveyed the boys in front of her.

"Hi," Otter answered, nodding. "Is Big Daddy around?"

"He stepped out." She looked absently at Arien's high tops, then up at his face. "Do I know you?"

"I don't think so." His smile was cute.

"That's impossible. He's from the future." Otter looked at Arien and winked.

"Oh," she said, "I'm from Utah."

Arien scratched his head. You could tell these people *anything* and they wouldn't bat an eye! He had never seen anything like it. Either they were all total cynics or they were the most gullible generation in the history of the planet!

"C'mon!" Otter said, turning to go.

"Peace," said the girl, smiling.

Arien nodded to her as he went out the door after Otter. "What is that place?"

"The '*I*' used to be in North Beach." They were continuing on down Haight Street. "It was a beer hall then. I was there once when Janice Joplin belted out a tune. Man! That was out-a sight!" Otter's expression took on a dreamy, faraway look. "That was awhile back. I hadn't even heard of her then. Wow, man. That was sooooo cool. She was, she was –"

"Awesome!" Arien helped.

"Yeah, man! She was awesome!" Otter was radiant.

She must have been pretty good, Arien thought to himself. "She's gonna be at Woodstock, Dude. We're gonna see that babe there!"

Otter looked at Arien squarely as they walked down the sidewalk and turned up a side street. He didn't speak. They walked on for a couple of blocks up a steep hill before drawing in front of a tall house on the corner of the block. It had great, big windows. They were very clear and clean and there were lots of plants and crystals hanging in them. Arien followed Otter up the steps to a wide porch with fresh-painted hardwood floorboards. There was an iron lever handle in the middle of an oak door of clear varnish over natural wood. Otter pushed the lever down. It rang like an old-time telephone bell. The large window in the top half of the door had a lace curtain in it. Someone moved it aside slightly.

A tall, elegant boy opened the door. He wore faded army style shorts and a white shirt rolled up at the sleeves; accentuating smooth, dark, tanned skin. His black hair was very, very fine and straight. It hung in a loose ponytail all the way down his back. He was barefoot, standing on an oriental carpet. He wore a gold anklet.

"Hello, Otter."

"Hi, Shasta. Arien this is Shasta."

"Arien," Shasta repeated. His piercing, dark eyes glinted appreciatively, and then he said to the both of them, "Would you mind having a seat. Zadkiel is here but it will be a few minutes before he can see you."

"Ok." There was a Victorian love seat by the door where visitors removed their shoes. They moved over to an antique couch of faded brocade and knurled wood legs. Shasta gracefully slipped out of the room into the great and rambling house. Arien let his eyes wander. There was a large bay window with a window seat in the immaculate room. It was full of daylight caught in crystal prisms and dancing on high walls and green leaves and on the hardwood floor. There was an exotic picture on one wall. It was a photograph of a middle-aged man with a rather large nose and a thick dark mane of hair falling on strong shoulders. Under his picture were the words, *Be Happy.*

Arien's eyes widened when he saw a small, cylindrical brass jar full of hand rolled cigarettes on an end table next to him. A smaller brass jar was stocked full of wooden matches.

"Pass 'em," Otter said, his eyes twinkling.

Otter took a doobie out of the jar, lit it with a match he struck with his thumbnail, and passed it to Arien. Then he promptly lit another one.

It was a very rich and spicy smoke. "Delicious!" Arien exclaimed, sucking the smoke deeply.

"Right on, man!" Otter agreed. "It tastes like Red, man. Zadkiel always has Panama Red around. It's amazing!"

"Panama Red!" Was this *the* legendary weed? Arien couldn't resist tearing one of the finely rolled joints open. Sure enough! This pot was red. It was really red like red hair!

"Who is this dude, Otter?"

"I've known Zadkiel for a long time now, man. He's real cool. Knows everybody. He's from South America. He speaks three or four languages. He's got this terrific pad here and a lot of young guys live here. Zadkiel's boys. It's a commune. He's like a –"

There were voices from the hallway. Shasta came back. A natty Black fellow with lots of beads and tiny crystals worn over a green velvet suit with very broad lapels was shown to the door. He weaved a little as he went, and chuckled to himself.

"This way, Otter, Arien."

Arien rubbed some ash he held in his hand into his jeans. He followed Shasta and Otter down a broad hallway with large, open rooms to the right and left. They turned into one of these. It was one more jewel in a tasteful chain. There was a dark purple carpet with swirling golden dragon designs in it. It had to be the most beautiful carpet Arien had ever seen. It lay in a room that was bordered on three walls with tall French doors that affected to put them outside into a garden, or an atrium. The doors were all open yet the room was warm. There were glowing embers in an open iron brazier that jutted from a polished marble-faced fireplace. A bristling bundle of smoking incense added a faint rose aroma to the space and the ash that slowly dropped off each smoldering stick was the only anomaly on the shinny marble hearth. A pair of overstuffed couches and chairs strategically faced off to take advantage of the fireplace and the setting. Otter and Arien barely sank down into the couch when Zadkiel entered the room.

This was about right. It wasn't so much the fellow's attire that set him off, though a floor length, striped caftan would have been noticed on the street, it was the aura of energy and mastery that the man wore as surely as any well fitted garment. He was probably in his late 20's or early 30's, by Arien's estimation, and this was pushing the gates of old, yet he sat down casually in a chair that faced his visitors and it made Arien feel at ease. He had a great cascade of dark, silky hair that hung loose over his shoulders. He brushed it aside where strands invaded his face. "Hello, Otter," he said.

Otter moved to pass Zadkiel the joint he still smoked. Zadkiel declined with a motion of his hand. Otter smacked his lips unconsciously. He held the smoldering doobie as if contemplating his next move.

"So how is everything in Portland?"

"Cool, Man. We're getting it together to take a trip back East. I just thought I'd make one last ride down here before we left to, ah, get something cool to take along."

"Where back East, Otter?"

Shasta leaned into the room to look at Zadkiel.

"Bring us some water please, Shasta."

Otter smacked his lips again. "Yeah!" He laughed. "Case of cotton mouth."

"We're going to New York State," Arien answered the question, "to the greatest concert ever."

"Oh yeah, Man. Zadkiel, this is my brother from the future. He's got us all going to Woodstock."

Arien blushed. Otter was running this thing into the ground. "My name is Arien." He got up and extended a hand to his host.

Zadkiel held him steady in his gaze as he took the offered hand. Instead of letting it go, as would have been expected, he turned it gently up, looking into the palm. "That's quite a break in your lifeline, Arien," he said after a few moments' inspection.

"You read palms?"

"Oh yes. I find it quite useful. May I see your other hand?"

Otter snapped another wooden match to relight his doobie and Shasta entered the room bearing a tray of tall glasses of ice water. He set it down on an end table near Zadkiel.

"Look. It's here, too." Zadkiel pointed. "This is your lifeline. It stops here, at a very young age. How old are you now?"

Arien enjoyed the attention. Though unpredictable, this man's manner was gentle. "Seventeen," he said.

"Well, that's about it!" Zadkiel laughed. "You're on borrowed time, kid. So what's this about the future?"

Arien was tongue-tied. It was Otter who helped out. "When we first met it was up at Blue Star's, in Portland. Blue Star just found Arien after an accident or something. Arien insisted he was from some other time zone, Man, like 20 years from now. It must have been some good Ozley, Man. Ha!"

Arien shifted uncomfortably. Zadkiel released him and he sat back down on the couch.

They all drank water. There was a hint of lemon in it.

"That's quite a story. Do you still maintain this?"

"I don't expect to be believed. I don't think I'd believe it, myself," Arien said softly. "But when I tell people most of them just seem to accept me as I am and I'm grateful for that at least."

"What's the future like?"

"Oh here goes." Otter said with a polite expression.

"Not like this." Arien shook his head strongly to emphasize his point.

"Is it peaceful?"

"No, Dude. President Bush gets us into a war about the time I'm history."

"President Bush." Zadkiel repeated it slowly. He smiled. "Go on. With whom?"

"Iraq. Iraq conquered Kuwait and all hell broke loose. So, President Bush sent the marines. Operation Desert Storm. That's it."

"Fascinating. What do the Russians do?"

"Oh, they just watch. They don't send no troops or nothin'. They tell Saddam to get out, too, I s'pose."

Zadkiel appeared confused. "Who is –"

"Saddam Hussein. He's a dictator. Like, Hitler. I know this because we just had it in Social Studies at the alternative school I went to."

"He's that bad?"

"Sure, Dude. Everybody's afraid he will attack Saudi Arabia. Gas might get up to a dollar and a half a gallon. "

"A dollar and a half a gallon!" Zadkiel was visibly impressed. The story had coherence! "You should write this up, Arien. It's good!"

"Thanks. It will happen. You'll see."

Shasta came back bearing a smooth, lacquered tray about two feet long with slices of melon, bunches of grapes, apples, a small bowl of nuts and cheddar cheese wedges arranged over the top. He set it down between Arien and Otter on the couch.

"Thank you, Shasta!" Zadkiel commended.

"Oh! Yeah! Wow, man. Thanks!" Otter reached to the board.

Shasta nodded cheerfully as Arien caught Zadkiel's reach. He confirmed the intention, and tossed him an apple.

"Well then, let's move back a little. Who gets elected after Nixon?" Zadkiel Bit the apple. It snapped between his teeth.

"I-I'm not sure. I never watched news much. I had all that in history, but it wasn't my favorite subject."

"You don't know?"

"Well - I think it was - it was Ford. Ford got to be President when Nixon had to resign."

"Ah ha!" Zadkiel hooted. "This is getting better all the time! But Ford? Ford who? Not Agnew?"

"Agnew? I don't know." Arien felt betrayed by his ignorance. This wasn't the first time he wished he had paid more attention to events.

"I asked him about the Beatles once; what they were doing in 1990," Otter declared. "That was a mistake."

"What's that music?" Arien drifted. He heard the delicate notes of a stringed instrument. It was non-melodic but harmonious; very pleasing.

Before anyone could answer he broke into a broad grin. "You know?" He laughed, "This is knarly bud, Dude!"

Zadkiel studied him, smiling faintly, his dark eyes intent. Then he looked over to Otter but the signal passing between them was of another matter. Zadkiel got up from where he was and went to a high and narrow bureau near the entry. It had lots of skinny drawers. He pulled one of them out entirely and handed it, tray-like, to Otter, who set it down on his knees.

Arien was very impressed. The drawer was sectioned by fine wooden dividers, like a jewelry box or a receptacle for special tools. In the various compartments were loose piles of assorted herbal wares – different kinds of marijuana, some odd, dried, cactus-like nuggets; there were mushrooms! – Arien had seen those before, in Oregon, and there were some capsules of something. Otter pointed at these.

"Is that spores?"

Zadkiel nodded. His eyes twinkled his approval of the spores.

Arien struggled with that one. He didn't want to ask too many questions and seem stupid. He settled on the nuggets. "What are these?"

"Buttons."

"Oh."

"You've never had peyote?" Otter asked.

"No. Is it like cid?"

"Well, it's psychedelic, man, but the difference is like coffee and tea, you know? It's a natural high, so it's not the same."

"Have you had acid?" Zadkiel asked.

"Oh, he's had acid!" Otter affirmed. He looked at Arien, who blushed.

Otter pointed at a dark, dry bud. It was more brown than green. "Columbian."

"What do you get for that now?"

"It's very good. Fifteen dollars, by the lid."

"That's gettin' up there." Otter pointed out.

"Ha!" Arien couldn't resist the outburst. "Is that all?! That is awesome! Damn! I sure wish I could…"

"You're stoned, man!" Otter laughed. "Too stoned to cop weed. It's like, man, like going shopping when you're hungry!" He looked at Zadkiel. "Is that why you leave the Red in the foyer?"

"Hey," Zadkiel feigned his defense, "if they can't get past the Red they have no business here."

"I don't see any of that," Arien observed.

"It's not for sale."

Otter clicked his tongue. "Will you swap us some buttons, for Arien here to try, and a lid of Columbian for two ounces of these other mushrooms?" He reached into the fringed leather shoulder bag he carried, that matched his outfit, and pulled out the Liberty Caps he had gathered himself in the fall.

"You had more of that last time."

"Yeah, but I'm taking some with us to Woodstock; some of Oregon's finest!"

"Sure, Otter. So what have you heard about Woodstock?"

"Mostly what Arien's has to say. We got it from Sarah Moon, too.

"Sarah Moon?"

"You know. She was hangin' around with Eric at the Hungry I there for a while. She knows the *Airplane*. I guess they heard it first even though Arien knows all about it. He remembers it from his history!" Otter winked.

"Ok. Tell me what you know."

Arien felt awkward but he didn't flinch. If ever he had confidence it was now, and it was confidence in his life as he had lived it, and Lord knows, it had been hard enough. Though his past had been stolen by an accident, his memory of those years was intact, and the pieces of his distant puzzle were matched in the eyes of Alex Danner, whom he had seen only this very morning.

"Are you going to see him again?" Tina asked.

They sat at the kitchen table of the apartment on Page Street. Arien was in love with this place! Contained in this pre-earthquake era apartment house was the strangest combination of art and life and their mutual imitation. Finally he understood the confusion of his new friends when he told them he lived in a group home.

He leaned back in his creaking chair, rolling his head against the wall just above the old, natural wooden wainscot. The shelves and cabinets, the floor, all was made of wood. It was so old timey! Gas jets still protruded from the walls.

"At first I thought so."

He'd seen the man in the picture on the wall before. The legend said, *"Don't worry, be Happy!"* But there was another picture, too. It was an exotic depiction of a blue-skinned boy-man with a cherubic smile. He was draped with a lei of flowers and dressed in a skirt of gold fabric and jewels. He posed in the step of a dance. He held a flute to the ready. And then, over the entry – as if to round things out – was a crucifix.

"What was it like with him?"

"Well, it was pretty knarly, you know? Your old man is the same age you are, like he's the ghost of Christmas past and yet, here I am with a complete stranger who sees things like some other Idaho and here I am, trying to make conversation with this dude; and all the while he's lookin' at me like I'm up to something funny, you know? And everything I said was jamming his head. Damn. Tina, he looks like me! It's pretty rad."

The radio was on in the hall that capped three flights of stairs. The words of a lilting rock song drifted into the kitchen.

"Who sings that, Tina? He sounds familiar."

"That's Steve Winwood. I love that guy."

"Have you met Zadkiel?"

"Yes. He's together, huh?"

"I never thought about this kind of stuff before," Arien began, "but, he seemed to have the key; whatever it is." His face was animated suddenly. The green eyes opened wide. "He's calm, first of all, soooo calm. He's like the stuff in the room, and yet –"

"Did he read your palm?"

"Yeah," Arien chuckled. "He said I have a short lifeline. I should be dead already."

Tina appeared concerned for a moment, then, relaxed with a winsome smile. "He must be right then!" She exclaimed. "He freaked me out when he read my palm! He was right on, right on." She nodded her head in affirmation. "So you're telling the truth." (She must be teasing me, Arien thought). "You have died! Only, only instead of going – Well, instead of going to the other side – you came here!" Her eyes danced.

Though Arien received his best audience so far with this lovely babe, he was reluctant to invest too much in her sincerity just now. He did ponder her explanation, however. Though it didn't really explain anything maybe it could help, somehow.

The teakettle on the stove began to whistle and Tim, a tall young man in his early twenties, with straw-blonde hair that hung in long, straight strands down his back, came to take it off. He rummaged through some tins of herbal tea that sat on a shelf over the stove. "Would you like some?" He asked Tina and Arien.

"Yeah."

"Sure."

"Get a cup."

Arien got up and turned to the large, rectangular porcelain sink nestled unevenly into the natural wood counter top. Various cups were piled there. A bunch of dried flowers and grasses had fallen in there also. He took the bouquet out and set it in the corner, balanced on the wood counter back. He rinsed out cups. He also marveled at how natural he felt here. He just met some of these people yesterday before hitch hiking to Berkeley. The folks here were friends of his Portland buddies. Otter lived here, once. They just called it "Page Street". Tim had said this apartment, along with at least one other household in the building, the Angels of Light, next door, had been regularly occupied communally since '66. They were part of an enduring tradition already, and they were proud of that.

An older man with graying hair cut short entered. He wore a black T-shirt and green army surplus pants. He was looking for something.

"Some tea, Old Joe?"

"Thanks, no." He went out empty handed.

"You guys staying for dinner?" Tim asked, as he stuffed loose dry leaves into a tiny woven basket. He lowered it into a pan with water from his kettle.

"Don't know yet," Tina answered. "If we do can we get something?"

"Sure. Get stuff for salad."

Arien felt uneasy for the first time. There had been no mention of his contribution. He had no money at all. "I'll clean up," he offered.

"That's cool, Man."

After tea was poured Tina and Arien were again alone. She searched him with her eyes. He felt a tingle that thrilled him in spite of a deeply ingrained reflex to shut it off. He really liked her! She was cute as a bug's ear; that, and everything else about her turned him on and, to make it all the more exciting, he was certain she felt that way too.

"Maybe I should go back with you," Tina mused.

He reached out for her hand across the table. God! That smile! She was so open and real and full of trust and innocence and yet a woman in every sense of the word; a woman of natural beauty. Cute. Cute. Cute! "Owww!" he squealed at her.

"Owww!" she countered.

He drew his hand back and clasped his fingers around the warm teacup. His thoughts drifted to that wild night before leaving Portland. He was with Tina, Otter, Blue Star and Jeff, and another girl who dropped by just when everybody was coming on to the orange microdots. The events that swept them along after that resembled an onrush of wind before a furious storm. It was the gust that causes great trees to bow and curtsy and show their light green undergarment of leaves and the world is suddenly changed. He'd had acid before but it was nothing like this. It felt like it would blow the top of his head off! First everyone seemed to get mixed up in each-other's thoughts, like melted brains all scrambled together. Somebody would say something and everybody else really felt it, too, as if it were their own words – or, at least that was Arien's perception. And then he and Tina got to hugging each other and got real turned on and it was like a fire that suddenly swept out of control, consuming everyone. "Oh God I'm hard!" Jeff had cried with gleeful abandon, but Arien could see the energy envelop all of them, like waves of heat on a hot black road, and turn a soft, undulating red before his very eyes; how the words that were spoken reverberated in his gonads! He strained against the bonds of his jeans; a young stallion, steaming, kicking against the door of the stall.

Now they were like one aroused creature; moaning, sighing, dancing as serpents of yin and yang cycled among them; each giving forth and exchanging the others' gender as the energy uncoiled; each knowing the others' experience from deep, deep within the core of their being.

Arien remembered Otter crying, "Holy! Holy!" It had all been so spontaneous and natural, and yet almost studied, reverential, blessed; a great orgasmic exploding sun of feeling, sensation, emotion, and abiding, transcendent love. He'd had a mystery lesson in primal generation. And here, days later, it still held a fresh fixation in Arien's mind and thoughts.

If someone had told him a thing like this would ever happen he would have recoiled in shock and disbelief. Impossible! But then, he would never have understood. He would never have known. Yet now he drifted in Elysian Fields, in an after glow of Love and Power in its purest essence. He had been greater than himself – an elemental masculine power – and he had known this in the company of others who had likewise opened a deep part of their souls' private place of being. It was by the grace of Priests and Priestesses of Beauty and Light. They were more than blood brothers and sisters now. This bond, this special secret they shared would surely bind them now and forever!

As they cried for joy, and caressed each other, and called each other Sister and Brother with a meaning and depth that Arien had not known could exist, as they blessed each other again, fresh in his mind's eye, he heard a voice in the distance call to him: "Arien? Arien? What are you thinking?" But when he looked at Tina there across the table he saw that she had already answered her own question.

"Wow," he sighed.

She held him steady in a warm and loving gaze, like pure sunshine, with little freckles on her cheeks.

He sighed again.

She laughed sweetly.

"No. I mean, totally rad! There's this guy in my group home - a staff dude, named Andrew. He must have been there!" Arien was awe-struck. Maybe more of the puzzle was fitting into place. But who is Andrew?

"Andrew?"

"I don't know, Tina. It's either Blue Star or Otter! It can't be Jeff, because --"

"He's Jeff," she helped.

"Yes. And..." He dropped off into thought.

"So you knew him in the–" she hesitated, "future?"

"Yes. He must have been there. Oh! Awesome!"

Later in the day they went with Jeff in his van to a market in the Mission to buy the fixins for salad. Otter paid for it out of a book of food stamps. On the way back, as the van chugged laboriously up lower Haight Street, Otter said to Arien, "You still don't have any currency, do you, man?"

"Yeah. I would like to contribute to all of this. I'd get a job, you know? But we have to be leaving before too much longer. I'd like to avoid the rush it's gonna be to Woodstock.

"That big a deal, huh?"

"Oh yeah, Dude." He moved unconsciously into the past tense. "There were so many people jammed up on the roads to Woodstock that some of them just didn't make it. I don't want that to happen to us."

"That would be a drag!" Jeff laughed.

"Well you don't need a job man," Otter remonstrated. All you need to start with is some of these." He pulled the remainder of his food stamps out of his shoulder bag and passed them to Arien.

"How did you get them?"

"Oh, it was easy. But you'll have to take your lesson from Preston."

"Preston?"

"Yeah. He lives next door to the Page Street Commune, at 1887. He gives free lessons for food stamps, and, if you take Preston's course on getting on Welfare, you're guaranteed, upon graduation, to be accepted! He's one of the Angels. These people are really out-a sight, Brother. You have to see them to believe it."

"Otter?"

"Yeah?"

"Is your name Andrew?"

Otter looked at him like he had gone daft. "No," he objected. "It's Otter. Why? Is your name Gus?"

Tina laughed. Arien couldn't help but smile, himself. "Then it must be Blue Star," he said certainly.

Otter shrugged. "Am I missing something, Man?"

"Likely, it's Blue Star," Tina said. "It sure ain't me."

Everyone was home for dinner (an unusual occurrence, it was overheard) and Arien met the rest of the people who lived at Page Street. Tim's babe was Karen, then, there was Beanie and Bob, Larry, Randy, and "Young Joe." Arien had already met Susie Q, Old Joe, Mikel, Janice and Paul. It was a large apartment, but still. This was a veritable army! It was a marvel how everyone could live in this place so harmoniously. He would not have imagined it possible before. At Youth Promise, the kids were always at each other's throats. It was a balancing act just getting through the day without a scrap. But this! He felt so comfortable here. Everyone made him feel at home. Without an exception he was accepted warmly, naturally, easily.

The kitchen was all steamed up with the cooking and the people. There was plenty of food. Tim ladled heaps of brown rice and red beans onto plates that Paul passed out to everyone. Paul was a short young man in his early 20's, about the average age of this crew. His face was cragged with the scars of ravaging acne. He wore thick glasses. But his bearing was proud, and set off with large mutton chop whiskers of dark, wiry hair. He wore a white shirt, rolled up at the sleeves, a black vest and black jeans.

On the table was a giant bowl of salad with a homemade tahini dressing. Arien helped to get it out to this multitude as it progressed into the broad living room with its high ceiling and bay window that hung out over Page Street. Before they ate, however, people set their meals down wherever there was a space to do so, and they joined hands in a rough circle extending all around the room. They fell silent. After a moment's passing, Paul intoned a grace: "Great Spirit. Mother and Father of All. Christ. Krishna. Buddha. Allah. Masters and Prophets: Share with us in the blessings we bring together. Give us our food. Guide us in love and friendship. Welcome our guests in peace. OM, Shanti OM."

Everyone sang out that last note; everyone, that is, except Arien, who listened with silent goose bumps. It was so powerful. It was so high. He barely resisted a tear that struggled to breach an eyelid. Then he could hear that plaintive voice again, singing from the radio in the next room in a distant, yearning voice that would find its way home. His eyes met Tina's. "Steve Winwood," she said. "I love that song."

Old Joe ate his food with his fingers. Arien watched him but Old Joe didn't seem to notice. Then he spied Janice who had been observing him. She smiled when their eyes met. "Hey, boy. You're pretty cute," she told him. He blushed; sure everyone had heard that.

Janice was a slim young woman with glasses. She seemed to go with Paul, who simply looked up and nodded at him when Janice spoke, but Mikel grinned broadly and said, "Ooo-ee- yeah!"

"Careful, Mikel," Susie laughed. "I think he came with Tina."

Tina smirked. Arien looked at Mikel, who still smiled at him. Mikel was a lean and graceful lad with sandy-blonde hair he wore down to his shoulders. He wore a tank top and cut-off shorts that revealed a good tan. He sat barefoot on the floor with his plate in his lap.

"Are you from Portland, too, Arien?" Mikel's grin was engaging.

"Uh – yes. I am." Arien was having trouble getting some salad on his fork. Other than Old Joe it seemed like everyone else was using chopsticks! They made it look so easy.

"Are you going to be around for awhile?"

"A couple of days maybe."

Susie Q sat to Arien's right. She nudged him and asked if he would pass the Tamari.

He reached for the bottle.

"Then back to Portland?"

"And on to Woodstock," Jeff drawled.

"And the toasted sesame seeds?" Susie Q asked next.

"New York?" Old Joe asked.

"Oh yes," Randy joined. "Otter told me about that last night." Randy used a fork, too. He waved it upright, as if to drive his point home.

Otter pointed. "Ask him. Arien's heard all about it already." He winked at Arien.

"There's going to be a super concert, right?" Randy pressed on.

Oh well, here goes! Arien thought to himself. He looked at Tina, who seemed to understand. "It's going to be the most rad concert there ever was, he began, "and there'll never be another one like it." He looked around at the faces in the room. Everyone was listening. Several were charmed by his words, and smiled, or caught an eye. "And I guarantee ya, now that you've heard about it, if you don't go you'll live to regret it."

"Wow!" Beanie exclaimed. Her blue eyes smiled in a freckled face. "That's just the way I feel about my mountains!"

"Here! Here!" Karen agreed.

"How many went?" Otter's coaxing approached the subliminal.

"Half a mill – ion." Arien caught himself too late.

Tina had a hand over her eyes as she shook her head. Then, she smirked at Otter.

Somebody coughed.

Arien looked at Old Joe. He merely ate. Could he have missed this?

"It sounds like you've been there already," Susie Q said.

"Oh let's go!" Beanie cried out.

"Home?" Karen asked her, grinning, "To Kalispell?"

Beanie pursed her lips and wagged her finger in Karen's direction.

Bob and Larry began a private conversation. "Larry, tomorrow would you come with –"

Tina caught Arien's eye. "This is a good time to drop it," she was saying.

"And who was there?"

Arien was becoming exasperated. There had to be limits. But before he could open his mouth Tina said, "Stop it, Otter. I believe him!"

Otter moved off the folding chair he'd been on, over to be close by Arien and Tina. He sat on the floor, holding his dinner, and he leaned forward so Arien could hear him. "I'd like to believe you, Arien, and you're cool, man, for a kid, and you don't seem like the type that would make something like this up. It's just that, well, it's pretty out-a sight, Man. You've got to give me that. And, well, maybe I'm hoping either you'll screw up somewhere, or say or do something that would convince me once and for all. Now don't take it personal, Little Brother. That's just the way I feel. Do you dig?"

Arien calmly took this in. Otter was sincere. He leaned back and took a swallow out of a gallon bottle of apple juice that was passing around. He wiped his lips with the back of his hand.

Jeff scooted up to be near them. He didn't say anything, but he seemed to have followed the gist of it.

"What do you think?" Otter asked him.

A noncommittal expression answered with a shrug.

Somebody turned the radio up for a song that was playing. *"Ol' Flat Top"* drifted in through the sliding door to the foyer. The door was slid back further.

"I want to go with you to see Alex," Otter said. "Let's go tomorrow."

"No. He hates hippies."

Now Otter looked exasperated. "Let Jeff go with you, then."

"Only if I'm invited."

The song continued, but wouln't come together.

The doorbell rang. Somebody was coming up the stairs. A few moments later an older guy, a medium-height, wiry man with a lot of hair on his face that fell to wisps and streaks of dark and gray down onto his chest entered the living room. He murmured quiet greetings and smiles to those who sat and stood near the sliding door, and then, after a spell, he shoved his hands in the pockets of his overalls and announced in a thin, reedy voice, "There will be a Free Bakery run tomorrow morning. I'm inviting volunteers. Whoever wants to participate, we'll be leaving at seven AM, out front. If you want to meet next door, we're having corn bread muffins and jam and tea before we go. Thank you."

He chatted again with people by the door, and then he left.

"What's the Free Bakery?" Arien asked.

Susie Q picked it up. "Oh that's a network thing," she explained. "All the houses and families, communes, whatever, chip in their stamps or their time. That way we can feed the people without copping to the system."

"Oh." Arien was puzzled. "So. Babe. If I volunteer for this thing, what happens?"

"Well," said Susie Q, "if you go you can help bake bread. It's soooo good! Fresh. Made with whole-wheat flour. And then – I've done it lot's of times – you go deliver it all over town. It's real groovy. Raymond's been doing this. Groovy, huh? That was Raymond. He lives at 1887, with the Angels of Light."

"With - uh - Preston?"

"And a lot of other folks."

After dinner and all the commotion of cleaning up Arien went next door with Mikel and Otter. He didn't know whether to look forward to this or what. Truth to tell he was feeling some apprehension. The Angels of Light. Who were these people? Would they all be like Raymond? He seemed so serious, dedicated, or something. Arien couldn't decide which.

The four long flights of stairs climbed upward through a sudden barrage of Supremes music. It was loud. There was shrieking and whooping. It reached pandemonium at the top landing. A sinuous young man with dark skin and black, curly hair pranced and danced around naked. His only article of adornment a long, red silk scarf. Another, shirtless, was barefoot and wore a skirt. His great shock of tight, kinky brown hair was tied back with an enormous pink ribbon. And there was another fellow in a dress suit with wide lapels. His white shirt was open at the collar. His tie was loosely knotted well below his chest. He also was barefoot. They jumped and shook and danced and twisted frenetically to the music.

Mikel cried out and jumped in with them, and to Arien's great dread the stark naked fellow leapt over and started twirling in front of him. Otter's grin could have busted his face. Arien jumped back - literally - back to the wall, his arms up in a defensive posture.

Mercifully the music stopped and everyone ceased their gyrations. "Hi Otter!" said the young man with the ribbon.

"Hello, Otter, and Mikel, and, who's your cute friend?" The naked one asked. He had a deep, silky voice. His large, dark, glossy brown eyes were slightly crossed. He stood panting. His slim, graceful form glistened with perspiration.

Otter opened his mouth but Mikel bounded in and introduced with one motion: "Charles, this is Arien, from Portland, that's Danny ," he pointed, breathless, to the young man in the skirt, "and this is Preston," he concluded, waving to the fellow in the suit. Preston wiped his brow with a handkerchief he pulled from his jacket pocket.

"Honey, you're so young! How old are you?" Charles asked. He cocked his head and raised an eyebrow.

"Seventeen." Arien lowered his arms but he vaguely resembled a cornered rabbit and was scoping an exit.

"My God!" Charles gasped. "And will you look at those eyes? My God! You have such beautiful eyes, Dear!"

"Charles, are you going to gobble him up now or wait your turn?" Danny rolled his eyes.

"Really!" Preston agreed. "You think this was the first chicken you ever saw. Excuse me." He bowed slightly and moved away into the kitchen behind them.

Danny, likewise, smiled at Arien and followed Preston.

"Well, come on in, boys," Charles coaxed, and he waved Otter, Mikel and Arien into the kitchen after him.

The layout here was the same as at 1889. What struck Arien, however, as he plunged in, hanging close by his friend, Otter, were the many similarities in style, though this was definitely more artful, subtle and harmonious. As with the Page Street Commune, Angels of Light kept an eclectic household with its own distinct style. He'd noticed the Indian bedspread and glass beads hanging in two of the doorways and the kitchen was set in a natural wood finish. There were some small posters, a crucifix, a lot of dried flower arrangements. Chopsticks bristled from a large mug on a shelf. The room had a wooden sink and was dominated by a large, unfinished oak table. There was, above all, an astonishing lack of anything plastic and the only appliance was an A-shaped antique toaster with manually operated doors at each side. It sat on the table alongside of a three-branched candelabra, with stubby candles in a ring of toasted breadcrumbs and solid drops of colored wax. An open cupboard revealed real china, and long stemmed wine glasses on a shelf there. Speckled corncobs hung around the room, and a row of hanging plants along the triple sets of natural wood-cased windows. The plants cascaded down nearly to the table and into the sink. Arien was especially taken by the clock that sat deeply into a frame between two of the windows. It shared space with all sorts of small objects and pictures. There was a red light in there and the second hand was a bushy feather.

There were two other men in the kitchen, both of them about in their mid to late twenties. Otter introduced them. There was Stewart, who was seated at the table in a leather reading chair, his fingers pulling at a wispy beard, and a big fellow who wore glasses, had near shoulder length reddish blonde hair and wore a tie-dyed T-shirt, whose name was Tom. He had a full, close cut beard, and he looked like a young Ulysses S. Grant, only heavier.

Both Tom and Stewart assumed a surprised and beatific smile when they saw Arien, who had by now surmised that all of these people were gay. For some incredible reason he thought about his birthmark. It seemed as if, perhaps, Tom was able to see it through his pants!

"So where are you from, Arien?" Stewart asked. "Portland, like Otter?"

"Yes." Arien nodded.

"He has the loveliest name," Charles cooed.

"Only he's from the future," Otter helped, with a smile.

"Yes. We can see that," Tom observed dryly.

"I wish it was my future, baby!" Charles blurted out, and some of them snickered.

"Yeah. Hummm," Mikel seconded.

Arien was feeling uncomfortable having all of these men fawning over him like this. He shifted uneasily.

Danny and Preston took a couple of wine glasses off the shelf and went out into the living room that was opposite the kitchen door. They both smiled at Arien as they passed.

Charles was standing close by now. He smelled like cheap perfume and perspiring animal.

There were footfalls on the stairs – a merciful distraction? A kindly face popped in the door, and moved aside, and the man who had spoken earlier during dinner next door, Raymond, peeked in also.

"Oh hear this!" The first one exclaimed in buoyantly rising and falling syllables. It was almost a falsetto voice. His smooth features and mid length dark brown hair with bangs in front suggested the young Prince Valiant. His face was animated. His eyes sparkled with expression. "I was hitting a pipe in Golden Gate Park, not a yard from the sacred breast of Hippie Hill" - he stressed those last words and his eyes rolled - "with a real hunk of a man I've had my eyes on for two whole weeks, and I've waited so patiently for a chance like this and who do you suppose saunters up out of nowhere, just as cool as slime on ice cream?" He paused here for effect. "Well. An officer of the law, that's who!" Arms on hips, he was a riot of indignation. "'What are you guys up to? Are you looking for trouble?' he said to us. I think he was surprised to see us. Certainly as surprised as we were to be so rudely interrupted!"

"I would have been disgusted," Stewart sneered.

"Oh, yes, Stewart. I was disgusted too, I assure you! So, to make a long story short, I said, no sir! We're looking for beef, not pork!"

Everyone burst into laughter. Arien laughed also, though he was astonished. These people were absolutely wild! He looked at Otter, laughing, glancing back.

When the merriment settled Raymond looked at Charles. "You're going to catch a cold, Charles."

"Yeah, and then you might catch it, Raymond." Charles frowned.

Raymond smiled thinly and left them.

"We're looking for beef, not pork!" Stewart repeated. They laughed again. "Oh Brian, you're special."

Brian glowed. He looked briefly at Arien with a glimmer of a smile. "Hello Otter," he greeted next. "Hello Mikel." He smiled warmly to them each in turn. "Goodies from Zadkiel?" He asked of Otter. Then he confided to Arien, "It's the only time we ever see him any more!" He winked at Otter and turned away. Soon his voice could be heard coming from the living room, retelling his story of the officer in the park.

"Otter, do you have any sweet Mary Jane?" Tom asked.

"Sure. Do you have papers?"

"C'mon. I have some in my room."

"Oh goody." Mikel said.

"Oh God! Those eyes just kill me!" Charles told Stewart as Arien slipped by to leave the kitchen.

Tom had a corner room with a south-facing window that looked past a ledge of the roof and on, beyond the corner of the house towards the park. It was dark outside now and this failed to do justice for all the hanging crystals in his window and the myriad plants that sat on or hung from shelves; but Tommy lit a candle and the crystals caught little sparks of light, like stars in the leaves, and ten thousand flickering shadows cast on stones, shells, assorted little figurines, metal objects, like shiny foreign coins, toy cars, miniature animals and bits of driftwood, to name a few of the things on a table there.

Except for Charles, who posed naked like a classical statue of some young Pan in the doorway, with his dingle dangling, and Stewart, who stood beside him, they all sat on Tom's bed. It was the only place to sit in that room. Tom scrunched himself up in a corner of the bed, up against the wall, making himself as small as he possibly could. Otter parceled out some of the weed that he always carried in a small leather pouch inside his fringed leather shoulder bag. He put it on a small, brass rolling tray that had some seeds and roaches on it. Before long Tom had one rolled and they were getting high.

"Say, Tom," Arien inquired, "Do you think I could catch a ride with Raymond into Berkeley in the morning?" He looked at Otter. "I'm going to ask Tina to come with me," he said.

"Ask Raymond." Tom coughed. Smoke boiled out of him. "I have nothing to do with the Bakery."

"And while you're at it now might be a good time to see what Preston could tell you about food stamps," Otter added.

"Oh there's nothing to it," Tom said with a wave of his hand. "Just be sure you have some money with you. You'll have to buy them so you can prove you can afford them."

This was getting confusing; either that or Arien was getting stoned. "Buy them?" He repeated, exhaling the rich, flavorful, primo Columbian smoke and passing the joint to Otter.

"Just tell them you have no further income in the foreseeable future. You'll have to pay at least ten dollars for thirty worth of stamps. You'll need an address, too. Tell them you live – where are you staying? Next door? – Tell them you live there. Stamps are real easy to get."

"Well. There you have it," said Otter.

Arien barely heard that. He was getting involved with all of the objects on Tom's table by the window. He picked up a beautiful shell. He had never seen such a jewel in a natural object. It was about a half inch in diameter. It had intricate designs seemingly painted on the glossy surface. Inside these designs were tiny blue squares, or rough squares, resembling turquoise set in ivory. "Rad!"

"Rad?" Tom asked.

"That's future speak," Otter offered. "Rad – short for radical." He had that damn smile on his face again. It teased, but somehow Arien knew he would have to bear with it. Otter really was his friend – his brother now; he had shown him so much. If Arien couldn't prove his history, at least he was determined to prove himself.

"Rad," Tom tasted. "Right on." The inflection was different. Rather than drawing out the *"on"* with a wavering intonation Arien might have expected, it was more like one word; one note. He finally realized something had been bothering him when people said "right on," and now he understood what it was.

"This dude's got a lot of out-a sight words like that. He's a trip, Tom. Very original." He grasped Arien by the arm and squeezed it playfully.

"Oh!" It was Brian's voice, shrill from the hall. "We've got another phone installed!" He exclaimed, nearly singing the words. Soon he was in the doorway to Tom's room. He looked over Charles' bare shoulder at Tom. "Are you going on another trip?"

Tom smiled like the cat that ate the bird. "I've got to take some acid back to New York," he answered directly. "While I'm there I can get some of that fabulous crystal meth."

"Tom, you're such a scammer." Otter said.

For the life of him, Arien couldn't see the connection any of this had to do with getting a telephone installed. Maybe he was too stoned to follow a normal conversation. It was all going over his head.

"Well! I hope we have this one for a few days at least!" Brian assumed the pose of mock indignation he had used earlier. "The last time, I remember I was expecting an important call when they came to take it out. Let's not let it happen again, Tom."

Tom smugly laughed. There was an air of delicious pride about him. He looked at Arien and asked, "Do you need to make a long distance call?"

"No." Arien was genuinely puzzled.

"Well I do!" Paybacks, Ma Bell!" Brian smiled and withdrew again.

"We can call and reserve tickets to Woodstock," Otter suggested, looking at Arien.

"We're not going to need any tickets."

"It's a free concert?"

"Tickets won't be necessary. Trust me." There'll be paybacks, Otter! Arien thought with a smile.

Arien and Tina snuggled close together in a bouncy old Ford van as it pitched and rolled over the steep hills of the city in the early morning damp. Raymond stopped at several houses to pick up people, and now was doubling back to the Bay Bridge, and Berkeley.

The van had no heat. They wrapped themselves in Arien's maxi-coat. Tina was sleepy-eyed. Neither she nor Arien had been quite ready to get up when they did, yet both were eager to see Alex, each for reasons of their own. They were too late, however, to have muffins with Raymond, so Arien's stomach growled. He wished for a moment that he could have used the morning to get his food stamps, but that would have to wait until tomorrow. It was Sunday now, April 20th. Tomorrow would be a school day and it probably would not be a good time to catch Alex.

"Where in Berkeley are you going?" Raymond turned to ask him.

"Derby Street."

"Down the Ave?"

Arien nodded. Raymond was another mystery. This fellow seemed so different from the other people in his house, yet he saw some looked up to him - like an elder. Arien could tell that by the space they gave him. It was not a physical space so much, but a mental one. During the previous evening while all the anarchy of Angels of Light in their habitat unfolded, Raymond had been busily banging away on an old typewriter, basically undisturbed. Come to think of it, Arien considered, avoiding thought of his appetite, all of these people were basically undisturbed by one another. And yet, they were as boisterous, as crazy, and as unique as anyone he had ever seen. What was the mystery of the cement that held them together? Why weren't they at each other's throats like the kids at Youth Promise? He pondered this. They seemed so easy with one another; so relaxed. They were each other's audience. They accepted themselves! Yes! That had to be it! They accepted each other when nobody else would. They were – brothers!

"Wow."

"What's that?"

"I was thinking about how all these crazy dudes can live in the same house together without killing each other."

"Do you know how, Arien?"

She's so rad! God, he was happy! Confused maybe, but happy. Last night they slept together – really made love together – for the first time. Oh, there was that acid trip with the others in Portland, but it was a different being they loved that night. Afterwards it was just like they'd been there. And then there were the times they fell asleep in each other's arms. There was a morning a few days ago when Arien was so hot he wet himself. She was so close to him. She smelled so sweet. He knew it was time – and he knew she knew! And that only served to get him all the more excited. But there was always somebody around them. He really liked this girl. He'd never liked a girl so much before. He wanted this to be something special, because it was. He waited to be alone with her. And waited. And – until last night. Finally.

They hadn't been entirely alone. The Page Street Commune was so jammed with people; freaks, they called themselves. But this time Mikel, Young Joe and Randy, who shared a room together, had all gone out for the evening and were still out when he and Tina awoke in the morning. They went out to a party with some of the Angels. Of course he was invited, but Arien had no desire to do that. Angels of Light were real cool; he was fascinated, yet he couldn't help but feel wary of them. It was all too new; a bit overwhelming. They were older and some of them openly lusted after his body. Grotey. Scary. Whatever. They were Gay and he wasn't. He was sure of that – to his great relief – especially after last night.

Otter was tired and rolled into his bag on the floor shortly after he and Arien returned from next door. Tina and Arien, well, they camped themselves down in Mikel's room. Oh awesome babe! And he was so proud. Before they shut the light off he showed her something special. It took a little boldness but her evident delight was worth the risk. With her finger, she traced the outline of his butterfly-shaped birthmark. She said it was hard to believe it wasn't a tattoo. It was too perfect. She kissed it. He throbbed so hard he thought he might burst. It could have been no secret to the others in the house unless they slept like stones. They squealed and laughed and entangled themselves together well on into the night.

He never answered the question. They dozed off. The conversation between others in the van only served to lull them deeper into the unconscious warmth of one another. They didn't awaken until Raymond called in his reedy voice, "Hey! You're here!"

Arien pushed himself to sit upright and looked through the dirty window to a dreary drizzle outside. They were actually at the corner of Telegraph and Derby!

"Thanks, Raymond," he said.

"You're welcome. Maybe next time you'll come help us bake, huh?"

"Sure, Dude. Thanks again." Tina and Arien both stepped out into the wet morning and for a moment, as the van moved on down the strip, they stood uncertain of what to do next.

"I never asked him for his phone number," Arien said. "I can't just go knock on the door." He walked hesitantly toward the house then stopped. "Besides. It's too early."

"Well, maybe somebody's up," Tina gently coaxed. "We're here. Let's go see if they're up."

"I don't know what will happen if Na - my grandma answers the door." Arien thought that no explanation would be necessary.

"She doesn't know you, Dude." Tina smiled when she said that. "You're not goin' to find what you're lookin' for hidin' in the bed, as my dad used to say."

Arien knew that Tina loved her dad even though, as she'd told him during the trip down, his problem with booze is what drove her away to begin with. After that there wasn't any going back, even though he hadn't lived at home for about a year. She'd quoted her dad several times now.

Evidently she preferred to remember the good times. Arien contemplated the contrast and the way a person's life seemed to be so connected to "Dad", what he did or didn't do, whether he was home or not.

Tina gave up on her home because of her old man. Arien lost his home, partly at least, because he never had one.

"It's early," he noted again. "Maybe he's not up."

"I'd knock on the door, Arien. She's not gonna recognize you."

"She might. I look a lot like her son.

"Coincidence."

"Yeah." He took a deep breath and went up to the door and rang the bell.

Sure enough, it was a woman who answered the door. As it opened, her eyes seemed to open too.

"Yes?"

"Hello, Ma'am. Is Alex - Alex Danner home?"

"He's up," the lady wavered. "I'll see if he's ready to see anybody. My heavens, boy! You look like somebody I know!" She was spreading her hands, devoid of explanations. "Who shall I say is calling?"

"Arien, Mrs. Danner."

"Arien." The name rolled off her tongue. It had been tasted. She turned away, a hint of reluctance, and looked again over her shoulder, not inviting the visitor in, but not closing the door either.

Tina came up alongside Arien. The lady disappeared in the house. "That was interesting," she said with some anticipation, but she was hardly prepared for the sight that finally came to the door. Face to face it was amazing!

Mrs. Danner was right behind him. Alex was silent. He looked at Arien with eyes that seemed glazed over.

"I had to come back one more time," Arien said to him.

Alex's mother stepped aside to better look at the two boys and then she looked at Tina who returned the signal. Yes. There was a remarkable resemblance.

"Would you like to come in?" The lady said at last.

"We surely would, Ma'am."

Arien looked passionately at everything in the room: the large, comfortable couch, love seat and two reclining chairs, the oversize "portable" TV with rabbit ears, the Chinese Q'uan Yens on the mantle of a fireplace. Had there been that many? It was so familiar. Most of the things he saw, locked in his memory, were now released (though it all seemed smaller than he'd expected). He felt an emotion unlike any other. It was more of an emotion that was oddly devoid of emotion, and yet containing them all. It had a feeling of deep serenity, dreamlike, as if he was out of his body, a visitor to another time before another life he'd lived in yet another time. He slipped his coat off and set it on the floor by the door. Tina followed suit.

Nanna went into the kitchen after Arien introduced Tina. "Would you kids like some pancakes?"

"Wow!" Arien remembered how hungry he was. "Rad!"

"Yes?" Her voice called out.

"Yes!" Arien and Tina spoke together.

Alex merely watched them. When he finally spoke he said, "I wondered if I would see you again. I thought maybe you were a dream or something. Tell me," he added after a pregnant pause, "Why did you come back?"

"I thought maybe I could ask you to stay out of the Marines, Alex."

There was another period of silence. It was longer than the last one. Alex grasped the arms of his chair as if it suddenly moved very fast. "That's the second time. I haven't told anybody that!"

"Please, Dude," Arien's voice cracked. "You're thinking of dropping out of school, aren't you? Don't do it! It's not just your own life you'll screw up!"

The smell of pancakes wafted in from the kitchen. The room seemed to brighten.

"May I use the bathroom?" Tina asked.

Alex nodded.

"That way," Arien helped, as Tina set out in the wrong direction.

Alex fidgeted.

His visitor went on. "I think I know why I came to see you, Alex; to tell you that. And maybe, maybe to know you a little better."

More silence.

"I've not decided to drop out. But anyway - you're too late."

Arien was about to speak but his thought suddenly derailed.

Tina was greeted by silence. "What happened?" she asked.

Arien sighed. "He signed up."

"I go as soon as I graduate," Alex whispered.

"Breakfast is ready!" His mother called from the kitchen. The three young people got up to go in there. Alex moved ahead and then turned to briefly stop the others. "Not a word of this to my mom," he said.

Tina's expression was blank. Arien nodded dully as they passed through the door.

The Danner's kitchen was a bright and friendly place that had a large window with yellow curtains. There was an archaic refrigerator with a rather fat yellow porcelain owl cookie jar on top. The owl had great big blue eyes. A maple wood table was set in yellow place mats with green cloth napkins and medium sized green glasses of orange juice at every place. A half grapefruit rested in small green glass bowls in front of every place too. Alex silently reached for the matching sugar bowl as he sat down and spread a white pile of the stuff over the top of his grapefruit. It was evident his mother recognized that something important was in the air but she chose to say nothing. She stood at the stove and poured more batter on the griddle that spanned two of the four gas burners. It hissed as the batter met the surface. She kept looking at Arien, who looked awkwardly back at her.

It seemed the gray drizzle outside was lifting. The room brightened from the light of the window. Arien's eyes wandered from the woman at the stove to the window. For a moment time was suspended as a fragment of memory drifted by.

"Thank you, Ma'am," Tina was saying. "It's so nice of you to have us in for breakfast."

Arien snapped back to himself. He took the sugar bowl Tina passed to him.

"Where are you from, Arien?"

"Originally from Berkeley here, but I've been living in Portland for a long time now."

"What's your last name? It's amazing how much you look like one of the family," she blurted out, folding her arms. "What a marvelous coincidence! Why, now I understand why Alex asked me if he had a brother. If I didn't know better, I would think so, too. Oh my." She turned the cakes on the griddle.

Tina looked up from her grapefruit. Her spoon stopped midway to her face as she looked at her companion.

"Yes. It really is something, isn't it," Arien said. He blushed. He hoped she wouldn't press him.

"So what brings you two down this way? Did you come just to see Alex?"

"We're visiting, Ma'am. Yes. In a way, I came to see Alex."

"Alex, you said nothing about this friend who looks so much like you." Mrs. Danner stacked plates with the pancakes. She moved efficiently around the room like an organist playing her instrument. The music smelled so good. Arien dumbly looked up at her as she set a plate in front of him. She had to slide his grapefruit over to make room. There was another flash of distant memory where this woman was barely older. It was difficult. Tina reached to help her, but too late. Mrs. Danner already had it down. It was as if Arien had frozen solid. He blushed again. Nanna had touched his hair.

Her fingers stroked and lingered at the back of his head as if disbelieving what was before her. Her son watched this intently.

Arien closed his eyes. His grandmother moved away to pick up two more plates, but after touching this little bit of him it seemed she moved in slow motion. Her expression changed. Words seemed to form on her lips but she held them back until she sat herself down at the table.

"Tell me about yourself, Arien."

"My parents died when I was young," he said, his voice edged with emotion.

"Oh dear."

"So I never had any real family. I had foster parents. Lots of them."

"You had no other family?"

"No, Ma'am."

"I'm sorry."

"So am I."

Alex quietly stared at his visitors as he ate, but now he dropped a bomb. "You said we're related."

Mrs. Danner seemed to apprehend the obvious. Her face darkened. "Your father was a good man, Alex," she said. "He never cheated."

"Maybe he did." Alex rocked back in his chair like a little boy, staring sullenly at Arien. "You knew so much about me!

"Momma, this is the second time I've seen him and he knew all about me!"

Arien blushed again. Tina shifted uncomfortably. "It's not like you think it is," she offered.

"I should think not." Mrs. Danner agreed, but her eyes betrayed confusion.

"How is it then?" Alex asked her.

"You wouldn't believe it," Tina responded bravely, "but your husband was not Arien's Dad."

Mrs. Danner sighed. She smiled thinly. "Of course not," she said.

8 — The Beginning and the End

"You tried to change the future," Tina mused.

"And I failed." Arien sat dejectedly, oblivious of the magnificent surroundings. Even though impossible things could happen he couldn't change the very thing he really would have if only he could. He was too late! It was so difficult to accept. What was the purpose of all this? Why was he so poised to recreate his destiny and here, his first attempt to do so was such a dismal disappointment? It was only a week ago Alex had visited the recruiting office! Just one week! If only he had gotten down here sooner! If only he'd had more time! With just a few more days to spare, and perhaps a bit more consideration of the matter he needn't have been so direct, at such great risk, and with such mixed results on a personal level. And yet now he had a believer. Tina was convinced of the truth of his story. Even Otter listened to her account of their visit to Berkeley with the greatest interest. He'd resisted all wisecracks. Now he sat silently on the bluff with them, and Jeff was there, too.

Arien felt shivers begin to come over him. He gritted his teeth. His view of the Golden Gate in the crisp, clear air felt oddly askance of his head, as if he were next to himself. "I'm coming on." His eye caught Otter's.

Otter nodded.

Jeff sucked air tightly through his lips. "Wow," he marveled.

Tina rocked her body rhythmically. She tapped out the rhythm with her palms on the grass where she sat. Her smile was blissful. The sharp sunlight glinted in her golden hair that puffs of wind wove into gossamer lattice. It changed in myriad kaleidoscope patterns from one instant to the next.

God! She looked just like those posters of mystery women, Goddesses surrounded by wild, swirling waves of hair in an intense landscape of psychedelic pigments. The blue-green sea and the billion white capped ridges whipped by the wind across its surface shimmered like a living curtain behind her; a lovely young Venus reclining on her green divan.

There was a visible light in her eyes. Maybe it was the sunshine in them? No. It was deeper than that. It was the sun inside of her. And beside her were these two knights.

Otter looked so strong, so vibrant. He was relaxed and confident. It radiated from his smooth, chiseled features, his dark close trimmed beard, and manly grace. He lay on his side, elbow in the grass, hand supporting his head. He began to nod along with the beat of Tina's hands. His nodding was so sensual. Erotic. Arien felt a stirring in his loins merely by connecting into the energy. He looked away.

Jeff was a picture of youth and innocence. He seemed so precious. Vulnerable. Open. He was wide open. Arien could "see" deep down inside of him. Way, way down deep inside. Jeff was pure inside. There were no obstructions, no masks, and no shadows. But wait! It was limitless in there! Arien was getting lost deep down inside of him. Jeff could afford to be vulnerable. He was vast!

"Wow!" Jeff marveled once again.

Otter tittered through his teeth. His jaw was tightly set. "The meaning of "Wow," he offered. "Do you remember the first time you knew the meaning? Wow: the one word that sums it all up!" He spoke generally to all of them. They smiled in agreement, caressing his message, wholly understanding.

Arien looked again at Tina. Leaving Jeff took merely an instant of thought. It happened so fast it precluded any investigation, but it revealed something. What was it? He felt a coolness. He was now outside of his friend! It had been "warmer" inside. Jeff said, "Far out! Ow! Wow!" He shuddered like he was having an orgasm.

But Tina! The sun in her! It was so bright. It blinded. It exploded in a flash before him when a beam of light, eye to eye, connected between them. In that instant it "crackled" like a little spark, an audible shock with terrific force. Arien was flung backward in ecstatic pulsing shudders, orgasmic, pure and from the source. Such power! There was such power here. "Ohhhh! Awesome!" he cried, writhing, as Tina wavered on her knees, her face flushed and radiant, her limpid pupils seeming to fill her irises in their mother-of-pearl settings.

Otter tittered again.

Arien felt a tingling in his spine, down in his tailbone. There was a rushing sound in his ears. It sounded like the ocean pouring over a cliff. Maybe it was the wind. Maybe he heard the sea below and beyond, way out to the distant curving horizon; yet it joined the sound inside of him. It was the same. Or was it in stereo? He tittered now, as Otter had done. The titter radiated outward into the universe. He would have sworn the universe was listening to him as he listened to it. It was a phonic version of the light that was in Tina; that was in them all.

Everything was vibrating now. Myriad sounds and tones reached his deep awareness. Arien sat motionless, erect, hands on his folded legs. His visual field sparkled with billions of infinitely tiny bits of swirling, shimmering points. He knew he heard them, too.

Arien hadn't taken LSD that much. Each time had been so different. It was a totally different and all-embracing experience, yet never had he penetrated so deeply into the mystery. It was all so real – more real than real! He didn't doubt it at all. How could he doubt whatever he was? Deep down within himself he knew he saw the Truth! He knew he would never forget this moment as long as he lived. It seemed to him his whole life had led to this very moment.

Arien strained harder to listen. He held so still that the rhythm of his heart slowed way down before it ceased entirely. Its thumping had been loud in his ears. He silenced it himself. He simply willed it to stop. There was no breath and no pulse.

The sound now buzzed and hummed in his ears. He'd heard sounds like this at a concert once. It was close to this. There were buzzes like the teeth of giant blades biting into forests of wood, like swarms of bees in vast clouds around his head. There were choruses. It sounded like voices, millions of them blended in a cosmic chorale entwined with millions of birds peeping and chirping and squawking and calling, and billions of clocks ticking and chiming. And the tingle in his spine was now a cool force, like a finger of flame with the chill of an icy mountain stream pushing inexorably upward to his head. The rushing within and without him was now exceedingly great and his visual perspective became a swirling vortex that seemed to reach up into the sky.

"It's like one awesome machine," he thought aloud, "but it doesn't think."

At this moment something inside of him touched him. He felt it. It was unmistakable. It could only have come from without. It was like a thought, in substance, yet a solid thing that did not originate from himself. And the quality of thought here, where he now perceived, was definitely a "physical" thing. And this particular thing touched him in the only possible place it could have to convince him it knew where to find him. How could anything have known to touch him there?

It does think!

The vortex sucked him up. There was no resisting it. Arien felt himself fold forward onto the ground as he buried his head in his arms and drew his knees up to his chin. In a blinding flash taut, translucent membranes of living flesh tore away before his field of view. There, a huge sparkling illumined ball of blue, with its green and tan escarpments and puffs of white rolled suspended below him in a vast inky blackness of a million pricks of light sharply piercing his being. The great planet rolled away an exceeding distance with an exponential velocity and soon was a mere blue jewel in the deep carpet of stars. As he slowly unfolded his arms a swirling spiral galaxy of a billion suns spun out and away from him.

I am the beginning and the end, he thought within his own ancient being (but he "said" them certainly).

Why have I come? How is it that I can know this? I am so very young!

Is this not good? Your whole life is before you.

And if this is truly forever, may I stay?

To what purpose?

Arien hesitated, an indulgence for some reason.

The choice is yours.

Then, will I remember this?

Yes.

And will I ever return?

Yes, as you are here with me, now. It is a promise.

My joy fills Forever!

And Arien saw so many things. His whole life he saw. He saw the beginning and the end, and they were the same.

Arien had his food stamps now. He followed Tom's advice and borrowed $10.00 from Otter, who always seemed to have the bread. And Preston outfitted him with an old gray sweater that had holes and frayed edges. "Wear this," Preston said, "and you won't be denied. It's irresistible." He'd grinned with a knowing wink and added, "Five of the last six applicants wore this very sweater to their interview, and not one was refused."

"Six now!" Arien proudly proclaimed to Otter. "How is that possible?"

"These guys are legendary, Arien. Do you know Preston convinced a whole panel of shrinks that he was too crazy to support himself? Yes. All true! He gets ATD, Aid to the Totally Dependent, Man, the absolute max, like a person who is totally blind and paralyzed is able to get. It's far out, Man, really far out."

"Rad."

"His teaching skills are nothing to sneeze at, either. He had a young student who was so convincing that they locked her up! Then, Preston had to pose as her doctor to get her released!"

"Really?"

"No kiddin'. And that ain't all, Man," Otter added. "Tommy there is getting welfare in three different names!"

"No!"

"Yeah, Man. And for two of his interviews he had the same social worker." Otter paused for effect. "He wore a disguise."

They both laughed. Arien was really impressed. In his case, the magic garment had done its trick. A phony social security card didn't hurt, either. Tom was able to supply him with that, along with some other papers that gave him a more believable birth date – and one with a legal age. He had thirty dollars worth of stamps now. Not bad for an hours' time invested.

Otter went with him downtown. They were crossing Market Street a short time after Arien's interview at the food stamp office. "Great!" he applauded, when Arien waved the little books in his face. Otter took one of them before Arien could pull his hand back. "We will donate this to the Free Bakery."

"But Otter," Arien protested, "We may need them."

What happened next was totally unexpected. "Listen, kid," Otter sneered with distain. "I don't have to know you!" They stood in the middle of the street where Otter came to a full stop. "You come a dime a dozen, with that selfish attitude, and unless you show some gratitude to your brothers who will use your contribution to feed the people you can high tail it back to your future, *Dude*! I don't know you. Do you dig?"

Arien was stunned. He had never seen his friend lose his temper before, and now, to throw this rage at him! Traffic bore down on them. At once his head swam with fear and shame. "Please!" He implored, red faced, eyes fleeting this way and that.

"No please! We're all brothers," Otter fiercely continued, totally oblivious of the onrushing cars. "But if you don't know this you'll never know the right thing. You can't ever be trusted. The Revolution doesn't need you. You're better off dead!" He thrust his finger in Arien's face. Cars hurtled past them. They brushed so close. A horn blasting into Arien's ear nearly threw him out of his high tops. Otter never flinched, but glared steadily; cool as steel, right into Arien's eyes. He could not weigh in that moment which was more terrible, the imminent danger of their situation or the righteous anger of his friend - or was it different sides of the same thing? He was overwhelmed. Mute and trembling he offered up all the stamp books.

"No. I don't want them!" Otter turned away and started walking to the curb. The light at the corner changed. The street was suddenly empty. Arien stood in the center, his gaze trailing after Otter.

"Otter!" he cried, chasing after. He could hardly believe what was happening. "Otter! Wait!" He caught up breathless. "Otter, you're right. I'm sorry. I'm sorry. I'm sorry, Dude. Really!"

"All right," Otter said directly. "Do as I've asked you then. And don't forget the house fund at Page Street."

"Yes! Of course!"

On the trolley along the way back to Page Street Arien regarded his friend. What happens to you? He admired this fellow so much. Loved him. There was nobody like this in the future. Otter went into him, as deep as Arien had voyaged in Jeff, though Otter was quite straight today. He went in and he found this little glitch inside, and he fixed it. He knew how. He'd magnified his power exactly as required. He used that traffic. Awesome! The glitch was gone! Arien knew he would never forget it. If there was anybody like this in the future he'd never seen him. Maybe he didn't know where to look. Anyway, the thought depressed him.

"What are you thinking?"

"You mentioned the Revolution, before, when you gave me Hell back there."

Otter's face was stony. His eyes sparkled though. "What about it?"

"It won't succeed."

There was a moment's silence. Arien could hear some old ladies chattering up near the front of the car.

"That's up to you, Arien."

"Nah. There's nothing I can do about it - or you, either."

"Man, we can do more than you know. Tell me: Are you the same as when you came here?"

"No. Probably not."

That's right. I've seen you grow like a weed. You have a spiritual life now. You'll never be the same again."

"But what's that got to do with -"

"Everything. That *is* the Revolution!" Now he smiled outright. "All that other stuff, that's Maya, Arien. It's not real."

Arien was about to argue further when he thought about his last trip in the park. He laughed at himself. He'd spoken to God, just like the hippies people joked about back in his own time. He thought about that moment he knew he would remember always, when he was in a place that was more real than real. He looked again at Otter. He had never admired anyone so much, except maybe Tina. But that was in a different way.

"I thought there for a little while I could be Gay," he said to Jeff. They were sharing a moment together, and a pot of herbal tea in the kitchen at Page Street. Tina was out somewhere with Janice and Otter was off on his rounds.

"Oh?" Jeff was growing a wisp of a beard on his youthful face. Somehow it made him seem even younger. He had gotten some honey in it. He rubbed his chin.

"Yeah, well, when we - we all tripped in Portland I felt turned on by everybody. I mean everybody, Jeff; not just the girls."

"Ha. Right. I know what you mean." He pondered his cup.

"But Tina. Now she's rad. I got the hots for her. More than that. I love her. A lot.

"I'll bet you're glad."

There was a double meaning. It was almost a surprise to hear Jeff, who seemed so innocent, so boyish, to be capable of that. "Oh yes. I mean I don't care what people do. I think I know how a dude could love a dude. I learned that much. I mean, I love you guys, you, Blue, Otter. I really like Otter. And, well, anyway I'm glad, because I want to live now. I never thought so before, but now –"

"What's wanting to live have to do with it?"

"Well, I don't want to get AIDS."

"AIDS?"

"Oh yeah, Dude. Very bad. A terrible killer virus that you get from sex. There won't be a cure. Once you get it, say, goodbye world. Like, in the 1980's, thousands, maybe a million people will die, most of them Gay, and, and hookers, and people who shoot drugs."

"Wow." Jeff contemplated the scenario. "Sounds like a plague. Well, hey! Why not try to stop it? If you know all about it?" Jeff was serious.

"Be real, Dude! Nobody'd believe me 'till it was too late. They'll think I'm bonkers or something, or it'd all be my fault when they find out I was right."

"But you could save somebody!"

"Maybe. If I can, I will I guess."

Jeff drained his cup. He got up and set it in the sink. "Well," he softly drawled, "I noticed Van Gough's got a tail light out. I'd better have a look at it before we head out again. We don't need a reason to get pulled over."

"I'm comin'."

Jeff's VW van was parked around the corner on the opposite side of Schrader. This funky vehicle amused Arien. It was an odd combination of sensible and practical with woefully inadequate power. It originally had a white top and green sides, but that part was now nearly covered with ocean wave and breaker designs that splashed along the lower sides all the way from a big silver half moon that was painted up front between the headlights. Van Gogh's windshield was made of two windows separated by a bar. The little sliding windows on the sides were dressed with Indian print cotton curtains.

All the seats behind the single, solid backed seat up front had been taken out. Jeff had a little galley set up at the back of the van over the engine compartment. Here was a single full-size propane burner attached to a hose that ran to a small refillable bottle strapped in the compartment below. A platform beyond the galley area extended forward enough to hold a small mattress that was covered with a green cotton sheet. The floor area in front of that had a ratty carpet with lots of cushions for people to sit on or lean against. Jeff kept an old, rusty green Coleman icebox there too. It had a cork stuffed in the drain hole that came out during the trip down from Portland and the melt water got some of their baggage wet. Along with that was a battered old olive-green army surplus jerry can, for water.

Jeff unlocked and raised the back door where he was able to reach past the galley area to a place under the mattress platform for his tool kit. Arien, who had no mechanical experience at all, admired Jeff's efficient get down to business approach to this little van. He took out a screwdriver and removed the small red lens cover on the left side.

"Yup. Bad bulb."

"That was easy."

"You got that right. I might even have a spare." He rummaged in a paper bag of stuff and soon found it. "Here, Arien. Go up and turn the key, okay?" He handed that over and Arien went up front and slid behind the large, nearly horizontal steering wheel. Van Gogh had a starter button rigged under the dash but the ignition key still had to be turned first. Arien inserted and twisted the key and pulled the spindly signal stick that jutted off the column.

"Yeah! Other side? – Cool, man."

"Say, Jeff? Where's the gas gauge on this thing?"

"Huh?"

"Where's the – Oh, duh. It's right here by the column." The door was ajar and now opened wider. "Hi, Babe." Tina slipped into the opening to stand next to him. Her long blonde hair framed her face.

He reached up to barely touch her cheek. She clasped his hand on its way down and held it for a moment.

"Hi there, Arien."

"Yo, Janice."

"What are you guys doing?"

"Oh, checkin' the van out."

"Has Otter said how much longer we'll be here?" Tina asked.

"He said nothin' yet. He told me this morning he had a hot tip on some clear liquid acid that was being offered pretty cheap, but he still had to hustle the bucks to make it."

"Say, are you planning to see Alex again?"

"I don't know. I don't know if I could take that just yet."

"You could call him next time; meet him some place."

"Is he the fellow you went to see in Berkeley?" Janice wedged herself in next to Tina.

Arien nodded.

"Man! Paul tells me things are getting hot over there. He wants to go with some of the guys to check it out."

"What's it about?" Jeff asked. He'd just come up to join the others by the front of the van.

"It's about some vacant land that everybody wants to make into a People's Park. The University wants a parking lot."

"That's bozo," Arien said. "Who's involved in this?"

"The brothers and sisters," Janice said. "The people."

"Oh."

"You wanna go?" Jeff asked, looking at Arien.

"I don't know." He was thinking about the proximity to Alex and Nanna.

Jeff moved away to close up the van in the back.

"There might be a real demonstration, huh?"

Janice grinned. "That's what he said."

"Wow. Yeah, I guess I'd like to see one of those. No doubt, if it's in Berkeley, Alex will view it as a communist plot."

"It probably is," Janice observed. She winked. Tina smirked.

They all went back up to the apartment. Mikel was in the kitchen filling up a pan of water in the sink. There was a huge pile of artichokes on the table. "Hi, Arien," he greeted, seeming oblivious of the others. He tossed the large heads into the pot.

"What's all this?"

Mikel wrinkled his lip in the 'oh, come on' gesture. "It's dinner, man."

"Oh wow! Where'd these come from?" Janice was visibly excited.

"Next door. The Angels are having a choker festoon," Mikel explained. "I dropped into some serendipity. There was more than even they could eat this time."

"How lucky! I love artichokes!" Janice said.

"Me too!" Tina agreed.

Arien demurred. He had never had an artichoke but wasn't sure if he wanted to admit it. An excited, "Ow!" from the stairwell helped him out. Somebody was being announced. Soon after that Otter made his way into the kitchen with a broad smile on his face. People looked at him for an explanation.

It wasn't the artichokes. Slowly, with understated drama, Otter drew something out of his fringed leather pouch. It was a glass vial, about half an inch wide and six inches long, with a rubber stopper on the end. It looked like it was full of clear water.

Gleeful wows and ows filled the room. It sounded like a schoolhouse closing early for summer. For a moment Arien wasn't sure what he was seeing, but then it dawned on him. This wasn't water at all. This was something *very* special.

"That's right," Otter assured him, as if reading Arien's mind. He held it up. "There's enough energy in here to transform the planet."

"My God!" Said Mikel reverently. "I've never seen so much pure liquid LSD in my life. Can we do some now?" His whole face pleaded. It was amazing how Mikel's face could adapt an emotion and own it.

"Maybe we can spare a little before we leave town, Mikel. But most of this has a very particular destination." Otter winked at Arien, who smiled and shook his head.

"Mikel, don't look so disappointed."

"Aw, poor baby!" Tina crooned.

The "chokes" were awesome. Everybody but Karen was there. She worked as a waitress most evenings. Along with the food, folks in the room were totally preoccupied with events in Berkeley. Old Joe suggested they all stay away. He'd heard Governor Reagan say on the news he would not give in to the radicals.

Arien listened and watched what was supposed to happen to artichokes before he tried any. "Do you think this is important?" he whispered in Tina's ear. He focused on a little sheen of blonde-white fuzz over her lip, conscious of how he kept noticing new things about her. She looked at him, questioning, then, with gathering intensity.

"The times - they are a changin'".

He knew she quoted Dylan. The way she said it didn't sound hokey.

She tore a fat petal off the large choke in her plate and slipped it between her teeth.

He felt troubled. Otter's words on the streetcar came back to him, *"All that other stuff, that's Maya, Arien. It's not real."* Just then he caught Otter's eye. He sat cross-legged on the floor several feet away, with Susie Q, Jeff, and Mikel between them. He grabbed some empty plates that were next to him and motioned to Arien as he suddenly stood. Arien followed him into the kitchen.

"Let's you and I wash and dry." He began clearing things out of the sink.

"Sure, Otter." What was this about?

"I hope you don't have any plans tonight, Arien, because there's somebody I want you to meet."

Later, Arien went with Otter to an apartment down in the Panhandle where a tall and lanky man lived. He sported long, stringy, very light blonde hair that was lighter than Jeff's, almost white, that was circled with a yellow headband. A long, but wispy beard hung from off of his chin. He looked like a Scandinavian - Mongolian hybrid in a yellow crushed velvet tunic, cut square at the neck, with an orange satin sash at the waist, and he also wore loose, faded orange cotton drawstring pants. He was barefoot. His blue-white eyes greeted them expressively in an oval face as Otter simply opened the door and walked in. He nodded and motioned for his visitors to sit down on some cushions ringing a low, round brass table where he also sat down.

Arien was puzzled. The fellow had been standing inside the doorway as if he and Otter were expected. Otter caught Arien's expression and smiled. He knew something. "Jamie? This is Arien. Arien, meet Jamie Sun."

The man called Jamie bobbed his head graciously. Arien couldn't tell how old he was. He seemed to be young and yet oddly mature. The eyes were too sharp for a young man. His tittering laughter tickled. It surprised Arien. That left him feeling foolish, but this man's apparent gentleness disarmed him - or was it charmed?

A woman appeared. She stood in an open passage to a hallway. She looked old to Arien, but she was beautiful. Arien had never seen such a fox be so old before. Her thick, deep gray hair fell out under a black beret. It was very long, luxuriant hair that reached all the way down her back, well below her hips. She had on a black turtleneck sweater and wore blue jeans and sandals.

"Otter!"

"Hello, Jennifer." Otter was obviously pleased to see her.

The woman acknowledged Arien with her eyes.

"How is the painting?" Otter asked her.

"It's finished."

"May I see it?" Her smile invited Otter to follow. He got up from the table and went with her down the hallway.

Arien sat calmly across from Jamie Sun. He let his eyes wander. On the brass table was a flat rectangular cake and a small pile of herbage. The cake looked like sticky black hash, the other was browner than weed. It was unmistakably tobacco. There was a pile of wooden matches there, too, and an obsidian pipe shaped like an elongated funnel. Jamie picked it up, opening the question to his young guest.

"What is it?"

"A chillum," Jamie said. "You smoke it like this." He stuck it from the end of his joined hands, between tight fingers, and he sucked through a fist.

Arien was flattered by the invitation. "Sure," he agreed.

Jamie picked up a matchstick and touched it to a tiny flame in a thick yellow candle that barely flickered there. The match flared. He held it to a corner of the cake and then peeled off some of the softened hash with his thumbnail, stuffed it with a pinch of the tobacco and passed the chillum to Arien.

Then Jamie lit another match, extending his long arms over the table as Arien fixed the pipe to his face the way he was shown. He sucked. It was hot and spicy. His head spun. It tingled. He giggled. The light in the room seemed to flicker as the pulse of a rush went to his head.

"Wow."

Jamie grinned broadly and bobbed his head again, only now with some frequency, like one of those little spring-headed toys in an auto's rear window. "You've really come a long way!" The words were like notes in his high-pitched musical voice. He seemed so delighted, like a little kid can be.

Arien smiled. He couldn't help it, though it was a shock – like cold water in the face; absurd - because Jamie's startling statement came off so naturally. It was like sunlight all around him. Then he was there in the room again. He was with it. His fullness seemed to illuminate the room. Arien could hardly believe it. Was he still in the same world?

Almost with reverence, he handed the chillum back to Jamie. Jamie stuffed it again with pinches from the tabletop and adroitly lit it himself. He spoke through the curling rings of smoke in his melodic voice. "It's very, *very* rare."

Arien didn't pretend not to understand. "How rare?" He asked, focusing on a gold ring with a large yellow, faceted stone that Jamie wore.

"Maybe once in a thousand years or so." Jamie's head bobbed in affirmation. He sucked more at the chillum until the end glowed brightly. "Sometimes it makes a difference. Sometimes not." His exhale was matter-of-fact, as if he had been smoking a cigarette, but the large sweet cloud of gray-white smoke didn't support that effect.

"Can you tell why it happened to me?"

"I don't know that. Just a cosmic accident, maybe. Maybe not. Maybe *you* know."

"What happens, then? Otter told me there were no accidents."

"Maybe. Maybe not." Jamie passed the chillum back to Arien. "It all depends on where in the paradox it originates, doesn't it?"

"I suppose." He gazed back as if from somewhere in a daydream. "How long will it last?" Arien pressed, trying to stay focused.

Jamie answered with another question, "Where are you going next?"

Arien held the warm pipe between his hands. It was burning on its own now. He drew on it. It felt hot in his throat. He laughed through the smoke that lingered around his face. "Woodstock," he said.

"Ha!" Jamie's eyes sparkled like two jewels in his bouncing head as he slapped his knees with delight. He twisted around to fumble for a moment among some cloth bags that were on the floor behind him. When he turned back to face his visitor, Jamie held one of these between his two hands. It was a bag of cobalt-blue velvet. It was tied with a fat, natural cotton chord. He passed it over the table. It was large, about as long as a forearm, weighing a couple of pounds, and very hard. It seemed to be curved, tapering from wider at one end to very narrow on the other. Arien hefted it first, and then, with a signal from Jamie, he untied the cord and pulled out a rather large animal's horn. It was a dark, nut-brown, three-sided and ridged with concentric rings. A hole was drilled through the pointed end.

"Bitchin'." Arien turned it over a few times. "Does it do anything?"

"You can blow it. But, not now!" Jamie's eyes danced as he lapsed into chuckles, as if amused with some inside joke. "It's very loud. Even the angels can hear it."

Arien was puzzled.

"It's for you. You'll know what to do with it." The words seemed to dance with the melody of his voice. He stuffed the chillum again and passed it back.

As Arien got more stoned he involuntarily receded into his head until he realized with a start he had allowed himself to drift too much. It was the strangest sensation. Jamie Sun was like a distant island now. Without anything being said he just knew this was so and that any further conversation would lack substance. But he did get away with an answer to one of his yearnings. He found an authority. For Jamie to have known anything at all patently guaranteed that much.

After that, Arien fell into a vague memory of Blue Star and something he said after that wonderful acid trip in Portland: *How do you contemplate anything greater than the miracle of yourself?*

He drifted into a comfortable place and rested there awhile. His friends were there with him. He loved them. It was such a good feeling. It was strange then when a distant stimulus formed into a body being nudged. His body. He had to find his way out to where this was happening. Otter was calling him.

"Yeah. Yeah. Okay." Did he have to open his eyelids? They were open. His eyes felt heavy and dry; lips stuck together. Stale. Out of darkness an unfamiliar room came into view as its pieces fell into place. The air was still and cool. Yes. They were at Jamie Sun's. They were there and Otter was rousing him. He could feel the smooth weight of Otter's fringed leather jacket covering him. It smelled good, like Otter. It had kept out the cool, still air in the dark, musty room.

Arien carefully stood up from the cushions that cradled him, handing the jacket back to his friend and, slowly remembering, he reached for the horn in its cobalt-blue bag, where it laid by his side. While his eyes took their time to focus, he let Otter lead him to the door. The real shock came when Otter opened it and guided him through into the morning outside. "Oh, wow," Arien said. They'd been there all night! Otter smiled at him. There was something funny about the smile. "Where were you?" Arien asked. They started walking down the early morning street.

"I was right here the whole time," he said.

"You weren't with Jamie and I."

"No. I was with Jennifer."

"Oh." Arien smiled now, too. "But I thought she -"

"- Came with Jamie? No. She lives there with Jamie but they're not a couple, if that's what you mean."

"Bitchin', Dude. I'm glad everything worked out so convenient."

Otter laughed. "Bitchin'," he echoed.

Arien was surprised to see most of the household was up already. People were making toast in the kitchen. The whole room, in fact, smelled like fresh toasted bread. Sitting at the table was Paul, Janice, Karen, and Tim, Old Joe and Mikel, and somebody Arien hadn't seen before, a hale young man, about mid-to-late-twenties, maybe six-feet tall, with long, wavy, dark brown hair. He wore a white silk shirt with an oversize collar. His navy bell jeans had patches and some embroidery over a front pocket. They were secured with a purple-colored web belt with a military-style plain brass buckle. His tennis shoes were blue with white stars. A khaki-colored army-style bag was strapped over his left shoulder. He wore a moustache over an engaging smile. He nodded at Arien and Otter and returned to a conversation he was having with the others. "Yes," he said, "I think they're going to be out in force. We need everybody. We've got to show them we won't be beat down this time."

Paul leaned forward in his chair, putting his hands on his knees with arms resting on his legs, sphinx like, poised, bushy black eyebrows furrowed. "I'll bet they call out the guard." He pulled a pack of Chesterfield's out from under his black vest and took out one of the filter-less cigarettes. He didn't light it, though. He held it like some object of concentration, and tapped the end of it with his thumb.

"Oh, hey, the Pigs busted into the Park early this morning. Man, they brought a bulldozer." He looked at Arien again, but held his gaze longer this time. "MDM will take the opportunity to pass out the newsletter I've been helping with," he continued. "That's why I need to get back right away."

He lifted a strap of his bag and took a folded paper out. Arien was a little surprised when it was passed to him. He looked over the cover page. The People's Coalition was announcing its relationship with the Movement for a Democratic Military. Here the visitor was paraphrased, and everybody was cooperating to bring about a big turnout for People's Park in Berkeley.

Arien was a little puzzled. But then everybody was involving him in things he knew little or nothing about. He supposed it was what was expected. Everybody had to be caught up in something; and, even if it was nothing at all, you absolutely had to be caught up with it. Arien wondered what he was supposed to do with the flyer now. Mikel helped him out. When he reached for it Mikel caught the visitor's attention and winked. It wasn't meant for Arien to see but he did, and he saw the visitor imperceptibly connect with Mikel. A slight smile stole the corner of his face.

"I'm Andy." He offered his hand.

"Arien."

"Like the Aryan Race, Man?"

"Like the God of War," Old Joe said.

Andy's smile broadened.

"I'm an Aries," Arien confirmed.

"Same difference," Janet shrugged.

"And I haven't met you, either," Andy said to Otter.

"Oh. Sorry," said Paul, as Otter introduced himself.

Some more toast popped up. Karen offered it to Arien and Otter, who both took a slice. They helped themselves to cream cheese and a jar of honey that was on the table. It was good, wholesome wheat bread. Someone had evenly sliced the Free Bakery loaf. As more bread went into the toaster, Tim reached into the big tin breadbox on the wood counter top and took out another loaf. He cut off several fat slices.

When Arien felt eyes on his back he turned to see Tina standing demurely in the doorway. I've been out all night and she's so beautiful and she looks at me with such trust and peace! She reflected his gladness. His heart quickened. He passed her his slice of toast. She ate some and handed it back. Ha! He watched how she caught a drip of honey on her lip; the way she licked her finger.

"So, how are we going to get there?" Paul asked.

"Van Gogh?" Otter suggested. "Is Jeff here?"

"He was a little while ago." It was Karen. She spread cream cheese on a fresh piece of toast.

"How 'bout you take some of us over, Old Joe?"

"Oh, no. I'm not going there to do that," he said. He raised his hands in 'nay' and fluttered them to enforce his point.

"Why not?" Andy asked.

"Because I can't run like I used to, and you need a good pair of legs to get out of the tear gas." He chuckled to himself. "No. That's for you younger folk."

"It's gonna be a peaceful rally, at the U," Andy said.

Old Joe guffawed. "You have to be kidding." His expression exaggerated disbelief. "Some of you run a good chance of getting your heads bashed at this one. No sir. Just look at Andy's rag there. It's all such a big deal. And, think of it, the Park has come to be a symbol to all these people on both sides of the issue. Governor Reagan, The

University and the City of Bezerkely's not going for it, and I've heard rumors National Guard units are on standby. You said as much yourself. You got nitro waiting for glycerin, Man."

"Well, you can take some of us over the Bay Bridge, can't you?" Paul asked.

"Oh, I don't know. You'd have to get back on your own. No one's going to talk me into hanging out there."

Arien was thinking Old Joe could be talked into it.

"What's that?" Tina pointed at the velvet bag Arien had wedged between his feet on the floor. He reached down to pick it up and loosened the chord around the neck. Everyone watched as he pulled the large, dark horn into view.

"Wow," Mikel said. "Water Buffalo."

"Where'd you get it?" Janice asked.

Arien handed it to Paul, who reached out. "Jamie Sun gave it to me."

"Wow," Mikel said again.

Paul put it to his lips, eyes twinkling through his glasses. Some people covered their ears. But, instead of blowing he asked Arien if he had blown it yet.

"No."

"Oh, then, here." He lowered it respectfully and passed it back.

"You're right, Paul," Otter said. "Probably Arien should blow it first."

Arien smiled a little sheepishly. "I don't know if I can."

"Well maybe you should practice outside," Karen said. Only now did she uncover her ears.

"How do you do it?"

"Like a trumpet," Paul answered. "Purse your lips and force the air out like this." The vibration of his example made a buzzing sound. "You just touch the mouth there and capture that. The horn will do the rest."

Mikel wore a puckish smirk. "You can bring it to Berkeley," he said.

"He's got something!" Andy exclaimed. "They have two way radios, right?"

"I don't know if that's what it's for," Arien fended. "I might loose it there."

"Yes," Old Joe agreed. "That and a piece of your skull!"

"Well," Andy said, "We still need to get all of us who are going, over there. It might be a good idea to arrive early."

As if on queue, footsteps up the stairs materialized with Jeff in the doorway. He barely got into the kitchen when Andy, on hearing Jeff's name in greeting, asked him, "Are you the brother with a van?"

"Huh?"

"He wants to know if you'll take us to Bezerkeley, Jeff." Otter said. Otter took his herb out and some papers and rolled a perfect doobie without even looking at it.

Jeff shrugged.

"If that's a yes, can we go soon?"

It took two hours before everyone was ready to go. Paul, Janice, Karen, Tim, Mikel, Andy, Arien, Tina and Otter all packed into Van Gogh with Jeff behind the wheel. Somehow Arien got to sit up front, squished between Jeff and Tina. He remembered some of the things Otter said, about life and Maya, and wondered why Otter was there at all. Arien felt quite excited, himself. He'd heard about the famous protests of the 60's. Maybe this would become one of these. Maybe he would get to see, first hand, what it was all about.

"Pigs followin'," Jeff drawled, looking at his side view mirror as Van Gogh chugged onto the Bay Bridge.

"Don't everybody look," Otter said from the back.

Arien couldn't resist twisting around but he didn't see anything through the small rear window that was blocked by people in the van.

"Damn," Jeff reported, "They're all wearin' helmets."

"They're Blue Meanies." Janice said.

"Yup."

Arien looked at Tina with a perceptible sigh.

"Oh shit," Jeff said. He started to pull over right there on the bridge.

"Bummer," Karen intoned.

"Are you carrying, Otter?" Paul asked.

"Me?"

Van Gogh was almost stopped when the patrol car zoomed right past with its light flashing on top.

"Yea!" Karen cheered.

"Shades of things to come?" Mikel asked rhetorically.

Arien noted the silence from this Andy dude. Andy. Andy –

Jeff merged the van back into traffic. Jeff didn't say anything the next time, but Arien saw another patrol car pass them with its light flashing, then two more, no lights, but going faster than the traffic. All of them were packed with men wearing white helmets.

"I don't know about this," Tina said.

"What's that?" Otter asked.

"Meanies convention over there," Jeff answered.

"Fuck 'em!" Andy snapped.

Arien looked out past the bridge into the bay. A few boats were on the water. A lot of birds were in the air. A lot; probably more birds than he had ever seen in one place at one time; little birds in a vast flock of them like a dark flickering river moving inexorably toward the Golden Gate.

"Awesome."

"Yeah. Check it out!"

Once over the Bay Bridge and onto the East Shore Freeway to Berkeley the police presence was even more marked. On Ashby, Van Gogh was pulled over, but the car drove off before an officer got out.

"They're confused," Jeff said, tightly gripping the broad wheel.

"We're pretty obvious," Arien remarked.

"We're free and legal!" Andy assured them.

"Almost." Arien couldn't see Otter's grin but he knew it was plastered over his face.

"Right on!" Tim chimed.

"Maybe we should head back," Karen said. "This gives me the creeps."

Engine at idle, Van Gogh filled with a billow of cigarette smoke as Paul lit a Chesterfield.

"Can I have one of those?" Arien asked, twisting around so he could see Paul. Paul ended up passing several of them out.

"I say we head straight for the campus. People will be there. Come on, folks! We're sitting ducks here!"

"Andy's right," Otter agreed. "The Pigs are crazed. We should be with other people."

Jeff laughed nervously as he slowly moved them away from the curb. "Know any good side streets?"

"Did you remember to signal?" Mikel called. He had a shit-eating grin on his face, Arien thought, Damn! This is exciting!

The steady wop wop wop wop wop wop of an Army helicopter pounded suddenly overhead.

"Heading due east. The Park, no doubt. Turn left down there at the light!" Andy was leaning over Arien's shoulder to see out the windshield. His breath smelled like spearmint gum. "Oh shit!" They could see a patrol car angled across the road up ahead. "Right! Here! Quick!

"Good. Now, turn into the alley!"

Jeff was doing the best he could. Van Gogh lurched, bounced and rocked.

"Okay, okay - slow here. Slow – Good! Right turn!"

Arien and Tina regarded each other. Arien might have been afraid for her, but her face was all lit up. She was excited as he was! Radical babe! They reflected each other's grin.

Andy directed them a little ways farther to where they parked, on Walnut Street, up a couple of blocks from campus. There were no police in the area.

"Good job!" Otter commended.

"Yes!"

"Yeah, thanks!"

"You're welcome. Glad you could be here. I think your van will be safer on this side," Andy told Jeff.

Everyone tumbled out and joined a gathering stream of people who were quietly converging onto the campus. Tim went back for a water jug.

The smell of Mary Jane and pure tension wafted in the atmosphere. People wore determined faces. Tina passed Arien a handbill somebody had given her. "Let's tell the University that we want the South Campus to remain a beautiful place of homes and parks...not...a place of ugly dormitories and parking lots," he pompously read aloud. "Radical."

Paul caught that. His eyes blinked through his glasses and a dead-pan face as he hunkered onward, as if driving himself into a heavy rain.

Tim got it, too. He smirked back with a shame-on-you motion of his fingers.

There were a lot of people gathering in the plaza. Knots of them were all over. Some people ran among them. Faces wore anger and dismay. Voices rose and fell as news and rumors spread like sloshing waves through the crowd.

The group from Page Street parked themselves around a large bench and planter box that was off to the side of the plaza. Some sat on the bench here and others climbed up to perch on the edge of the planter, above everybody. Andy slipped away but returned a short time later. "They got the whole area around the Park sealed off," he announced.

"Something ought to be done about it." Tina said with a fist raised tight.

"Yeah! Yeah!" Arien agreed, laughing.

A hush came over the still gathering crowd as somebody standing on the flight of steps in front of the building there started shouting through cupped hands.

"Students, Friends, Comrades, they've put a chain link fence around our Park!"

A great shout of "NO!" went up.

"I can't even get into my dorm!" Somebody yelled.

Next, after a few spurts, pops and sputters, the speaker's statement, "They've blocked off the whole area!" went over a loud speaker that had just been set up.

Arien's laughter subsided. The rush of this crowd was a genuine thrill. There had to be several thousand packed in there by now! Most of these people were older than he was. There were some hippies his age. College students still seemed like a distant race. Everybody was rad, though; kind of like kids would look later on. Lots of jeans and T-shirts. A smattering of pea coats. Tina, standing by Arien, took his hand. His heart swelled in his breast. He felt light. Dizzy. How did I get here? His awareness withdrew to her. She took a doobie a person near in the crowd passed her. People were always passing her things. Oh, she wasn't a bombshell but she was perfect. She didn't wear tight or skimpy clothes. Plain dresses. Turtle neck sweaters. No make up. The sparkle she had was all her own. All real.

She pinched it tightly between her fingers and took a hit, smiled, winced, passed it to him. It was burning down the side. He dropped a tongue of saliva onto a finger and daubed it on the doobie to stop the run. He drew slowly.

"...Dan Siegel." He heard the person introduced over the mike. There was a smattering of applause.

Arien hit it again. It tasted pretty good.

The speaker launched into a story about the Park, recounting events. His words captured listeners. "...They tore down perfectly good housing that citizens and students could afford to live in!" he explained.

It looked like Otter was about to move near when Andy and Mikel came to stand by Arien's other side. Arien looked at Andy. "I don't think so," he mused out loud.

"Huh?"

Arien passed him the doobie. "You don't look like anybody I know." He smiled, but he really wasn't sure. This was the first person by that name he'd run across.

"Oh?"

"Pretty good, isn't it?"

"Oh. Yeah." Andy coughed. He passed it to Mikel, and then he pulled a handful of the People's Coalition flyers out of his side pack and passed them out to everyone nearby.

People were shouting now. Arien looked back toward Sproul Hall. "It's our Park, right?" the fellow up on the steps baited.

"Yes! Yeah! Yes!" the people cried.

"So, let's go down there and take it over!"

"Yeah! Yeah! Take the Park! Take the Park!" It was becoming a roar.

Arien looked around at his friends. He could see it in their eyes. Something was happening. So much anger among so many people. So awesome!

It was just like a pot boiling over. It spilled and splashed whooping and shouting on Bancroft, where it spattered, surged and flowed into Telegraph. God it was exciting! It felt like driving, pounding, defiant music. Screaming Punk, Arien thought. He flashed a wide smile to Tina, who held his hand. He looked around. His friends were all together. Wow. Rad! He looked to Otter who was so alert. He seemed to be listening for something, almost as if all those people were not there and he was walking and listening intently on his own.

They moved a couple of blocks down the 'Ave' when up ahead there was confusion. Arien heard people cry out over advancing mayhem. Lots of angry shouting drowning out an amplifier. White helmets visible over heads at the front. They straddled the Avenue. Off to the right he could hear a pop, pop-pop. A cloud of yellow smoke billowed thickly upward, wafted by a thin breeze into tendrils of smoky fingers, grasping bits of people. Coughing. Rage and screaming. Protesters in front folded onto those behind them. Some ran this way and that. It reversed the general direction of movement. They backed up a block toward campus.

Arien had let go of Tina's hand. He could see her running next to him, surging with a large group from their part of the march. Rather than return to the University, where a lot of the people behind him were going, his group headed to the left, down Dwight. As they rounded the corner Arien heard a great crash behind him from the Bank of America on his right. He could just see the shards of thick dark glass cave in and fly, like spattered fat in a cauldron. It was where he had stood with Alex. It was where he saw their reflections and something of the yawning gulf between them.

Andy howled. He disappeared after that.

It was a long block to run. A police car, red light flashing, suddenly bore down on them. It was right in the middle of the street.

The large knot of people, maybe a hundred in all, seemed to open like an amoeba and close behind the speeding car. It was as if it happened in slow motion. The car approached. Arien was just scoping a direction to escape from being run down when the air filled with a hail of flying objects. Bang bang crash! As bricks and stones hit, the rear window blew out first; then the sides. Finally the windshield sank away in a thousand crystal fragments.

The car stopped to a wail of screeching tires, dipping forward with momentum, lurching backward as tires furiously reversed. Arien was sure he saw sparks and smoke coil out from burning rubber! No more than twelve feet away were the whites of a startled policeman's eyes gawking through the hollow space over the dash as his car withdrew backwards down the street, maybe faster than it came!

"Damn!" Arien cried to Tina.

"Yeah!" she howled.

"Revolution Babe!" He beamed at her.

There was yelling and cheering and more things in the air; more crashing, breaking glass. People were trying to reach the Park by another way. They'd gone down this shorter block. Students' faces were in windows here. Many hung out over sills and ledges, craning to see. Some waved. A few books and magazines were thrown down.

In a moment everything changed. Arien couldn't tell where it came from, but a black object whizzed by his feet spewing yellow-white snaking, billowing, and dense, stinking smoke. It smelled like fizzling matches with a liberal sprinkling of rotten onion and vinegar-soaked, black pepper. His eyes were suddenly on fire! It hurt! It stung! He gagged, tried to hold his breath, gasped and started coughing uncontrollably. His stomach felt like it was about to heave. Unable to see clearly, he lurched this way and that, trying to make out the identities of running legs in the cloud. Somehow he stayed upright. Somehow he moved far enough away to breathe again. He felt sick and dizzy.

"Bastards!" He coughed, bleary eyes trying to focus. When he saw a group of dark-suited, helmeted men in uniforms it was almost too late. Arien sprinted like he never had before! The wind in his face stung his eyes as legs flailed beneath him. He had no way of knowing whatever on the sidewalk caused him to stumble just then saved his head. He could only hear the whoosh of something cut through the air. He barely heard the faint crack on the skull of whoever was nearest. The only hope of escape was to run like the wind.

When he stopped, gasping, heart pounding in his heaving chest, trembling with a finger-stinging dose of adrenaline, in whiffs of acrid air and cries and sirens and shouting and shattering windows and the pop pop, pop-pop pop and bang of - gunfire? - Arien realized he didn't recognize anybody anymore! "Oh God!" He gasped again, but this time not for lack of air.

Where was she? His eyes darted this way and that for something he could recognize. He heard a pop - smack - whinny next to his ear.

Those are real bullets!" somebody cried out.

"Shit!" Arien realized he had circled all the way back to Telegraph. Now there was a wall of police efficiently sweeping everything before them, just moments away from where he stood. He looked out over the phalanx of white helmets, the surging and catcalls from windows and rooftops, the fleeing people. Arien had never seen anything so terrifying and so exciting in all his life. He feared for his friends. He feared for himself. Yet, someplace deep inside he exulted at the mayhem while desperately wondering where Tina, Otter, and the others were now.

Just then Andy and Tim, running by, saw Arien, and stopped right there.

A brief moment of appreciation glinted in their eyes as they looked around and at each other. Andy and Tim took great gulps of air. Nobody could see which way to go. One was blocked by a surreal mist of gas. Arien scouted another but four cops with gas masks on motorcycles were parked in a cluster just behind it. The only other way open, an alley across the street, looked too far to get to in time.

Oh damn! They were so close! Others, who were also trapped, only closer to the moving wave, were being smashed mercilessly to the sidewalk by baton-wielding officers. Arien, transfixed with extreme excitement, fear and horror, was sure he saw a pair of glasses shatter on somebody's face. Blood literally splashed out of the unfortunate head, like a crushed turnip.

"In here! Quick!" A hand grabbed Arien by his shoulder and pulled him backward, off balance, into the darkness of a hallway. He heard the door slam shut as he fell on his ass and a few pairs of feet jumped and scurried over the top of him. There was banging on the door but it passed and moved away. He was on his feet. He tumbled up the stairs after the person - or persons - that had pulled him inside. He saw Andy already at the top, turning to look after him. On the second story there was a door open to the flat roof. As soon as he passed through it, somebody shut the door behind him and turned a key in the lock.

There were others on the roof; a group of nine or ten people beside himself, Tim and Andy. Some of these were throwing bricks over the side. There were little piles of brick, cement block and rubble along the low wall edging the roof. It hid their bodies like a rampart.

"Smash the Pigs!" Andy screamed, rushing over to the edge. He grabbed a cinder block by the low wall, and placing a foot on the rim, raised the block up over his head. Arien heard that pop-pop popping sound again. He thought it funny the way Andy tossed that block. He practically dropped it, almost hitting himself as it landed, dunk, on the roof at his feet, when he buckled and slumped down by it. "Ow ow ow - oh! Oh fuck. It hurts! Oh fuck! Ohhhhhh fuck!"

"Jesus! He's been shot!" somebody gasped.

A bright red stain began to spread under Andy's left armpit, right through his white shirt. His hand reached around, almost to his back. Twisting in agony, he clutched himself. Arien could hardly believe his eyes. Andy looked so afraid; so shocked.

It was a real war! Arien had no idea! He'd heard about the Civil War. He'd certainly known of Viet Nam, but this? No one had ever told him about this! A real battle on the streets of an American city was happening all around him! Those were *real* bullets!

"Why didn't I know about this?" he cried out. "Why wasn't I told?"

The wounded young man clutching his underarm tensely rocked himself, striking his head against the wall with a soft, thunking rhythm. Briefly, he looked up at Arien. "Throw it for me, huh?" he pleaded.

"Sure, Dude. What the Hell?" Arien grabbed the block, and setting his foot on the rampart for balance, raised the block over his head as Andy had done. The line of police had already moved away. But a car was down there. It didn't look like a police car, but it didn't seem to belong there, either. Arien watched his missile fall. He saw it land on the car like a baby in a blanket, slamming right on top, crunching deep into the metal. At the same time the windshield changed color, from a glassy reflection to sugar-white. It slumped inward, to a concave geode of worthless glass nuggets. The car stopped. People came out. They were police. Covering their heads, they ran as a hail of objects rained down on them. People on the roof cheered, raising fists high in the air.

"Smash the pigs!" Arien screamed. "Take the Park! Ah ha ha ha!" So much he felt then. They dared to shoot people! *Shoot* people! He shook with the rage. He cursed over the wall, "You mother-fuckin' bastards…"

"You better get down now," Tim said. He stood back by a dingy skylight. He beckoned.

"Yeah." Arien backed away. He bent down to the fellow at his feet. "How does it feel, Andy?"

Andy's complexion was now white as paper. "Oh God, ow. Ow!"

"Can I see it?" Arien grasped Andy's trembling wrist.

"Oh no. Oh no, Man."

People were gathering around now. "Here, Man!" A fellow handed Andy his bandana. Andy carefully stuffed it in under the hand covering his wound.

"It hurts. Oh God. I can't breathe."

"Lay back," Arien said. "Get your head down." He helped Andy move. Arien was sure he felt some force tingle up his arm when they made contact. It was like a current; a cold animal current of fear and pain. His arm trembled, but he held his hand out to cradle Andy's head, to stop it from hitting the wall anymore.

"He needs an ambulance," a bare-chested teenager observed. The kid had several bands of beads and a silver peace sign draped around his neck. His jeans, hair and body were dirty and sweaty. He was breathing hard.

Now all these sirens could be heard. Arien realized they had been there all along. In all the noise he picked out the sound of sirens, fire, police, and ambulance. It seemed impossible.

There was so much blood! Arien knew he could hold that tighter. He moved Andrew's hand away from the wound. What scared him was Andy let him do it. Blood oozed through the bandana and between Arien's fingers. That's when he noticed there were really two holes in Andy's body. The bullet hit Andy under the armpit, on the edge of his pectoral, against the rib cage and exited under the left shoulder blade. The hole in his back still bled freely. Arien thought he might get sick, but he held his breath, and then let it out slowly. That seemed to help.

"I need more bandage!" He hollered. "We have to stop this up!" Arien pressed the wounds tightly with both his trembling hands. Blood flow slowed.

Tim took his shirt off.

Two more bandanas and a hankie were passed down. Someone else passed another T-shirt. Arien placed these over the sopping area and wrapped Tim's shirt under Andy's arms. He knotted the sleeves together as tight as he could, letting Andy yelp in pain. The effort took his mind off of fear. He just wanted to help so badly he nearly cried. This side of him was frantic. There was another side of him that still couldn't believe what was happening. It was kind of numb from there; distant and dreamlike.

Some people moved to the wall again. They shouted. "Man shot up here!"

Arien couldn't see what was going on.

"No," Andy said. "I can't let the pigs take me."

"Does anybody know a doctor?"

"We could get him to the clinic."

"How?"

There was a bang from the street below. It sounded like a shotgun.

"You need a doctor," Arien said. "Who cares if the pigs help you now?"

"I do. I do, man. I'm - I've - got - warrant for - dr - draft - evasion. No way, Man. No -" His breath grew shorter; more rapid.

Arien got that sick feeling back again. He was so afraid for this fellow. Something had to be done! Fast! "Come on," he said, looking up. "Let's get this guy to the clinic!"

"In Scouts, we learned how to make a chair," the unwashed young man said. "We can carry him down the stairs."

People rallied to that. The teenager was telling some others what he had in mind but they were going right to it. Andy grimaced and cursed as he was gently lifted into a human cradle that laboriously moved him to the door off the roof. Arien stayed by his side, between Tim and the teenager, to be sure the bandage stayed on.

It seemed to take forever to get Andy down the steps. They almost dropped him at the first landing. At the bottom they were more careful. Three guys supported him while somebody opened the door and Arien looked outside. He searched both ways, like a crossing guard - very carefully.

Two policemen were running back up the middle of the street toward campus. One of them, without hat or helmet, looked up at rooftops as he ran. He tripped and stumbled on the street, got up and started running again. Briefly, his eyes met Arien's as he passed. There was no connection. Only eyes. Arien couldn't imagine what they saw. He moved back inside the open door. He looked helplessly at the tumble of young men inside. They set Andy down on the floor, cradling his body to keep it from fully feeling the cold, hard tiles.

It stank in there. It stank of sweat and blood and raw fear.

Tim stared. "Is there a telephone?" he asked. "I'll go look for somebody with a car," he added right after. He pursed his lips as if about to whistle, or kiss the air.

"Yeah, Dude." An odd image popped into Arien's head. In his mind's eye he saw Hendrix. *"'Scuse me while I kiss the sky..."* the singer crooned, leaning forward, face up to give the sky a little kiss. Arien saw that in the movie, *"Woodstock."* He was pretty sure he'd seen it there.

Tim was by him and out the door. Arien could hear his feet patter away until they were absorbed in a shattering window, a police siren and the wop wop wop of a helicopter chopping the air in the near distance overhead.

"Damn!" He cried. "Can we get Andy inside anywhere?"

He heard keys jangle on a landing of the steps above them. "Yeah," a voice called.

"Ow ow!"

"Shit!"

"Easy! – Easy now!"

Andy was carried back up a flight. They took him in a room and laid him on the bed inside. It had an iron headboard and footer. They laid him on his right side, away from the wound. The bed was by a window over the Ave. Arien, the shirtless teenager, another young man in collared shirt, slacks and penny loafers, moved the bed away to the opposite wall.

"Ohhhh. Ow. Ohhhhhhh, shit," Andy moaned. As he lay there some color flushed back to his cheeks, but his brow paled under beads of sweat. His eyes brimmed with tears. Blood had gotten into his hair. It clung, glistening to his neck and jaw.

Arien brushed the hair back. Blood streaked the back of his hand.

"Here's some water." The fellow who had the door keys offered Andy a cup. Andy flinched and shuddered in pain. The cup was placed to his lips. He took a small sip.

"Thank - thanks."

"Jesus, Andy, hang in there, Dude. We've only just met. I'd like to get to know you better," said Arien. "You've got to show me you can throw a cinder block." He reached out to Andy's hand.

"Yeah. Far out, Brother."

"Far out," Arien repeated. "Brother."

He broke into a wide grin. He repeated the phrase, "Far out, Brother." A giddy, drunken feeling washed over him. So relieved he was. It was amazing. This guy didn't look at all like – But, now, at last, this had to be him! That voice, that, "far out."

"Is somebody going to stay with this guy?" The young man with door keys set the cup on an upended orange crate that was next to the bed. The crate was stacked with textbooks.

"Yeah," Arien said. "I'll hang here with him. This guy's my brother - and he's gonna live long and prosper!" The sparkle in his eye was so clear Andy looked up at it with a grimace that stood in for his smile.

"I'll be back on the roof," the student said. "There's not much here, but if you need anything, help yourself."

"Thanks."

Andy barely nodded.

The student went out. Soon, others who had come down began to leave, one by one. The former Scout was the last one. He had been standing near the bed with his hands in his pockets, staring with intense interest at Andy. When Arien said Andy would live long and prosper this other fellow looked at him as if he wasn't so sure about that. If faces could make words it would have been "not likely" in plain English.

A racket could be heard from a few blocks away. It was a helicopter flying very low.

"What's happening outside?" Arien asked him.

The kid went over and looked out the window. "Nothin'. Street's empty."

"So, Andy, how long have you known the Page Street folks?" Arien asked, trying on a distracting question. He sat in a ratty armchair facing the bed. He had to move it a little so Andy could see him. He pushed it with his feet.

Andy's eyes closed. A single tear stole down the side of his face. His breathing was labored. Arien moved to the bedside to see if the bleeding was still under control. It looked like it. The bandages hadn't soaked much more. He considered moving them aside for a closer inspection but decided against it. He thought there must be more he could do but he didn't know what it was.

A small clock radio sat on a simple three-drawer dresser on the opposite wall. Arien went over and turned it on. "I don't believe there's any park worth getting shot for," somebody said. The voice sounded tinny, but vaguely familiar. It bore a British accent he thought he'd heard before.

"Well, John," asked the announcer – his voice was much clearer – "You've chosen to stay in bed. Do you have some advice for the people out in Berkeley? What should they do?"

"You can't fight the meanie on his terms. You don't stop insanity with more insanity, you know. Stage a festival, or something. Chant Hare Krishna. Stop violence with peace."

"Thank you, John. Speaking with John and Yoko from their bed-in, in Toronto. This is KPFA. Stop violence with peace!"

The sound of banging and a lot of glass breaking, along with some whoops and shrieks came up from the street below. The boy by the window slid it open so he could lean out and see more. Arien joined him. A group of about twenty kids ran down the opposite sidewalk at top speed. Several of them carried lengths of pipe and baseball bats. They swiped at storefront windows as they dashed along, a free-form rhythm of symbols and drums.

"Damn!" Arien said impatiently.

"Out-a sight!"

"Maybe, but how's anybody going to get in here to bring Andy out?"

The kid shrugged.

"Look. It's taking Tim too long. Maybe he got into trouble. Anyway, I think we need an ambulance. I've got to find out if we can get one in here. Will you stay with him until I get back?"

The kid lowered his voice. "Do you think he's going to live?"

Arien's - "YES!" - was much louder. "Damn straight! I *know* he's going to live!" Will you stay with him?"

"Sure. I'll be right here."

"Andy, I'm going to get help. "You're going to be alright."

Andy nodded slightly. "Th–ks, Arien."

"No problem, Dude. I'll see you later."

12 – And then they kill you, like in Berkeley

Arien's plan was to find a telephone. Or, if necessary, go right to the police and have them call an ambulance. Outside, though, he was afraid of the police. Their behavior seemed too unpredictable. Arien had no intention of getting beaten or arrested. He started running down the Ave, away from campus. There was too much activity up that way. He tried a few shop doors but they were locked. Some smashed windows were inviting, but Arien decided against that. This mission was too important to blow it doing something stupid.

Ahead of him there were a lot of police so he ran down a side street, around that corner, and on down a few more blocks, dodging an occasional cruiser and likewise, avoiding knots of protesters. He grew more frantic as he went. This was taking longer than it should have! Telegraph Avenue was to his left now. He went that way again, nearly out of breath, weaving through a car dealership where some new Pontiacs sported busted windows. Across the street, on the same side of the Ave, was a Texaco station with a public phone.

He was about to go for it when a large group of protesters formed from several clusters of people that spontaneously merged here. "Free the Park!" Somebody shouted. "Free the Park!" The chorus of voices called. A Berkeley Police car came out onto Telegraph just then, from the street Arien had to cross. It was going too fast and barely missed running some people down as they scurried out of the way. The response was immediate, however. The little crowd roared like an angry beast and closed around behind the car. Soon auto glass was everywhere as people beat on the car and blasted it with rocks and a terrified officer was forced to abandon it. People grabbed him, attempting to pull him down when he drew his pistol. He whirled around like an actor in a street dance trying to watch all directions at once. Protesters backed away, some with hands raised in the air. Others were already rocking the car, converging on it like heaps of ants on a picnic plate. "Off the pigs!" – Some of them screamed. Arien, remembering his own vital mission, saw the police car heave and flip – Ka-CLACK – over on its roof, as he dashed into the street from the big Pontiac he hid behind. Bang. Bang, bang. He reflexively twisted, slid and rolled under a parked car just when the window above him splattered. It cascaded in bouncing glass nuggets about his feet as he pulled them under. The shots came from another direction. It could come from anywhere! "Bitchin'," he said out loud to the undercarriage of the car.

Oil and dust in his nostrils was now met with a portentous whiff of gas from across the Ave, and a sudden 'whomph' sound as the derelict police car became a ball of fire and thick black smoke. There was cheering before people scattered. A helicopter was soon chopping overhead and after that a contingent of twenty five or thirty tactical officers in helmets and flack-jackets, riffles, shotguns, radios and other gear double-timed into position. Slowly, Arien dragged himself out from under the car, and very slowly, quite visibly, as if it were a perfectly normal day, he strode over to the gas station to use the phone.

It appeared to be dead. There was no dial tone. Arien felt like he'd burst. "Shit!" He hit the side of the long, black, dial phone with the flat of his hand. The pair of officers walking towards him from across the street made him especially nervous. He thought of running. "Stay cool," he said to himself. He ceased thinking. *Be cool. Be cool,* repeated in his brain.

The officers were there in no time. One of them socked his Billy club into a gloved hand with an immanent gesture. He looked so ready and willing to wield it. He did this as the other one spoke. "You'll have to clear out of this area."

Arien could see his reflection in the officer's impenetrable dark glasses. He swallowed, summoning courage. "I- I'm trying to call an ambulance. A friend of mine was shot. It must have been a mistake. He was just looking out a window and somebody shot him. It's pretty bad. Can you help me?"

"Where's the victim?"

"A couple of blocks up the street." Arien pointed toward campus.

"Come with us." Arien followed the officers over to a captain who held a radio. The officers exchanged information. The captain got on his radio then turned to Arien. "We can have an ambulance from Herrick back here in five or ten minutes," he said. "It will need an escort on Telegraph."

Arien stifled panic. What would the people on the roof do? Might someone else be shot? How about Andy? Andy was so paranoid of police. What kept Arien together was a certainty he couldn't explain. He just knew in his soul he played a critical role in whatever was happening now with this fellow, Andy.

"No!" He barked. "No escort. Please. People might blast you. It will hold you up. Please. They won't mess with an ambulance. I'll go with it. We'll fly a white flag. You gotta listen! Dude! You gotta listen!"

Arien didn't know what the captain's grin meant but it melted when he turned back to his men. As if to support Arien, an officer came up whom Arien overheard say, "They're hitting us hard from the rooftops."

"Damn. Why didn't we secure them this time? Doesn't anybody know this isn't the way to run a riot?"

"Probably not, Captain."

Standing in this place was making Arien nervous. Here he was in a veritable hornet's nest of meanies. Some of them looked at him as if they'd just as soon crack his head. The captain moved away and was busy directing his men. One officer came up the Ave pushing a couple of kids ahead of him. Both of them had their hands cuffed behind their backs. When they got up to about where Arien stood he told them to stay right there if they didn't want to get shot. They looked so scared and sorry. One of them had fresh blood on his face. The other looked like he would cry with an ounce of encouragement.

"Yo, Dudes." Arien addressed them.

"You talk like a colored man," the one with blood on his face said. "They got you, too, huh?"

"I hope not. I've got a friend who's been shot and I don't know where my babe is, or the people I came with." That sank in some. "What are you here for?"

"Caught us shopping," the bloodstained one explained.

"My old man's gonna trash me," the other worried. "No tellin' what he'll do."

"Run."

"And get shot?" He looked incredulous.

"No. Run from your old man."

"How? They'll call him to come bail me out. He'll trash me bad."

Arien was about to say something else when a large green and white ambulance actually arrived. It stopped in the middle of the Ave behind the line of police and waited. It looked like it was big enough to haul a hippo. Arien ran up to the open passenger window. The driver, a young man, leaned on the broad, white steering wheel with both his arms and his chin jutted out the window. He was looking intently at the scene up ahead. It was a no man's land. The street was full of bricks and trash. Knots of people ran this way and that. Strong whiffs of gas made the eyes water.

"My friend's been shot," Arien told him.

"Where is he?" The driver straightened up. He seemed ready to roll.

"Up there."

"Up the Ave? I don't think this baby's going up there."

"No! It's cool, Dude. You've got to go," Arien pleaded. "He's hurt bad."

"Do we get an escort?"

"Then we'll get rocked. We better just go."

The driver hesitated. "Ok," he said. He looked excited, really. His expression said it all.

"One more thing."

"Yeah?"

"These guys come with us."

The driver looked over Arien's shoulder to the curb where the two boys in handcuffs stood. He cracked a smile, then buried his head in his hands as if to hide it.

Arien whirled around to the hapless fellows at curbside. "Quick, Dummies, get in!"

They looked at each other and back at the ambulance, then at the officer who had brought them up. He was on the other side of the street. His back was turned. "Shit!" The fellow with the bloodstained face squealed. In an instant they were by the door. Arien swung it open and pushed them in. The driver turned on his light and sounded a little whoop on the siren. The blue line parted for the vehicle to pass. As it lurched forward, one of the boys fell back inside. He laughed as he fell. There was no way he could hold on.

"Thanks, Dude!" Arien beamed.

The driver shrugged. "This whole day has twisted my thinking," he said. "What have we got?"

Arien told him what happened to Andy. The driver called it in. Now, as they cruised up the Ave, dodging rubble as they went, Arien could hear the commercial radio playing. The volume was low and hard to hear with the occasional whoop of the siren, but when he heard the tinny voice on the telephone being broadcast he reached out and cranked it up. This time he knew, with a thrill, who was speaking.

"The students are being conned," the voice with the British accent said. "It's like the school bully: he aggravates you and aggravates you until you hit him. And then they kill you, like in Berkeley..."

"Damn! That's John Lennon!" The driver exclaimed. He had to slow down at Dwight Way and Telegraph where there was a huge contingent of police ringing an open space as big as a city block. A brand new chain link fence stood tall around it. A bulldozer and some construction workers were gathered in the near corner. It looked as if they were as much trapped as protected.

Arien scrunched forward to gawk. So, this is the reason for all the fuss!

"...People are finding out the hard way," the Beatle continued, "The monster doesn't care – The Blue Meanie is insane. We really care about life. Destruction is good for the establishment. The only thing they can't control is the mind, and we have to fight for sanity and peace on that level. But the students have gotten conned into thinking they can change it with violence and they can't, you know. They can only make it uglier and worse."

The boys in handcuffs were scrunched in the isle between the driver and shotgun seats. There was a motion from the back. Another EMT had been on the ride. His upper right arm sported a winged-motorcycle tattoo under the short sleeve of his shirt. He made some remark about the handcuffs. Arien wanted to listen to the radio. Damn!

"Can you get them off of us?"

"Maybe." He disappeared again in the back of the vehicle. The boys craned to watch him rummage in a toolbox he pulled from under a cabinet. "Voila!" He said with a grin, brandishing a serious pair of bolt cutters. "These have come in handy a few times."

"Out-a sight, Mister!"

"Are we lucky or not?"

"This is your lucky day," Arien said. "Stop here! Andy's upstairs in that building."

When the ambulance stopped, the rescued boys got out and scurried away. Both of them turned before disappearing, flashing waves with grateful grins.

Even as the EMT's yanked a gurney out of the ambulance Arien wondered what happened to Tina and the others. He looked up at the window over the street. There were two worried faces looking down. One of them, the youngest, who was there when Arien left, shouted, "Jesus! Hurry! I think he's losin' it!"

"That's impossible!" Arien said out loud as he followed the men up creaking stairs to the room where Andrew lay.

Andy's face was damp and ashen. The responders hustled to cover it with an oxygen mask. They were efficient, focused.

"He's lost a lot of blood." Gently, they moved him to the gurney. The younger responder, who drove the ambulance, looked up at Arien. His eyes said it all. This one's close. There's not a moment to spare.

Arien fairly reeled as he took it in. He could have been on acid, seeing this. He could have been rushing on canned nitrous. Who was this guy anyhow? What was the point? He thought of something

Jamie Sun said: ""It all depends on where in the paradox it originates..." Maybe that was chance, too. Maybe 'Andrew' was just a lucky dude.

"You want to ride with him?"

The older fellow shot a glance at his partner, but said nothing.

Arien surely felt the current of the day's events. He wanted so badly to know where Tina was. Is she good? What is she doing now? He hesitated. Oh, shit, "Yes," he said. "Thanks."

Siren wailing, they skirted the riot area, passing through several roadblocks. Arien rode in back with the older man, who busied himself with checking the obvious aspects of Andy's condition while Arien simply grasped a hand. It was cold and clammy to the touch. Arien was no doctor but it was evident Andy was pushing his border. At this point he was unresponsive.

It didn't take long to get to the hospital, but once there they had an unnerving wait. Several vehicles were ahead of theirs before the emergency entrance at the rear of the building. When they finally did pull up to the door, the EMT's yanked the gurney out into a chaotic scene. A photographer with long hair was being pushed away by a nurse while an intern waded towards them through a press of injured and attending people. In the doorway beyond, a doctor assessed injuries waiting to be treated. He had to shout to be heard above the clamor. "Well, open the cafeteria" Arien heard him holler, "We can lay them on the tables in there!"

Arien couldn't tell if the EMT's with Andrew even said anything, but the press of people parted to let them through. The doctor bent over Andy as he was wheeled forward and peeled back an eyelid. "I want this one in ICU," he told some attendants who took the gurney from the EMT's. Barely blinking, he moved on to look at a police officer with a bloodied eye.

Arien got as far as the elevator before a nurse came up to him and said to go to the lobby and fill out whatever paperwork he could on his friend's behalf. She daubed her forehead with a handkerchief to exclaim, "To think we just had our first disaster drill! And look! We have a real disaster!"

13 – Herrick Hospital

It was a long wait in the lobby. It seemed dark. The lights were on but they illuminated some other world, not this one. This one was dark. Arien sank numbly into a white plastic chair, having chosen one with wrought iron armrests. There were other people: a worried-looking old lady with a restless young girl, a few hippies and student types. Quite a few people obviously connected with the protest came in on their own two feet. Sometimes they would be accompanied with a group of friends. There was a lot of talk in the air about buckshot. It wasn't a very big room and it seemed to press everyone together. At times a loose line stretched out past the doors.

The magazines were cool. In spite of his considerable fatigue and anxiety they attracted him. The ads were fun. Arien hadn't spent much of his time reading magazines. His country was such a different place now. Funny. Life Magazine was trying to interpret the "counter culture" to its readers. It didn't seem to report what was really going on. They weren't seeing it as Arien did. Was it deliberate? Arien supposed they just didn't have a clue. He thought of something Tina said a few days ago, about how cool it would be if everybody took acid one day. "Then, everyone would get it," she said. "Then they couldn't deny what they knew. You can't fake it on acid," she said, repeating a maxim Arien had heard spoken before. Arien wasn't so sure. He'd known a few kids who took acid in his own time. Arguably, it wasn't nearly as strong, but still, there didn't seem to be any need to deny anything. Why bother? When it all came down to it, what difference did it make?

He wished he knew the phone number of the Angels of Light. He knew it was listed under some business. When Otter told him a business phone didn't require a deposit the mystery of the long distance calls and plane tickets Tommy ordered and charged to the number was resolved. God! He smirked. I should have written the damn number down. Why didn't I think of that?

Ha! Angels of Light! When the phone bill comes these idiots will ignore it, he realized. Eventually, "Ma Bell" will disconnect these people with the enormous bill. They'd explain how the responsible party just up and left one day telling no one where he went. Practically the next day they'd simply order another phone under a different name. It was really incredible.

A nurse came out into the lobby. "Mr. Danner?" She called. He got up and went to her. Her expression calmed him. "Your friend is going to be alright. He lost a lot of blood. He's had a transfusion, but the bullet missed anything vital. It did rake a couple of his ribs and chipped a piece off the scapula. The doctor said he won't be doing any gymnastics for awhile." She smiled.

"Yeah, I guess not. Uh, can I –?"

"He's resting now. You can see him tomorrow."

Arien hesitated. Should I spend the night? He decided against it. More than anything he wanted to get back to Tina and the others. He wanted to tell them what happened to him and to Andy. The nurse turned away.

"Ma'am?"

She continued moving away as she looked at him.

"Thanks."

As he headed for the entryway his passage was blocked by a group of people who were just entering through the glass doors of the lobby. They were upon him before he recognized any faces. He was too surprised, and relieved, to speak.

"Arien! Great! You're already here! How is she?" Jeff shouted. He hurried over and gave Arien a big hug. Otter was there next, then Tim, Karen, Paul, Janice and Mikel gathered close around.

"You look like shit, Jeff. What do you mean? Andy's here. He took a bullet today." Jeff had a deep red shiner under his eye and a big puffy sore over his left cheekbone. There was dried blood matted in his hair.

"Yeah. We guessed that." Tim said. "But I didn't know where they'd taken him."

"What happened to you, Dude?"

"I'm sorry." He stroked his little blonde goatee. "I nearly got arrested. They let me go after a couple of hours." He wore a fatigue shirt that didn't fit. The sleeves were halfway up his forearms.

"Is Andy okay?" Mikel asked.

"Yeah, Dude. After awhile, when you didn't come back I went for help. The dudes in the ambulance said it was real close. He lost a lot of – " It dawned on Arien that somebody was missing. Twice he looked at the faces gathered around him. He felt dizzy. His jaw dropped. "Where is she?"

"She's *here*, Arien," Otter said. "That's why we came. When we heard she was -"

"Why? Where? Oh damn! I've been here the whole time!"

"Come on!" Otter said.

"What happened, Dude? What happened?"

"She got cracked on the side of the head, man. The pigs beat her," Otter told him this as they found the stairs and bounded up to the second floor. "That's why Jeff looks so banged up. He jumped right in and took it for her. Then the crowd rained rocks on the bastards. Shit, Arien. It was out-a sight."

"Oh bogus! I wasn't even there!" Arien cried in anguish.

Otter stopped on the landing. People bunched up right there. He gripped Arien's arm and held him for an instant with that hard stare of his. "It's okay. Don't blame yourself. We were in a dangerous place. It was chaotic, Man. You were lucky you got away. Remember that, okay? Got that?" He gave Arien a gentle shake.

Arien's head spun. His eyes wouldn't lock with Otter's.

"You love her, right?"

"Yeah," he said. It surprised him, but he said it. He really did love her. He loved her so much it hurt now. It was the old feeling that crowded around him again, a fear and revulsion of that deep, grinding, aching pain, all alone with it, powerless to do anything about it.

"Ohhhhh…" He groaned.

"Then we'll go see her now, and you can love her some more!"

Now their eyes met. I love you, too, Otter. "Yeah," He merely said.

Busting through the landing door they headed down the hall. "Where is she?"

"207."

The door was open. Arien knew that was Tina though it didn't look like her. There was a big, white bandage wrapping her head. What face showing was bruised, puffy and red. One eye opened as everyone gathered around her bed. When Arien kissed her, her lips twitched into a little smile. "Hi," she whispered.

"Oh yeah, Babe." He kissed her freckled cheek again and straightened out some golden hair on the pillow. Sudden tears spilled off his face and dropped, one, two, on the sheet beside her. "Oh damn! I'm sorry. I'm so sorry."

"It's cool, Dude," she answered with another twitch of a smile.

"What are all these people doing here?" A voice from the doorway demanded.

"We came to see Tina," Paul told the RN standing there.

"I'm sorry, but there's too many people here. This is not a circus. This girl needs her rest."

"We love her," Arien answered without looking up.

"You will all have to leave immediately!"

"We'll wait for you downstairs, Arien," Otter said softly. "Good night, Tina."

Voices chimed in:

"Good night, Tina."

"Get well, girl."

"See you tomorrow."

When everybody was gone the nurse still waited by the door.

"Can I stay with her?"

"No, son. But you can come back tomorrow. She's going to be fine, so don't you worry.

"Can I stay just a little longer?"

"Five minutes, then. That's all. Do you understand?"

Arien sat on the side of her bed and hugged her as best he could with his head over her heart and his arms along side of her. He sniffed through the gathering mucous in his nose. His chest heaved with a great, aching pain. Oh! How he hated that feeling! Once, he swore he would never let himself feel that damn pain again. "God, Babe, you're precious. I want you better so bad. I wish I was there with you. Oh, Tina, I wish I was with you! I wouldn't have let this happen."

Feebly, she put her hand on his head.

"Time to go now." The nurse was back.

"I love you, girl."

"Arien?" She whispered.

"Yes?"

"Where am I?"

"Oh, Jesus, Babe…"

The nurse cut him off. She tapped him on the shoulder. "Come on! Time to go! If you love this girl you'll let her get the rest she needs."

Everyone was waiting in the lobby.

"Can we come back first thing in the morning?" Arien asked Jeff, who carefully probed the side of his face.

"I don't know, man."

"What do you mean, Jeff?" Arien was caught off balance by the unexpected answer.

"What he means is, we might not be able to get back," Paul soberly interjected.

"That's right, Arien," Otter agreed. "Regan's called in the National Guard. They'll likely have every way blocked off."

"Just driving Van Gogh here was a mistake." Jeff shook his head.

Arien's eyebrow was up. "Huh?"

"Van Gogh looks just like Jeff, now, too," Mikel answered. "Pigs stopped us. We thought we were all going to the slam, man."

"Well, what happened?"

"Come on. I'll show ya," Jeff drawled as the pack of them filtered outside.

Arien was dumbstruck when they reached the vehicle in the crowded parking lot. The passenger side of Van Gogh's windshield was hopelessly shattered into little nuggets barely holding together. A slender rectangular hole about five inches long accentuated the center.

Jeff lightly scratched one of his bruises. He wore a puckish expression. "War mobile," he said, rocking back on his feet with a sorry grin, shoving hands into pockets.

"Ha!" Arien put a hand on Jeff's shoulder, squeezing with his fingers.

"Maybe you should leave it like that," Karen said.

"Nah. Eventually I wanna see what's comin'."

"Did the pigs do that?"

"Yeah, Arien. Before they let us go one of 'em just whacked it with his Billy," 'See you with this one-eyed van here again and you're all goin' to jail!'" Jeff quoted.

"I'll be damned! That's gotta be illegal!"

"Police brutality," Janice offered up.

Tim petted the damaged window. "Poor Van Gogh," he consoled, in a soft, soothing voice.

"Aw," some of the others chimed in.

"We'll fix it, Jeff," Otter said.

"So, what are we gonna do, Dudes? – I want to be here in the morning," Arien generally asked.

After a short conference, they decided to keep the van right where it was. Everyone would spend the night in Berkeley. That way there would be no hassle getting back to see Tina and Andy. Otter had the phone number at the Angels of Light. He said he would call to leave a message for the others at Page Street. "I'll be back in the morning," he announced then. "We all can't pack into the van for the night. Do you want to come with me, Arien?"

"No thanks, Otter. I'll stay here."

"How 'bout you, Jeff?"

"Nah. I want to be with Van Gogh, in case somebody tries to tow him away."

"Possible. Cool. Try not to worry too much," he said to Arien.

"I'll go with you," Mikel said.

"Cool. Later."

"Later, Dude."

They all watched Otter and Mikel walk away.

"I don't know about you guys, but I'm hungry enough to scarf road kill," Jeff said.

"Yeah," Karen agreed. "If the crows haven't beat us to it."

"I got a few dollars. Let's check out the cafeteria."

"Forget that, Tim," Arien said. "They made it into an emergency room."

"Well, I got some brown rice stashed back here and there's probably enough fuel in the bottle. All we need is some water. The jerry's empty. Somebody wanna go an' fill it up?"

"I will." Arien waited while Jeff pulled out the water can.

Jeff and Arien camped there in the parking lot for three days in all. Tim and Karen made their way back to the city the following day. They were able to catch a ride with Tina's mom, who came from Marin, where Tina grew up. Arien thought this woman seemed a little out of her element when he met her the first time in Tina's room at Herrick. By some fluke everyone had gotten in to see her. Otter brought a bag of oranges so all except Tina and Arien were peeling and eating one when Mrs. Deacon came in. She was tall, and wore a smart tweed skirt with matching jacket. Every hair was in place. She seemed shell-shocked at first, sizing up her daughter's companions. Then she pulled herself together and the group around the bed parted to let her through.

"Hi, Mom," Tina acknowledged wearily as her mother bent over her.

"Dear, dear! Oh Christine, look what has become of you!" Her tone was an odd mixture of horror and remonstrance. She carefully arranged herself on the side of the bed opposite Arien. She stroked her daughter's exposed cheek and shot a territorial glance at Arien, who felt too hollow to get it. He may have appeared stupid to her. He was holding Tina's hand and wouldn't let it go. "How did this happen, child?"

"I don't know, Mom."

A policeman hit her, Ma'am," Jeff offered.

"Why? What in the whole wide world were you doing?"

"I don't know." Tina's puffed up purple face looked like it would cry.

Arien squeezed her hand a little tighter.

"Well, I want you to know – all of you – this is not a good place to be! I had a heck of a time getting here. My God! It's just like a war zone!"

"We've been here since yesterday," Arien said. "Figure if we leave, we won't be able to get back."

"You're probably right about that. And who are you?"

"Arien."

"And were you with my daughter when this happened?"

Arien felt a stab to his heart, as surely as if driven with a hatpin and then yanked from side to side. "If I had been it'd be me in this bed," he rued.

Mrs. Deacon seemed to soften. "Well," she said, looking down at Tina, "The doctor told me you're not out of the woods yet. You've had a very serious concussion." She looked up at everyone. "Do you think it's alright for all of you to be in here?"

"Sure," Otter said. "We have good vibes." He stuffed a large section of orange in his mouth and wiped his lips with the sleeve of his fringed leather jacket. The whole room smelled like an orange.

"Good vibes. Oh, dear. Christine, if only..."

In the next moment Tim asked Mrs. Deacon if she would take him and Karen back to the city on her way home – and anyone else there who wanted to get out of Bzerkeley. She said, "yes," without seeming to register.

Paul and Janice stayed on through another evening in Van Gogh, which was still crowded because Otter and Mikel came to sleep there, too, that Friday night. Paul wanted to be sure his friend, Andy, was going to be alright. The prognosis was good. He would have to spend a week or two in recovery after the operation to patch him up, but as the nurse told Arien earlier, nothing vital had been hit, and after the transfusion his initial recovery was rapid. The color was returned to his face. He sat up in bed, his left arm snug in a sling, and he couldn't breathe deeply without pain and so spoke in soft, clipped sentences.

"I want you to have this, Andy," Arien said, the first time Andy was allowed visitors. It was on Saturday afternoon. Andy feebly extended his right hand to take the Swiss Army knife Arien offered him. The name, "Arien," was scratched into one side, and "1990" on the other.

Paul, who was there at the time with Janice, nodded his approval of the gift. Andy's eyes seemed to double in size. "Wow. Man. Thanks, Brother!" he said. "I always wanted one of these! Are you sure you want to give it away?"

"Oh yeah, Dude," Arien affirmed, with a whimsical smile. "The red handle is for the blood you spilled in the Revolution. Think of it as a Purple Heart, since I don't have one of those to give you."

"Say, man. What's 1990 for?"

"Oh, Dude, you'll just have to wait and see." Arien winked up at Otter, who entered the room. "I found it up in Oregon, in the Columbia Gorge."

Otter said, "Say what, Brother?"

The next day brought the protest to the Hospital.

A lot of people were there and it was hard to get through the parking lot to the building. Some people had signs. Others chanted. Someone yelled, "Stop the War in Berkeley!" Loud, in Arien's ear. He just left Otter and Jeff at the van. How does he do it? Arien mused, pushing through a dense throng of people in front of the door. Just a short time earlier Otter showed up before either Arien or Jeff had awakened. They'd been up late, smoking pot and drinking beer with some kids who had a set of bongos.

"Knock knock! Jeff! Got you some windowpane!" Otter called. "Come get your windowpane."

"What's he goin' on about?" Jeff threw off the blanket he was curled up in. He blinked his eyes and scratched his head. "Acid? Now?"

Arien snorted. Jeff's wake up drawl was comical with his tousled head and bruised face with its purple-black shiner complimenting the perfect cowlick.

"Come on," Otter enticed, "Nice, fresh windowpane." Arien wondered if tripping at the hospital was a good idea.

Jeff stretched to the door latch. "Oh! Otter!" He grinned and squinted at the sunshine and Otter in the opening. Otter held out a section of Volkswagen windshield between extended hands. New rubber gasket was wrapped around an arm.

14 – A quiet place of sanity

It wasn't all that needed fixing. At the hospital on the day before Tina was released she was getting some exercise in the hall when Arien, Jeff, and Mikel came upon her.

"Hiya, Tina." Arien held her close in greeting. He missed being with her so very much. It was almost bearable with the press of people in Van Gogh at night, the comings and goings and impromptu parties near the parking lot, getting stoned, goofing, sharing news with students and sometimes, the world. Earlier, Arien had accepted a brief interview with a reporter from "<u>The San Francisco Chronicle</u>". But now he pressed his nose into the side of her neck and drew a deep breath. Her scent made him tingle all over. "I want you, Babe. I want you out of here," he whispered.

"Where?" She asked, like an innocent doll. "Am I going home?"

There was an awkward silence. "I'm so sorry I left you." Arien finally said. "I didn't see it. I didn't see it coming." Tears welled up in his eyes.

"Say, let's go down to see Andy. Why don't we all go?" Mikel said.

They headed down the hall. Tina kept up fairly well.

"How do you feel?" Arien studied her.

"OK." She had a faint smile on her face that seemed incongruous. She kept looking down and off to the side and at one point reached down as if to pick something off the polished floor. Otherwise, the movement of the people around her swept her along as Arien, too, was swept along.

Andy's room was full of flowers, small, bright red flags, get-well cards, even a few books and magazines. There was barely space for a small paper cup of water on the roller stand next to his bed.

Sitting up, Andy had a vaguely contented look. A thick little book, barely wider than his fist was nestled in his free hand, held open with a thumb. His eyes were half closed as he drifted with music from a transistor radio on the bed with him. *"Some pills make you large and some pills make you small, but the ones that Mother gives you don't do anything at all."*

"Not a bad idea," Mikel observed. He bent over and gave Andy a squeeze and a kiss on his forehead.

Andy cracked a smile. "I think I'll give it a few more days. Guaranteed bummer to trip in a place like this." And to Arien he said, "So how's the brother who saved my life?"

Arien didn't shrink. "Chillin'," he said.

Andy chuckled then checked it, wincing. "Great word." He lifted his right hand for Arien to take it, letting the little book fall away.

"He's got more where that comes from," Jeff helped. "Otter calls it 'future speak'."

Andy still grasped Arien's hand and looked up into his green eyes. "Man, I was so scared in that room. It hurt so much. I thought I was going, Brother, I really did. But, you were so sure. You were a rock!"

Arien nodded.

"Did you cling to that rock?" Mikel asked with a sardonic grin.

"Mikel? If I wasn't stuck here—" There was laughter as Andy let go of Arien's grasp to ball his fist. "But, yup. I sure did!"

"Ah! You've been reading the "Gita," Mikel observed, nudging the little book. It had a light pink, thin paper cover. "Where are you?"

"Oh. Man. Just read a surprise. Wasn't Buddha's contribution the Middle Way?"

"Yes. And the Eight-fold Path."

"Well, well here I read…" He fumbled with the little book. It was an effort. His visitors waited quietly for him to find the place again with only his right hand to turn the pages. "Ah… Krishna says, Arjuna, this yoga is not for him… who eats too much, nor for him who does not… eat at all, nor for him… who is given to too… much sleep…, nor… for him who… is   ceaselessly awake." His speech grew more measured as he labored through each sentence a phrase at a time, with evident discomfort.

"How does it compare with the 'Quotations of Chairman Mao'?" Mikel wore a smile that harkened to a matter between them.

Arien had never heard of either of these books. It might as well have been gibberish. He searched for Tina who was off in her own thoughts.

"It doesn't… But you know? … A mind is not… easy to make."

"Shall it be rice or curry?" Mikel quipped.

Arien stifled an impulse to leave them. He was sure he owned some time with this fellow whose destiny so precipitously crossed his own. "Why not curry with rice?" He asked. His smile masked his ignorance.

"Clever!" Mikel commended.

"Synthesis seems… to be… the name of the game,… though I don't know." Andy probed. "Tell ya, guys; getting shot… makes you think. All ideas… do not… go together."

"'War is Peace'. George Orwell." Mikel added, turning to Arien and Tina, "We've been at odds over this, but he may be coming around." He winked.

Mikel offered his room to both Andy and Tina for when they got back from the hospital. He said he could stay with a friend in the Castro for the time being. It turned out to be an unnecessary invitation. Andy, now a hero of the Revolution, said he'd been invited to recuperate at a pad near the U in Berkeley where he'd been crashing with a cell of Fidel Castro look-alike, neo-Bolsheviks.

Tina ran into some unexpected asylum. She was released first. Arien knew her mother wanted her to come home to recuperate but Tina insisted she felt good and would take it easy. Back at Page Street she sat at the table in the kitchen a lot, pretty much being Tina, but every once in awhile she would look curious, like she saw somebody where nobody was, and once Arien caught her talking to the thin air. She merely smiled at him when she realized he was with her.

"Who are you talking to, Tina?"

"Oh I know you don't see her."

"Who?"

"She lives here."

"Do you know her name?"

"No. She speaks to me, but I don't know what she's saying. I can't hear her."

"Can she hear you?"

"I don't know. I think so."

"Have you seen her before?"

"I think so. Once or twice."

Then, there was the time Arien found Tina looking for something like her life depended on it. She upended things and opened everything in a fruitless search, but when he asked her what she was looking for she hadn't the slightest idea, like snapping out of a dream. It was pretty weird.

She had no memory of the injury. Tina recalled running with Arien and the others when the tear gas started exploding all around and that was it. After that she had to be told what happened.

Sometimes Tina would get real sad, sad enough to make her cry. There was no explaining it. Arien was usually able to rouse her out of it. He'd kiss her and hold her. He worried about her. It kept him awake at night. He wanted her back the way she was.

A couple of days later Tina's mother came by to see her. After visiting for a while she became upset at something Tina said – or maybe it was the way she said it. She began to insist Christine come home with her to Marin. Arien caught the conversation as he passed by the door to her room. His heart skipped a beat. He wanted to be with her and not have her be anywhere else. He poked his head into mother and daughter's space. Mrs. Deacon leveled her eyes at the intruder.

"This girl is need of a quiet place of sanity to get better. She has had a serious blow to her head and she is not quite right. I'm taking her home!"

There was nothing Arien could do. He was perfectly helpless while Tina's mother hustled her daughter out of the Page Street house. It was all so fast and "in-your-face" that before Arien could gather himself, his babe was headed down the stairs. She looked up at him before disappearing around the landing with an oddly serene smile.

He followed them down the steps and out into the street. "Call me, Tina!" Arien cried. She was bustled away in a late model Volvo sedan. She left without a goodbye hug. He didn't even get a number where she could be reached!

"Bummer," Tim said. He stood on the steps with Arien, along with Karen and Randy, who were the only other people around the house at the time.

"Christ!" Arien shouted. "I've gotta know where she is! I can't even follow them!" He was flushed. Wild eyed. "Damn! I should have looked at the license number! Did any of you see it?"

"You don't know where her mother lives?" Randy asked, hands deep in his pleated, gray pants' pockets. "Try the phone book."

"Good idea." Arien pulled himself together and ran up the stairs.

A dog eared, 1967 Bell Telephone Bay Area Directory that lived on a shelf in the foyer wasn't much help. There were no Deacons listed in Marin. He knew she was there, somewhere. Where? Frantic, Arien began going through whatever stuff she had for some clue. Nothing. Nothing at all! When he pulled out a T-shirt with holes in the nipples from a duffel of hers he started to cry. He just couldn't stop it. All of the frustration with himself over letting her get away, indeed, not being there when she was hit to begin with, and the worry he'd felt over her condition, this preposterous, abrupt separation, and not knowing where she was going; it was too much.

His heart began to burn. He felt a blackness closing in around him as he sat on the mattress where they'd slept. It was like passing out; a kind of stupor. Numbness. He barely acknowledged the arm come around him as Karen sat next to him. She held him as he sobbed.

"What a lover," Randy said sympathetically, standing in the doorway.

Tim came in after a while with a cup of hot tea. "Relax, Arien," he advised, passing the cup. "You'll find her."

Arien took the thing and wrapped his hands around it like it was all the warmth in the world. He rested his head on Karen's shoulder. He felt so stupid. Gradually, with no apparent recourse, he collected himself and inched back to the wall, to lean against it and stretch his legs out on the covers.

"This is quite a shirt!" Karen said, matter-of-factly. She spread it over her knees.

"It's Tina's."

Karen clucked. "I've never seen her wear it."

"She just wears it for me."

Tim came in with another cup of tea for his girl.

"Does she have any mail?" Tim asked. "Maybe there's a return address."

"Uh. No."

"How 'bout the hospital? They must still have her home address!"

Arien seized on that one. He returned to the phone book to look up the number.

"Wait!" Karen put her hand on it. "They won't give you her home number unless you are a relative. Don't even try it until you know what you're going to say."

"She's right," Tim agreed. "Maybe you should get Preston to call for you."

"Nah, I'll say I'm her brother."

"Yeah, but her brother would know where she lives."

Arien saw that well enough. Impulsively, he swiped at the phone book with an open hand, knocking it to the floor. A moment's awkward silence followed. "OK." He said, finally. I'll try Preston.

Preston wasn't home. He, Danny, and most of the Angels at 1887 were off for a free theater dig tonight with Hibiscus somewhere in North Beach, or so Stewart told him. Arien still panted from his rush up the stairs where midway he nearly collided with Raymond, who seemed put off when asked if Preston was there. Raymond carried an unwieldy stack of boxes down and they had to carefully navigate past each other.

"I just got home from work," Stewart said, "or I would have gone, too."

"What's Hibiscus?"

Stewart regarded Arien fondly from his corner chair in the kitchen. "Not what, who. Hibiscus is doing liberated theater with the girls at KaliFlower and whoever else wants to dress up, for that matter. The show is making quite a splash." He touched the tips of his fingers together over a crossed knee. Stewart was the most conservative of the Page Street Angels in appearance. Where Raymond looked rather like an old-time farmer in his overalls, Stewart wore manila-colored cotton duck pants and a white shirt and tie under a v-neck sweater-vest. Stewart called to Raymond as he passed by the doorway. "Can I help you with any of that?"

Raymond disappeared into the large room opposite the kitchen.

"He's moving out," Stewart said with a sigh. "It was all so sudden."

Arien could barely think about anything but Tina's whereabouts. He was about to get up.

Stewart fumbled under the vest and pulled a pack of Pall Malls out of his shirt pocket. "Cigarette?"

"Sure." Arien relaxed back into his chair. Stewart ejected a couple of cigarettes from a tap on the red pack and passed one to the visitor. He lit them with a big Zippo lighter that had an imposing click of lid. They both looked up to see Raymond hovering in the doorway holding an old black-enamel typewriter. "This is it," he said with a grim smile. His beard looked like it could get caught in the roller.

"I'm sorry, Raymond."

"Yes, Stewart. So am I." Raymond's thumb fidgeted with the nickel-plated return lever. "I never thought tuna fish would do it."

"If not that it would have been something else. It's been getting out of hand."

Arien drew on his filter-less smoke. It had an earthy taste and carried a rush to his head. He blew a smoke ring and wondered at the uncharacteristic evidence of dissention in this house. He had to know. "Tuna fish?"

Raymond was about to say something but shifted his weight with the typewriter and then turned out to the hall and went on down the stairs.

"Tuna fish?" Arien repeated.

"Raymond saw it on the shelf." Stewart explained. "He said he won't live in a house that's been corrupted with commercial canned fish meat. The house took a vote last night and Raymond lost."

Arien fidgeted. "Bogus fuss over shit," he said.

"Well, I don't know, Young Stuff." He crossed his other leg. "It's principles. It's what sets us apart from the Bourgeois system out there. Raymond is a revolutionary."

"Seems pretty stupid to me."

"I guess you would have voted with the rest of the house, then, huh?"

"Look–" Arien took a deep drag off his smoke, "On the other side of the Bay there, people got their heads smashed in over fuckin' tuna fish?" He got up from his chair. "I'll be back later, Dude. I need to see Preston."

Once outside Arien decided to go off for a while to be alone. It was a sunny day, yet the air was crisp. He'd left the greatcoat in the apartment upstairs and considered going back for it but blew it off, not wishing to engage anyone else. He headed up the panhandle toward the park.

Golden Gate Park was a wonderful place with its open meadows and tall stands of eucalyptus. Any time of day it seemed there were always a lot of people there, biking, jogging, juggling, or taking in the sun in the shelter of clusters of vegetation or the rumps of little hills. Arien didn't recognize anyone and that was just fine for now.

An occasional gust seemed to render the proud trees reversible and from pea green they went to yellow, flickering gold as their tops greeted wind. It was like a huge Impressionist painting bursting into life. It lifted his spirits some. When a bum asked for a quarter he accepted the dollar food stamp note Arien offered. A guy on a ten-speed bike slowed down enough to pass Arien a fat, smoldering roach before speeding off down a winding path.

Arien could already recognize the full-bodied flavor of Columbian Jane. It wasn't something he knew in the world he was from. Not particularly spicy, or heady, the stone yet had some depth. A couple of kids a bit younger than he, coming down the trail stopped by him, barely exchanging nods or indulging any skip in time for Arien to pass it around. So much of existence in this place was familiar, unspoken and taken as given, even expected. It pleased him. He could do this. He felt like he belonged in his life in a way he couldn't recall ever knowing before. He wasn't sure if it came out of him or it was just this place and time, its rich, aerated soil nurturing his deepest roots, the conscious and unconscious, blending and reversible, like the green and golden coats on the trees in the park.

That one inch roach got the three boys high. No words passed between them other than a short "Dig your sneaks" from one, who took in Arien's high tops. When the roach was finally cast away the other boy raised his hand to Arien, too high for a shake. Arien wasn't sure what he was supposed to do. "Gimmie five!" The kid said.

"Oh." Arien flipped his right hand over, lifting it up as the other came down with fingers spanking by. He smiled as they nodded and strode away.

Just then Arien spied Otter among a small cluster of folks on the bank of a hill about 100 yards off. It looked like a deal was going down. Otter counted bills and stuffed them in a pocket as Arien drew up.

"Yo Dude."

"Hey Man."

The other people drifted away.

He told Otter about Tina being snatched by her Mom.

"Bummer."

"Yeah." Arien resisted the ache it invited.

"I say, let it hang for a few days. It might do her some good. Then, we'll go scoop her up."

"I don't know where she is, Otter."

"Ah. We'll find her. Think of it this way, I'd say we're about ready to head back up to Portland. We don't need to get stuck here and gather karma. That could cost us. So, we'll have to find her. Simple as that." Otter pulled a roll of Life Savers out of his jacket and offered one.

"How?" The worry on Arien's face seemed to darken the landscape as the sun slipped behind a passing cloud. Orange taste exploded in his mouth. An herbal buzz could really excite the flavors.

"Have some faith the two of you are together, Arien, so events will prove it."

Otter's manner of thinking out of the box had already mastered Arien a few times. So now, Arien let it all go for the moment. Another gust upended the leaves above them into a curtain of pea green and gold. The sweet spice of eucalyptus filled the air. He folded his arms for warmth just as the sun sprung out again. This park was big enough to swallow him.

"Otter – you're awesome!"

"You show some potential yourself, young Brother."

Otter began walking and Arien followed. They moved through the wide entrance of the park and passed some benches that faced the head of Haight Street. A very big and tall old fellow in a black turtle neck sweater and beret was settled on one, talking to a young, teenage girl in a plain dress. Otter stopped before them and reflected back the warm, wide, toothy grin the ponderous, grey-haired, round-faced man gave to him. A captain's beard bordering the edge of his chin accentuated the roundness of the face. It was a kindly face.

"Otter! Nice to see you again!"

"Hello, Eric! Arien, meet Big Daddy!"

Arien had already heard about Eric Nord from Otter since visiting the "I" before. He stepped up and took the big hand that was offered.

"And, where are you from, Lad?"

"Oh, down from Portland, with Otter and a few other folks."

"We're going to Woodstock together," Otter said.

"Ah, yes! I heard about that from Grace," Eric said.

"He means Grace Slick," Otter confided to Arien, though it didn't make any connection with him. "Are you going?"

"I don't think so, Otter. There's a lot to attend to here. I don't think it practical for me to go anywhere like that just now."

The girl who was sitting on the bench with Eric smiled up at Arien. He could tell immediately she was a runaway. He'd seen them in Portland and surmised they were the same all over the earth. This one was particularly wet and Arien couldn't help but look from her to the big old man beside her.

"Oh, this is Betty," Eric introduced, likely catching Arien's angle. "She's recently arrived and I may be saving her the trouble of reinventing the wheel."

Otter chuckled. "Welcome, Betty Baby," he said. "You're a cutie."

Arien thought 'Baby Betty' was more like it. He said, "Yo, Babe."

Betty shyly smiled her greetings.

"Yes, she is a cutie," Eric indulgently cooed. "Betty's from Nevada."

Betty nodded.

"How did you get here?" Arien asked her.

There was a barely perceptible wince. "By car," she said.

Eric's expression became more serious. "And that car may be cruising for her somewhere in the city," he confided. "You're safe now, Betty."

She nodded again, biting her lower lip.

"I suspect so," Otter agreed.

This connection Arien had no trouble making. He shuddered. He surely grasped the ways of bliss cookies since his life began anew in 1969. But, the tear gas, Andy's gunshot wound and Tina's cracked skull were beginning to have some effect. The added weight of this young girl's recent and apparently dark reality simply slid him further into opened eyes. He was reminded of something a much older Andy had said to him that day in the Columbia Gorge. *"But it was not all sex and drugs and rock and roll. There was pain and struggle; hungry times - injustice."*

124

Just then another man who was also pretty old to Arien ambled up. He was rather tall and sported a shock of grey hair under a tweed tam and wore a wool tweed sport jacket. He, too, had a turtle neck sweater under the jacket. He looked agile and his eyes were sharp as jewels.

"Lawrence!" Eric greeted. "I thought you were in New York."

"Eric! How goes the day?" It was a sure and pleasing voice.

"Quite well, really. Lawrence, have you met Otter?"

"You do look familiar, son." They shook hands.

"I saw you in North Beach one day last summer," Otter recalled. "You were doing a reading for everybody. It was really out-a sight, too"

"Ah, yes, thank you, but you know, I see a lot of people. You do look familiar, though. Been nice to meet you – again!" He smiled graciously.

"And, this is Arien."

"How are you?"

"Chillin'." Arien took his hand.

Lawrence was caught for a second, peering into green eyes. "You're an especially beautiful kid," he freely said. "Guard that." And then he turned to the girl. "And who's the lovely young friend beside you, Eric?"

"This is Betty." Betty did offer her hand to the man. His manner seemed easy and relaxed. "Lawrence," he said, "Lawrence Ferlingetti. Are you new in town, child?"

"Yes," she said.

"Well, you stick with Eric here. You've found gold, my dear."

"I will."

"Eric Daddy-O, and hep cats, I must be going. So long. No wrong. Be strong."

"And you!" Big Daddy said, as the rather animated fellow strode away from them.

Arien could feel some energy go away with him. "Who is he?"

"A poet," Otter informed him.

"And a very rare one, at that." Eric said.

"Knows everybody." Otter added.

"Maybe it's the other way around." Big Daddy pushed himself up from the bench. "Come on," he offered. "I'm hungry. Let's go to the "I" and see what we can rustle up."

The door to the "I" was open as it usually was. A small group of people were practicing a Yoga breath technique in the large front room. The leader, a young, dark-skinned man in a saffron-colored silk tunic, barely nodded to Eric as he strode around them with his little train of friends. Through a set of doors in the back was another, smaller room that extended for the width of the building. It had a few more mattresses on the floor on one side, and a kitchen area was on the other.

"Arien?" Eric inquired, "Are you German?"

"Uh, no."

"He's an Aries, Eric."

"Oh." He chuckled. The small old refrigerator had some pans in it with leftovers. "I don't know," he demurred, rummaging. "This is questionable. How about we go down the street? I'll buy us all a hamburger."

"I'm hungry," Betty agreed.

"I don't eat dead cow, Eric. But thanks."

It sounded good to Arien but Otter's refusal presented a dilemma. The issue was a sleeper. It had been awhile since Arien had any meat. Some of the people at 1889 ate it but not in the house. A can of tuna caused a genuine upheaval next door. This had to be one of the most difficult adjustments for Arien so far. Both chopsticks and vegetables were rampant. He hadn't expected that. Gathering gumption, and appreciating on some level that Otter would be displeased, he still accepted Eric's offer. "You can get some fries, Otter," he said to rolling eyeballs.

Eric Nord chuckled, and then they were slipping by the yoga class as it was winding things up with a deep "OMMMmmmmmmmmmmmmm......." The OM filled the large old front room of *The Hungry I.*

"He's new," Otter observed, out on the sidewalk.

"Yes. Shri Jaya just started the Yoga classes."

'Cool. Well, maybe I'll check him out sometime."

"He'll be right there, Otter."

Otter turned away and headed back up toward the park while glancing a last remonstrance off Arien. No words were needed. But Arien simply nodded and followed Eric and Betty the other way. Dead Cow: one, veggies: zero.

They ducked into an alcove of a place not far down Haight, on the same side as the '*I*,' which provided a counter top and stools for patrons. The air smelled like hot greasy food. A fat man in a T-shirt behind the narrow, light-gray counter was red-faced and furious, muttering under his breath and pushing a towel around like a detested enemy. Beads of sweat crowned his brow. Perspiration from under his arms soaked his dingy cotton T-shirt.

"What'll it be?" He growled, but not in a menacing way. Rather, he looked comical to Arien, who scanned for Big Daddy's response.

Eric slid onto a stool with a serene expression. Somehow his tall, broad body fit onto the stool. "Burgers all around," he said.

"What do you want to drink?" The fat man demanded.

"Dew?" Arien asked.

"Do? Do what? What the Hell do you want to do?" The guy fussed. He glowered. He shook the dingy white towel as if to strangle it and looked like he would bust a gasket.

Arien wondered if he would be held responsible when the man fell down dead over this.

"Oh now," Eric soothed. "How 'bout a 7-up, son?"

"Right." (Whatever it took to appease).

"Coke," Betty said.

"Damn it! Do you want fries? Do you want fries with that?"

"Yeah, Dude, 'n ketchup."

"Dude, who? Do I look like a dude to you, fer Chrissake? Ketchup. Ketchup. Damn stuff's right there in front of your face. Chrissake. Running out of it, too. Got-a order more ketchup. Damn it. Should have ordered it yesterday! Why didn't I order it yesterday?"

The muttering trailed off as the fellow tussled his way between the tight spaces of his isle. He turned away to throw three patties on the grill and drop a basket of fries into spattering hot oil.

The sizzling burgers smelled good. Arien's tummy growled. His mind wandered speedily through dead cows and tuna fish, bricks, bullets, typewriters, Page Street and "Bzerkeley."

"So, what have you been up to, Arien?" Eric asked.

It sounded like small talk but Arien heard something else. "The Revolution," he said. "But I'm wondering, just what is that, anyway?" He fiddled with the ketchup bottle that was a mere reach away. It seemed this man would know as much about the Revolution as anyone alive.

"Everybody has their own Revolution," Eric said right off. "Isn't that so, Betty, girl?"

"Uh huh."

"Don't peel the label off the bottle, please!" The cook hovered from fifteen feet away. While he spread lettuce, sliced tomato and sliced onion over opened buns on heavy china plates, he watched the bottle in Arien's fingers. "Got-a order more. *Why* didn't I order it yesterday?"

"And when lots of people are doing that all at once you have what's going on outside."

"But, it happens all the time, huh?" Arien twirled one way and then the other on his stool, pushing off a rail at the base of the counter with his feet as he fixed on Eric's eyes.

"Suspect so. Different times for different people, and not everybody's revolution is successful."

"Hmmmm…"

Plates were slapped down in front. Arien didn't wait. His first bite was almost too much to chew. "But it's not just one revolution," he said, as soon as there was enough space to articulate.

Eric looked back with an expression Arien couldn't read. Here was a mountain of a man who felt right as the solid hills. How totally unusual! He was an old dude, but he was a cool old dude! Arien felt safe. Had he ever known an adult who felt like that to him before? He was suddenly glad for Betty; for the both of them.

"Appreciate the lunch, Dude"

Eric nodded warmly.

"Say," Arien said between bites of fries, "do you think it's possible to travel through time?"

The cook was taking the order from another patron who had just sat down. "The kid's a nut cake," he abruptly confided to the man. "Travel though time. I get nuts in here all the time."

"Please pass the ketchup?" Betty asked.

"God damn it. Should have ordered it yesterday! That one won't last all day. I'll have to order some *more*!" Eric started to reach for it but the fat cook snatched it away and dropped it noisily in front of Betty on the other side of him. Arien actually looked at the man's ears, half expecting steam to escape them.

"Time marches on," Eric responded. "We can't stop getting older." That wasn't what Arien was after, but then Eric added, "Perhaps there are other universes and one could slip between them." And then, "I may have peeked into the past, once."

Betty spoke up: "Oh really? What happened?"

She's alive in there, Arien thought. It was his question exactly.

Eric grinned. He wiped his lips with a paper napkin he'd pulled from the stainless dispenser with some difficulty. "I was watching a play about the framing of the Constitution. Interesting play, really. Some line was recited and it got me to thinking, and then it was as if I was transported to another place. Instead of the theater I was in a big room with no furniture, but it had very tall windows and expensive, fancy molding and it was full of people dressed in old-time clothes."

"Wow."

"I've never told anybody this."

"What were you doing?"

"Just looking at everybody, I guess. We were all afraid of something. Fear, fear and uncertainty were the over-riding issues. But nobody spoke about it. It was the proverbial elephant in the room."

"Hmmm… Dude. Rad. Do you really think you were there?"

Eric heaved with a long breath. "I don't know if it was that. Maybe something in the play reminded me of another lifetime. Maybe I was there again for a moment."

"And what happened?" Betty asked.

"I just came back again. I was sitting in the theater watching the play and I was surprised to find myself concluding we are very fortunate to live in this country, all things considered, because wherever I had just been, the problem was not addressed. I just knew we could not get to that next step and stand on our basic rights. There was neither liberty nor security. It was terrible!"

Arien said, "Dude. There's so much that's not right! There's so much crap and they shove it down your throat and nobody seems to know what's going on and nobody gives a flyin' fuck."

"Quite so. But you know, young Arien, Thomas Jefferson said the government ultimately belongs to the people and we have a right to change things we don't like."

"Will there be anything else?" The fat man asked.

"Nah, nothin' will ever change. It will get worse." Arien grew morose.

"No thank you, Sam. We'll take the check."

"Time travel! The kid's a nut house," the cook groused.

"It already has changed," Eric continued, gracefully ignoring the irrelevant mutterings. "Things change all the time. I think by that I should say it boils down to you and me, and Betty here, too. We just have to do our part to put some purpose in what we do and that changes the world."

Outside on the sidewalk Arien looked up to the big, tall, gracious man who had just treated lunch. "Thanks, again, Eric!" He said. "Hope to see you again."

"Yes, you're welcome. It was very nice to meet you, Arien. Perhaps something will come of it someday."

Arien shook hands with Big Daddy, 'Baby Betty,' and was off. Ready or not thoughts of Tina pressed upon him again.

16 — Marin

It really rankled that he didn't know where she was. In one swoop the delights of the city by the bay had lost their keen appeal and it now bore a hollow and empty face. The hours of the afternoon weighed upon Arien. There was nothing he wanted to do but be with his girl. Oh, he might have jumped at a fighting chance to keep his Dad out of the Marines but that was getting to be blood under the bridge. It already seemed so long ago. It was like, Pre Riot and Post Riot and they were not the same. Arien felt changed all over again. People and places and things! How they messed with a dude! And this was not even taking LSD or God in Heaven into account.

He did return to Golden Gate Park to look for Otter but his wise friend wasn't there. The search eventually took him to the place on the bluff where they tripped and Arien was sure he'd spoken with someone a lot like God, by most definitions. This was as holy a place as Arien could identify. He sat in the grass, drawing his knees up and wrapping his arms around them as much for security as for warmth. He felt alone and so very small. What did all of this mean?

The sun was lowering over the horizon and the chill in the air deepened its bite. With chin rested on his knees now he couldn't possibly make a tighter ball of himself. He rocked a bit, forward and back. "Oh God!" He exclaimed aloud. "God! What are you? How can you be so close and so far away? Why? Damn it! Why? And, why now?" It was not supposed to be like this! It was like the terrible thing had just happened; it was still so fresh in his mind.

Arien's thoughts recalled the sparkling-perfect day and his beautiful Tina with the sunshine in her hair and the awesome light in her eyes. The thought of that pretty head being cracked by a Billy club while he was not there to protect her tormented him. It made him feel sick, like a cork screw churned in his stomach.

A nasty, needling thought that waiting or looking for her might actually cause him to miss Woodstock was no help. Would he actually do that for Tina? He knew the time to go was fast approaching. He knew Otter was pulling things together; Jeff was as ready as ever. The house at Page Street, as hospitable as any place he had ever been was awfully crowded, none-the-less. These people were like his family, yes, but it was not his home. It wasn't where he was going. He was a guest. He felt like a guest, now more than ever.

Yikes! It was cold! He shivered.

The thought of hanging in the city without his closest friends was inconceivable. It would be like swimming in that vast ocean out there as far as he could, all alone, freezing, tired and aching and maybe going perfectly crazy with panic as he sank, unable to muster just one more breath to say he was sorry just one more time. Tormented by such thoughts, Arien did a very impulsive thing. He stripped off all of his clothes and stood up, bare feet connected with the grass, to face the sun. A flashlight would have been warmer than its fading bronze light, but he accepted that with the chill breeze off the sea. He stretched out his arms and stood rock still. He worked to blend his thoughts with the cry of gulls and the distant, rushing murmur of ambient ocean.

Arien reached inside himself then and drew out the sound his hosts used in their circles before dinner. It was the word from the Yoga class at *the Hungry I.* It just seemed right. It was mysterious and heavy enough and came with no cheap associations from his past experience as a boy in Portland. "OoooooooooooooooMMmmmmmm......" he called. It was loud, almost a yell. It helped him first ignore and then resist his shivering reflex, loath to surrender before the relentless, pressing extremity.

He made the sound again, determined to lose his anger and frustration. That man at the diner was frustrated as Hell. Arien would cringe to invite any comparison, even saying his cause weighed so much more on the scale of things. His experience of total bliss with the Being in the stars was yet too fresh and special to be subject to his stupid questions. How could anything in his little life be *that* important? But this thought was a struggle. His affection was so strong and seemed too perfect to permit any interruption. That was no option.

"I'll begin again," Arien said to the falling sun and the sky and to the ocean. "Start over. Begin with what I know now. I'll take what Otter told me, and Jamie Sun and Big Daddy. Om-shanti-Om," he called. "Om-shanti-Om. Take her! Take me, too! Take all I was and all I am, oh God, oh damn it. Damn it! Take it all! I give it back!" He screamed now, at first silently to himself and then out loud, and some of his tears actually fell on his chest, smacked by the wind and already cold as water from melting ice. He began to shiver uncontrollably.

Gulls called loudly as the sun sank behind the curve of the west. The sound of waves in the distance grew crisper and then the wind suddenly slackened, becoming still for a moment before it completely changed direction. It rushed to chase after the melting orb. It was mercifully warmer at his back and against his limbs. It smelled first of cut grass and eucalyptus and then the odors of the city. Cooked food, automobiles, cigarette smoke, marijuana, odors of the whole world behind blended into the breeze and now murmurs of the city rushing to the ocean after the sun. Arien pulled his clothes back on, ran in place and rubbed his arms to warm himself up, and by twilight he was making his way back through the park at the Golden Gate.

Lights were coming on in the shop fronts on Haight as Arien headed down the street. He passed the *"I"* but didn't stop. He knew Preston wouldn't be home yet if he was off doing some theater thing, but the big house on Page Street seemed the right way to go. His thoughts turned to his friends there. He could help with dinner or something. At the top of Schrader Arien was surprised by a familiar face. Jamie Sun was climbing up its steep slope to Haight with the woman, Jennifer, he lived with. Arien was sure he could feel Jamie's gaze before he noticed who it was. The dude's magnetism was incredible!

Arien flashed a skater salute from his own future time, with the inside fingers contracted. They drew together and stopped to look at each other before anybody said anything. Jamie bore a child-like serenity, his wispy smile accented by his unusually long, light blonde lower lip hairs that were delicately braided through a small amber bead. Arien thought it looked truly rad!

Jennifer's black beret was swept down at a slight angle. The collar of her Navy pea coat was turned up. She was such a fox for a gray hair! She had a neat smile. Arien thought she probably would have looked cool in a flour sack. If she'd offered to kiss him, he would have said, yes. He hoped Tina wouldn't mind.

"Is Woodstock calling you?" Jamie said, finally breaking their pleasing silence. His expression grew sharp and serious under a floppy, yellow-wool cap.

Arien wasn't sure what he should say.

Jamie continued. "Sometimes, when there are obstacles, help comes from unexpected places."

Arien hesitated. There were the obvious connections in what all happened in the days leading to today, but what would Jamie Sun know about that? These two people were looking at him. "Should I be going soon?" he replied, dangling a question. He felt kind of dumb.

"What do you think?" Jamie asked.

"Dude, I don't know what to do now. My girl has been snatched by her mother and I don't know where she is. I've got to find her. Tina's coming with me to Woodstock. No way is she staying!"

"Walk with us."

"Sure."

They continued on down the street, passing people who apparently knew Jamie because greetings seemed to line the way. It was an unusual thing to Arien. A lot of people knew Otter, but the sense of anonymity that generally accompanies a public street was starkly lacking here. Twice, Arien was about to say something further about Tina when somebody greeted them and it was snatched from his lips.

When they were almost to Ashbury, Jamie Sun slowed their pace. He singled out a girl who walked in the same direction just ahead of them. "Ask her," he said, pointing at her back.

"Huh? – Ask her, what?"

"Ask her where your girlfriend is." Jamie's expression was sober.

Jennifer seemed surprised initially, but then broke into a broad smile. She nodded her head. "I'd do it if I were you," she coaxed. The smile was stuck on her face and her eyes had a delighted look that made her appear much younger than she was.

This is nuts! Arien was not an idiot. The girl was a complete stranger. She could not possibly even know Jamie Sun! When Arien hesitantly tapped her shoulder she turned her head with a guarded look of alarm.

"Excuse me. Do you know where Tina Deacon is?" Arien felt very stupid. He braced himself to get shot down like some kind of dork.

The girl's sense of intrusion melted and morphed into surprise and a tentative smile. She actually smiled! "Do I know you?"

"Uh-uh. No way, Babe."

"Well, how do you know Tina?"

Arien was flabbergasted. How could this be happening?

Jamie placed his hands together prayerfully, bowed his head and sweeping forward, continued on down the sidewalk with Jennifer shrieking with excited laughter along side of him.

"She's my babe. I want her," Arien heard himself say. His head was spinning.

"Oh, my God!" The girl exclaimed. "I didn't know she had a boyfriend! Wow. You do look a bit young, but, gee, you're cute. Good for you, Tina honey!" She laughed to herself. "So, you're – you're –"

"Arien."

"Wow. Groovy name, Man. I'm Linda." Linda was dressed preppy, with a beige cashmere sweater, plaid skirt, socks and penny loafers. Her black hair was short. The anomaly was her hippie bead necklace and she wore a number of silver bracelets on each arm where the sweater's sleeves were pulled up. They looked expensive. She was a bit stocky, but appeared nice enough to Arien. Like Tina, she was probably about eighteen.

"And how do you know Tina?"

"We were buddies all through High. I haven't seen her since taking on UCLA. Far away and no time anymore, you know?"

"Well – uh, do you know where Tina is now?"

"You don't?" She was befuddled. "What's going on? The last time we were together was last summer in Marin, at Jackie's going away party."

This couldn't be right, Arien was thinking. The connection is too close, too close. Jamie Sun wouldn't have taken it this far for… But that was a ridiculous thought.

It hit him! God! He got it. "This is unbelievable!" He said, "You must know where her Mom's house in Marin is!"

"Duh," Linda said. "Do I? I practically lived there, especially in '66, when my Mom was in the hospital for three months!"

"Jesus. This is so rad." Arien was truly blown away. How the heck did Jamie Sun not only know, but make the connection and everything? The timing! It was too much. It was impossible!

"Can you take me there?"

The girl hesitated, but seeing the earnestness coming off Arien's face…

The boy from the future grinned from ear to ear. They were flying over the Golden Gate Bridge in a perfect, baby blue '56 T-Bird. Even with the top up it was a thrill. Arien loved the bucket seats. It was the first time he had ever ridden in one of these. He swept his hand over the metal dashboard in front just to be sure it was real.

"Are you having fun?"

"Oh yeah." He remembered the first time he saw a Bird like this when he was still a little guy and he wanted to ride in it so bad.

He still couldn't believe what was happening. The car had been parked down on Ashbury. Linda recounted her side of the coincidence. She was on her way home to see her folks in Marin when Arien tapped her shoulder. It was just a fluke that she came to the Haight earlier in the afternoon to drop off a friend she knew from the U that she happened to meet downtown.

Arien tried to explain how they met but Linda didn't buy it. She was not happy that her passenger didn't reveal the true connection instead of feeding her this nutty story with a hippie wizard in it and all. Things just didn't happen that way. Arien surely understood, so he charmed her as best as he could, and he asked questions about Linda and Tina's old friendship, and that got the subject changed.

The road led through picturesque Sausalito, though vision was limited in the dark. They stopped at a 'Flying-A' for gas. Arien could make out the ocean from here. In fact, from a rising mist in the close, deeply-dark horizon the ocean and the bay were likely near enough, except for this big hill rising up behind a cluster of white houses tastefully illuminated by outdoor lighting. And then they continued on up some winding road into the County. Arien had no idea where he was. They drove for about half-an-hour more and then turned down a dark street lined with large trees and branches that hung over the road. And then Linda pulled over to the curb in front of a great big house with multi-paned windows framed in iron and an ivy-covered, brick entryway. It was illuminated by a giant, old-fashioned lamp with an iron frame, very impressive to Arien. He'd never even been in a house like that. It was like something from an Ivy-league campus. Tina was here? She was in this house?

"Well, here we are." Linda looked over to the silhouette of handsome boy beside her.

He was dubious. He was actually here. What now? This stage came up so quickly there hadn't been time to do a plan. He scratched the back of his neck. "I just can't walk in there."

"Oh. Of course." Linda had a knowing look. "We could go to my house and I could call Tina from there. It's just that, well, my folks will be home."

"Yeah, so?"

"I guess I could call Tina and tell her I'm coming over. But, I'm just getting in to see my parents. It doesn't make sense for me to be running off right away. Come to think of it, if you need to see her without her Mom knowing…" Linda concentrated. "Tomorrow would be better. If Edith Deacon goes anywhere it's usually in the morning. That would be the best. Well, Arien, what to do with you in the meantime?"

"I could just get out here and hang in the woods, I guess." Arien was serious.

"Oh nonsense. Good grief, Boy. If you weren't Soul-Sister's boyfriend, I'd have no problem with you staying in my bed tonight!" Her own boldness made her giggle to herself.

"You're rad," Arien said. His smile came natural. "Do you smoke pot?"

"No, Hun. Don't do it. It makes me paranoid."

"Too bad. I don't have any. A hit would be awful rad right now."

He opened the window and hung his arm out as the T-Bird pulled away from the curb. The crisp air smelled damp and woodsy. Linda cranked up the heat. She made a U-turn at a driveway ahead and drove on back to the main road.

"Do you do anything, Arien? Going to school or whatever?"

"No. We're just going to Woodstock."

"Where's that?"

"New York State. It'll be a mega-rad concert."

"Oh. 'Mega-rad,' huh?" She smiled to herself. "Groovy. Wow. I haven't heard about it. New York! My God! That's a long way. How are you getting there?"

"My friend, Jeff, has a VW bus."

"So, where did you meet Tina? How long have you been together?"

"At Blue Star's – uh, pad, in Portland."

"Oh, yeah. Tina said she had Portland friends. They get up to Seattle, too, she told me."

"Don't know that." Arien considered it. Maybe there was a lot about Tina he didn't know. He wanted to know more, lots more. He was sure he would be keeping this girl up all night.

Linda's home was at the top of a really long driveway bordered the whole way with a white rail fence. Aside from a couple of horses behind the fence, barely visible in the headlights, Arien couldn't make out anything else in the dark. The wood frame colonial was over two stories and a large, detached garage with three bays sat across from it, linked by a breezeway, and there was a cobblestone court in front where a '69 Cadillac 4-door sedan was parked. Everybody seems to be so rich in these parts, Arien thought. He felt out of place.

"Stay here," Linda said, pulling away from the yard-light poles and shutting down the car. "I'll think of something and get back as soon as I can." She opened the trunk and pulled out a suit case and then went into the house though a side door.

Arien waited a long time alone in the dark in his leathery bucket seat. His tummy growled. He was thirsty and thought about cigarettes and doobies. It was more than enough to keep him awake and uncomfortable. Food, smokes and plenty of pot was always around. At Page Street all a guy had to do was be there. If he wanted anything somebody else probably did, too, and soon enough it was happening. Outside of that special environment and away from his friends there Arien found himself feeling rather like a helpless fish in a bucket. He was just beginning to wonder if he would be spending a hungry night in this car when someone came out of the house. It wasn't Linda.

Whoever it was came straight for the Bird. There was some relief in seeing a young dude. He came over and tapped on the window. Arien rolled it down.

"My Sister's tied up," he said. "I'm Danny."

"Hey."

"My room's up over the garage. You can stay there with me tonight." Danny had short black hair like his sister. Arien guessed he was about sixteen. He was a good-looking kid with a solid build.

The garage was full of toys. Besides some vintage car with wire wheels, under a canvas cover, and a Triumph TR next to that, there were a couple of motorcycles, about four 10-speed bikes, a tall surf board against a wall, baseball stuff, golf clubs, a basket ball... To Arien it was a peek into Santa's house at the North Pole. A set of steps went up along a back wall and ran to a landing on the second floor into a loft as spacious as the garage below.

Upstairs, Danny pointed at one of two beds, on the end of the big room. It was the one that was all made up. "That's for friends. That's you," he said. "Hungry?"

"Oh yeah, Dude!"

"Fridge over there. Leftovers. Snacks. Help yourself."

Arien had to make his way around a pool table to reach the refrigerator. There were some barbequed chicken leftovers on a dish covered with foil among the items there and he went for that. He held it up.

"Eat it," Danny said. "So, how did you know my sister?"

"What did she tell you?" Arien came back over with the plate of chicken and sat down in a rocking chair closer to Danny.

"She said you told her some impossible story and she hopes you're not hiding anything she should know." Danny sat at a desk on the opposite wall. He cranked the chair around to face his visitor.

"It's true, and I'm not."

Danny leaned back, tilting the chair on two legs. He raised his arms and locked his fingers behind his head. "Tina, was in the hospital?"

Arien winced. "Yeah. We were over in Bzerkeley for the demonstration, and she got hit in the head by a cop."

"No kidding?"

Footfalls were on the steps and soon Linda was with them. She sat down on Danny's bed. "Got everything you need?"

"Think so."

"Have a toothbrush?"

Arien shook his head in the negative.

"I'll fix you up. I called Tina."

"Wow. Cool. What did she say?"

"She said she just woke up." Linda looked away.

"And? How's she doing? What? What?"

Linda giggled to herself. "She said she woke up and wondered what the Hell she was doing at home! She said she didn't have a phone number to call you. She asked me to help her get out of there!"

"Oh! Awesome! Oh so rad! Oh man! Mega radical!" Arien was beside himself. He jumped up and began pacing, still holding the dish. "Well?" He said. "What are we going to do?" He set the food on a desk there with a small portable typewriter in its case, the lid flipped back against a window behind it. He wiped his hands on his pants. He looked comical. Linda and Danny grinned at each other.

"I was right again!" Linda pronounced. "Edith has an appointment with her hairdresser tomorrow morning. Tina is supposed to go with her, but she'll say she has a headache and wait for us."

"Will she tell her Mom?"

"I don't know, Danny. Maybe she'll leave a note."

"And hope she doesn't say who helped her," Danny added. "You don't want to be on her hit list!"

"Oh, you're right. I don't." She laughed.

"It was easy," Arien said with a wave. "She was waiting in the driveway and she rode on my lap in that T-Bird all the way back."

Tina's expression was thoughtful. The smile she carried through most of Arien's report was wistful by its end. The sweep of her golden hair hung down over her brow. "I feel better," she said. "When I walked into my house something snapped me back. Sometimes my head still throbs, but I'm here." Her gaze at Arien passed a note between them and Arien's connection with her was a portrait in solicitude, relief and gratitude.

"Wow," Jeff said. "That's so far out! Now I see why you didn't share the whole story 'till we got here."

"Didn't I tell you how amazing Jamie is?" Otter looked to Arien and then the others. "Now you get to see it for yourself!" He reached to the basket lid on the grass between them for another wedge of Brie. He set it carefully on the slice of crispy green apple he was holding and pushed it between his lips.

Jeff poured more white wine from the classy bottle into his metal camp cup. Their celebration on Tina's rescue and likely recovery was nearing its end. The breeze was light over the water off of Land's End. Gulls called. 1969's maturing sun felt warm and pleasant on their faces. There was only a hint of fog just where the water met the beach. It hung a foot over the sand; wispy stuff.

"I spoke with Blue Star last night," Otter said between chews. "He's pulling his trip together. And Andy told me he wants to go with us, too."

Jeff had a sip from his cup. "Hmmmm... That's a lot of people for Van Gogh. It might be a good idea to put the extra seat back in."

"He said he would help with the gas."

"That's great Otter, but gee, man, three-thousand miles is a heck of a run."

"Maybe we'll come up with another car," Otter said. "Blue Star's got an old bomb, but I got dibs on a Mercury in Portland that would be a nice drive."

"Cool," Arien mused. "Andy's got to come with us."

Otter focused on him. "So, what happened back there in Berkeley, Arien? You sure planted a flag on him. He told me how you saved his life. You seem so young and green, Arien, but something you got runs deep."

Tina grinned and reached for Arien's hand.

"Babe, do you remember when I was looking for this guy before I met him? Remember when I wondered if Andrew was Blue Star's real name, or Otter? You, too, Dude. At first I thought it had to be one of you."

"No shit!"

"I remember," Tina said. "It wasn't long after we got here."

Otter stuck his index finger to his tongue and then held it up over his head to scribe one in the air. "So! We finally have something, but you know there're other more probable explanations." His look was defiant but the spark in his eye made some room, maybe for the first time. Arien didn't miss that. The thought crossed his mind to remind Otter of what Jamie Sun said. He let it pass.

"I was thinking maybe we could leave tomorrow, but they want to have a party for us at Page Street on Saturday," Otter told them. "What's your take?"

"Sunday, then," Arien agreed. "We need to hit it, Dudes."

"All ready Jeff?"

"Ready as a van can be, man."

That Friday night just before dinner Brian came panting up from 1887 to tell Otter he had a long-distance phone call. Brian said it was important, to hurry, they were holding the line open. Otter was slicing tomatoes in the kitchen. He handed the knife to Arien and busted out of the room.

Paul leaned over the stove, frying fish patties in a pan. "Some of the guys from Flat Bread are coming over to play at the dig tomorrow," he announced over his shoulder, eyes following Otter's hasty exit.

"And the Angels are doing a little show for us," Mikel noted.

Arien's musings took him to an odd place, like a momentary trance. Somehow he knew he would not see the show. But, since he could think of no reason why he focused back to the kitchen. He pulled the cutting board of tomatoes across the table to himself and picked up slicing where Otter left off.

"Groovy," Karen said. Some butter had gotten on her thumb and she'd stuck it in her mouth like a toddler.

Jeff sliced the bread. He took the butter dish from Karen's free hand and set it by while he finished dividing the heavy loaf. He looked over at Arien standing on the other side of the table. "Van Gogh's all gassed," he said with a little wink.

Arien smiled. "I can feel it all around me, already." It barely expressed his rising excitement. The mega-major road trip was finally about to happen. He could hardly believe it. It was just another day away. He peered at Tina, who was at the sink, and she caught his glance with the edge of an eye. She had that glow about her. She was on to his feeling. They could have been standing together with a wire between their brains. It was like it had been before and Arien's happiness over that now vied with his excitement. He was about to splay open the last tomato in the bowl when there was a pounding from the stairs.

Otter burst into the doorway, gasping for breath. "Blue Star's in – some kind-a trouble. We – we have to go! We have to leave tonight!"

"Oh wow. What?" The murmurs went all around stunned faces in the room.

"Don't know any details, but the call was from Tommy Jensen." Otter furrowed his hair with nervous fingers of both hands. "He said, now they can't find him!" He stood as if deciding which direction to turn, then threw his hands in the air. "Let's get packing!"

Karen shooed her hands at Jeff, Tina and Arien. "I'll make sandwiches. Go!"

"Does anyone know where Andy is?"

"He may be next door," Paul said. "I'll go and see, Arien."

It was a real scramble. Suzie Q expressed her disappointment that Page Street's house guests would miss their going away party but found a way to be useful, helping to get bags that were mostly ready, in any case, down to the van.

Jeff arranged stuff so tools and water would be handy. Yesterday, he decided to replace the green sheet covering the mattress with a tan canvas tick. It would wear better and be easier to smooth out and keep tidy. Everything had been carefully run through during the week and the only thing to be concerned about tonight, really, was not forgetting anything they had in the house in the sudden rush.

And, Paul returned without Andy.

"Where the hell is he?" Otter fretted. But then composing himself, "Guys, don't forget to take a moment, close your eyes, and think about what's in your packs and still upstairs."

"Oh, wow," Beanie chimed. "We had gifts for you! Hold on! We'll be right back." A lot of folks took off with her.

Tina began to arrange the duffels, packs and hastily rolled sleeping bags to make room inside the vehicle.

After a while people returned and some others showed up and all were pressing around Van Gogh. Susie Q passed a small bag to Tina. Tim and Paul flanked the center doors. Both lit cigarettes. Even Old

Joe, awakened from a nap, was there. Mikel, who was over at the Angels', turned up with Tommy, Brian, Preston and Charles.

"I'm going to miss you, sweetie," Charles told Arien. He pinched Arien's cheek.

Arien returned a sheepish grin. "Anybody know where Andy is?"

"Does he have anything upstairs?" Otter asked.

"Yeah," said Bob, who had just come to stand alongside Beanie. "He stashed a pack and sleeping bag in our room this morning."

"Let's get it!" Otter and Bob ran back up to the apartment.

Karen showed up at the curb with a paper shopping sack bulging with sandwiches made from the aborted fish patty dinner, and there were bananas, oranges, and some nuts and candy from the house.

"Wow, Karen, that's so cool!" Jeff told her. There were murmurs of thanks.

"Allow me to make a little donation," Preston said with a grin and a short bow. He reached in the pocket of his tweed sport jacket and pulled out a handful of food stamp books that he summarily dropped into the bag of food. There was applause from some in the group.

Randy had just walked up Page Street from the Panhandle. He turned the corner to see the assembly around Van Gogh. "What's happening?"

"These heads are going to Woodstock a day early," Paul said. There's been a Problem with Otter's friend, Blue Star, up in Portland, and he needs to see what can be done, I guess." He flicked ashes off his cigarette.

"Oh wow. They'll miss the party we're having for them." Randy said with disappointment.

"Have it anyway," Arien heard himself say. "We'll think about the good energy here and it will help us".

Old Joe stroked his short, graying beard. "Spoken like a young sage," he affirmed.

"Yes," Paul said and Tim nodded in agreement.

Then Otter and Bob returned with Andy's baggage. Folks moved aside to let it be set in the van.

There was some searching of faces among the group about to depart and the little crowd that was there to see them off. Arien was touched. These folks were true friends, from beginning to end. It kinda hurt to say goodbye.

Mikel stepped up to face him, standing by the front passenger door of the little bus. He removed a plain leather-thong over his head, struggling a bit with his very long, straight, strawberry hair. A slender, shiny 'letter' about an inch and a half high dangled on the end of it. "I want you to have this," he said, reaching over Arien's head until it rested in the center of his chest. Arien peered down to study it. It was pure silver. It looked a lot like the number three only it had a small crescent with a dot in it on top and what looked like the small letter s, in longhand, coming away at the bottom. It was delicate, and lovely. Mikel took hold of Arien's shoulders and eloquently searched his eyes. "It's the OM," he said, "In Sanskrit. The sound of everything."

Something seemed to rumble in Arien's head when Mikel spoke, like a memory that tags a certain smell. He wanted to chase after it but the clamor of the moment called him back to the group.

Other gifts were passed. Karen and Beanie both presented Tina with quartz crystals. The smaller of the two, slender and purplish, dangled on a fine silver chain. Tommy passed a small drawstring bag of sundry medicinal items to Otter, who likewise, dug in a pocket of his fringed jacket for something Tommy could take away. Paul threw a pack of Chesterfields through the open window onto the front seat. Brian handed a bundle of rope incense to Otter. Randy shrugged and pulled a bill out of his pocket that he passed to Jeff. "For gas," he said.

"Safe trip, now." Mikel said.

"Thanks! Thanks a lot," Arien answered, fingering the OM against his chest. "It's so rad."

"Fire it up!" Otter said to Jeff. The moment had come.

Arien stifled a rush of panic. "Wait a minute!" He cried out. "Aren't we forgetting someone?"

"We'll pick him up on the way out."

"Where, Otter, where? You know where he is?"

"Get in. It's time."

Jeff slipped his slim body behind the wheel, punched the starter button that was rigged under the dash and Van Gogh sputtered to life.

Arien and Tina took a spot together on the mattress behind the front seat. They stretched their legs out. Otter got up front with Jeff.

With some "byes" and waves they lurched away from the curb.

"Pick him up on the way out," Arien said, absent-mindedly to Tina.

"I know. Where does he get that?" she giggled. "His stuff is here, anyway."

"Maybe we could trade it for food it in the Midwest." Arien said.

Down where he sat Arien couldn't really see where they were headed. The light was fading and streetlights were coming on. He listened blankly to the exchange up front.

"Where are you going, Jeff?"

"The Golden Gate."

"Let's take a little detour, first."

"Just say which way, Man," Jeff drawled in his patient Texan.

"Hang a U-ie. Get back on Oak, to Castro, and go down to Market Street."

Arien's body pressed against Tina's as Van Gogh pitched and rolled this way and that. Then the gargle of the engine picked up. After a spell Arien could feel the next turn. They hardly passed a few blocks when Jeff muttered, "You rule the world, Otter. There he is!"

"What?" Both Tina and Arien crouched up as best they could to focus through the windows and sure as the Land's End fog, there strode Andy's silhouette with the arm in a big white triangle on the other side of the street.

Van Gogh's horn cried out with a long bleep until Andy looked up, saw them and ran over, dodging a couple of cars.

Arien flung the side doors open and the young man he'd snatched from certain death in Berkeley stepped in. "Hey guys. Thanks," he said, finding a place between bundles in the darkness.

"What?" He'd caught Arien and Tina's bemused expression with enough streetlight filtering in through the windows. He fussed with his shoulder bag. The catch on its strap had come undone when he pealed it off over his head. "Hate that," Andy growled.

Van Gogh was again at speed and they tumbled forward with renewed purpose.

"You might as well get on Fell and catch 101 in the Park," Otter said.

"Yep, on the way."

"Where we going, Guys?" Andy asked.

"Portland," Otter said.

"Shit! What gives? I thought we were leaving on Sunday! Hey, we need to go back! My stuff's at Page Street!"

Tina giggled.

We need to understand the mystery of Otter, Arien thought.

18 — An image, bloody and horrific

There was some debate on the highway to take. Route 101 hugs the coast and has majestic vistas, a moot issue at night and it is not the fastest way to go. However, Jeff favored it because it favored Van Gogh. There were more places to stop if necessity required, and this was always a consideration when road tripping with a VW bus. Otter was torn. The twists and turns, the hills could be interminable, but more brothers and sisters were beginning to populate the little towns along the way. A decision had to form by the time they reached Petaluma. They could strike off east from there toward Napa, and eventually hook up with the Interstate.

Andy fussed with something. Tina grabbed the flashlight Jeff kept by the middle doors and switched it on. They watched him reach awkwardly into his army surplus shoulder bag and dig around in it until fixing on something. The shiny blues harp he brought out went to his lips and with a few sharp puffs of air it emitted a pleasing, plaintive wail that morphed into a plausible one-handed rendition of *"Me and Bobby M'Gee."*

Up the road the people in the van grew quiet. Arien had questions but he kept them to himself. He figured he'd have answers along with the others when they got to Portland. Blue Star had gone missing. That was all anybody knew.

His hand found the OM dangling from his neck. *'The sound of everything.'* Where had he heard that before? A smile crept over him.

Tina's head rocked on his shoulder. She'd dozed off. Her breath actually smelled sweet. He timed her breathing to pull it into his lungs and steal away with it.

"OK, what do you think?" Otter's voice drifted overhead.

"101" Jeff said.

"You called it."

"Arien, you asleep?"

"No." He whispered, not wanting Tina to waken. She'd curled up next to him with an arm wrapped around his thigh. He stretched against the seatback and peered blankly into the darkness of the van's lurching interior where Andy snored. Jeff's words floated above him.

"What was it like to come here from your time?"

"There wasn't much to it."

"Did you see anything?"

"A flash."

"Was there any sound?"

"A crackle."

"Was it loud?"

"Can't say."

"I saw a flying saucer once, when I was a kid in Texas. It was here, then it was way over there, like a light beam, and then it was gone."

"And?"

"I've thought maybe that's how it did it; it moved through time, you know? It stopped the clock. Not even light could move that fast. Otherwise, anyone inside would be crushed by the Gs."

"Did it make any noise?"

"No. It was totally quiet."

"Were you high?" Arien's chuckle was barely audible.

"I know what I saw!"

There was a precious silence.

"Jesus, did you grock that?" Otter could be heard asking up front. Jeff didn't respond.

"The time-bandit doesn't believe in flying saucers!" Otter roared. His wild, infectious cackle shook all through Van Gogh.

They were a few hours up the northern California coast after a gas stop and found a place on the beach south of Crescent City, to eat. Tina and Otter carried blankets. Tina spread two of them in the darkness and they set the others down off to the side. Andy had the paper sack in his available arm and Arien brought a canteen and cups. Jeff followed with a flashlight that was turned off as soon as folks were settled. It was cold and breezy but clear, except for a wispy haze over the water that reflected starlight. The fish sandwiches went around. Arien passed on the first doobie Otter produced. Instead, he opened the little wax paper package of assembled edible, contemplating with his nose. Other than the muffled rushing at the ocean's edge, crinkling paper and pleased murmurs, quiet reigned. He took some of the blanket Tina offered to spread over his lap. Chewing and feeling his good food, he stuck a fingernail between front teeth to dislodge a thin, bony sliver when somehow, like falling out of balance, he drifted to another space in his mind between waking and dozing, and the land and the sea and then the plum-dark curve of the horizon and the inky sky.

And then it fell on him like a bridge in an earthquake: An image, bloody and horrific, seared across his inner-eye, smeared and splattered, red and gory and Arien recoiled with a cry! His heart raced.

He gagged and coughed violently. Tina jerked up with fright. Otter was behind him in an instant pounding his back with an open hand and forearm. There were other sudden, discernable commotions as friends sought to know or find a way to help.

Arien gasped for breath. He perspired in the chill air. He jumped up to walk away in the glow of Jeff's flashlight.

"Stop, Arien! Arien?" Otter came after, taking hold of his arms.

Arien wept. He couldn't control it. He suddenly recognized who he'd just seen! He fairly reeled with the incredible vision. He'd hardly known the fellow but, for an instant, he did know his wrenching, terrible, pitiless pain.

"Jesus!" Otter exclaimed, pulling the boy to him, where he fell apart weeping against the fringed-leather jacket. Otter nestled his head like a child. Tina was there, wrapping her arms around his waist. Jeff kept the light low, and Andy helplessly kicked the sand.

"You were chokin', Brother. It's okay."

Arien couldn't begin to share it. How could it be? But, it was so vivid and unexpected. He knew he couldn't possibly have dreamed such a thing. It simply had to be true!

It was too traumatic. There was no going on with his dinner. He nearly barfed what he'd already had. His only desire was to curl up in Otter's strong embrace. He hoped Tina would likewise, not let go. They would protect him and block the horror and maybe even soak some of it out of him. Deep inside, he thought that was a selfish thing to hope for, but he'd just had the terror of his life. Jeff and Andy eventually returned to the blanket to fitfully finish their meals.

"What happened? What happened?" Tina pleaded. A reflection of the horror was in her expression.

"Oh, no! No!" He cried.

"Arien, what's this? You have to tell us! You scared the shit out of me!"

"I'm so - so sorry, Otter," he panted.

"Sorry? Sorry for what? Tell us!"

"He's – so *dead*." Arien sobbed.

A series of wavelets rushed the shore like a sigh. It cut past the silence and deepening dread in slow, rhythmic pulses.

"Who's dead, Arien?" Jeff asked from the blanket. Otter didn't press but instead went limp around him, and Arien could feel a rush of tears splash the side of his face. Otter staggered back and sat down heavily in the sand at his feet.

Tina froze.

"Oh Kali, Kali," Andy keened.

Jeff said, "It can't be!"

"We have to go!" Otter stammered.

"It doesn't matter now," Arien said softly from his heart's most hollow chamber. "I think we have all the time we need."

After a dreadful, rock-quiet drive further on, Otter couldn't resist stopping at a pay phone by a roadside eatery up in Crescent City. The place was closed, but a light shone over the aluminum niche where a skinny phonebook dangled. After several tries feeding and retrieving coins he got through to Tommy, in Portland, and the terrible crime was confirmed. Arien heard later, when 'Tommy J' asked how he'd found out, Otter told him they traveled with a true seer.

Details were sketchy. It was difficult for Otter to recount what he'd been told, but everyone cried with him as a fractured story congealed from wounded words. Blue Star was indeed found by friends who were frantically searching for him. After the police took over, people grew wary of the questions into his connections and began to duck or split town. It was sincerely recommended that their party avoid Portland altogether and keep on their mission. There was nothing they could do. Nor was it known if there would be a remembrance of any kind. Something very scary had gone down and Blue Star's whole community felt uncharacteristically vulnerable.

For a long while Otter sat on the sill between Van Gogh's splayed-open side doors, his head in his hands, partly illuminated by the stark light cast from the phone stand on the store's outside wall. Jeff hadn't stopped the motor. His arms lay across the wheel as the engine's low gargle vibrated the vehicle. Tina sat alongside Arien in their spot against the front seat back. Andy carefully peeled a stick of spearmint gum from its foil wrapper but held it in his hands. He stood outside to take in heavy breaths of air, then to exhale with a barely audible chanting murmur.

"Who did it, Arien?"

Arien, still stunned, said he didn't know.

"Why, didn't you *see* who did it?" The tone didn't accuse, it pleaded. Otter looked like he would break apart.

The next words were measured. "It was part of me that did it and another part felt it, so, I couldn't." He rolled his head wearily against the seat back.

"Do you think you could have?" It was unexpected for Jeff to have asked.

Arien tensed. There was no way he was voluntarily going back to that place.

Near twenty minutes passed when Jeff shut the engine off and an hour was away before anyone stirred. Only a few cars came along during that time, but one slowed way down.

"Otter!" Jeff called, tempering his volume. "Cop to the heat."

"He was my good brother!" Otter sighed.

"Second time he's gone by and now he's watchin'."

Arien was deep into himself. There was nothing to say. It was all out there for everybody. He avoided contemplating any way that evil thing could have happened from fear of being sucked back into it, and yet he searched through his past for an inkling of this extraordinary experience. There was nothing. He was blown beyond his borders to a new room in the house.

Or, Arien finally crept to the little boy in his head and a distant, buried memory. He cowered under a table where he went to get away. If he'd hastened to the preview in his mind's eye he would have had time to escape, but it paralyzed him. The man his mother knew came in and saw him and reached under, taking hold of his shirt hem and furiously yanked him out from under there, ripping the shirt, and began to slap and hit him and hit him and… But he knew! Arien knew because he *saw* the jerk and felt his energy before it slammed into him! Oh so distant and buried. He was so alone with a broken boy's heart, full of the terror, rage and hurt of the abandoned.

Arien said, "Wow," summoning his private self to comfort him. But he let Tina in. She found his eyes, stroked his hair, put a hand on his knee.

Andy's occasional chant grew loud enough to be audible. *"OM, Na-my-ah, Shivai."*

"The heat!" Jeff said again. "We need to kick some bootie."

"No!" Arien heard himself say. "Move, and it's cat and mouse."

Otter didn't budge, nor Andy.

You're not even lookin' at 'em." Jeff despaired. Then, he got out of the car, went over to the phone and dropped coins in.

Arien had to lean forward to see him. He nodded his head. "Good move."

"He's driving away," Andy said.

Jeff hung up the phone, his change rattled down, and he put it back in his pocket. "I couldn't stand that, just had to do something!" He explained when he got back in. He turned the key and pushed the starter in. Van Gogh shook to life. Otter swung his legs inside and Andy got up front.

Otter sat on the other side of Arien and they wrapped their arms around each other's shoulders and just then Andy's hand came over from above and set it to the side of Arien's head, fingers in his hair. Tina snuggled into him from that side. Though Jeff commanded the ride, Arien felt him, too. It felt so warm and beautiful. They were together in the mystery of one-another and the awful sorrow they shared.

A bit down the road, Otter fervently wanted to hit Portland, but to Arien's surprise, he surrendered to, "No! It will resolve itself later." It might have been the tone of voice which had the conviction of a seer.

"Which way, now?" Jeff cried. He was choked up again, enough that Van Gogh wandered all over the lane with the driver's bleary eyes.

Otter said, "Take me to the nearest bridge so I can jump off."

Arien rose to the occasion. He hadn't come this far for nothing. "Jeff," he ordered, "Go for Grants Pass. We can buck east from there."

"Damn. You're amazing." Andy said.

Everybody was ready to crash by the time they reached Union Creek, a little town where signs pointed east to Crater Lake. Jeff found a place a few miles past the town when a picnic table dimly loomed in the headlights at a bend in the road. He pulled past the sign that said "No overnight camping," tucking Van Gogh away at the rear of a local park where a tight cluster of pines rendered them invisible in the darkness. He didn't have to say anything. He just shut off the engine.

The middle doors opened and soon enough Van Gogh's mattress swallowed them all in that ancient blanket of dreams.

In the early morning, the travelers washed up, each taking a turn with the white enamel basin. When Jeff was ready, he yanked out the stove and perked up coffee. They hauled a strong Colombian blend that had a welcome aroma and a powerful kick. Then, he dug up bowls and canned milk while Tina managed to parcel a small avalanche of cornflakes from a family-size cereal box. A few bananas were passed around to complete their breakfast.

They were quiet except for the crunching and slurping. Otter and Arien were the loudest. Otter took turns following his spoon to looking at Arien. The others stole their glances, too. There had been a big change with little fanfare. It hung in the air over the stout, dew-drenched wooden table like the Goodyear Blimp.

Arien's paper napkin was soon damp and hung from his fingers like cloth. He liked the way it cooled his lips. He held it there. Maybe they won't see me behind it. He couldn't explain it to himself and he expected that's all they wanted now, like a craven hunger not to be satisfied with cornflakes.

Tina retreated to what seemed a stoic patience, to offer no demand. She was really so good to him; predictable, but not in a way that could ever be boring. Perhaps it was in the way they flowed together. She gave him his space and an honest respect, taking him as he was and delighting in his surprises. He'd wanted to make love with her as soon as they were awake but the proximity of friends ruled it out. If Arien was anything, it was not oblivious to vibes.

"Who's got the smokes?"

"Here, Arien." Jeff tossed the Chesterfields. Otter struck the match and pulled another one out of the pack on the table.

"I think I'm hooked on these things." It was Arien's little joke. His first dance with Lady Nicotine was soon after his twelfth birthday. He remembered bringing cigarettes to school in the seventh grade and managing to have two or three every day into the high school years without getting caught.

"They're not easy to shake," Andy concurred.

"I'd quit in a minute if I didn't like 'em." Arien blew smoke rings over the table, chasing that last draw with a shot of coffee.

"So, we're right here, kids," Tina said. "I say we see the lake."

"Hell, yeah," Arien agreed. "I've never been."

"It's everything I imagined it would be!" Arien was so impressed with the perfect little world of the rim and the dazzling, deep blue water spread out beneath them. It was like no color he'd ever seen short of the cobalt corona of planet earth he gathered once, in his soul, on its wondrous journey to the stars.

"It's a holy place," Andy agreed.

Nature had its way of tapping Arien's soul. He felt himself expand into the magnificence all around them. It made him teary. He sucked freedom and wonder down into his lungs and it squeezed a leaping heart. Tina took his hand and inexplicably, Andy took the other, awkwardly, for the sling he wore. The young man had to reach across his body to not turn from the view. Likewise, Otter and Jeff stood as close as they could in a silent display of affinity. Arien distinctly felt them draw off of his energy. It was suddenly and infinitely expanded, bottomless and inexhaustible. It was an extremely powerful moment. He was high as an eagle, soaring on flakes, cigarettes and coffee in awesome majesty. They hadn't even had their day's first doobie.

I love you. I love you all so much. Let me feed you. Let me heal your poor, sorry hearts. Arien swooned, in awe of himself now, fairly pulsing with energy and awareness.

A big Oldsmobile pulled up to the curb near the traveler's viewpoint. A couple of children got out of the car. They, too, a little boy and his older sister, were drawn into the magnetic sphere. They came up and stood by the group at the crater's rim, staring not at the lake but at the sandy-haired youth with vivid green eyes.

Their mother hurried at first, but slowed her pace as she came near. Then, Dad came over, ostensibly to gather up his family and lead them to a sensible location. But the parents came to stand there looking confused, especially Dad. Arien could see the wheels turning in the man's head. He was draging for something to say. His wife already was lost in a relaxed and blissful smile, her gaze fixed on the jewel of deep, blue lake below them.

"Well, ah, that's really something, eh?" The man finally said, shuffling in place.

Arien felt a deep current of compassion press upward. It swept him along in a veritable river of empathy. He'd never felt anything like this before in his life and he could not have explained it but he knew it like he knew light and shadow, taste and touch, sound and silence. Helpless, they drank him like thirsty vampires, friends and strangers alike. But Arien was up to it. The more he gave the more he had to give. It bubbled up from within and washed over him, filling the whole lake and its enormous bed.

"It's rad," he said.

"Well..." The man gathered himself together. "Come on, Gang. Come on, let's check out the lodge."

The little boy reached up to touch Arien's pant leg before reluctantly turning away. His sister kept looking back. Their mother took Dad's hand and they made their way back to the car.

"Fuckin' A!" Otter declared, stepping away with an open mouth.

"Jesus!" Andy agreed. "I felt that, too! Oh, man, bliss-me-out!"

Tina searched his eyes. Jeff swooned dizzily to the low stone wall. A pair of ground squirrels scampered over his lap to drop away on the crater side of the wall.

"Man, have you been helping yourself to the acid?" Jeff asked.

Arien chuckled. "No, Dude. This must have been me, buck naked."

"I'll eat cornflakes every day now for the rest of my life," Jeff said.

"Don't forget to have the bananas with 'em," Tina advised. She slid her arms around Arien and hugged him like he was about to take a train to the war. Arien traced the sides of her head with his hands. He kissed her lips with passion, and still hungered to lie with her.

From the lake they connected to Oregon 97 north. The dearth of chatter in Van Gogh spoke volumes. Jeff drove again. Otter rode shotgun. Andy, Tina and Arien relaxed on the mattress, propping themselves with their bedding and duffels. Andy munched on some dried fruit. The engine droned. Arien overheard Otter say, "He was a Buddha back there."

"Contact high if ever there was one," Jeff answered.

Arien entertained a vague worry that he couldn't yet define. It lurked, seeking an audience from behind his own veil. It was Tina who kept him centered, that and the after-glow of a moment that dissipated like mist in warm sun, with traces still present but invisible, about the time they'd turned away from the gray-faceted, stunning blue jewel that was Crater Lake, in Oregon.

"Andy, there's something I don't get," Arien said, breaking a long silence. They tracked through scenic high desert and ponderosa country.

Andy had inadvertently jerked his shoulder getting in after a gas stop. He now lay with his shirt off, arms splayed-out face down on the mattress while Tina gently kneaded the muscle around the wound on his back with Tiger Balm. "Yeah?" He focused on his questioner.

"Well, Dude, what got you involved in Bzerkeley? When I met you, you were passing out flyers."

"It was a Commie newsletter." Andy chuckled to himself. "These guys are so serious. They wear berets, fatigues and boots –

"Tina, wow, that feels so good."

Tina dipped her fingers into the little red tin for more of the waxy, aromatic balm. Its menthol punch was filling up the cab.

"What did you do?"

"I illustrated the rag and helped type and print them and pass them out."

"So, are you really a Communist, Andy?" Jeff called from the front.

"Oh, I just have to see things for myself." He caught his breath with a little spasm of pain. "The best way to do that is to get involved."

"So, answer the question," Otter said.

"Why? Are you Senator McCarthy?"

Otter laughed. "Answer the question or you will be in contempt!"

"Ya, mein capitan."

"That's, 'ya' you're a Communist?" Jeff pressed.

"Nah," he admitted. "The comrades, they're grim, they have no sense of humor. I think, if they got their way, things would be worse than they already are."

Tina asked him, "Then why are you involved with them?"

"Well, I'm not. I'm going with us to Woodstock. Let me present Exhibit 'A' to the Senate panel." The half of Andy's face that could be seen had a smile on it and the eye wore a twinkle.

Arien said, "I'm still confused."

"Look, Little Brother, there's a revolution going on. It's like a war to stop the war. It's a fight for freedom, to do our thing. Those who are with us are the friends. Then, like I said, I had to see it for myself. You wouldn't believe it, the full one-eighty!" His voice grew more excited, laughing. "When I was in high school I went to John Birch Society meetings!"

"Oh, you're kiddin' me, no!" Otter protested.

"Oh, yeah. My cousin was a member and she got me to go to meetings. When I read 'None Dare Call it Treason' it told me my country was in mortal danger. We were infested with Reds!"

None of this made any sense to Arien. He listened, guarding the impulse to pepper with more questions.

Then Van Gogh hit something and the left-front wheel thumped loudly. Jeff swore under his breath. "That's what I get for not payin' attention."

"Ouch," Otter acknowledged. Then, over his shoulder, "That's a trip, man. Some folks travel the world. You travel somewhere else. What did you get out of it?"

"Oh, Tina, that was fantastic. Thanks!"

Tina pressed the lid on the Tiger Balm tin and sat back against the engine wall. "You're welcome, Andy. You're our hero of the revolution, after all."

"That's another thing," Otter inserted. "I think the real revolution is inside a man, not out on the streets."

Arien shook his head. "I'm thinkin' it's both. It's inside and it's outside."

"Right on, man!" Andy cheered. "Yeah, kid, it's on every level in every person that makes a choice."

Arien continued, "Big Daddy told me it was at different times, too, because everybody's at a different speed, or something like that, and when the times come together with lots of people it goes to the streets. Who's got a smoke?"

"It starts in the head," Otter argued.

"Chicken n' egg," Jeff added.

"Scrambled eggs," Tina said.

"I think I love you." Arien told her.

"Oh, you *think* you love me?"

"And I think I love you," Andy chimed in and Arien caught it like a turnip in a catcher's mitt.

"So, did you finish college?"

"Damn it!" Jeff said.

"Close, Otter." Andy was thoughtful. "Then Tim Leary came along and I turned on, tuned in and dropped out."

"Righteous," Tina cheered, slapping him on the buttocks.

"Oh, you bitch, woman! That's not fair."

"Damn it. It's pulling," Jeff observed. "It doesn't feel right."

"What was your major?" Tina asked.

"History, Philosophy minor."

"I'm looking for a place to pull over." The beating engine changed its tone. Van Gogh was slowing down.

As soon as they came to a stop the passengers stepped out as much for relief from the rising heat in the car as concern for its problem.

They were parked about 30 feet off the road by a cluster of second-growth ponderosa where Van Gogh had a place it could live for a while. There was a light breeze that didn't relieve the heat very much.

Jeff wore a sorry look. "Shit. Look at the tire already!"

"Yeah, it is wearing fast," Otter agreed. "We may have bent a tie rod back there."

In a moment, Jeff was under the car, grabbing and shaking things. "Aw, Damn it! I should have been watching out."

"You've been doing great, Jeff. Don't beat yourself up," Andy soothed.

"Yeah," Arien agreed. "Shit happens."

"I like that!" Tina said. "Shit does happen, doesn't it? And this is a-happening."

"You're a funny girl, Tina," Otter told her. "You two are made for each other."

"Well, we're knee deep in it, y'all," Jeff groused. "This has to get fixed."

Andy stood shirtless in the bright sun. A pesky fly cased his body, landed briefly on the Tiger Balm surface, and buzzed away. "Where are we?" He asked.

Jeff crawled out from under the axle and headed for the back door.

"Last I looked at the map, we were a few miles short of La Pine," Otter said.

"There ought to be someplace to get help there." It was more of a question than an assertion. Andy stood back while Jeff popped the hub cap and Otter took the jack and set it under the front-end. It was very hot right there in the bright sun and its reflection off the vehicle. Arien grabbed a blanket from inside and held it up to make shade.

"Good idea. Thanks!" Jeff obliged. "Andy, there's some clothes pins in the car kit. Get 'em, huh?" Soon the blanket was clipped at top to the rain channel and the bottom was tied with string at the corners and that was looped around some rocks to hold it out. Jeff removed the wheel, consulted briefly with the *'Idiot's Guide…'* and had the damaged tie rod and a steering knuckle bushing off the car in short order.

Otter determined he'd hitch with Jeff to find the parts. It was understood two people hitching might slow them down, but Otter wouldn't accept leaving Jeff alone in case it took a while. Besides, he had money to cover costs. He did empty his fringed-jacket of contraband and left a draw-string belt pack with his baggage, opting to carry only what could be eaten if they ran into fuzz. The others would have to make themselves at home and wait.

There wasn't a lot of traffic. It took nearly an hour before somebody stopped. Otter and Jeff mounted the cab of an early '60s Dodge pickup and before long they became a glimmer on the road's far horizon.

Arien lit a Chesterfield and offered a puff to Tina. She smiled. "You know I don't smoke."

"Try it! Try it, little girl! It's good for you!" They laughed.

"Cancer sticks," Andy said. "Give me a toke."

Arien complied. "Go for a walk?"

"Nah. I'm feeling tired and achy. I'll hang." Andy sat on the center-door sill, wiping sweat off his brow.

Arien hoped his nonchalance would be accepted at face value. Tina was happy to accept the invitation and they set out in the direction of a rocky out-crop studded with ponderosa pine and juniper.

They were barely out of sight of Van Gogh when Arien took Tina's hand. She turned to take his other hand. Their faces flushed as they kissed. Her lips were so sweet and soft! They kissed and tasted each other. Arien inhaled a deep, full breath of her, so suddenly intoxicating. Quickly, feverishly, they peeled off one-another's clothes.

"Oh, God, you turn me on! You're such a beautiful girl!" He exulted, holding her light, supple flesh against him; her dream-blonde hair catching sparkles of sunlight, her freckles driving him absolutely delirious.

"And you are the most beautiful boy I've ever seen." She replied, exploring a lithe body with tender hands.

"Ow!" he cried out in his most squeaky voice, gently pinching her cheek.

"Ow!" she replied.

Their coupling was the center of the world, a euphoric swirling, rhythmic-pounding, sweating, shrieking high. Arien stretched through their climax together in utter blindness, his every sinew focused in the sensory explosion of being within and around her.

Utterly spent, in a sweaty tangle, they fell to their knees among the clothes scattered about them, and stared into each others eyes for the longest time.

Arien and Tina returned to discover Andy had set up the stove and put on a pot of rice. There were some carrots that Arien set to peeling and when that was added, along with luke-warm cottage cheese out of the cooler, Tamari and sesame seeds, it was a decent and filling meal. This type of entrée was not so strange any more and Arien found himself looking forward to it. There was enough for everyone, but they determined at twilight that the guys wouldn't be back this day. The leftovers were covered with tin foil and set in the cooler even though the ice had completely melted.

After dinner, Arien made a small pit on the side of the van opposite from the road. Andy advised him to be careful to dig a good hole into the ground and sweep duff and pine needles away from it, which he did. The sticks and bits of branch he'd gathered were very dry and caught immediately, making very little smoke. They all settled down cross-legged on a blanket next to it as the evening cooled and stared into the flames.

Coyotes yapped out on the desert flats. The night was clear and starry.

"Do you know where they are?" Andy casually asked.

"Not a clue, Dude."

"But they're alright?"

"I suspect they are."

"Do you think you'd know if they weren't?"

"Andy, I don't know anything. Shit just happens and I'm along for the ride." He selected a few sticks from a small heap behind him and tossed them on the flames.

"I don't know if I buy that, Arien. You tune in a lot more than you let on."

"Whatever, Dude."

The next day was born cloudy and threatened rain, but it never did. Arien awoke alone in Van Gogh with Tina. He wasted no time waking her up, kissing and climbing on top of her. Being so close to her like that put his amorous beast in gear. She was irresistible. In the course of their subsequent romp he snatched a view of Andy peering in through one of the side windows. He turned away, pretending not to notice. He wondered about it later; where this was going, among a few other things in the pack he carried.

Andy was moody for a while that afternoon, but he seemed to move past it when they sat around the fire that night. He pulled out his harp and wailed a few tunes. They smoked joints, swapped stories and sipped rum from a flask Andy picked up at a roadside market where they'd last bought gas. Andy asked Arien again if he thought Jeff and Otter were okay. "I think they are," Arien said. "They're probably waiting for parts."

His hunches were right. The guys returned the following day just after noon. Everyone was happy to be back together. The shade went up and Jeff picked up right where he'd left off.

"Another day and we would have had to go find water," Tina said to a pair of legs sticking out from under the little bus.

"Yeah, a swim would be great just now," Arien added.

"The Deschutes is just up the road," Otter said. "We could hit it."

"Good idea to me," Jeff agreed. "And I had a shower last night."

Arien was taken by the speed the clothes came off and they were all in the water. He'd never actually pondered modesty and this time was little different but for a sense of recent changes. He found himself resisting arousal and haste seemed essential toward that end. The energy had gone everywhere and lit him up, with no part of him immune. Everybody stole their glances and he read their hearts by the light of eyes; affection, pride-in-fellowship, surprise, even hunger. It was all very quick to occur and for Arien to process. He watched it flash across the screen of his mind as his body took to the snappy water and found its footing among loose pebbles and slippery stones. There was some horse-play; a need to make contact, though Andy held back. Arien was up to that. He was feeling very full there in the river.

Refreshed and back at Van Gogh, a pleasant surprise awaited. Jeff held the door open for him. It was the driver's door. "Want to give it a go?" He offered.

"Oh, rad!" Arien exclaimed. They finally asked! He hesitated by the opening. "I've never driven a stick."

"I'll show you." Jeff assured him. "It's not hard. It's like drivin' any other car but you're more involved with it."

Arien got in, pretty excited. He stared at everything, cataloguing the driver's space, reviewing its parts and their uses. He put both hands on the wheel, grasped it tightly and turned it this way and that, laughing like a little kid. "Vroooooooooommmmmmm," he said.

Jeff looked askance. "You have driven a car before, right?"

Arien flushed. He'd been busted. "Aw," he said in a sorry tone, "maybe we could do this some other time."

"This is that other time," Otter said, with a chuckle from the back.

"Go for it, Arien!" Tina cheered behind him.

"I can hear it now, at our funeral," Andy chided, "they died doing what they insisted!"

"Well, at least there ain't much traffic," Jeff reported in a soothing manner. "Arien, turn the key, step on the gas and punch the button, there."

"I know, I know. Okay." Arien had seen it done bzillions of times. He gathered his courage and soon Van Gogh was spitting awake.

"Lighten up on the gas, now, but press it a little bit, up and down at first, so it doesn't stall. The signal's right there. Push it forward. Look in your mirror."

Arien did all of that and then some. He wanted so badly for it to be perfect.

"Press the clutch, left peddle there and grab the stick…"

If anyone were watching they would have seen this thing lurch forward from the roadside, rock back, jump forward, stall out, restart, shoot onto the highway and proscribe a perfectly curvy hurdle ahead.

"Oh, this is so rad!" Arien exulted. "This is so rad!"

"Now fourth. Put it in fourth!" Jeff instructed, unconsciously wiping beads of sweat from his forehead with a sleeve of his T-shirt. "Watch the road, man. Keep it steady!"

Laughter came from the rear. "Ah, screeching tires, broken glass and twisted metal!" Andy melodramatically intoned.

19 – Gary, Harlan, Luke and Sally-Ann

Arien's driving through the small town of La Pine was sketchy. He coasted through the red light because he couldn't remember how to stop without stalling. Then, Jeff had to tell him to watch his speed. By then everyone was concerned they had too much to lose if they got stopped.

"Your ID won't fly," Jeff commented dryly.

"We're lucky the fuzz is at the doughnut shop," Andy said.

"We wouldn't make the concert," Otter pointed out, "or the next couple of decades in freedom, if he wasn't."

So, Jeff reclaimed the wheel and ferried them north, through Bend, Redmond, and then east to Prineville, where they stopped for gas and considered their options for the approaching night.

"Ochoco National Forest is just a bit further," Jeff noted. "We can get in there and camp for the night." He stood by the pumps, waving the state's map in his hand.

"Three sixty-five." The attendant was a curious teenager in stovepipe jeans and cowboy boots. He made a half-hearted effort not to stare at Van Gogh's passengers, and peeked through the windows as best he could. He pointed Tina to the bathroom, inside. Andy followed her.

Arien wondered at these '60s kids who tended to wear their baseball caps on straight.

Otter gave the fellow a five-dollar bill.

"Where you from?"

"San Francisco," Otter told him.

"Wow. Cool. Where you headed?"

"We're going to a concert in New York State."

"Wow! Man! That's a long way for a concert!"

Jeff set the map down on an old, red Coca-Cola cooler where the light from a window behind it made the map easier for him and Arien to read. "See," he pointed, "The Ochoco's right here."

"Hey, guys," the teenager asked, "do you need a place to spend the night?"

As a silent connection passed among the three outside, the young attendant counted change and added, he would be off in a half hour, he didn't live too far from the road, and the travelers were welcome to spend the night there.

Arien was fine with it though it appeared Otter was looking for a reason to decline. Jeff shrugged. "I don't see why not."

When Gary's shift was over, Van Gogh followed his rusty station wagon a few miles to a weather-beaten old farmhouse he shared with three other young folks from the area. One was a waitress at Brownfield's Café and two stacked lumber at Hudspeth Pine, though they were presently laid-off for a few days. There was not a hippie among them, but except for Sally-Ann, who was about to leave for work, they all took hits on an unlikely meerschaum pipe Gary immediately offered his guests while Harlan passed out cold cans of Coors to people.

Arien still looked for the tab on the top of the can that invariably wasn't there. Sodas, beer, there was no way to open them without a tool. He smiled to himself, waiting for the church key to get passed around.

Their hosts seemed somehow out of place if not out of sync. Arien soon learned Gary was the first among them to drop high school, then his friends, Harlan, Luke and Luke's girlfriend, Sally-Ann, followed soon after. Their original idea was save a few dollars to move to Portland, but Luke was recently drafted and with his Army induction coming in a matter of weeks, they decided to hang together here until the big day.

"Fuck that!" Andy said, toking on the moldy weed in the pipe. "You should just resist the draft, man. Don't go." They were all standing around in a kitchen with dishes stacked in the sink and Superman comic books on the floor among scattered socks and a cardboard box full of beer cans and soda bottles.

"Not an option," Luke grunted, chugging on his beer. "My Daddy's a good shot, and I'd rather take my chances with the Viet Cong."

"Bye," Sally-Ann said. The dark-haired girl came up to peck Luke on the cheek and went out the kitchen door. A rumble of car with bad muffler could be heard outside.

"Well, skip town. How can they have a war if nobody shows up? Your dad will get over it."

Luke's answer was a quiet grimace.

"Please forgive our friend, Andy, here." Otter said with a straight face. "He just wants to save your life."

Andy passed the pipe to Gary.

"I don't wanna be no draft dodger," Luke grumbled, looking at the floor.

"Just don't leave a kid behind," Arien sighed, ushering a change of energy with unanticipated intensity. "He won't thank you if you don't come back."

Tina stepped in the awkward moment to follow. "His father dies over there," she phrased it. "He knows something about this."

Otter started to speak but stopped himself, dipping into his jacket; instead, he took out some herb and yellow Zigzags to roll it in. He stood squarely on a worn-out edge of carpet where he put papers to tongue, shaking out his consistently clipped bud like a trapper with his powder horn, and with supple fingers, twirled-out three perfect doobies. The guys who lived here were visibly impressed.

"Oh, wow, Arien," Andy broke in, "I didn't know your Dad died in Viet Nam!"

Jeff laughed. "Hot damn! That's right, you didn't know that, Andy. But then, the first time we met was at Page Street."

Arien shuddered. He slurped his beer with an unnatural thirst. It tasted pretty watery. A sharp bite of bitterness began to vie with his interest in the conversation. Yet in the morning of this fantastic quest he smarted with a familiar pain that he hadn't felt for a while now. How could I forget? Maybe what happened to Blue Star brought it all out.

Tina was right on top of it. "Arien, Dude, you couldn't help it. It was too late,"

"No, I could have tried harder. I should have gone back one more time. I could have crashed through him with the magic! I might have laced his water with acid and blown his mind. Oh, fuck!" He stood on the verge of a swoon and pushed between them to the kitchen door. "He needs to beat himself up," he heard Otter say before the door slammed behind him.

Outside, Arien drained the can and pitched it in the darkness. He strode to a fence line where the barbed wire stopped him and a 4x4 post was the companion he would have. He hit it with a fist and when he felt the stab of a sharp point sink into the flesh at the edge of his palm, he held it there, twisting it, taking the explosive *OW, OW, FUCK* inside of him, bathing, as it were, in the white-hot torment careening up the length of his arm against the perverted force of his will. Oh, God, that hurts! Oh, God, that hurts so good!

"Stop it, Otter!" Arien heard Tina say, closing the kitchen door behind her. "Arien? Arien?" She called.

A twinge of shame came over him. That's even better, eat that too, ass hole!

"Arien, can you hear me?"

He could sense her connection to his energy, like knowing when somebody stares. She stepped closer. Maybe if I'm still, if I make myself real small, she won't find me.

But then Tina was there and she wrapped her arms around his tummy from behind. She squeezed him tightly to herself and rested a cheek on the back of his neck. Next, probing, her hands found his before he could hide the impaled one. She must have felt the slick, warm wetness. She gasped. "Shit, what happened? What did you do?"

"So, what's this concert you're headed to?" Gary asked, and Arien obliged with his standard advertisement, even slipping into the past tense. His friends listened with some amusement. Tina's knowing nod met with Otter's bemusement and Jeff allowed all to see a snarky grin. Andy was the only one who seemed to be out of the loop.

It passed over the heads of their hosts. Slim, lanky Harlan scooped eggs off the griddle into a dish that went around the little table and the other chairs they'd brought up close to seat everybody.

"You'll want to bring a tent or something dry to sleep in or, you can just go naked in the rain." Arien added with a sure smile. He unconsciously pressed the gauze wrapping his hand where a fresh, throbbing red spot seeped through to the surface.

"You might need a tetanus shot," Luke pointed out.

"You're not the first to suggest it," said Andy. "I thought it needed stitches, too."

Arien chose to ignore that. He had to suppress his wincing-flinching urge. He let it remind him not to think about Alex anymore. He wasn't buying Tina's view, for that matter. He had to have missed something. Only so recently he'd seen such cosmic things. A key had to exist somewhere and he'd missed it.

Harlan switched the light over the stove off just as sunshine broke through the kitchen window's dusty glass. It was like that switch turned the light on outside.

Luke was staring at him. Maybe everyone was, for different reasons. "Negative energy brought that about," Otter said with a detached tone last night while Andy had been full of sympathy. It was Tina who'd helped to wash out the wound and bind it up tight with some medical tape Jeff got out of the road kit. Gary offered to run Arien to Doctor Jones, who lived a few miles down. But, he'd declined while accepting with his friends the invitation to roll out their bedrolls in the house.

"Are you registered for the draft?" inquired Luke.

"Eggs?" Harlan asked Sally-Ann, who was barely out of bed. She still looked half-asleep. Arien watched her yank a can of Coors out of the refrigerator, but it wasn't for her. She passed it to Harlan, who smiled and cracked it with a little opener on his key chain. It must have been some joke between them.

Sally-Ann said, "Ugh! Not now."

"No," Arien replied to Luke. He slipped his throbbing hand onto his lap where no one could see it.

"He doesn't exist," Otter said.

"He's an alien," Jeff added with a wink.

"He's from the future," Tina said, giggling. Arien reached out to poke her in the ribs, but she evaded it.

"I'm not eighteen, yet." It struck Arien that he could lose touch with how old he was. He guessed he could probably figure it out by adding his days in 1969 to his time in 1990, which was around six months into seventeen plus a few more weeks – here.

"You're all up early," Sally-Ann said. She yawned and made her way to the coffee pot that was plugged into the wall and percolating with periodic, croaking eruptions of brown liquid, spitting and splashing under the glass bulb on top.

"Yeah," Gary agreed. "Arien and his friends are leaving this morning."

Arien reviewed that in his head. Why not Otter and his friends? …Tina and her friends? …Andy…? And, it was Jeff's van, after all.

Gary sopped up egg yolk with his white bread toast. "Well, maybe we should all go to Woodstock, too." he said.

"Damn it, Gary," Luke protested.

"Oops. Sorry, Luke. We talked about all of us signing up," Gary explained, "even Sally-Ann."

"Jesus!" Andy scoffed.

"Can you buy Coors in New York State?" Harlan asked.

"It's against the law in New York," Otter responded. He accepted a splash of coffee Sally Ann offered.

"It should be everywhere," Andy added. Some chuckles circulated. "Joe Coors is a Nazi bastard."

Harlan blinked at him.

Otter set his cup down and pulled a couple of pre-rolled joints from the recesses of his jacket. He snapped a match to life and soon they were making the rounds with coughing and sunlit, churning clouds of exhaled smoke.

"I'll be eighteen in about six weeks. I go right after that." Luke's eyes met with Arien's. They had a distant look.

"My Dad signed up and there wasn't a thing I could do about it." Arien said with a sulky tone.

"Maybe you weren't supposed to," Tina told him. She shook a few sugar cubes out of a small Mason jar on the table and dropped them into her cup. She looked at Arien with some exasperation.

"You're eliminating on us now, Man. Kick it free." Otter warned, in his most defining tone.

"Was your dad an officer?" Andy asked.

"They told me he made E-4 and served two or three tours over there."

Andy looked confused.

Otter assumed the trace of a smile.

"Here's where we enter the Twilight Zone," Jeff warned.

Tina said, "It's complicated, Andy."

Arien wondered when this situation would work itself out so he wouldn't have to bother with it anymore. The novelty was wearing. But the inestimable trade-off was feeling accepted. Weren't people reinventing themselves all the time? Then again, he could see an uncomfortable clash of common sense with the impossible become more acute with actually believing it.

"Well, I can understand if you don't want to talk about it," Andy retreated.

Arien was ready to be relieved, but Luke picked it up. "When did your father die, Man?"

"I wasn't born yet." Arien could only guess if his terse treatment would settle the issue or add to the confusion.

"Wow!" Harlan exclaimed, raising his eyebrows. "I didn't know we were there such a long time ago."

"Really. The French were still in Viet Nam, then," Andy noted. "Same war, different invader. "

"What happened?" Luke pressed.

"No, Luke" Sally Ann countered. "This may be personal."

Arien nodded. "It's okay," he answered. "I don't know, anyway." That did touch a sore spot deeper than his throbbing hand. It smarted to admit he didn't know how his father died, and he didn't appreciate how it so easily could. Arien was beginning to watch his own behavior and noted its changes from patterns with more limited choices. In his former life, he might have made something up, or clammed-up, or flashed a temper. Honesty felt better than any of these, for all sorts of reasons. Then, he knew Otter didn't suffer petulance, or any of her offspring. He'd called it 'elimination.' How do you argue with this?

"That sucks, man." Harlan said.

Arien was grateful when the conversation drifted elsewhere, and then breakfast was over and it was time to pull it together and go. What was apparent then to the travelers was the yearning now kindled in their hosts. They hung about Van Gogh as if to arrest it in a timeless farewell.

"Send us a postcard," Sally-Ann said. "I want to hear all about it."

"You'll have to turn on the radio," Arien advised. "It'll make the news, just like the walk on the moon. "That's one small step for man..." he said, mimicking the famous words as yet to be said. "And, years from now, when you're forty and old, you'll be able to watch the video cassette," he said that with a grin and sparkle that plainly impressed.

"You're amazing!" Andy exclaimed. "Where does he get this stuff?" Andy looked around to Otter, Jeff and Tina, who probably should have shrugged and left it there.

"There's something about Arien you don't know yet, Andy," Tina said, lending depth to the mystery. She stood alongside the van with a hand shielding bright, morning sun from her blue eyes.

It was Gary, Luke, Harlan and Sally Ann who shrugged.

Otter looked at them. His comment was, "This boy is special." Then he turned to the others. "Get in. Shoo! In the van!" He ordered with a grin. "We got-a split."

Jeff slid in behind the wheel. "Get in here, Arien. Watch me for a while and see how I keep it in a straight line."

"Dude, you're on!"

The motor spit and rumbled. The departure committee outside waved. Sally-Ann threw a kiss.

"Maybe we'll see you at Woodstock!" Gary called after the little bus as it jerked forward. Arien couldn't resist turning to check Luke out. He waved, too, but with a troubled face.

Arien really did watch Jeff drive it. So intently did he focus on the timing and coordination that kept their motion steady, he almost missed Andy's "No fucking way!" shouted from behind. Andy's laugh was sharp. "What are you guys –? Jesus! What a load of crock!"

"Ask him, yourself. Go ahead!" Otter pressed. Arien now focused on that.

"Arien, you know what we're talking about?" Andy's breath fell against the back of Arien's neck. Sometimes, he is close enough to bite me.

"I wasn't listening, but let me guess."

When he didn't, Andy explained what Tina told him. "…And, she said it with a straight face, and Otter not only didn't laugh but said it might be true!"

"It might." Jeff said, hanging over the steering wheel with a grinning glance at Arien.

"So, when's your birthday? And, please tell me the truth!"

"March 22nd." Arien turned to look him in the eye.

"March 22nd, what, Arien? I want to hear *you* say it!" Andy brushed a dense forelock of brown, wavy hair from his face. It had the effect of driving the point forward. He was animated, intense, and sincere.

"1973," Arien said, flatly.

"You little shit!" Andy turned away and sat back down.

Oh well. Arien couldn't do anything about this one. It would just have to work itself out. He returned his attention to Jeff, who was shaking his head with a trace of smile.

"Cigarette, Jeff?" Arien reached into the shelf under the dashboard for the pack and the Zippo that was always there.

"No." Jeff focused on the road again and the scenery.

The country was pretty cool. It invited the eye with colorful open spaces of desert maroon set in volcanic rock and pumice. It was scattered with tough-scrabble grasses and junipers in clumps or standing out alone, and there were dry stream gullies and cow trails left and right. Here and there was the rusty old husk of a vehicle wearing decades of abandonment with a dignity that blended perfectly among the surroundings and only the occasional, destitute farmhouse was more evocative.

Arien pulled the vent window back to blow out his smoke. The subtle rush of tobacco satisfied. The sweet outside air mix enriched its honey-sour taste. These moments with the habit were not common but seemed to underwrite his pleasure in it. Cigarettes were neat to hold and fondle between the fingers, too. But his chest felt dirty of late. There was an incidental irritation as well, with a cough. For now he would put off the tug-of-war invited by thinking about it and enjoy the smoke.

Something else had to be put off. The perfection of the moment, the motion, the sunshine, his friends, was otherwise imposed upon by the tenderness in his palm, which was warm to the touch today. It tied him to a memory and a side of himself he'd just as soon ignore. That a rash, impulsive temper could tether him so! He'd thought maybe, just maybe he was past it now; the acid these last weeks, with its fantastic revelations, had blown it out of his brain but was finding the wiring was still there in its iron conduit, buried deeper than he knew, and a little shock and grief and fright was what it took to find it again. Some ash dropped into his lap, and he absently rubbed it into his jeans.

Jeff yawned. "I don't know why but I feel like crap today," he said.

"Getting sick?"

"I'm just tired, like I didn't get any sleep. Maybe I drank too many beers last night."

"Are you drinking water, Jeff?" Otter called from behind.

"No, Otter. Maybe that's it. Say, Arien, my man, ready to give it another go?"

"Twist my arm, Dude."

Before starting again, Arien shut off the motor and went through the motions of shifting gears, pressing pedals and making sure he had it right. He was discovering that to watch somebody drive was not the same as doing it yourself. Timing was very important. It had to be second nature, like walking and chewing gum without biting your tongue. After getting back on the road, he slowed and stopped, then picked it up until he was sure he could master it. His passengers were patient and evidently relieved to see he was at least being a serious student.

I must be doing okay, Arien thought sometime later, considering the lack of wisecracks and the fact some of the riders actually dozed off. This was so cool! He loved the kick of the motor, underpowered as it may have been, when he pressed the gas pedal, and the beauty of the rural landscape they passed. Their route ran through and skirted north of the broad swath of Ochoco National Forest that lies like a lid on mid-central Oregon, a land of ponderosa, mostly proud and tall, and the lonely open country of before. The day was beautiful. There wasn't much traffic.

Arien noted the license plates of passing cars. "You'd think we were in Idaho," he observed.

Jeff had a jacket between his bouncing head and the door frame he'd tried to rest it against. His eyes were sleepy slits. "Not yet," he corrected.

A refrain from the U2 song, "*I still haven't found what I'm looking for*" came into his head and Arien began to tap it out on the steering wheel. He barely sang it, thinking along with the words, and that caused him to back up. "Let's see," he said, talking to himself. "It goes like…" and the words began to take their melodious form over the engine's cadence.

He was pleased with his rendition. Singing out loud wasn't something Arien was accustomed to doing, but the miles passing under Van Gogh lulled his awareness to a dreamlike place, held between the tension of the road and an ongoing, solitary sense of confidence and gratification. Driving a car was a new and wonderful thing to do.

"Cool, Arien!" Andy praised. "You have a sweet voice. It's a neat song, too."

"Hey!" Tina leaned over the seat and silkily slid her arms over Arien's shoulders to knead her fingers into his breast. It tickled some, but it felt good all over. He pursed his lips in a little kiss up at her, but he didn't remove his eyes from the road. "How's the owie?"

"Rad."

"Are you having fun?"

"Oh yeah."

"I'm sorry we spaced getting you a license to go with your Angels' ID, Arien," Otter told him. "We need to get you one if you're going to drive much."

Scary thought. It was limiting and seemed so unfair. "I'm doing pretty good though, ain't I?"

"Oh yeah. You haven't rolled us yet."

Arien placed a hand over Tina's. She kissed him on the ear.

"Jesus, Babe," he blurted. "I'm poppin' one."

"How many is that for today, hot dog?" she whispered.

"Lost count back in Prineville." He grinned, combing hair out of his eyes with his fingers.

"Oh God!" Andy said. It probably wasn't meant for Arien to overhear but he did.

"What?" Otter asked him.

"I think I'm in Hell."

Signs for both Umatilla and Malheur National Forests began to show up about the time they topped off the tank in John Day. The little bus seemed to attract more attention here for some reason. There were lots of stares that made the travelers nervous, Otter in particular. Andy said he knew a spell to deflect attention from an object. "Well, let's give it a try," Otter suggested, "or we're going to get this puppy repainted like a business coup. We've got a lot of country to cross and we don't need any hassles."

It was evident Jeff didn't approve of that idea, but he held his tongue.

A short conference had them opt for Route 7, to Baker. Shortly after the turn-off they stopped at a picnic area in the forest for a stretch and some lunch. Jeff pulled a 16-inch 1 x 8 pine board out of the kit to lay-out saltines while Tina peeled a bit of mold off a block of yellow cheese before slicing it. Arien rummaged through the dwindling items in the box and was happy to find a couple of tins of sardines. He cranked them both open with the little keys stuck to the top of each tin. Otter tossed several pairs of chop sticks on the board, too.

Andy stepped out of the bus with a smoking twist of rope incense and while folks busied with setting out lunch he walked counter-clockwise around Van Gogh with it, while muttering an unintelligible Sanskrit incantation. The light, musky odor hung about the area for want of any breeze.

"I can still see Van Gogh," Arien told him when he sat down at the picnic table.

"Of course you can see it, Pin Head. It's not a spell of invisibility."

Arien chuckled to himself. This was easy.

"You're quite the skeptic for a guy with powers, not-to-mention a wild story," Otter said.

"Spells can work, Arien," Andy informed him between crackers. "I was with a friend once at my dorm and didn't want to be bothered, so I invoked the flaming pentacle to keep people away, and then I forgot all about it. It made me wonder a couple of weeks later why nobody stopped by! There were always people coming by. I couldn't figure it out.

Arien took a sip of water from the tin cup he shared with Tina. "So what did you do?" A ground squirrel had been making preliminary advances from his fallen-log redoubt and it finally made a dash for a bit of cracker Arien tossed in its direction.

"Well, I cancelled the spell, I banished it, and that very day I had visitors!"

After a chuckle, Tina asked, checking out the little critter, "So, where do we go from here?"

"I'm thinking we could pick up 30 in Baker City," Otter said. "It runs down to Huntington, and from there it's pretty much a straight shot east."

"We still have the rest of June and all of July," Arien pointed out. "Woodstock's in the middle of August. I want to be there early, but–"

"Yes," Otter noted, "We all expected to spend some time in Portland." A painful silence followed.

Ever so briefly, Arien allowed himself a peripheral consideration of his terrible vision. It was still way too fresh to take head-on. "Helter-skelter," he said under his breath.

"Oh my God, Arien!" Otter blurted, making eye contact with Andy.

"What's that? I missed that." Jeff was carefully lifting a sardine out of the tin with his chopsticks.

"I can't explain it, but there's some kind of connection."

"With what Arien?" Otter's expression was strained. "A song in the White Album?"

Arien pondered the question. "It's not so direct," he said carefully. "You can't put a name on it. You can't nail it to anyone, but some people let it happen. It's the energy. I could feel the energy." He shuddered.

"Everything has an evil side. It was bound to come up sometime," Andy observed. "We live in a world of polarities."

Tina tossed the squirrel another bit of cracker. It was promptly stuffed into widening cheeks and then it sat up, sniffing the air and looking cute, certainly asking for more.

Otter sighed. "I don't get it. LSD is too beautiful."

Jeff sang a line from *"Itchycoo Park."*

"The Small Faces," Tina noted for Arien.

"It isn't supposed to go that way," Otter said.

"It's too beautiful," Jeff said.

Arien got an uneasy feeling in the pit of his stomach. Polarities. He hadn't been familiar with that word before, but he knew instantly what it meant and it opened a memory. "First there was Woodstock," he said. "It was *so* beautiful. It was like a promise. And then, the promise was broken. I almost forgot that."

Andy leaned toward him. "What promise was broken? How?"

"With another concert. I can't remember what they called it, but I can say this, don't mix the Stones with Hell's Angels."

The silence was deafening. Everyone just looked at him. Then Andy broke in. "But that's ridiculous. That's a very unlikely mix."

"He's a boy seer, Andy. We should know that by now." Otter warned.

Arien chose his words carefully: "I could say I'd lived it, if it didn't happen before I was born." Then, after a moment, he shook his head and said, "Damn it."

"What, Arien?" Tina asked.

Arien's frustration was evident. Here we go again! "Why don't people just let me be?" He pleaded, staring down at the table.

"Dude," Andy said with a slight taunt to his voice, "You're the one with the sage pronouncements. Don't you see? You do it or you don't."

"I think he *is* doing it," Otter countered. "We just have to be patient. I can only imagine what he must be dealing with."

"Excuse me," Arien said, rubbing his sore hand and promising himself he would keep the lid on this time. He shot a grateful glance at Otter before getting up and spooking the ground squirrel. He placed a hand on Tina's shoulder, with a gentle squeeze, to tell her he was alright. The folks at the picnic table quietly watched him stroll off.

He came on a walking trail and took it down a-ways to a draw where the vegetation grew dense and greener. Arien could smell the water before he saw it. It was a lovely spot where a spring fed into a broad beaver pond. He sat on a bench there that had somebody's name carved into the back, "In Memory of my friend, John McArthur" he read. As he gazed over the scene, a good-sized trout jumped out of the water and fell back with a splash. Sunlight topped the ripples, expanding with them over the surface in delicate, golden rings. Birds twittered. Insects buzzed. Then he saw the osprey lying unnaturally on its side by the edge of the water. Arien had to check it out.

The body looked so fresh the inquisitive lad actually felt it to find if it was still warm. It wasn't, but it couldn't have been dead for very long. Its head flopped aside when Arien poked it. It was a very large bird with gorgeous feathers.

The long night wore heavily on Arien through the dim lights of the van and the painfully hesitant slap of its single windshield wiper. It barely revealed a hollow road through glistening fragments of broken light smattering both halves of a windshield. A dull, luminescent reflection from the speed gauge remained. It was a ghostly companion in some parallel world hologram that hung suspended outside in the darkness. "Vdo," he read. "Vdo. Kaplunkit. Vdo." Jeff once said the radio had been 'kaput' since he owned this magic bus. Man. Some tunes would be 'gear'. What a quaint word.

Again, he sang phrases of that song by U2 under his breath.

The rain drove in waves that lessened to a bare sprinkle and charged once more in ferocious drumming drops, forcing him to slow down, as if that were possible without entirely stopping, so he could see. And then a moment's stark flashing revealed a world in its great halftone panorama; the shimmering, snaking road clinging to forested slopes in sheets of rain, the gray metal dash, the white of his knuckles on the broad wheel, dangling osprey feathers hanging from the rear view mirror, a glimmer of golden hair in the corner of his eye.

Incredible. You'd think the boom blasting through the air would wake everyone - but it didn't. They slept like sacks of damp grain. Andy snored a little. Otter wheezed. Jeff was invisible in his silence.

Arien yawned. The air was thick and humid. He could smell their bodies, especially the sweet one pressed against him.

"Being with you," he whispered, in contemplation.

Oh, Tina. His heart felt too full, like it would crowd his lungs and restrict his breathing. He tried to think back to how it happened; of when he knew. It was something he hadn't felt before, and it snuck up on him, a Robin Hood that brought so much floating good feeling to his poor soul he pitied the rich man it had to come from. He could not bear thinking what it would be like to lose that once it was tasted. His deepest dread approached when her Mom stole her away. It had to be the worst thing that could possibly happen. If it were not for Jamie Sun! Oh, in spite of everything, he acknowledged such incredible luck! God! So this was love! Am I really ready for this?

His shoulders ached. He tried to stretch and flex the muscles in his arms and back without disturbing her. He shifted his feet one more time. The beating drone of the engine wavered then restored its rhythm. Another flash. Another crack and boom. That one was really close! Rad. He could still see the country in his head after the brilliant light faded. And he hadn't even closed his eyes! Candles would be brighter than those stupid headlights, he mused. They just pointed to where his eyes had to adjust to the darkness.

"Wow!" It was a low exclamation from behind him. He could feel a hand on the back of the seat and breathing push the sluggish air against his ear. "Are you okay?"

"Yeah, Andy. Thanks."

"If you see a place to pull over just do it."

Just do it. Arien smiled to himself. "Who was Nike?" He knew Andy would likely know the answer. Andy was into that stuff.

"Oh, ah, a Goddess, bro. Goddess of Victory. Greek. She had wings. Why?"

Tina stirred and snuggled. She hadn't awakened. Arien stretched and flexed again, this time more smoothly. The beating engine hardly wavered. God it was fun to drive! Even this torture was fun. It was so new a thing. He rubbed his eyes. "I'm good," he said. "I'll drive a little longer."

His feet felt clammy in Keds. He hadn't worn his High Tops since leaving the city by the bay. They were stashed away in the pack. He'd cleaned them up and bought new laces. They were being saved now for special occasions. Arien didn't want to wear them out. They were the only pair of High Tops in the world.

He decided he could use a cup of coffee.

"Where are we?" Tina yawned. The light from the sign, "Family Restaurant - Fine Food", was in her eyes. It glowed blue neon against the log wall in a halo of moist air.

Arien hadn't shut off the engine yet. He put the van into reverse and rolled it back a few inches. He felt so proud of himself. "Coffee," he said. "Anybody want anything?"

"Ohhhhh.." Jeff groaned from the rear. "I gotta' go bad."

"No thanks," Otter said.

"I'll go with you." It was Andy. The double doors on the side of the van swung open. He stepped outside, brushing his hair with the fingers of his free hand.

The two of them walked in the double doors at about the same time. For some reason Andy hesitated when they were inside, but Arien, not connecting, began to walk toward the bar. There were people there, all ages, a lot with cowboy hats, sitting on stools or standing by them, and some folks were scattered at tables in the broad room and in booths around the perimeter. Arien thought the red and white speckled tiles looked odd. The song *"What We're Fighting For"* was on the jukebox. The singer sounded Country. Arien reached the bar where a man, about sixty, in a cowboy shirt and string tie, looked at him with a stony face.

"I'll have a coffee with cream and lots of sugar, to go, please." There was a long moment when nothing seemed to happen, but the song was very clear, filling up the large room with a taut, thin veneer over deepening silence.

The singer was asking his momma what we were fighting for.

"Tell me something, boy. Do you have anything against our men in the service?"

Arien was puzzled by this man's question. "My dad died in the Marines and left me in Hell," he said, putting a dollar down.

The man didn't speak, but the answer got him moving. He poured coffee in a paper cup and set it in front of Arien with a glass jar full of sugar and a small bottle of cream along with 75 cents change. As Arien stirred ingredients he felt the tension finally come over him like a cold draft. He turned to see Andy, his slinged arm thrust out like a tie-dyed triangular shield, blocking Jeff who was just now coming through the entrance. The neon light overhead glowed pale blue on Jeff's matted, sleepy face. The door closed, shutting him out.

Some guffaws could be heard from the other side of the room. Andy glared at Arien. His message was unmistakable. Arien left the change on the counter. His reluctance was turning to measured alarm. He thought he heard somebody say, "Queer." He stopped at this and looked among the people in the room seeking the source. So intent he was he didn't notice Andy cross over to him. "C'mon, Arien," Andy coaxed, lips barely moving. His voice was so low it could not have been heard by anyone else.

Arien measured his words, "I'll rip his fuckin' face off." His rage he allowed so quickly; so easily. It settled uncomfortably like a dissonant relative one is loath to see, who never comes to enjoy anything, who it would be hoping too much for him never to return whenever he says goodbye.

Arien stood solid as two young men from the nearest table pushed their chairs back. The one with a baseball cap said it again: "Queer."

Andy was smooth, intense. It was not the toughs slowly closing the distance but apparently his friend's intransigence. Arien's free hand was already balled into a fist. He would have thrown the coffee, but Andy was pushing him out of the room as he stepped into the no man's land between them.

A moment's desperation gripped Arien. His friend will take the fall! Andy was recovering well from his wound, but he was in no shape for a brawl!

"Mahh - ha!" Andy loudly shouted, his free arm flailed out, palm open with outstretched fingers. "Ohhhhhhhmmmmmmmm. Ohhhmm, Shri Ram, jai Ram! Jai, jai Ram!" There was such resonance in his voice! The cowboys actually looked confused.

Arien felt like he had just been blown into space. Was it his own doing? It had to be! It had to be his astonishment. Andy's iron stare would have stopped a mad bear, he thought, forcing back the spontaneous grin. He felt like he was in a dream as he and Andy walked out of that place.

He stood under the neon outside, as if to catch his breath. Locking eyes with Andy he felt a shudder creep over his elated senses. "Ooohhhmmm Sri Ram, jai Ram jai, jai Ram," Andy said. Arien couldn't take his eyes away from his friend. And yet, out of a far corner, did he see the door move outward, and then close again?

"Arien. Let's go now. Man. Let's go." He motioned for Otter to get back in the waiting vehicle.

The doors in the side of the bus swung open. Andy gently pushed Arien from behind.

"SO awesome!" Arien rhapsodized into the tightly packed vehicle.

"Let's kick some bootie, Jeff," Andy said with conviction. Jeff was already in the driver's seat. "I've gotta piss, man. My teeth are floatin', he protested, but the little motor obediently putted to a start and Van Gogh rolled away.

If Arien could have found the word it would have been "choreography". It was like that. Smooth. Rehearsed. Professional. That was it. Professional. He brimmed with pride and newfound admiration for his friend, his brother, Andy.

They went another ten miles before stopping again. Jeff just pulled over and busted out to pee alongside Van Gogh. He'd even neglected to set the brake and there was a frantic moment with people banging into each other as they scrambled for the lever. Everybody got out to stretch this time. Arien and Tina stepped away into the darkness. Muffled voices could be heard behind them. There was no traffic on the highway. The rain was over but heavy drops still fell in the damp dark woods all around. The thick air was full with the scent of soggy earth and green things.

The silence between them was long; two silhouettes in drippy space, holding hands.

Tina spoke at last: "Penny for your thoughts."

"Penny ain't worth much." He kissed her cheek. The world seemed to spin.

"You said it's worth more in '69." He couldn't see her sly smile, but he could hear it in her voice.

"Right on." Arien's version was from the future, where "on" had nearly the sound of two syllables. "I was wondering what will happen to me, I guess."

"Why, Arien?"

"Well, Babe, you know how I tried to change the future; how I was too late. I know my old man's gonna die over there in Viet Nam. He'll be a young dude, still, with a cool old lady, and a little boy he'll never see. Well, back there on the road, I was thinking. I was thinking about some of the rotten breaks I've had in my life; of some other things that I would change if I could. Well if I could, I would have already. You know what I mean? My life would have been different."

"And you wouldn't be talking to me now, Arien."

"That's right, I guess."

"So maybe you did change things. Think about it. Would Andy be here without you? Whatever will come of us has yet to happen, and your dad did see his little boy, though he wasn't so little, he still got to see something pretty special, you have to admit. Maybe he'll know before... Maybe he'll figure it out."

"Yeah, but, how come I never tried to help *me* any? How could I let some of the things happen to me that shouldn't have to happen to anybody? How come I never rescued myself?"

"Is that what you want to do?"

"I think it is. You know, Tina, since I've been here - it's like I've been given another chance. I don't know what might have happened if things just kept going the way they were. I was so pissed all the time. I didn't think I was worth a big heap of shit, you know?"

Tina rested her cheek on his shoulder and put her arms around him.

"And now I think about all that time that was wasted. Those times I cried inside when I should have been a happy kid."

"We stoppin' here for the night?" Jeff called from the road.

"I don't care. What's everybody else want to do?"

"Let's move on," came faintly through the humid air.

Jeff hollered back, "Andy wants to move along further. I guess he's drivin'."

Andy slipped carefully behind the wheel, resting the tethered hand on its edge and feeling for the gearshift next, in two distinct steps.

Arien watched from his shotgun seat and wondered if Andy would be able to do that for very long. Tina got in back. She said she was tired and needed some room to stretch out. The motor clattered to a start, and the little bus lurched back onto the highway. Arien stared into the dim light ahead. The darkness was comfortable. He slid the window back and stuck his arm out in the air and caught the damp wind in the palm of his hand as they came over a grade, and went faster and faster down the other side. Van Gogh whistled.

"You're cool, Andy."

"Thanky, Spanky."

"Tell, me, will ya, what the heck you did back there?"

"Damn, I don't know. Ram came through, I guess. Ram was an incarnation of Vishnu. He was a warrior, full of courage and power. I was thinking about that. That's all. I didn't know what else to do, Arien."

Arien contemplated it. He chuckled to himself. *"I didn't know what else to do."* It was wonderfully absurd. "Well, what about Jesus?"

"Say, what, Brother?"

"Where does he fit into all this?" A big bug thwacked the windshield and splayed out in liquid directions. Van Gogh was flying!

"It seems like it's all different forms of the same energy. You have different forms of God that speak to us like idioms in language. That's what I've been thinking. And they really don't translate very well. A whole cultural context goes with it. You know what I mean?"

"No," he said, really trying to understand.

"Well, Jesus is great for love; he's a healer and let's not forget sacrifice. And, there's a lot of other sides to him, too, which helps to explain his appeal. There's all the mythic stuff from the old days and all the expectations that come rolled up with that. It also explains how so many people into Jesus have so much to disagree about. Everybody gives him this awful burden, though, don't you think so? How often do you hear people say they want to help him out a little? They just tug on his sleeve about every little thing. People won't take responsibility. So, he just hangs there, like raw meat all of these years, since he was alive."

"Wow. I've never heard it explained like that. Like, everybody dumps on him."

"Exactly. For pure compassion, though, Buddha's hard to beat. He includes all living creatures. Do you have such compassion for living things anywhere else? Oh, Mohammed scolded people for mistreating their beasts of burden. That was a real breakthrough, too. And, the brotherhood of Muslims is a very powerful thing. The Koran says that basically, everyone is equal. There is no justification for racial bias. That's a really special thing!

"And for the pure perfection of divinity that inspires a sweet-as-nectar devotion to the energy of God, I think of Krishna." Does that help you any?

"Andy, where did you learn all this? For a while there, I thought you were just a Commie." Arien laughed. "Maybe we should have stayed there a little longer. You might have healed them! They would now be full of peace and love!"

"And they would have had to come with us to Woodstock," Andy said. "And this van is packed out, already. "Whoa – what's that?"

Arien strained to see what Andy was looking at. He was hitting the brakes. The eggbeater in back was winding down to a lower rpm. It took awhile to come to a complete stop.

"What's up, Andy?" Jeff drawled.

"Open the door. Somebody's getting in."

"Huh?"

Arien stuck his head out the window. He saw a formless mass scramble up from the darkness towards their van. He marveled how Andy could have seen this guy. He was wearing an army rain poncho and had a dark wool cap on his head. Jeff turned a flashlight on and opened one of the doors in the side. A very young face peeked in, breathing heavily. Long, wavy light-brown hair, matted and damp, cascaded out from his head onto his shoulders as he peeled off the sopping poncho. "Out-a sight!" he cried joyfully, seeing Jeff first, and then Arien and Andy up front. He clambered in through the narrow opening, pulling a duffel bag in after him.

Arien thought he could hear Otter say something as the light went out back there. Then a hand was on his shoulder and there was breathing near his ear. "Man! It's been too long since I had a ride. Nobody would stop." It was a boy's voice, still more in his nasals than his breast. Arien guessed he was about thirteen or fourteen.

"Nobody stops for you when it's raining, and you can forget it after dark," Andy agreed. "Where you headed?"

"A place just north of Buford, in the Medicine Bow. I'm camped with some family there, the Tree Family. They took me out 'cause I got sick. Appendix. Anyway, I'm fixed now, and I'm goin' back. How 'bout you?"

"We're going to Woodstock, Dude."

"Oh. Where's that?"

"New York State," Andy said.

"You like hitchin'?" Arien asked.

"Oh yeah. Nothin' to it." The boy yawned.

"My name's Arien. This is Andy, drivin', and that was Jeff who let you in, and Tina and Otter's back there, too."

"Out-a sight. I'm Clayboy."

"Clayboy? Where'd you get a name like that?" It was Otter from the darkness in the rear.

"We hung out at Geyserville a lot last year, before we headed out this way, and –

"Oh, hell, let me guess," Otter interjected. "You got into the mud."

"Yeah! You been there?"

"Yeah, Man. It's a groovy place, huh?"

"It's out-a sight!" His hand dropped from the back of the seat and he projected his voice to Otter, in back.

Otter seemed to have been everywhere, Arien thought. Then it grew suddenly quiet. "How far is Buford, Andy?" The engine was beating up another hill, straining noticeably with the added body, and Van Gogh was slowing to another crawl. In the dimming headlamps the night sky seemed to brighten just a little, and Arien could make out dark silhouettes of mountain peaks on the near horizon.

"Hey, I don't know. We're a little ways past Rawlins, I think. You'll have to check the map."

"Andy?"

"Yeah?"

"Do you believe in Jesus?"

"I guess, when it comes down to it, I do, though I believe we're all children of God, not just him. Why?"

"Well, I'm not so sure. I got to do something he didn't do. If he was who he was supposed to be he could have solved a lot of problems by being able to move around like I did."

Andy was silent for a while. There was only the hacking engine and a faint rattle of gear in the back. The color of the sky broadened to purple in the east and the outline of mountains became more defined. Arien twisted in his seat to see the kid they had picked up. Clayboy was curled up against the doors, dead to the world. That was fast.

"Some of it defies understanding, Arien. Once, I thought I had it figured out, but the mystery is too deep. Every master has his own power, his own approach to the problem. Maybe you want to reveal another one – or two, for all that. You know, there are yogis who have been seen by people in more than one place at one time, who could materialize wherever, and medicine men that could see what happened miles away."

"Do you believe all that?"

"Oh, yeah, certainly. And your vision of Blue–"

"So, Andy, do you believe me?"

"Rationally, no way, man. It defies reality. If yogis could do the things they do, I suppose anything's possible. But, I can't think of a single example of something like this ever happening before unless, of course, it was reported to be something else. Can you? You're - you're just such a normal kid, I guess, except for your story, that is. But the evidence is flimsy. The fact that you got them believing it, unless they're just humoring you, is like some kind of weird church thing. And, some of the things I've heard you say will take a long time to pan out. You could be like Nostradamus, or something. Tina's convinced. She said if anybody were to see your old man they would be, too. I believe her, I guess. What she had to say about your trip to see him was pretty far out. But, Christ, that guy could still be your brother, or there's some other explanation.

"Then, Otter told me that Jamie Sun says you're the genuine article. Otter puts a lot of stock in whatever Jamie Sun says. He says he's seen that guy do things that defies most people's definition of reality."

"I'll second that with a true experience, and Otter's got talent, too. You weren't that bad, either, back there." Arien shook his head with the recent memory. Some of his lengthening hair got into his eyes, and he pushed it back. He could see Andy was looking at him. The day was wakening. Facial features could be seen now and the world around them was taking on a twilight, gray-scale definition of long-needle and lodge-pole pines, juniper and tumbled bluffs and boulders among broadening rocky meadows. The roadside flowers still lacked any visible color but luxuriant tall young grasses hinted at their early summer green by the way they caught the light in a trillion shimmering diadems of dew.

Andy reached over, barely touching Arien's face with the tips of his fingers. "You're really beautiful, Brother," he said. His eyes seemed to glaze over.

"Thanks." Arien thought he'd heard something like this said before. Could it have been in his other life?

"No. I mean it. You look a little like God when He was young." His fingers were lodged now under the cut of Arien's jaw, tracing down along the side of his neck. "Like an angel; not man or girl or boy, the Eternal youth, maybe. I suppose I've thought so since we met at Page Street, but I needed to tell you now."

"Yeah." Arien gazed back at him. Andy was pleasant, spontaneous, loving. And when he turned to look back at the road he thought he saw a tear in Andy's eye. For a moment he was baffled and then withdrew deep into his own thoughts.

"The turnout's up there, just past the construction," the boy said. He awakened only moments before. Arien, dozing, became aware the sun had cleared the crest of the mountains and wide-open country.

"I'll take you off the highway," Andy offered.

"Take me in, man, and the family will be grateful. If you're not in a hurry, you can hang out with us." He seemed to talk into his nose like he had a little snuffle and it made him sound even younger than he looked.

Arien sat up stiffly. He wondered about this boy's story, seeing he was so independent for his age. He was probably a runaway, and fourteen years old might be pushing it in the clarity of morning.

Andy looked ready for a break. His eyes were dreary. He leaned into the wheel and yawned, "Either way, we need a change of drivers. My whole right side is like one big throb for doing all the work." He looked at Arien who shook his head. He always wanted to drive but was ready to stretch now, too. "Did you hear that back there?" Andy asked. "I need a break."

"I'll drive," Tina said. "I don't mind if we stop first. We have the time, don't we?"

"Yeah, we're doin' good," Arien said.

"Sure." Otter and Jeff spoke almost at once.

"Say, uh, Clayboy, how much further is your camp from here?"

"About a half hour."

"Good," Andy said. "I'll just take us out where we can pull over for awhile first."

It was more forested here again, especially as they wound their way past road repairs and out into ranchland where long-needle pines ringed the nearby meadows and climbed the hills. They continued as directed, now up a long, well-maintained dirt and gravel road steadily increasing in elevation. The sun was out in force today, too, raising moisture from the previous evenings' weather system into waving tongues of wispy golden-white evaporation. Its phantom tendrils clung along the edge of the road and over the meadows and bare crowns of still-sleeping trees. Obstinate patchy fingers and spots of snow hugged the landscape's shadows and folds and sugar-dusted ridges. The sky was clear and blue. Everything was washed and fresh and full of sparkle.

Andy pulled the van to the side of the road and finally stopped. Both he and Arien vacated the front seat for a stretch outside in the sunshine. Otter poured water from the jerry can into the enamel basin that he set up in the doorway to wash his face. Jeff took a walk out to a cluster of trees with a roll of TP. The boy gravitated to Tina, who took some blankets outside to shake and fold. He helped her out. Arien, watching, admired the way things got done and needs were met. Nobody barked orders or put anyone down. It amazed him. He thought about what could have caused it. It wasn't human nature as he had known it in his "other life". He visualized a period of darkness before waking to some entry level of Heaven.

A powerful urge suddenly erupted into Arien's awareness. He went over and reached in Van Gogh's back door for his small duffel on the edge of the stove platform. It was where the water buffalo horn was stashed with some of his stuff. Tina saw him walk by with it. She sent Arien a knowing glance as Clayboy stacked blankets in her arms. Arien nodded back to her as he passed. He walked up an embankment and struck off towards an inviting meadow beyond the cluster of trees where Jeff went.

It was a lot further than it looked. When he reached the center he gazed back to see the van and the people he left around it appearing rather small. It was quiet. He could hear a bee hovering nearly twenty feet away, and the tweets of birds in the aspens growing here, and a scattering of spruce around him. Arien untied the cotton chord closing that cobalt-blue velvet bag and removed the horn. He took a deep breath of fresh, clean air, pursed his lips, started forcing breath between them, and then brought the horn up with both of his hands. It sounded a crisp, tenor note Arien held long as he could. The note did seem impossibly long, and only slowly faded in echoes from all directions. There were other notes, too, catching Arien's attention before all the echoes faded. Rasping, yet familiar sounds, came up swiftly from behind him, speeding over his head, fanning up and out like jets at an air show: Three very large, glossy-black crows, flapped and cawed furiously, rushing further and further away, their raucous voices blending with the last feeble reverberations of sound. Their synchronistic presence grabbed hold of Arien's attention with a clarity that spoke as surely as any words. He understood it perfectly. It was like the time at Jamie Sun's, when he knew Jamie appreciated who he was, and with such matter-of-fact certainty; and there was only acceptance to do about it.

He stood there awhile, savoring the moment until he guessed his friends were probably waiting. It was time to go down. Time. He wondered about that. Everything seemed so tied up with time. If those crows said anything it was that. It was time. Time for something. Arien sighed.

"Why me?"

When Arien got to the van Jeff was behind the wheel with Tina sitting shotgun and Clayboy squeezed in between them. Tina wore a perturbed expression that barely softened when Arien poked his nose in the open window.

"What's the matter, Babe?"

"It's nothing."

"No, it looks like something."

"It's nothing," she said again. Arien shrugged and got in through the middle doors that had been left open.

Van Gogh putted to a start and rolled back onto the rutted track of a road.

"Just keep on going up this a way," Clayboy snuffled.

Arien nestled down into a pile of bedding that was against the front seat back. Andy and Otter both faced him. Andy opened the fat little coarsely-printed holy book he'd read from in the hospital. The "Gita" he called it, whatever that was. Otter lit a doobie and exhaled a vast cloud of smoke. He got red faced and coughed with all of his might.

Andy smirked. "It's just another kind of Bogart," he noted.

Arien nodded, accepting the doobie from a hacking Otter.

Andy pointed at the cobalt blue bag Arien set beside him. He said, "Something happened up there, huh?"

"Something. And it was perfect." He drew carefully on the doobie. The smoke seemed to fill him. He let his head fall back with a rush of the stuff. It was very strong. It tasted like something he'd had before. He tried to remember where.

"Y - yes," Otter agreed, getting hold of himself. "I saw the crows, Man. That was cool. Good timing, Man."

"Timing's the essence," Andy added.

Van Gogh lurched and jostled as the road became suddenly rough. Small rocks kicked up by the wheels tapped the underside with a series of little pops. Arien stole another quick hit and passed the doobie to Andy. Boy! That's tasty bud.

"What is this, Otter?"

Otter's eyes twinkled. "Remember the visit to Zadkiel's?"

"Oh wow, cool!"

"Hey! Don't forget us up here!" It was Tina. Her voice had an edge to it. Arien was struck by the realization he had never heard any irritation out of her before.

"Whoa, yeah!" Andy got up unsteadily and hunkered over Arien as he passed the doobie to Tina. "Sorry."

Arien winced, feeling he should have done that.

It was well beyond the half hour's projection, but rather more like a couple of hours of increasingly bumpy, rutted roads to get in the vicinity of where Clayboy was going. Arien barely overheard Jeff say they were somewhere in the Medicine Bow National Forest.

"That's right, like I said" Clayboy told him. "We've been camped up in here for over a month."

"Wow. Cool, Man. And that's chilly cool, too. Doesn't look like winter knows it's over."

"You get used to it," Clayboy said.

Van Gogh lurched to a stop and Arien didn't hesitate to open the doors in the side. Andy's relief was visible. The pitching, heaving vehicle caused him considerable discomfort.

It *was* neat. From where they were the view dropped dramatically to a green valley and blue shadowed, white-topped mountains beyond. Clear air smelled of spruce and a faint whiff of wood smoke. The dimension of silence only deepened in a rustle and wisp of breeze in the crowns. Sunlight sparkled in the bushy green branches, and on last year's matted yellow grass.

The forest camp to where Clayboy led everyone was a cluster of tarps, tents and lean-tos built into the side of a steep hill where winter snow clung stubbornly to the ground in shaded enclaves. Streamers of colored cloth swayed from low branches in a festive effect, and a large rack of elk antlers from a bleached-white skull on the trunk of a tree presided over the broad fire pit. Several young men and women and a couple of children ambled about. A swarthy, shirtless old man with gray in his ragged beard was the first to greet the visitors from where he sat on a fireside log. His bare, weathered feet looked tough enough to wear out shoes from the inside. "Ho, Clayboy! Who have you brought us?"

"Howdy, Tree! These brothers picked me up on the highway."

"Welcome, friends!" He looked carefully from one to the other of Van Gogh's passengers, as if for something he should remember. "Have a seat. Would you like a cup of Joe?" He gestured to a tall, sooty, enamel coffee pot resting on a flat rock at the edge of the pit.

"I'm Tree." He offered his hand to Otter, who was nearest, and he glanced more appreciatively at Tina before returning his eyes to the others.

Names went round, Otter, Tina, Andy, Jeff, Arien, who said, "I'll take you up on some of that brew."

Tree reached for a tin cup lying on its side on the ground. He poured a bit of coffee and swirled it around to rinse out dried up sludge already there and filled it to the brim with the stuff. Their eyes locked when he passed the cup.

"What did you say your name was? Your young face looks awful familiar."

"He is one of the twelve people in the world," Andy observed.

"More likely the thirteenth." Otter said.

"Siege Perilous," Andy agreed.

The lad cradled his cup with both hands and seemed to think about it before he took the first sip. "Arien."

Tina smiled inwardly and sat down with him on the log. She seemed to have moved beyond her irritation.

Jeff said, "I'll have some coffee, too, thanks. Be right back. I'll get more cups."

Clayboy hugged a few people and then sat himself cross-legged on the ground. He was plainly home.

"Maybe it was in the dream." Tree aimed his words at the fire pit before looking at his visitors again. "Yes. That's it! I saw you in the dream!" He wagged a finger in the air with excitement.

"That's rad," Arien mused.

"Jeeze! It's coming back to me. The 'thirteenth,' you said. Ha! How right you are! You were all there; and then some!" Tree poured coffee in the other cup that was near him along with a splash for Jeff.

A slight breeze wafted through the treetops. It bore the piercing, lingering whistle of a red tail hawk. Colored streamers and bolts of cloth swayed from branches. Wind chimes tinkled in the woods. Other residents of the camp were drifting in to stand around. There were nods of greeting and some names exchanged.

"Ho, People!" Tree addressed them, "Remember the beautiful dream I told you about?" There were further nods. "Here's someone that was in it, now! His name is Arien. Whoa." He rolled his head in wonder.

"What was he doing in your dream?" Tina asked.

A tow-headed, barefoot tyke in a hooded jacket poked his stick into smoldering embers. A little girl, her face streaked with dirt, squatted to watch. Campers crowded in to listen.

"Let's see. Oh my. It was a beautiful dream, and I told everyone, didn't I? I was on our little mountain; Old Rock, we call it. That's where we go up to pray. And, I heard the blast of a horn. It was very fine, loud and long, and for a while I pondered that, in the dream. Then I saw a procession, a gathering. There were countless people in it, thousands and thousands of them. The road was jammed with traffic, like rush hour, but it was way out in the country. It didn't make any sense. Why are all these people here, I wondered. Maybe it's the Second Coming!"

Tree swallowed some of his coffee and motioned for visitors to sit. "It didn't make any sense, the part about the people, I mean," he went on. "The thing that was happening wasn't what was happening. I mean, it was like everyone was there for something but not the thing it was all about. That is, except, for a handful, or so it was in my dream," he reflected. "Very few paid it any attention, like they had no idea what was important. You might say it was a bit of paradox. But, this lad, the one right here, wore a crown of leaves. He took his place in a circle. I saw them in the dream! There were others, too, who are here now! Tree paused and fiddled with the ends of his beard. "And, somebody told me they'd come from far away and only they knew what was happening."

"Awesome," Arien said with a brief smile. His friends were in rapt attention, but Arien's bemused smile melted to wonder as Tree finished this tale.

"And I wanted so much to find out more about the honored young fellow, but some pesky crows making a ruckus woke me up."

The travelers stood or sat as if frozen in place. Only eyes connected. The campers contemplated their visitors. Otter shook his head and chuckled to himself. Andy brought a hand to his chin and unconsciously bit down on some fingers. Tina put an arm on Arien's knee. Jeff stared down into the reflection in his cup. The wind chimes could be heard again, off a ways.

"Maybe he's really Parsifal," Andy said with a chuckle. His eyes met Otter's.

"What do you make of it, Arien?" Otter asked him.

"Look, I'm goin' for the music!" he blurted out. "No bozos, no cops, no rules, no appointments, just my friends, and some slidin' naked in the mud, and some cid and some weed and the music. I don't know about any more." His befuddled protest even got a surprised grin from Tree. But, on another level Tree's marvelous little story had shaken him.

He put his cup down on the log and got up to relieve himself, but he also needed to get away, as he often did when this stuff just bubbled up and didn't stop until it practically swirled over his head. There was a lot to sort out. He didn't feel comfortable being an object so often.

Some of the campers who were nearest held out their hands in greeting or just to touch him as he passed. There was a lovely young woman with short, dark hair named Aspen, a big, thirty-something fellow with a medium-length, dark-brown beard, in overalls who called himself Oak and another, lanky, young man with shoulder-length red hair who introduced himself as Willow. He wore a grey wool touring cap that looked like it came out of the 1920s.

"I'm beginning to see a pattern here," Andy said, shaking Willow's hand.

"Yes. Tree is our leader," Willow answered seriously. "He dreams truly."

Their gaze followed Arien as he disappeared down a trail.

Arien came upon a fine coast of stream. A little blue plastic boat and a yellow rubber duck sat on a rock with the damp heap of a child's T-shirt there. Here the sun slanted warmly on rocks in defiance of snowy patches in the wooded shadows and it sparkled among the rivulets of the current. He stripped off his clothes and jumped into a deep pool from a fallen log that hung out over the stream. The icy-cold water really stung at first, but the rush to his body was so refreshing after all the time in the van. Here, he could tread water and exercise and dive to the bottom to feel for little rocks and watch the blur of small fish in there with him. The water was so pure and clear. He drank some even as he splashed and did somersaults over and over. It felt really snappy.

Still dripping, body red and tingling, he laid his clothes over a broad rock and spread himself out on top to catch the rays and gaze up at blue above and little bright white wisps of cloud very high up. It seemed he could stare right through them still higher, to where the blue grew hazy to purple-indigo and then inky black where stars glinted sharp as knives. He shut his eyes and melted into the warm glow. He dozed.

"Mind if I join you?" It was the gentle voice of his road brother, Andy.

"Be your own guest, Dude. There's enough rock." He raised a knee a little self-consciously but then set it back, flat on the rock as it was, hiding instead behind his closed eyelids.

"Going to get wet, first." Carefully, Andy unwrapped his arm from the sling and slowly undressed by the side of Arien's rock. Getting the shirt off was no little trick. Tremulously, he climbed down to the bank and waded into the water. "Wow. Brisk." He laughed.

"You get used to it pretty quick." Arien opened one eye to see the exit wound with its fresh pink scar on Andy's back just as he slipped into the water, huffing and screaming a little bit, too. His movements on that side were jerky, but it was healing well. By 1990 nobody will notice as long as his shirt is on, Arien thought. It also occurred to him he would probably never stop being blown away by thoughts like this. It was almost too 'far out' to fully appreciate. But, this moment was right now. It was real. Here they were beside a crispy stream in the Medicine Bow where a bright, warm, sunshiny day contended with defiant clumps of snow lurking in midday shadows. Maybe the rest was all a dream, a fantasy, a hallucination. After he was around long enough he would begin to remember his real past. Yes. Surely he would. Then he could get his real social security card; his driver's license would be legitimate; he would have to register for the draft. That thought grabbed him.

"There's fish here!"

"Yup."

Andy ducked under a few times. Arien could hear him splashing, louder, nearer.

"Dude! I'm gonna whip your ass!" Shocked by cold water, he sat up. Andy laughed and dunked back under.

Arien folded his arms around his legs and watched his friend come out of the water with brightly reddened skin to sit along side. He sat close, very close. Arien was about to give him more space as a wet limb, cold as the flank of a fish, came up against his, but Andy reached his arm around the folded leg and pressed them together, knee to knee.

Arien's inhale was slow, measured.

"I love you, beautiful Brother," Andy said softly from under the bangs of his dripping hair.

"Uh, yeah, Dude."

"Lay back down."

Arien blushed, hesitated and then gave in. He closed his eyes and peered into sun-ruby lids as a palm lightly rested on his navel and fingers stretched out to tingle through the hair at the root of his manhood.

"Hey! That's got to be the coolest birthmark in the world!"

The hush in Arien was the center of the earth. He watched himself like the boy coming on to acid, that same fight or flight tension as an irresolvable extreme when finally broken in the transcendence of letting go, dying, and seeing bare, fluttering branches over his face. A bird called keenly from the woods.

Gentle fingers trolled up from his knees, barely touching the skin. The dancing, tingling on his thighs elicited the sweetest, irrepressible moan. He tensed, subtly writhing.

Arien felt the press of breath, so subtle, and drops of water on the taught plain of his tummy and a growing part of himself devoured into a warm, moist place. He dared not open his eyes in the passing moments but his trembling was gradually calmed with whispers and touches of tenderness and skill.

With sudden lush pleasure pulsing through his body, Arien gave himself in the bright sunshine day. It seemed so right, so natural, the gurgle of the stream, the scolding of a jay, the smooth, sensual rock beneath him, the scent of water, earth and pines, wet hair dragging, softly tickling across his exposed skin, and some fresh, damp, electric animal that he allowed.

Arien heaved and sighed.

Andy, tasting, kissing, touching, moved up to rest his head on Arien's breast where he held him so snugly, entwining their limbs, thrusting himself once, twice into the fine young fellow's flank and leaving hot jets of yearning there, between their bodies.

For a long while they lay like that.

"Do you molest all the kids?" Arien said with a smirk on their way back to the camp.

"Hey, you're going to be royalty, remember? I prefer to molest a prince, especially pure honey, like you."

"In the stories I've heard, the knight takes a princess."

"Or, it was the queen, Arien."

"Then you're pretty confused, Dude."

Andy laughed. "I just hope you will still respect me in the morning."

"No, Dude. I will tell all the kids this knight is a cock sucker."

"And I will tell them how much you liked it."

"And they'll like it, too!" Arien said.

It was darker in this thick section of forest. That and growing hunger quickened their pace.

Tree Family's Camp was a different place at night. The glow from the fire lit up tall trunks like columns in an ancient temple and flowing cloths in branches were the pennants and standards of a prehistoric, Druid universe. The great antlered skull of elks' spirit seemed to come alive, its hollow eyes danced again in flickering reflections. Torches placed here and there illuminated the pathways. Voices chortled in darkness and from glowing faces and children scampering about, or staring into the fire. Some of the young men and women sat on fireside logs with bongos and dunbeks, flutes and symbals and the music they made bore a sound as old as the Word.

Arien closed his eyes as the light and warmth of a spiraling, whirling tongue of flame and sparks of settling logs cast its rosy glow through his eyelids. For the smallest moment he was back at the stream, and he could smell a young man's damp hair tousled on his chest, and feel the weight of this fellow's head in a place where only Tina was allowed. He grimaced like a skydiver jumping for the first time out of a perfectly good airplane. Do I know what I've done? Do I even know who I am? What I am?

Otter once said to him that if a thing felt right it probably was. Was this the truth? Was this the simple truth lost in all the rules? Was this freedom? Had dropping acid loosened his moorings that much? Was the drug to blame? Under any other circumstances, with anyone else, it couldn't remotely have happened, or... could it? The doubt was there. For now, Arien snuggled with Tina and felt particularly randy. She loved his attention and hung close to him. This evening he truly felt like a visiting prince, and Tree, wrapped against the crisp chill in a great fir robe looked every bit the tribal chief.

A gallon bottle of cheap red wine was making the rounds. Arien could hear Jeff telling Tree about their trip to Woodstock, and he'd set the bottle down on the ground between his legs.

Tree reached for it. "Tell me more about Arien over there. Where is he from?"

Jeff helped Tree to the bottle. "Berkeley, originally, and then he lived in Portland in a half-way kind-a house, I heard him say."

"Half-way to where?" Tree held the bottle up to his lips with both hands while he drank.

"He's a splitting image of young Dionysus," Andy said, aside to Otter who had three joints in his lap and was manufacturing yet another.

Otter smiled, nodded. "Smoke this," he ordered, thrusting one up, "and beseech Dionysus to get Tree to pass that bottle." There was a stick in front of him that was long and one end burned close to the coals. Otter pulled it out and lit all of the doobies, passing them right, left and behind him.

"Your generosity gets you the power hit from every one of these," Andy observed, sucking in smoke as Otter slid onto the ground to lean back against the log. "From such a height you must look down upon us!"

"The bottle!"

"Oh."

The drumming rolled from one player to another. A few girls danced, arms outstretched in mudric gestures, waving and undulating their bodies with the rhythms. To Arien there was something forever about them. He'd been here before. He'd always been here and always would be. He cuddled his Tina and kissed her, pushing hair back from her face and sinking his fingers into it, luxurious, silky.

Somebody offered a wooden salad bowl full of nuts, dried dates, figs and raisins to Tree, and he let go of the bottle long enough for Andy to gesture to Arien and to Willow, nearer, to pass it.

"Half way to freedom from jail, I suspect," Jeff drawled in his sultry East Texan.

A little boy grabbed the bottle of wine and had a draught before Andy could wrestle it.

"Kid's got the right idea," Otter commented. He pulled a hip flask out of his jacket and filled it when he finally had the bottle, before passing the wine further along. "Maybe one of these pretty women is available," he considered, looking around. "What's her name? Aspen?"

Clayboy was furiously beating on a tall wooden drum. He had perfect timing. He anchored the drum between his boots and held it with his knees. His forehead perspired with exertion, but he was often leading, and the others followed and occasionally nodded their approval. For a young boy, he appeared to occupy a respectable place in this family.

Tree would not be distracted. "So, tell me about Woodstock," he asked Jeff.

"Arien says it's gonna be the biggest concert ever. Maybe half a million people will be there."

"Hmmm. And, it's in the country?"

"Yup. Upstate, in New York."

"You got room for more?"

"Oh hell, no!" Jeff laughed. "We're crowded like sardines as it is. You'll have to find another way, yourself." The Texan came out most whenever Jeff drank alcohol.

"You stopped for Clayboy."

"Yeah, but we dropped him off here. It's still a long way to Woodstock. Say, don't you people have any vehicles?"

"Yup, three, including an old school bus, but none of them are parked here. They might give our camp away." One of the doobies reached him and he took a few quick hits. "Wow. That's very good!"

"Well how 'bout this drummin' here? The racket should draw an ear or two."

Tree passed the doobie to Jeff. "Ah. Drums after dark can come from anywhere, and the rangers go home to bed at night. Besides, the forest soaks up the sound."

Jeff rolled it carefully between his fingers to loosen a blockage. "And the fire y'all have? That there can come from only one place."

"Yeah, but it's pretty deep in the trees, too, and, what the heck? You live a little!" Tree gestured at the primal scene around them.

At that they both giggled like little kids.

Tree offered Jeff the bowl of healthy munchies and he readily accepted. "You know," said Jeff, "the school bus might be the ride of choice for y'all."

"Let's go," Arien said to his girl. Her face was flushed with her youth and contentment and looked so lovely to him in the firelight, her blissed-out blue eyes, her pink, freckled cheeks and saucy twist to her lip. Holding hands, they moved away from the pops and fits of the fire and the people, and the drumming receded to an exotic play of sound, motion and shadow in the trees. They made their way to a small clearing under bright stars where Tina had earlier taken their bedroll. They stripped in the chill night mountain air and hurried to snuggle under covers.

Arien was so turned on he could barely contain it. He felt so sexy, so desired by those he loved, so full of himself. He was all over her, kissing and drawing her scent. She squealed with delight and they tussled and rolled, several times throwing the covers off and having to pull them back again.

Crows wakened Arien. They called in raucous spats from branches directly over his head. Crisp morning damp kept the covers drawn up high. The crowing seemed to be hinting, but Arien felt unable to grasp whatever it was about. It troubled him. He had so much! He had friends, love, an immediate purpose which thrilled him through and through, yet there was a missing part. What was it? His past? His future? His thoughts were drawn to that house on Salmon Street in Portland. He shuddered, feeling much as the moment at Blue Star's on that wonderful night when accepting a hit of doob was to cross some threshold, where painful existence was rejected, and he tried to latch onto anything else, like even thinking about it now in his ongoing but still-fresh fullness might jerk him back there to Hell against his every fiber of being. Oh my God! That would be so horrible! The idea took a sudden shape, fully formed like a fearsome ghost there to haunt him.

Why now? It scratched at the door left by pain and anger that seemed to close with acceptance, with love, with purpose and hope.

He realized Tina watched him alongside, her expression blank, assessing his sudden well of tears.

"What?" She kissed his cheek.

The crows called.

"It's so scary, Tina," he said. "I think I have something to lose for the first time since I was a little boy.

Breakfast was a big steaming pot of oatmeal with nuts and raisins and honey to put on top. Arien was hungry enough but held off from greeting people as long as he could. He and Tina started with strong coffee from the ubiquitous camp pot settled on its rock in the fire pit. He was grateful for the smoke drifting into his eyes. He could shut them. Tree kept looking at him. It made him self-conscious.

Andy was mostly quiet, concentrating on the Boy Scout mess kit truncheon that held his mound of oats. He stood off more than usual, hanging nearer to Otter who was disposed to chat with lovely Aspen. Jeff shared an amusement with one of the children.

"We goin' to Woodstock, Tree?" Clayboy asked.

"We have to get to work on the bus, Clayboy. Think we can do it in time, Oak?"

Oak shifted in his wide pair of overalls and rag wool sweater from where he sat on the log. "I'll need to get to a bank, scare a little bread to fix the radiator, sure."

"Maybe these folks can take you to town." He motioned to his guests.

"Maybe." Jeff smiled up, the child astride his lap now.

Arien still struggled with his ghost as he ladled a heap of oatmeal for Tina. She stole glances. He was not himself. He put barely a dollop of food in his own bowl.

"I can't eat this much." She tried to scrape some off into his bowl, but he moved it away, and she chased it nearly dumping it all, and finally they laughed.

"OK," he said, pecking her cheek with his lips.

"The crows were back this morning." Tree observed, shoving a spoon at his enamel plate. His rugged bare feet extended out from a spindly folding camp stool that looked about to give way under him.

"They woke me up 'fore I was ready." Clayboy said.

"Me, too." Oak joined in.

"I sure heard them," Andy admitted.

Otter nodded.

Arien said nothing.

"I think they're here for you, boy." Tree continued. He was so serious.

"Not likely," Arien whispered. It was meant for Tina whose expression betrayed nothing.

"What do you think they mean?" Andy asked. He finally faced Arien for the first time that morning.

"They carry messages. They're eyes and ears," Tree said.

Andy accepted that with a knowing nod.

"Who for?" Otter asked.

"The boy here, and the others who know him."

Arien sighed. He wished for a moment that he could start again, go back to Blue Star's place and make something up to explain the circumstance. By now he knew how easily he could have done it. But it was way too late for that. It was like he'd cast himself in some kind of concrete that dragged after him now wherever he went.

When Arien asked for the honey, Willow, and two of the girls who danced the night before, nearly collided in the rush to bring it to him. This did not escape Otter's attention. "Did you check that out?" he whispered to Andy.

"Honey for the honey," Andy replied wistfully. "Can't get there fast enough."

"Maybe Tree is setting him up."

"Seems straight to me."

Aspen shifted uncomfortably. She was close enough to overhear. She smoothed out a wrinkle of a loose-fitting cotton sari under an open fatigue coat and set her tin plate back on her lap. "There was some talk about him yesterday afternoon," she volunteered. "Your friend there," pointing at Jeff, "told us he claims to come from the future." The thought dangled like her spoon, hovering halfway to her lips. "Maybe that's the real set-up."

"Could be." Otter said, appraising her. He sipped some black coffee, sloshed it through his teeth and spat it out.

"Only, Tree dreams true."

"So I've heard. Woodstock is like that dream. Especially Arien's version." Andy agreed, again locking eyes with Arien.

"Tree dreamt about me before I came here with Charlie," Aspen added.

"Charlie?"

"Charlie's not here anymore. Tree dreamt that, too."

"Maybe he makes it happen," Andy suggested,

"No. It's just some part of him knows. He's like that, you know."

Willow offered Arien more coffee.

"No."

Tina?"

"Sure."

Willow took her cup to set on the stone, freeing his hands to pour.

Arien entertained mixed feelings about such conversations as just went down. He couldn't deny a certain pride in so often being the center of the subject, but it felt totally ungovernable.

The rest of breakfast evolved into chores. People gathered bowls and cups for washing. The east-bound were considering a time of departure when Tree requested a favor. He told them of his decision to go to Woodstock. They would take their old school bus, but needed transportation to get it going. Would the travelers mind the delay?

Tree suggested Oak be delivered to wherever their bus was parked, pick up its radiator, then run it to a shop west of Cheyenne. It might take a day or two, driving there and back and waiting for the repair to get done.

"We've three-fifths of the country to cross yet," Otter said. "We still have a couple of months, right, Arien?" It was a rhetorical question. By now, everyone knew the opening date was in the middle of August, but they also were aware of Arien's imperative to arrive early.

"Would you mind the run, Jeff?" Arien asked his friend.

"I guess not. These folks have been good hosts to us." He smiled at Tree who nodded appreciatively. "Come with us, Arien?"

Before Arien could answer, Tree asked if he would stay behind. "I would like you to see Old Rock, where we pray, lad," he said.

Arien was curious about that but another side of him resisted what was beginning to run like an expectation, and not just to Tree; that contrary to his highest hopes for an experience of wild abandon, he was being prepped for some role to play. It was like a wondrous golden thread, yet weaving a growing entanglement that ran all the way back to that strange night at Jamie Sun's. Oh Jesus! What was going on?

He shifted uneasily, unable to say yes or no.

Otter broke into a grin. "He fights with destiny."

Arien's eyes widened. "You bitch!"

There was laughter all around. Was it that obvious?

"I'll go with you, Jeff," Andy said unhappily. "I'd like to rummage in Cheyenne if there's any time to kill."

"Otter?"

"Nah. I'll hang." He tilted his head.

Tina's staying was a given. Arien had unconsciously taken her hand and so together they stood.

Arien, Tina and Otter took what personals they needed from Van Gogh, Oak climbed aboard with a box of tools, Jeff beeped the horn, Andy resolutely waved and the little bus putted away down the rutted mountain track.

The walk back to camp was quiet at first.

"I really thought you would go, Otter." Arien said at last. He shifted his duffel from one arm to the other.

"I've an interest, here."

"Let's see. Could it be a certain tree named, Aspen?" Tina probed.

"Maybe."

"You'll love her and leave her." She chided. She had that sparkle Arien yearned for, even when it was all his.

"Probably." Otter chuckled.

"Heartless bastard," said Arien with a smirk.

"That's me."

"It's so groovy," Tina gushed as she stared into the flames, her fair complexion soaking up light in rich tones of yellow-orange.

That word always made Arien want to chuckle at least, but he agreed with her. The Tree Family's Camp was awesome at night anyway; on LSD absolutely luscious and magical. The velvet darkness had great depth, a quality, enhancing every vivid lick to leaping tongues of flame and their busy, strobing patterns dappling branches and tree trunks. There was a pulsing rhythm about it Clayboy captured with eloquence on his drum. It was alive as certainly as everything else.

Otter caught his glance. He sat beside Aspen and turned away from their shared secret just in time. His nod said, "You're welcome." He was the meister with pure liquid. He'd responded when a sharing was required. Not an hour ago he'd gone around with his vial and eye dropper and folks stuck out their tongues for the true Eucharist, surely. Old Tree actually kneeled and that surprised Arien and then most of those who came after did also.

This stuff, Arien pondered, liquid omniscience, had dropped onto his tongue and for ever so brief a moment made it the center of his consciousness! The tongue assumed command, both awake and aware, and it reviewed its responsibility and conducted itself perfectly, with flawless memory and calm deliberation. And then the inexorable current flowed into the esophagus, where awareness expanded and watched the scene around itself like any person, the eyes, the nose, the taste and feelings re-routed, as it were, until the "Seer" opened into his stomach and filled the length and breadth of Arien's body, when the capital of his mind was restored to its conventional location.

"I wonder about those big dinosaurs, with their little brains. Maybe their whole body was their brain and they could have been awfully smart." He smiled as he said that. It was profound for him to say.

"And they lived in peace," Tina replied, "happily ever after."

Arien's eyes met with others' now. Willow sat between two girls who leaned against his shoulders. He worked his jaw with 'acid indigestion' (An Otter-word that delighted Arien.) His subtle smile was proud. The girls were both dreamy-eyed, stoned, in a good place.

A young woman nestled with little ones. She was tripping, too. Her eyes said so. They had a loving intensity that surely embraced her kids and then everyone else. The children were animated in their blankets. They pointed at things and giggled. It was a classic contact high, since an earlier enquiry Andy made established that feeding acid to little children was verboten.

Tree's dark eyes burned like coals. Their intensity hinted a wildness, unknowable, vaguely unsettling. He hunkered under his heavy fur robe. Its effect was total, with his somewhat disheveled hair, a beard with streaks of gray that appeared to be longer than yesterday, and a winding vine walking staff that leaned against his shoulder, he was all the prehistoric chieftain, or a wizard out of Tolkien.

Catching Tree's eye summoned him like a sidewalk beggar. He made his way over, past several others who faced the fire, one hand clutching the robe tight around himself and the other his staff.

Arien was so high. He wished Otter sat by him, or Andy was here; true warriors. The Revolution was Otter, if a person could sum it up. He was a free man, and Andy had a grasp of magic and subtle things. Arien did not know if he could run with Tree on his own, without his friends. Should he even care? One arm pulled Tina closer to him as Tree sat on the other side.

"Good acid. Clear as morning dew."

Another young man joined Clayboy with a drum and the blended rhythms wound through vastly heightened senses to dance with flames on faces and the streamers of cloth flowing under branches, and rolling sparks rushing upward to join all their brothers and sisters in the Milky Way.

Arien shuddered with a delicious rush responding to Tree's words, his body a tightly coiled spring. He gritted his teeth. He bobbed his head and tapped his Keds against a rock. When smoke crossed his face like an abrasive wool blanket he held his breath and shut eyes tight into a splash of sparkle and kaleidoscope patterns.

Arien fell into the drumming. It made dappled patterns of colored light over his head, like Christmas bulbs through a hazy filter. Or, was it the firelight?

Something else began to congeal into view. Arien couldn't quite make it out. He concentrated with tightly closed eyelids, certain there was indeed a thing to see in a shimmering, blood-red, fleshy veil of a billion tiny corpuscles that swirled furiously about. A little focus seemed to stretch and tear it and pull it apart. He saw a shimmering, like a bright, sunlit, silver tray caught in bedrocks of a rushing stream. As the image came into focus, Arien saw it take form in his thought, but it was not *his* thought. Was it his body? Was it the fabric of nerves and tangle of axons, dendrites, and synapses? And he felt it almost certainly was, and the cacophony of a billion crickets was surely the racket they made in his head. But the sharp image that finally settled-out revealed blood-red treetops of a forest, greening as it took form, and a lofty pinnacle of rock exposed to an open sky. It had a reddish, sandy color. He still couldn't tell if the image was *in* his brain or about him. Sounds quieted, blending to a static tension. His space felt soft but the vision of the rock face was very clear. He was there! It was framed with tall trees and the sky was a deep, dark blue.

Abruptly, he was back. He stared into Fire, most ancient entertainer, shuddered with another rush, so strong it flung his upper arms outward and shook his hands in a spastic convulsion.

"I'd like to show you Old Rock." Tree said.

Arien clamped down involuntarily on his teeth and giggled to himself. "I think I've seen it already."

Tina smiled at him. "Yes, I felt that," she said.

The hike there came a little later on. Tina had just gone off to the latrine in the woods and left Arien with drumming and leaping flames and vivid impressions from surrounding faces, one after the other. Tree's gravitation tugged until his guest sprung to feet with a will of their own. He was flying, full of power, body feeling both light and expanded as air yet compact as granite rock. He actually saw it, a true force, dense, gray hurricane that furiously rotated to a fantastic speed, like the magnified hyper-ball of a frenzied pen rocketing over some inner plane, with his intention, and it seemed to hold the will and force of his being tightly together. And, the denser the ball, the faster its rotation, the more solid and invincible he felt, as if his falling feet could pulverize the very stones beneath them.

He wanted to run just to spend some of the energy. He felt like he could have run to New York State, but trembled on his legs instead, with hesitation, like a nervous foal, as he checked his forward motion. His thought for Tina was 'I'll be right back,' stepping carefully around people clustered by the fire pit and nodding to Clayboy who was drenched in sweat and the haze of its collision with the crisp night air. He scanned for Otter, but both he and the girl, Aspen, had already gone off somewhere. No matter. He was moving now, irresistibly.

Together Arien and Tree, the fur robe pulled snugly around him, the tip of his staff finding its meter, picked their way through a deep blanket of darkness on a trail into thickening forest. The voices and firelight became muffled, distant. Here and there a star or two sparked through momentary openings in hovering branches but it was impossible to see the ground. Regardless, he followed the gravity of Tree's body before him or alternately along side of him at a quickening pace that should have slammed them both into something solid, but this didn't happen. Every step was sure. Not a root, boulder, twig or finger of snow barred the way. Sometimes, Arien stepped high and then low. Sometimes he veered to the right or to the left or ducked down without any need for sight. It was spontaneous and automatic. It was a strenuous yet thoroughly thrilling pace. To move so quickly in total blindness! His breathing took air that felt somehow solid, once inside and outside, around him, and his feet simply knew their way.

They were climbing now. It required more air and more heart. Arien could not recall a stronger, more powerful pulse. It worked as a fulcrum between breath and step, pushing him forward like a rail car. It was Godlike. Effortless. He perspired and it cooled him perfectly. His mind was blank, receptive. There was only experience in the moment, feeling the man next to him in the solidity of the air more than hearing his steps, and never touching him. They didn't speak but they were very much together, sometimes more, sometimes less. Arien could feel the other man with a surface tension like a tugging moon on the sea. Communication between them was through the experience of the moment and the proximity of their bodies in motion on the trail.

At one point, just before they came up into a close clearing where the stars clustered busily between tall silhouettes of trees and dense, dark, massive formations, Arien reached out a hand to mingle his fingers in the fur of some wild animal easily as big as a very large dog, to gently stroke it as he whisked by. His high-pitched, excited giggle never escaped his lips but blended into their footsteps and their breaths and the silence around them. God knows what the hell that was! A wolf? A big cat? He embraced the impressions of the soft, short fur at his fingertips, a warm body under his palm, structurally plastic, quivering with warmth and energy, and continued to feel it when it was no longer there, like the bright light that lingers under closed eyelids. It didn't move away as the humans continued upward, and yet Arien could sense its receding gravity and its being and understand its knowing and its curiosity and lack of fear. Oh Rad! He was on acid now where everything is wondrous and everyday reality can be exposed as the ultimate imposter.

Now it was very steep. He was vertical on all fours, and he would reach in total blackness and there was a hand hold or a place for his foot and never did either he or Tree break their swift hiking stride. Arien could feel his heart squeezing in his chest, like the cavity was barely big enough for it do its marvelous work. He breathed to the top of his lungs and his heart contracted like a piston with a strong, upward pull. He could hear the blood coursing furiously behind his eardrums.

Gathering moisture clung to the nape of his neck and the narrows of his chest. It was an enormous effort and wonderful. His body felt so strong and fluid and wore its invincible youth to utter perfection.

At length they stood at the top. Below and for a very long way was utter darkness, and above were a riot of bright, sparkling stars, then one, and another, shot away across the sky with a fabulous streaking tail.

"Awesome!"

"One for each of us," said Tree.

They sat for a long while, Arien getting as comfortable as he could, crouched in a niche between a cleft of boulders in a lap crusty snow. Night closed around them with stillness. For awhile the climb up and then pure force wielded in Arien's mind kept the chill air at bay. Indifferent, now he blended with the freezing temperature of the night. He allowed his thoughts to go still as the Watcher in him focused through an exponential lens where darkness expanded into softly layered fields of seeing and being. It was so deep and beautiful, stunning. The light of the stars sang with high-alto voices and beckoned in limitless possibilities for expansion. "Oh Hell! I'm so young!" he blurted.

"You are a pup." Tree agreed.

"Why me? Why am I being all this?" The answer had to be somewhere. It was the other side of the question, after all, and if he could ask the question…

"I think you're finding out who you are." Tree said.

Arien's body shuddered. "I want to have fun. I want to be free. I'm just a kid." He was suddenly very sad.

"You're being guided. Don't fight it."

Who are these people? They seemed to come from anywhere and yet they knew so much, but it wasn't at all the kind of knowledge that enslaves. A voice in his head answered, *"We are ourselves."* Surely, the voice was his, or was it? Or, was it the sound that interpreted these bundled flashes of light and feeling that shot through the matter in his skull? Heavy, heavy stuff, as they said in this peculiar time.

"Oh rad! I know so much, too!" He knew it. He felt it. "I Am It!" He cried out. "I'm all of it! And, when I'm through with this planet it will never be the same!" A sense of power filled him again. It pulled him from sadness like a rocket lifting off from the surface of the earth, slow at first, but inexorable and faster and faster.

Right then a really big meteor shot out from the sky over them. There was a russet glow on the tips of nearby ridges that appeared to lift their rippled features out and float them over the velvet darkness. It lit the wide-eyed faces of the boy and the old man on the rock. The fireball streaked to the ground in a strange other-worldly scene, parting the airs, its greenish, phosphorescent, glowing tail trailing with a fantastic, sweeping whoosh from the arc of the sparkly sky. When it hit behind a ridge maybe five or ten miles away there was a spectacular white flash. The night's silence deepened first to a hush, and then a loud, sharp "crack," like a riffle shot, resounded and echoed off the ridges and canyons.

"OH AWESOME!" Arien cried. He jumped up, hooted, hollered, and danced. This was *way* cool!

Tree's laughter bubbled outward. "Ho! I never! Who would believe that one? They'll say it was the acid!"

"It was!" Arien joined in the laughter now. Could such a so-rad thing happen? But it had!

"A man can live a lifetime and never see that." Tree pondered. "So, I'm glad about going to Woodstock, young stuff. If you're going there it's a place I need to be."

An icy breeze came up. It was first announced by a subtle pressure change that registered somewhere in Arien's tripping head. It was followed with a rushing in the treetops, distantly, then closer, closer; that finally embraced the bodies on the promontory like a cold bath. Arien held his arms tight to his frame. There was nothing to warm. He'd merged with the air.

"Take this," Tree said from the darkness all around as he wrapped the boy in his heavy cloak. It had a dead-leafy, earthy smell about it, and it warmly embraced him like an actual hug.

"Ahhhhh…" Arien pulled it over his head like a tent. He surely heard this exchange go down inside: But, Tree, you need it!

No, lad. I'm plenty warm.

Hours passed in stillness. Arien roamed his mansion's halls. He played with the workings in his head and his body, first quieting the very rhythm of his heart to absolute rest. It began with an exhale that established the perfect equilibrium of air pressure with his body's mass. Whole minutes passed. It expanded his awareness with a blinding flash, filling the forest and the hearts of myriad creatures. As he moved among them they grunted and stamped, rustled, hooted and yapped. All his body filled with the awareness and knowing of a thousand pairs of eyes and ears to focus the vast consciousness of a supra-life with a great receiver of being. His heart with kinship, then, was the most brilliant lamp in his house.

A stirring finger of attention reanimated his heart. Lubdub, lubdub. The sudden rushing of blood at the base of his ears sounded so loud it was like waves crashing on the beach.

At one point he gazed through an opening of the cloak into the majesty of the firmament. Stars shimmered like a billion jewels in the deepest limpid pool of night. "Tree, I think I got it!" he exclaimed. "Everything I am inside is out there! I'm at the window of what's above me, all around and below me, and what's inside of me and they're like, like – reflections of itself!"

Tears brimmed over Arien's eyelids and trickled down his cheeks. He blew air between his lips as the wind came up and pushed against the hardy, furry barrier about him. It receded with his inhale.

Arien hummed. The sound began to fill him. In the sound's reflection he perceived an unexpected stillness. The life around him coursed through him, and he knew what was and what was not, and he knew he was now alone on that high stony knoll with all of the company in the world.

"Tree!" he called, reaching out, first feeling a foot on the ground and then the body it belonged to beside him. It was very still and unnaturally cold.

The boy's OM was loud. It filled the canyon, its echo reverberating to a very great distance. In the twilight of morning he knelt over the old fellow and closed his eyelids. Then Arien laid the great cloak over the body and the staff on top. He placed rocks around the edges to keep it all together. It seemed so right.

'No,' he thought, before his descent. 'I'll take the staff down with me, and it will speak to them.'

Only a few people were about when Arien came near the camp. Now a decision was in order. He still wondered what he would say to people. The best he could do was to focus his attention. On the parabolic tail of his powerful trip was a space between everything, wide-open, blissful, but the bird still flew. He headed for the fire pit that smelled of fresh coffee and where a pot of oats was coming to boil. There was a young woman there. Arien couldn't remember her name. He drew forward and looked at her. She greeted him with a dreamy smile that told him she'd also been up all night. And then a subtle question in her eyes, regarding the staff he carried, prompted his voice. "He's gone," Arien said gently. "Tree has passed on."

The woman stuck her thumbs in the hem of the jeans she wore. She connected, searched his face, and processed his words. Arien could see the machinery at work.

"Heart attack, maybe. Or, out of his body and decided not to come back. I don't really know. It was probably a short while after the fireball. He's up there on Old Rock. No way could I get him down, myself, but, if it was up to me, I would leave him where he is. It was a really *beautiful* place to die." He tried to pass Tree's staff to the woman. She raised a hand to stay him.

"Will you tell them for me?" Arien asked, uncertain, pulling the staff back to his side.

At length she spoke, "Sure, I will."

He turned away, hesitated, "I'm sorry. I forgot your name."

"Kelsey."

His next stop was his camp where Tina already slept, wrapped in bedding, a trace of her yellow hair exposed to the new day's sun. He bent over to kiss her forehead. Blue eyes blinked open. They were still dilated.

"Oh Babe, Tree died last night."

"Wow, really, Arien? Oh wow. Heavy! What happened?"

"Maybe it was a heart attack, or he left his body and decided not to come back. I think it was a short while after a killer fireball."

"Oh, wow," she said reverently. "I saw that!"

"Did you hear it hit the ground?"

"No. That must have been out-a sight!"

Arien laid the staff beside their bed. He pulled his Keds off and picked up the covers enough to climb in with her. "I'm too pooped to pucker," he said, a phrase he'd borrowed from Jeff. The moment he stretched his body out it shut right down.

"Goodbye, Tree," Tina said, looking up at the sky.

It was sometime in the late afternoon when he awoke, called from sleep, as it were. The forms displayed against the hazy sky were human. They were looking at him, all in a circle, down to where he'd slept, men, women, children, the Trees. But, it was Otter who knelt at his shoulder. "I've seen Tree's body," he said.

"Oh, yeah." Arien stretched self-consciously. Tina was awakened by his voice. She propped herself up on her elbows. "He never said a word, Otter." Arien spoke loud enough to be heard by others who stood around. "I was out there, Dude, in my great big world, and then I knew he wasn't there anymore. I just knew he'd gone. It was rad, really." His mind drifted. He was thirsty. He had to pee. "But, you know?" Arien managed to say, "The last thing he said to me was he wanted to go to Woodstock. I'm sorry he won't get to go."

"The whole Family says you made a good call. Old Rock will be his resting place."

Willow spoke next. "More rocks. We covered his body with more rocks. We'll hide the trail better, too. Only we will know that place." Folks crowded closer, to hear. "There's one other thing."

Arien blinked, scratched, sat up. There were a lot of them at this camp when taken all together, maybe 20 or so with the kids. What did they want from him? He wondered, waiting.

"You have Tree's staff."

Arien was caught off balance, unsure of what to say. He reached for it and thrust it forward.

"No, that's just it, it belongs with you now. You were the only one with him at the end, though some of us have known him for years. He was our brother and our father, too; our teacher. And, he dreamed true. You were the only one there with him on Old Rock when the fireball came. We want you to have it."

Things were different after that.

When they finally crawled out of bed, Arien and Tina grabbed a bottle of Dr. Bronner's from their travel kit, a towel, and worked their way to the swimming hole through a camp subdued in mourning. An acid night left Arien with the typical rangy feeling of old sweat and greasy hair. As soon as they were screaming in the freezing water, they saw Myrtle, a young woman Tina had connected with their first day here. She stood by their clothes on the bank. "I can swap these out for something fresh, if you'll let me."

Tina balanced herself, shivering on a rock with a bemused grin. "Wow," she said.

"OK, whatever," Arien agreed. The cold, fresh water actually felt great. Stuff in the pockets of the jeans he'd worn really didn't cross his mind until the bathing and splashing was over. The Bic, which no longer worked, a cat's eye marble from the bay window at Page Street, a rubber band, a cowboy bandana he'd been wearing like a headband, his wallet with the impossible laminated ID and four dollars and sixty-seven cents were in the same pockets of the practically new jeans that replaced his own. In place of his T-shirt was a light, gauzy cotton pullover with string at the collar to cinch it up. There were fresh, clean socks, too. Only the sweater he'd worn was still the same.

Tina chuckled, seeing Arien ponder the socks. "Arien," she called, stepping out of the creek, "Have you ever heard the definition of a rich hippie?"

"No, Babe."

"Clean, dry socks!"

When Tina got to where she'd left her clothes, she held up a long, flower-patterned skirt and cotton blouse for Arien to see. "Righteous!" she declared, after putting them on. "They feel perfect. This was so nice of Myrtle."

They were barely back at the smoky camp when a plate of hot scrambled eggs with canned corn beef hash was offered up. Otter was there along with Aspen, Clayboy and most of the others. Arien was famished. He dug in and with acid's very physical afterglow, felt his body absorb the food and turn it to energy nearly as soon as it hit his stomach. "You're always right, Otter," he said, shoveling it in. "Eggs are the perfect food for LSD."

"Notice anything?" Otter asked, confidentially.

"No, Dude." Arien was bugging on the delicious pleasure of rapid absorption.

"There's not enough eggs for everybody."

Arien looked around, confirming the observation. No eggs anywhere. "Oh. Wow," he acknowledged, feeling humbled.

"Go for it, Brother. I think people here have a need to serve you now. You have their staff. But it works both ways. Just do us all a favor; keep a clear and modest head. Share what's yours. Don't take everything that's offered and insist on pitching in."

"Otter, I don't understand."

"Work on it."

A part of him did understand. He sat up in darkness on his bedding after a day of family chanting and prayer, thinking back to that meal and beyond, to the top of Old Rock and the things he'd seen and felt there. He was very connected and it was quite impossible to deny it. It was dull around the edges just now, like a hand one sleeps on and whatever sensation there is seems to belong to somebody else. But soon, it tingles, wrenching through its own local catharsis as the hand rejoins its wrist and then the arm that's attached.

An owl hooted overhead. He couldn't quite go where he had been only so recently into the true heart of forest creatures, and now not even that one, but he could sympathize. He knew. Up there in the tree was a fellow being in the choreography of existence. On the Rock, Arien tasted a share of a higher being, a creature that found its awareness in the body of life, itself. He pondered questions that rattled between his ears. Where did this creature go when he was just being Arien? Exactly, how was access accomplished or denied? Were drugs a requirement? What made him any different? – Other people didn't ever seem to deal with problems like this! And, why did people and events strive so earnestly to shape him, prepare him, lead him on? The side of Arien who just wanted to go to Woodstock and be a kid was about ready to have a tantrum. However, it was difficult to ignore such a blatant imposition as 'higher consciousness.' There was a deeper, more ancient side of this boy who yearned for connection, understanding and relevance. He'd stumbled into a space in his head he hadn't known existed and now it loomed over him like the mighty tsunami of the Cretaceous comet.

Tree's role with these pilgrims began to dawn on him. God, I've got to get out of here! He thought, feeling the tantrum. His higher side fought back, there must be a reason! Was the owl talking to him? He didn't own the words to answer but he couldn't sleep that night, either.

In the morning, Arien and Tina arrived at the kitchen lean-to to find Clayboy making passable pancakes. The kitchen was out of honey and there wasn't any syrup but Tina had a small jar of honey from the travel kit and went back to their bags for it. That was when Aspen asked Arien when he thought his friends would get back with Oak. Arien was about to blow it off with Babe, how should I know? But he answered instead, "This afternoon," before he could stop himself.

Catching that, Otter looked up from his plate. "I'd bet the farm he's right," he said to Aspen, who shared the log with him.

Tina got back with the honey and gave it directly to Arien. He screwed the lid off and was about to pour some over the cooling pancakes when he remembered Otter's favor. He passed the jar instead to the person nearest him and by the time it came around again what remained of his breakfast was stone cold and there was very little honey left.

Arien planted himself on a high knoll and leaned on the staff he'd brought along. Tina came up right behind him and then Otter, with Aspen, and Clayboy was the last one up. They'd been hiking for a couple of hours and just doubled back at a brisk walk on a rocky trail winding its way back to camp. They expected to arrive in time either to be there for Van Gogh's return, or shortly thereafter. Arien said nothing about it since breakfast; it was Otter who suggested the hike and who was keeping it to something of a schedule. There was a great view from here. The wedge of national forest they could see was a classic Rocky Mountain panorama of russet bluffs and canyons set with clusters of tall pines and open spaces covered with still-brown grasses. They could see a lazy tendril of gray smoke from the camp, below, that hugged the treetops, and the snaking trail running to the camp, and the reflected sun glinting off lumbering windshields a long way down on the jeep trail.

"That's the bus!" Clayboy pointed.

Tina waved. "Think they can see us?"

"Probably not," Otter said.

Tina pulled a scarf from a knitted shoulder bag and waved it. "Woo hoo, woo hoo!" She hollered, jumping up. It was silly and everyone laughed.

A few tiny people could be seen now as they made their way down to the vehicles. The folks on the knoll grew silent.

"Oak's gonna die when they tell him about Tree," Clayboy rued, verily speaking their thoughts.

In the distance, the folding doors at the front of the bus flashed as one of them pitched the bright ball of Sol's reflection. The biggest of the tiny people stepped out and was shortly surrounded by others that came to meet him. Arien couldn't be sure he actually saw the big man fall to his knees to bury head in hands, but he certainly felt it. Tears fell down Aspen's cheeks, and Clayboy suddenly looked so despondent.

Arien sighed. Tree had been loved. He was the anchor to these drifting folks. He'd given most of them their names and their purpose.

They'd prayed together, to the Great Spirit, like an Indian tribe. They'd moved from place to place to stay ahead of the rangers but wherever they stopped, their home was a fervent isolation among natural surroundings with a face tens of thousands of years old. Now Tree was gone and all they could do was give his staff to a mere boy and a mysterious stranger at that. What were they thinking?

Otter was watching Arien, not the people down on the trail. He moved closer to stand by his side, opposite Tina. "Your friends are here, to keep you strong," he said.

"What do they want from me, Otter?" He lifted the staff for emphasis, feeling its twisting vines with their rough, barky surfaces as the object seemed to merge among the fingers of his hand. It was a strange sensation since he wasn't tripping and his senses had been otherwise behaving themselves.

A cloud drifted in front of the sun and the landscape's colors grayed-over as a group of western jays fussed all about in an obnoxious vocal duel. "Raaaah, raaaah!" they taunted.

"Clayboy, come here a sec." Otter called. The lad ambled over and stood by with a somber expression. He dug his hands into the pockets of a pair of Army surplus pants. He wore a spare blue jean jacket and sneakers with no socks.

"What would you like to see happen, now that Tree is gone?"

Clayboy's tongue unconsciously traced his upper lip. He pondered a bit. "We need to keep together."

"Why?" Arien asked. "What does it matter?" And then he saw a haunted look blink out from the sockets of this young boy's skull, and it was hard not to follow the thread.

And, the boy went right to it. "I, I've been happy, I guess. I'm home." His eyes welled up. He shifted on his feet, sniffed and spat.

Aspen came up behind Clayboy and wrapped her arms around his tummy and rested a cheek into his head like a loving mother sharing their grief. Comforted, the hollow in his eyes diminished to serious and steady. The fussing jays packed their chattering further up the hillside above the knoll while the gathering gray above them rolled up more of the sky and the temperature fell along with it. Eyes went back to the people on the trail, below. They were making their heartsick way to camp.

"Are we ready to go down?" Otter asked.

"No."

"What do you want to do, Arien?"

"Dude, I'm staying here for a while, clear my head."

"Want us to stay with you?" Tina asked.

Arien didn't answer. He had a mind to invite Otter and Tina to stay, and send word for Andy and Jeff to come on up. These were the people closest to him, after all. But, he realized there was no way to say that to Aspen and Clayboy, so he resolved to tell them he'd like to be alone, and he'd ask Otter to leave him with a doobie or two.

Arien's pacing worked the dirt beneath his feet. In his mental process he assembled his friends, his travel-mates. It crossed his mind he'd suggest to them they just slip away in the dead of night, but that thought left him awfully uncomfortable. In the last few days he'd really come to like some of these folks. They accepted him, too, perhaps to a fault, and they held nothing back. They totally respected his connection with Tree. There had been no apparent resentment there and that said something about their sense of security in their relationships, who they were, and what they were about. Arien may not have been ready to articulate all this, but he grasped it, none-the-less.

He sat down on a rock and shortly scratched a line in the dirt between his feet with the end of the staff. "I'm this, I'm that," he said aloud, tapping the staff on each side of the line. But then he sank the staff into the line itself. "Whoa!" he marveled, revisiting the sequence of his perceptions the other night on Old Rock. He understood it would be the height of insincerity to deny, or attempt to ignore, any of it. But where is this going?

Arien tried so hard to grasp it. On the rock beside him were three doobies Otter left with him, along with a little pile of wooden matches. He scratched one against the rock and caught a good light the first time. The spicy smoke tickled his nose and a head rush trooped right behind his inhale. Knarly. A fleeting smile responded. Though it quickened his breath it relaxed him overall, transcending the psychic predicament by letting a physical dimension balance things out. It's a good tool, he mused. This is such a good tool.

The jays were back. They were distracting. Funny, how it seemed whenever Arien tried to meditate, just when it felt like he was getting somewhere there was a distraction. A noise, an itch, someone talking to him; it was always something! But a little deeper into his stone the issue receded. He coasted on the free ride. It doesn't matter. Endorphins flooded the space between his ears, and it felt too good to be down.

The sky was now going cloudy everywhere. A large bird, hawk or eagle, circled off in the distance.

I could use a brother up here.

"Hey."

Arien twisted to see the source of the word behind him. Andy was coming up. He was huffing from a rapid ascent. "Jesus! You're perfect!" Arien declared, truly relieved to see him.

Andy's arm was not in the sling, but he moved stiffly. It was plain the shoulder still hurt. An uncertain expression barely became a smile. "They told me to leave you be. I couldn't. It's been days already, and I hate it. Now that I'm back, I think I still hate it."

"It's rad, you're here."

"Thanks, Brother. I wondered."

Arien passed the roach up and Andy took it and sucked in a few quick hits. "I got a problem, Dude."

"Does it hurt like mine?" Andy took a last hit as the roach dissolved into sparks and flaky bits of ash.

"Well, maybe you can help with mine, first, since it concerns a lot." Arien worked the end of the staff into the line between his feet. He regarded his friend, unsure of the nature of the problem he'd brought up here. "I haven't thought about running anywhere since I left 1990 behind, but now–"

"Wow, man. What gives?"

Arien hefted the staff up and back down to the ground. "This, for one thing."

"Oh, Arien, that was Tree's!"

"No kidding."

"What are you doing with it?"

"Good question."

"What was it like Arien? They said you were the only person with him."

"I was trippin', Dude. It wasn't like much. The last thing he said – well, I don't know if he said it, but, I heard him tell me he was warm enough. He gave me his fur cloak up there on Old Rock."

"And?"

"I knew he was gone after he left, because there wasn't anybody there with me anymore."

"Whoa, out-a sight!"

"So, Andy," Arien said, shifting on the rock, "now, I can't figure what I am, you know? Like, Dude, am I all of that?" Arien pointed at everything around them, starting with the sky and ending with the rock they sat on. "Or, am I this?" He patted his chest with the flat of his palm. "Or, is it this?" sticking a finger to his forehead, between his eyes. "And, Dude, I honestly can't say if I decide anything. It's like, everything's already been decided!"

Andy was pensive, listening.

"And then, I know all this stuff lately, stuff I shouldn't be knowing. I knew you guys would be back this afternoon. Don't ask how I did. I just did! What am I supposed to do with that? It's scary."

"That's a sidi, a power, man. You're coming into an inheritance. Doesn't it feel good, even a little, Arien?"

"Well, you know, what have I done to–" The words failed him. "Something's still broke after…" He shuddered. The vision of a grisly murder was yet too fresh and horrible to mention.

"Hmmmm… I'm guessing here, Brother. You could be resuming a place you left in a past life, you know? That comes up from time to time. Then, the scary part, well, maybe that's a lack of experience. You've got little to work with and nothing to relate it to."

Arien sincerely listened.

"So, you just have to be patient, and live it out. Have faith that you'll rise to the occasion. You know, Arien, my grandmother used to say, 'The good Lord never gives us any more than we can handle.'"

"Unless it kills you," Arien said with no expression. "And people die all the time."

"Touché," Andy grinned. "You're a smart kid." He grew more thoughtful. "You've had no preparation. But, you're a natural, Arien. You've hit some Buddhist issues: finding what you are or what you're not. Buddhists meditate with, 'Neti, neti,' 'I'm not this, not that;' your destiny may be knocking, big-time. Then, you smacked into deep truth and you're really taking it on."

"I've listened to you guys talk a little about meditation," Arien posited. "How come every time I try to go there, there's all these distractions? It's like, whatever it takes, until you have to give in."

"Ha. I think I have that one." Andy shifted his weight. "It's in the Bible. Be mindful, I don't give all that much weight to the Bible, Arien."

"No? Yeah, so?"

"I was always interested into comparing religions, but for me, LSD altered my understanding of what it is to be spiritual and that makes the Bible seem to take a wrong turn almost right away. But, there's still a lot of useful material in it."

"I'm glad you see it that way," Arien said with open hands.

"Well, there's a line in Genesis that refers to the angel with a flaming sword who guards the gates of Paradise." He waited for his words to sink in.

"I didn't see any angel."

"Arien, we're talking metaphor. It's not literal."

"You know a lot about this stuff," Arien commented, trying to make sense of what Andy said. He wasn't even sure he understood all the words Andy used.

"That's a distraction, right there, and *I* see an angel. He's sitting right here on this rock next to me."

Arien lowered his head. *He doesn't take me seriously.* "Stop it."

"Oh, Arien, think about it! The angel has a sword because God, according to the story, wants to keep you out of Paradise. Think of it this way, it isn't a place in the sky but the space between your ears. When I think of the meaning behind a flaming sword, I think of determination, of will. In old magic, the sword is the tool of your will. God's Will is the ultimate version of what was made in His image. The world responds to the Law that has been set down. I'm thinking, our nature, human nature is the sense of that Law."

Arien retraced the line in the dirt he'd made with the staff. "So, the distractions are stronger than me and that's the angel?"

"You're on it now, Brother. Think of the distractions as an intelligent force. It wraps around your thoughts like the ocean covers a sunken ship and that ocean I'm talking about is the entire universe! It knows how to match your very best, because this is the point where your best meets everything else. You just have to go deeper, under the words."

"Then, why even bother? It's hopeless!"

"No, it isn't. That's just it. But it takes real work. It's like a test of your commitment." Andy scratched a match just to hold it and watch it burn. "And, it may take something else. The Church calls it Grace. It could be just giving in, but if that's it, your timing has to be perfect, letting go not too soon, not too late. Maybe acid is a kind of physical Grace. Otherwise," he went on, "we may be forcing our way in, blasting by the angel with a pass that used to be reserved for the immortals. But I think I get Satchidananda. Sooner or later you still have to pick it up and do the work, live it out, stand for your true visions."

"Satcha–?" The name rang a bell for Arien, but he couldn't place it.

"Satchidananda."

A light breeze moved cooler, scented air up from the forest and canyons. It carried the cry of the resident red-tailed hawk. Arien took a deep breath and gazed out into the distance.

"About a year ago," Andy continued, "I was in New York City, and I saw a swami there, a really amazing guy – his name's so cool. It means, 'Essence, Consciousness, Bliss.' Anyway, he said you can't take a pill to become a doctor. Likewise, a pill won't make you a yogi. It takes ongoing study and practice."

"Well, these people here, the Trees – Andy, I think they want something out of me and I can't take a pill to catch up to that old man they followed. I wish I could. Besides, doesn't what I want count for something?"

"Let's look at it another way. I think the difference between us is basically this: I may know a lot about the myths, the Mysteries, I've read a lot of books and take tons of notes. I've made it my life to study it since I left college, too, and Otter's great to bounce off of, because he's so there and must have been born just to make connections, but you, Brother, you don't have to read about it. You're probably living it and you're making it look easy! People respond to something you've got even if they don't know that's what's happening." He stopped to gaze intently into Arien's deep green eyes. "You know that's right, don't you? And, it doesn't hurt you that you're so fucking beautiful. It's a given, like the surroundings. Catch my drift?"

"So, who am I?"

"Ah, the age-old question." Andy chuckled to himself. "I'm working on it myself, Bro. The key may have to do with a man's purpose. Now you – you're still a mystery, really. I've been going through various archetypes."

"Andy, you make me feel stupid." Arien twisted the end of the staff into the dirt.

"Nah, this is not so hard to follow, Man. The philosopher, Plato, brought out the idea that the Gods and their myths are archetypal people and events that are close to the core of what it means to be human. They set the tone or the pattern." Andy helped himself to the second doobie and another match from the pile and struck it. They both took a good hit. "Where was I?" He laughed.

"Uh, archetypes?"

"Oh yes. I can give you an easy example," he went on, blowing out a cloud of smoke with his next words. "Eros, the son of Venus, Goddess of love; when you're struck by his arrow madness takes over. You get dizzy and crazy and the one you love is the most perfect creature in the world, and you feel like you're the only person alive to see it and feel it just like that, so, it has to be totally true, you know? Nothing else matters. That's an archetype."

Arien took another, long draw on the joint and held it out to take away.

"I'll give you another. When I say, think of a drunk, who do you see?"

"Not you, Andy."

"Righteous!" he agreed. "But you see somebody in your head, right? And, you know, that's basically the same guy everywhere; that drunken guy is the same in every country. We all recognize his face. He's an archetype, too, but in this case it's not a God or Goddess but a demon." Andy's next hit was a little easier. He seemed to contemplate his exhale. "Now, these Gods and demons live inside of us but they are older than we are and they know the ropes. Think of it, they've been around forever and we live only for a short stack of decades. It's extremely hard to outsmart them and get your balance back if they ever get hold of you. Rub your bottle the right way and they pop out like genies. Sit on that bottle too tight and sometimes it explodes in your face and fucks up your whole life. And if they do take you, pray it's the Gods and not the demons that own your body."

"Wow. You got a great stoned rap, Dude," Arien laughed. "So, Andy, you're looking at arch-uh-archetypes to make sense of me?" Arien was pretty high at this point and his friend's brainy lecture was becoming a comfort, though he had no idea how much of this he'd be able to remember, later.

"Well, yes." Andy, curiously, looked suddenly stricken.

"What's the matter, now, Dude?"

"You don't get it, do you?"

"Get what, Andy?"

Andy looked away. "I love you, damn it. You're the most beautiful kid I've ever seen in my life. It's making me crazy." There were tears on Andy's cheeks. "I don't know what feels worse, being with you or not being with you."

Andy had been sitting close, but now he leaned into Arien, put an arm around him, and softly sobbed.

"Dude, I love you, too, but…" Now another issue clamored. He'd allowed this twenty-something man to get very close, maybe closer than any man would ever be again. His thoughts turned to the creek and the wet body on him and his intensely erotic experience there. He hadn't mentioned it to Tina. He expected he would at some point. Not that he thought it should matter. He was just being himself on one more adventure.

"But…" Andy echoed.

"I love you like my own brother, Andy. Not my girl." Arien had both hands wrapped around the staff. He realized he'd yet to study it. The way the vines - there were three of them - wound around each other and over a thin sapling trunk, or a branch at the center, was quite remarkable. It felt trim, tight and solid. It appeared unlikely it grew that way, but Arien couldn't be sure. The top was bound with leather lacing that ended in a setting for a smooth, mostly round stone, like a beach stone, dark black with a natural, white-quartzite eye in it. The bottom part of the staff had a hardwood plug about an inch in diameter at the base, and tapering up, lashed again with leather to attach it. It felt good to hold but Arien had to wonder if it ultimately belonged to him.

Andy pulled a bandana out of his pocket to wipe his nose and took a deep breath. He stuck his index finger to the center of his forehead and said, "This!"

Arien gazed up at him, quizzically.

"You're this. I call him, 'Watcher,' but your heart's attached. He's past, future, present. He could be a girl, too, for that matter. I'm thinking of a line that was inscribed on the Temple of Isis, in ancient Egypt. *'I, Isis, am all who ever was, is, or shall be. No mortal man hath ever me unveiled.'* At least that's the way I see what we are. The day-to-day is likely an illusion, a dream." His expression was suddenly numinous, passionate.

"Right on," Arien said with his futuristic inflection, and he smiled.

The hike down the trail was thoughtful though hurried. A dark blot gathered in the deepening gray and the air cooled some more. They'd gathered up the matches and last doobie and smoked it on the way. There wasn't much conversation. At one point where the width of the trail allowed, Andrew walked with his good arm around Arien's shoulders. Its weight bore a curious accumulation of emotions, where Arien found himself connecting with hurting at a very deep level. Ouch!

Pain can be used, Arien thought. It welled up from him as if packaged like an instruction. He felt gratitude for this closeness yet didn't know if he should be ashamed or joyful. It warmed both his body and his heart and he accepted that was partly who he was, both a body and a heart. It did, however, add an element of worry. Arien apprehended a gathering host of powerful forces that both beckoned to and threatened him, as a towering desert mesa might intimidate an experienced climber.

Raindrops barely followed behind them when they strode into camp where a good many folks were hanging out under the tarp of the kitchen lean-to. Otter and Tina were there, and Jeff, who got up from a make-shift bench of boards and wooden fruit crates, to come over and hug Arien in greeting. "We brought back a bunch of food and stuff," he said. He handed Arien a Hershey bar. It was larger than expected. Arien immediately tore into it. He was glad people fussed constantly about the righteous diet but made little protest over sweets. White, processed sugar occasionally came up for criticism, as it had once in a while at Page Street, but exceptions were always made. The chocolate was a delicious rush on top of his high.

Arien felt a pair of eyes against the back of his head. He turned to see Oak looking him over. The big man was sitting on a stump. Arien missed him on the way in. He nodded, making the connection and went over to him. "I'm very sorry about Tree," Arien said. "I was just getting to know him."

Oak's eyes were rimmed with red. He regarded the staff the young fellow held. "What does it feel like to hold that?" he asked.

The question was unexpected. Arien thought for a moment that fell suddenly quiet. Everybody listened to hear what he would say. He forced his way through a sneaker-wave of stoned paranoia. "It's knar-knarly, Dude. Sometimes it feels like my hand's touching the ground but I'm holding it right here." He raised it up. "And sometimes, it's like, I'm not sure where my fingers are. It's hard to explain." He stuck it easily in the crook of his arm to get at the remainder of the chocolate.

Oak daubed an eye with the back of a fist and blew some air through his mucous. It was almost a snort. But his grieving demeanor relaxed a little. There was a subtle but immediate change in the energy. Arien pulled out his bandana and Oak accepted it to blow his nose. Most didn't seem to notice but Otter did, and he smiled when Oak handed it back and Arien just returned it to his pocket. Tina grinned at Jeff. Andy was looking out into the rain.

The shower let up after dark. The night air was cool, damp and richly redolent of everything that makes a forest. The fire was built up to a crackling roar and everybody assembled around it for a council.

"May I have the staff," Oak asked Arien. "It's custom to pass it at our councils." Arien readily complied. Oak took it and held it up, quieting everyone. "Brother Arien has said it's time for them to continue their journey," Oak opened, in a voice deep and resonant. "We have been with the staff from the beginning. We need decide if we're letting it go on without us."

Otter stood alongside Arien and Tina. His eyes met Arien's. They held the same, steady gaze they'd ended an earlier talk with. "They're going to want to follow you, Arien," he'd said. This was shaping up to prove it. Arien told him he would make up his mind later, and Otter said he hoped it would be an answer everybody could live with. Now, some resolution was indeed taking form. Arien thought of Tina's contribution to that discussion, to just let things play-out and see. She'd made it sound so simple.

"To begin with, I put the question to the Stand," Oak said, turning. It was an endearing segue, though Arien fretted that might become his name among them. It was not the first time he'd heard it.

Jeff responded promptly. "We would surely be a sight rollin' down the road," he held. Oak raised the staff, reminding him to take it. "Oh, right." Jeff set it before him, folding his hands over the top as Arien did, and then seeming momentarily distracted by it, he continued, "We need to think about it and the attention from the townies and the heat."

Clayboy loaded the fire with an armload of damp wood. It settled, popped, crackled and billowed with dense gray smoke. The light of the flames shone through on focused faces. Willow raised his hand for Jeff to pass the staff to him. "We have food stamps, some money and supplies, but that won't buy us tickets to this Woodstock thing," Willow said. "Where would we go?"

There were murmurs, several hands raised. It was passed to Arien. He rested it over a shoulder. "I think we'll hardly be noticed," he said. "There'll be a zillion people, and busses and vans and cars and helicopters, even. And the gate will get crashed. We won't need tickets, People, believe me." He wore a near-devious grin. "But, we don't want to be late or we won't get there and yes, we do need to think about how we take the road."

A palpable sigh ran among them. Arien was seeing it their way. They would all go to Woodstock. A few of the listeners were joyfully tearful.

"Now, I have a question. Who is 'the Stand?' I hope that's not *my* name."

A few nods and chuckles circulated. "Ha. It's all of you who came in the painted bus," Aspen said. "You're the Stand, the Stand of Trees!"

"That's fair," Arien retorted, "because I like my own name."

Oak was grinning now. "Might you consider a new last name, then?" he suggested. "How about Arien Wood?"

"I got that plenty," Arien said. Andy smirked back, Tina covered her face and some of the little kids laughed though it was debatable they knew what was funny.

"Uh oh," Oak interjected. "No, it has to be dignified, if that's where this is going." He brushed the front of his overalls with his big hands and scattered the thought with stout fingers. Otter appeared to like seeing that. Oak's laughter came easily. "Let's see," Oak continued, gesturing for Arien to pass him the staff. "We can add an 's.' Arien Woods? Then there's Arien Forest, or, how about, Grove?"

"Like a Sacred Grove," Andy added, seriously.

"Arien Grove," Arien considered.

"That's it!" Aspen called, clapping. There was applause and a few cheers went up. A tall, serious, dark-haired young fellow with a full beard, whose name Arien had only recently heard, stepped up with a tightly bound bundle of wild sage that smoldered like a Jamaican spliff. He waved it over Arien and all around him to encircle his body in its pleasing, aromatic smoke. "May your name be blessed and loved and remembered," he intoned.

Arien nodded his head shyly. "Wow. Rad! Thanks, Hawthorne," he said. Then he leaned toward Tina. "This might make you Mrs. Grove," he confided. She poked him in the ribs, and they giggled and swatted at each other.

25 — "I may be officially crazy now"

With everyone working hard it took two and a half days to load up the camp. Most of it was densely packed in the long rack on top of their worn but worthy International school bus.

Willow took charge of a group to camouflage the site. After over a month of continuous use by the Tree Family it took some doing but it was agreed by early afternoon on the last day that a good job had been performed. The area looked natural and unmolested. They'd taken ash from the fire pit and scattered it, except for a small jar of it that Oak said they would take to Woodstock, for Tree, along with a lock of his hair. The ring of stones were scattered all about and the blackened sides turned down, fresh duff, leaves and branches covered the camp and some of the moms and children had re-planted tufts of grass taken elsewhere to make even the trail there appear unused.

Oak grappled with the logistics. It had always been his job, along with Tree, who previously decided things in their commune that were not practical to drag-out for a consensus of the whole group. Now it was Oak, Arien, Willow and Aspen who were deferred to. On the first day of packing up Oak sent Willow, one of Willow's girlfriends, Laurel, and Jeff off in Van Gogh to bring up the other vehicles they had available, from where they'd been stashed. They showed up with one. It was a standard GMC step van that would be the rolling kitchen. It carried an LP gas stove, ice boxes, and a set of racks to hold canned, sacked and boxed bulk-items. There were also mechanical and building tools. The other vehicle was an old Willy's Jeep wagon that would have taken too much time for needed repairs so it was left behind.

The bus itself, a 42-passenger, had all the seats behind the first set of four in the front removed for carpeting and people to stretch-out on bed rolls at night. There were hand-sewn curtains over the windows that hid the travelers from the eyes of 'townies.' For all, a casual observer would see only the driver and a few people up front, and the invasion of grocery or hardware stores would be planned discretely in advance to be kept at a minimum.

Now there would be three vehicles. Otter suggested they not travel too close together, but keep each other in sight and plan places to rendezvous ahead of time if they became separated. When all was ready everyone stood around waiting for something, eyes fixed on the young fellow with the staff. Oak stood near. He leaned to Arien's ear. "Can you give us a blessing?" he whispered.

"Oh, wow. Yeah. Uh, Hawthorne? Would you do that thing with the sage for us?"

"That thing with the sage," Oak repeated, disbelieving.

People chuckled approvingly. The tall fellow appeared pleased to hear his name called. He stepped out from a cluster of friends and pulled a fresh smudge bundle from a small canvas backpack, obviously ready. Otter snapped the match to light it. "Blessings Be!" Hawthorne announced when the edge of the herbal bundle flared up. He held it briefly flaming and then jerked it in the air to blow out the flame. It transformed into a small cloud of smoke that Hawthorne carried down the trail past the step van, the bus, and on to Van Gogh, with everyone following in single file. Arien was impressed with the simple beauty and dignity of the procession. Aspen had a pair of little brass bells. She held them by ribbons tied to their handles. They bounced together as she walked, jingling along the way.

"From Sunday, who enlightens our minds as you reveal our way," Hawthorne intoned with his steps. And, Monday, be our lamp in the darkness, and Tuesday, protect and defend us. May Wednesday ensure good passage, and Thursday keep us together, and may Friday fill our hearts with love and Saturday, Old Father, may you bring us home." Hawthorne made sure he stood between the wind and the VW, to catch it in the smoke, and then he circled clockwise, and doubled back to the van and the bus where they began.

When all had circled the bus there was a group Thank You for this place in the forest that was for a time their home. People left tokens, pennies, crystals, stones. The Trees were finally ready to depart.

"Why don't you take it, Otter?" Jeff asked, with an upended hand by the driver's door. Otter shrugged. "Ride shotgun," he said to Aspen, who stood with him. He got in while Arien had to console himself with the realization that Otter hadn't been behind the wheel yet. So, he snuggled with Tina in their accustomed spot, leaning back against their duffels. Some bubble gum was passed around. Jeff pulled his sneakers off and stretched out opposite them. Andy, his back against the doors, poking at his teeth with the little white plastic toothpick out of his Swiss Army knife, regarded Arien with curiosity. Arien gazed back, waiting.

"I've been wondering what you were into in, uh, 1990." He turned the small, red object over in his hand.

"Deep shit," Arien answered, but with a twinkle in his eye. He felt secure in the moment and they were on the road again. The miles between here and the greatest rock concert in history were closing. This is all that mattered now.

Van Gogh swayed and lurched. It probably moved faster than it should have over the rough, mostly downhill track.

"Guess I'll wait 'till we're on the highway to catch some Zs," Jeff said, sitting up.

"No, I mean, what were you into? You seem to be into music, man. Any bands you like?"

"Traffic," Arien said, grinning. "Stevie Windwood." He poked Tina in the ribs and she sprung at him. They grabbed at each other, laughing.

"Help me, Jeff." Andy said, shaking his head with a strained smile.

"Shall I tie him up so you can torture him for information?"

"Maybe Otter has some truth serum in his pharmacy kit," Tina contributed.

"I have just the thing," Otter said over his shoulder.

"I'll get it!" Tina said. She struggled to stand and then to crawl over to the front seat but Arien cried, "No!" and tickled at her until she fell back down on top of him with more laughing and tussle.

"Ah, children!" Andy sighed.

"Daddy's gonna spank you if you don't behave!"

"Then why should I?" Tina laughed.

When they settled down into a cuddle Andy tried again. "What are your favorite movies, Arien?"

"Oh Dude, you're gonna love Star Wars. Luke Skywalker's cool. And, Obewan Kenobe, R2-D2, and Chewbacca – Ha! Get me a light saber and I'll fight against the Evil Empire and Darth Vader! And, if he's closing in, we'll go into star drive in the Millennium Falcon to escape certain doom." Arien thrust-and-parried with the air. "I loved that stuff." The van grew silent as passengers tuned in to Arien's report. Otter slowed it down some to take the ruts and bumps easier.

"What's he talking about?" Aspen asked.

"Listen." Otter whispered.

"And, E.T. – the Extra Terrestrial. ET call home," Arien quoted in ET's cute, froggy voice. "Rad flick." He reached to take Tina's hand. "I'll take you to see 'em, Babe."

"What else?" Jeff asked.

Arien chuckled to himself. "Back to the Future! Wow. Imagine that. Tina, in that flick this dude, Marty, goes back to see his parents!" He grew more serious. "But that's how you know it's the movies.

Marty changes everything, and they all live happily ever after. Damn. Well, my fave was Star Wars, anyway. And, the Empire Strikes Back and Return of the Jedi. Awesome flicks. You had to wait years between them, though.

"Did you ever see 2001?" Otter asked.

"No. I think I heard of it."

"Jesus, Arien. You have to see that one," Andy recommended. "Best space movie ever made and maybe the best movie ever made."

"Better than Beach Blanket Bingo?" Otter asked.

"Better than Gone With the Wind?" Tina chimed in.

"Just wait 'till you see Star Wars,' Dudes."

Aspen leaned toward Otter. "Is he talking about movies that haven't been made yet?" She asked him.

In Nebraska, the caravan stopped for the night at a state campground called Johnson Lake, which was off of the highway. Some of the family grabbed their rods and went down to the lake to fish. Others concentrated on putting dinner together. Arien felt it was his duty to pitch in. He could hardly believe himself. He actually wanted to be involved and jumped into the tumble of the people from the bus and the step van. For the next two hours he washed and chopped vegetables, collected scraps for disposal, and even carried a poop bucket to the latrine to pour its contents and rinse it out.

The love and gladness that was beamed back at him was worth more than if he had been paid in real dollars. It seemed to pour into his body, energizing and refreshing him. It looked as if Tina was at odds to keep up. At one point, Arien told her to take a break. She wouldn't, and he sensed it might have had something to do with all the energy and attention engulfing him. He caught Otter's approving glance as his friend approached with two respectable fish, a decent walleye and a white bass that would have made anyone proud. "This can help flavor the stew," he said.

Andy got involved, too. But, he seemed to hang back with a collection of stolen glances. Arien suspected his shorts only aggravated the issue. He'd borrowed them earlier to go swimming. They were as spare as a pair of men's briefs and left him feeling exposed like the classic dream of being naked in school. But Andy's attention held a yearning, flattering as well as unsettling. These couple of months among people who behaved as they were, without mask or guile, invited a fascination that made his head swim.

Oh, but Otter provided the right amount of ballast. "I couldn't miss it," he opened. "You're royalty, man."

225

Arien said, "Dude." It wasn't a question. It merely acknowledged what was heard. He brushed the fine, sandy hair out of his eyes with one hand while the other lowered a spoon into his bowl of stew.

"Now, Arien," he whispered, "gather that energy and don't spend it on your ego. Gather it about you and wear it like old Tree's cloak." People sat everywhere. Some were spread out over blankets on the ground. There wasn't enough space at the picnic table where Otter sat opposite Arien, with Andy sitting alongside.

Tina didn't say anything. She blew over her spoon to cool the next bite. She listened.

Arien was about to ask why, but the thought only opened to the answer. It was like a voice he'd heard before, some time ago. Where?

So you will grow strong enough, the Voice said, almost as if it were audible. It was more a sense of the meaning, a few flashes of light and staccato pulses of feeling interpreted by his own thoughts. It may as well have been a foreign language, but perfectly intelligible. The rush startled him. His head spun. He stood, suddenly gasping for air as his heart went thumping in his throat.

"What's the matter?" Tina called after him.

"Whoa!" Arien sat back on the bench, facing away from the table.

"Breathe, Arien," Otter instructed. "Don't forget to breathe."

"What happened, Otter?" Andy followed, very concerned.

"Only Arien knows that, but you were gone, huh? The breath helps ground you."

Amazing. The dude is so right there. He turned, flinging his legs one-by-one, back over the bench and under the table. They looked at him. "I may be officially crazy, now," he told them, with a sheepish grin. "Somebody just spoke to me in my head."

"What did he say?" both Andy and Tina asked together.

"He agrees with Otter."

In the twilight, Arien skipped stones over the water. He actually had to say he wanted to be alone because people tended to follow him around. One, two, three, four, he counted, five, as the skipper slipped over the placid surface. He rummaged in his head, just above the silver water. A fish jumped up and smacked the surface on its return. Mosquitoes buzzed near the back of his neck. The evening felt close and warm, a nice change from the still-freezing nights in the Medicine Bow. He found the place that matched his thoughtful mission. It transported him to the spot off the trail at Tree Family's Camp where he'd drawn a line in the dirt. What side of the line am I? Who is the Effector and what is the Effected? There is motion. There is will. He could visualize that tiny, incredibly potent ball of force he'd seen tripping. There is duality. It is a focus of forces. Focus. Focus. Arien shuddered with a sudden inkling of an enormous, lurking power that could easily snuff his candle. How can I be gentile to what may kill me? He meekly thought. Then, he shuddered again, feeling so exposed. It will kill me, he owned.

Arien inwardly smiled, clenching his teeth, facing his death. "I dare you, fucker!" He felt it stalking him from the other side of every breath. Such a novel consideration this was! He'd never truly bothered with the idea until now, when it dawned upon him that he had so much more to live for than he'd ever thought possible.

He walked to the edge of the water and looked down into the occult calmness, certain that in the barest natural illumination he could still make out his reflection. The force in him, that was surely his; his life, his awareness, his focus and an inexplicable yearning, welled up like magma in a long-sleeping volcano. I'm not even stoned!

"Oh God, whatever you are, help me. I can't do it myself." Arien spoke aloud to the silent, brooding lake. He felt the pricking, bloodsucking mosquitoes, one and then another, sink their tiny spears into his back through the T-shirt. He resisted an inclination to twitch, turn and swing at them. He was them. They needed him and his need to connect with that, All of That, and with everything that made it up, froze his body like a stone.

He sank deeply into the lake of himself. If I don't choose you I'm nothing. I'm outside, forever, he clearly thought. You die in me. It's death. Who am I to kill you?

But in this question you have done it again. It was the "Voice," the thing that was more a flashing of light and feeling and as it coursed freely through him he knew what it said. *Accept the words you are knowing,* it went on. *They are obvious. Do not be afraid. It is the choice you must make but you will.*

Arien fairly reeled with all this. What or how was far again beyond any previous experience, other than the fantastic adventures he'd had with LSD. And then, on the other hand, it was so matter-of-fact. When? He asked it, barely believing his own boldness. When will I make the choice? He pressed. When I will live – or, or die?

Jesus, he mused. It's the same thing. One is on the back of the other!

"I'm afraid of being so big!" he admitted to the water's edge.

The mosquitoes were bad enough, the Stand, minus Otter and Aspen, spent the night in Van Gogh. Jeff had some netting he'd saved from an old Army surplus jungle bivouac and it came in handy now. He hung it over the opened center doors so folks would have air along with some respite. Arien lay awake on top of his bedding for a long while, staring up into the darkness, contemplating his strange experience, and probing his inner life for signs of any madness. There didn't appear to be any, but, how is one to know? Every so often a dude hears a story about someone who flips out. They hear voices. Did they know they'd flipped? Can I tell the difference between a good voice and a bad one? He wondered. Can I tell you to beat it if you tell me to kill someone?

No answer pended. He knew he was alone, if being with his friends could be called that. Tina's hands were wrapped around his bare shoulder, a tiny cushion to her soft cheek, her breath steady on his skin. Andy, on the other side, rested a foot against his. It seemed natural enough at first but it followed when Arien slightly moved. The pressure was the same! Surely, he sensed some electricity there. The tension held it fast. He stilled his breath on the back of a long exhale to resist the gathering erotic rush, and it slowed the beating of his heart. He remembered how it was done. Arien's senses quickened. He could hear the distant roar, like tumbling breakers on a far-away beach.

Andy was exceedingly still, but something of his yearning, his excruciating need and enormous torment broke through. "Oh, Brother, don't." Arien whispered into the darkness, more to comfort him than to stop him.

"Please?"

When Arien failed to answer he could feel the rhythm of the body beside him, and eventually the straining, tempered catharsis, and what may have been a sigh or a sob and then sleep.

Hell. He stood alone, feeling rushed. The motors purred at the periphery of Arien's hearing; Van Gogh, the bus and the step van. He'd finished relieving himself but he wasn't ready. His thought was how curious the Tree Family's vehicles ran without names. He mused it was likely that would change. He waited for someone to whoop at him. Hurry! We're all waiting for you! But no one did.

Arien lingered, indulging their deference. It seemed like everything that happened only gave him more. It was heady, all the little things that added up. His soiled clothes were still being replaced with clean; he barely thought of hunger or thirst and the need would be met, and probably the headiest of all were the small comforts, the sensual things, and the building erotic energy. How it fed his sense of himself! It was turning him on. His breathing came deeper.

"Oh, heck," he said to the back of the tree. "How I love you!"

Arien wore an unreadable face when he stepped up into the shotgun seat. Aspen had joined with the others in back, working through a tune on her dulcimer to the accompaniment of Andy's harmonica. Otter guided Van Gogh out of the campground and onto the highway. His vibe was a little unsettling. *Does he know?*

"Are you still hearing voices?"

Arien had to reel it backwards to bat away the paranoia. It took some facing up. The words to a Christmas song jingled around his head, *"He knows when you are sleeping / he knows when you're awake."*

"Otter, do you know what I'm thinking?"

"No, Arien."

It was a big relief to hear that. This 'connection' thing still had its privacy screens! But what about the *Other*, the one who'd spoken to him? Was that privy to everything?

If we are engaged I will know your thoughts and you will know mine.

Arien looked out at the passing countryside. *What is this voice? Who is it?*

Be still, and know, Arien was certain it said.

The music behind him fell silent.

"Otter, yes. But it's like a – a necklace. Yeah, a necklace of pictures in my head, and they're packaged with feelings, and they…"

Arien grasped for the words, "The pictures shoot through my mind, and they have the truth of something I did and remember." This was very hard for him to put together and say and he wasn't sure now if he had. "Do you know what I mean?"

"Yes, Arien, I think I do."

"Wow, man!" It was Andy. "You're channeling, man."

"Too weird. I may be losin' it, big way." Arien rubbed his hands together. Should I be scared?

"Man, there's this lady who does that. What's her name, Jane, Jane–?"

"Oh wow!" Tina chimed in. "Yeah, Jane Roberts!"

"Cool, Tina. Seth. She does Seth. Do you know his name, Arien?"

"Seth?"

"No, man, the name of the person you're channeling?"

Of course he'd wondered about that. It was all too 'out there,' anyway.

"I don't know that one," Otter admitted.

Arien looked at him. "But, do you know any?"

"Jamie Sun told me to get in touch with my spirit guide, once. Then his name just came to me. Kylian, that's his name."

"Dude, you're so on it, no matter what it is." Arien said with genuine admiration.

"I wish, Arien. There's a lot I may not be very on about."

"No. You're on it, Dude. Trust me."

Otter's begrudging grin was met with Arien's big, grateful smile. Then Arien said, "Damn."

"Yeah?"

"I just wonder why we bother. Everybody already knows everything. They already are everything."

"But they don't know it," Jeff finally said. "They're dumb as rocks."

"They already know everything!" Arien protested.

"They don't know that they know, then," Andy pushed back.

"What do they know?" Otter pointedly asked.

Arien didn't answer, drawing a total blank.

"What do they know, Arien? Do you know?"

He felt as put on the spot as he could be. He felt, well, dumb as a rock.

"If everyone knows what you say they know, why don't you know what it is?" That sparked some laughter.

It's not for my head! Arien felt dizzy.

False, the Voice insisted. *If it were not for your head you would not be having this conversation.*

I don't want to make any mistakes.

Then you will not learn anything new.

Arien felt himself back away. It's so clear! But I do want to learn. He felt his own duplicity here. He might just as well have bitten its hand. It was like his book was open to the numbered plate at the center-fold. The Voice could see right through him and knew that he knew. Arien was a little afraid. But then, he felt the Other's inward smile.

You are learning.

"Arien? Are you with us?"

"Yeah, Otter."

"So?"

"Otter, what's medicine?"

Otter was driving to the caravan's rear. The bus, in the lead, had just gone out of sight and the step van was about a quarter-mile ahead. The road had a crispy, new look. It rolled on through heaving plains that stretched to the horizons of every direction. A bright sun cascaded through the windshield to suffuse swinging osprey feathers in a golden glow among its finest filaments, like the soft brilliance of an Aladdin lamp turned down as low as possible without going out.

"What do you mean?"

"They dispense it at the infirmary?" Tina presented the obvious with a smarmy grin. She looked up at him with the face he loved to kiss. Her eyes danced for him.

"I don't think that's what it is, Babe." But he suspected she already knew that.

"Put it in a context," Andy suggested.

Arien spoke slowly as if he were reading off of a page. "This constitutes the first lesson in which the medicine has a purpose," he said, "and the wise one knows what it is. Nor is it to be regarded as a purpose contrary to the law of life."

"Wow, man. That sounds magical or alchemical. Don't you think so, Otter?"

"Sure."

Tina asked, "Where does that come from, Arien?"

"I'd like to know that, too," he said. "It was something he told me."

Iowa was an ocean of corn bridged with route 6's ribbon of pavement, where hurtling traffic on the road generally left Tree Family's caravan consigned to rear-view mirrors. The wide open plains seemed to gather closer here somehow. A sign on the roadside announced Chicago's distance, 350 miles.

"Wow," Jeff called, "first sign to the big city!"

"Didn't think I'd be this way again so soon," Andy said. "Last year at the Democratic Convention I managed to dodge the damn bullets and, boy, it was a blast." He rode up front with Jeff. Arien dropped his cigarette into the little green Coke bottle he held. It hissed as it soaked up residual brown liquid at the bottom. He stared into the rich, curling smoke in the bottle where his thoughts turned to their last stop, outside of Omaha. They'd turned off the highway back there to shop at a roadside stand offering early vegetables, and spying a grassy area under tall, spreading oak trees by a creek they'd corralled the vehicles to stretch and rest in the shade. The little ones got into a game of tag around the tree trunks and some of their elders had joined hands in a spontaneous circle. They called to Arien to join them. That he did, and during the OMs they chanted there came another one of those visions that could match an acid vision for its truth and clarity, only it came on quicker, though mercifully, with less of the intimacy than the murder of Blue Star had been.

He'd said nothing about it, having been stunned by the breadth of the experience, like something out of the movie they would make about it. And, there were so many ways to feel about his vision; he couldn't begin to describe it, especially to himself, without a great deal of contemplation and even a fair share of apprehension. At the time, there was no word from 'the Voice,' but the presence of the Being on the other side of his thoughts was sensed as given, as were the reasons why so many people came to this particular festival, with all its high expectations. Arien guessed some would leave Woodstock with less than they brought, ripped-off by their drug of choice, the rain, a lost item, a false expectation or whatever, while others would set forth from the hive like kindled flames, to venture into the world with little but their holy light. Arien grasped these people actually had a shot at something worthwhile. He used to wonder what that could be to the point of jumping off a bridge, or getting his hands on a pistol to blow his sorry brain away. Here, it dawned on him, big time. There it was again: polarities in action, maintaining a balance that runs through all things, from the most trivial of the mundane to the majesty of All That Is!

"Penny for your thoughts."

"Oh, Tina, it would take a billion." He sighed.

You are not alone, said the Voice.

"Will you take an IOU?"

"I'll have to check with the loan department." He laid the bottle down on the floor by a paper sack with grapefruit peelings and candy wrappers in it. He watched the tendrils of smoke diffuse into a gray haze inside the thick, green glass and mere wisps of it curl out, like the tentative sense of his place in the scheme of things.

"I think there'll be others like me at Woodstock."

"Maybe half a million?" Otter grinned. "I mean, you did say there will be a lot of people there."

Arien chuckled.

"Or, do you mean royalty?" Otter pressed on.

"I think so."

Otter nodded.

"Time travelers?" Tina asked.

"I don't know, but they'll be special somehow, like all of you."

"I suspect so," Otter mused, appearing impressed with the lad's diplomacy. He snapped a match to light a doobie and reached over folded legs to stick the match in the bottle. "You've infected us, you know?" He leveled his gaze into Arien's eyes. "Like, we all have our own bags, man, but for now they're hitched to yours. Ain't that right, people?" He took a deep hit and passed the doobie to Tina.

"Yes," Andy agreed, speaking over his shoulder. "You're such a sweet baby, Arien Grove. I hardly remember who I was without you and we have to protect you and see you get there in one piece."

"Shit, there's plenty of company who believe that now," Jeff added, with his eyes fixed on the road.

"Hmmm. Interesting to think of it that way," Otter said.

Arien had a toke and rocked his head back, closing his eyes. Van Gogh grew silent other than the beating of the motor. He didn't see Andy reach over the seat back for the doobie, wince in pain, and then try again with his good side. That was when Arien reached up and passed it with a little push from his thumb. His exhale was slow. He coughed. The rush swirled peacefully into a spontaneous meditation.

"Dudes, we're on this trip."

Tina laughed. "Good bud, Otter."

"No, not just to Woodstock," Arien corrected, "a trip through our heads and the world fucks with it. We're stronger than that."

"You're a cussin' yogi." Jeff said. Laughs went around.

You already know it is there, you just have to teach yourself. It was the Voice again. It held as tightly to the other side of his thoughts as the back to the face of a playing card. *When you are here you are God.*

Arien was shocked at first. This idea was too sudden, too unexpected.

You think this is blasphemy? Is this perhaps why the people of the world are afraid? Well, step out of there into Paradise.

Then God kills himself, Arien said to the Voice. Maybe this is why I'm afraid of him.

Does he really kill himself or does he free himself?

"Wow," he said out loud. "This pot's like food, Otter. It makes it possible for me to get there."

"Where are you going, kid?"

"Damned if I know, but I'm going. It is scary, though."

"Why? What's there to be afraid of?" Otter's tone was very earnest.

Arien scratched for the words. "It may be a test of my power, Dude. Maybe this is like a cross, like with Jesus or something. I think I get it! I must have known for a while, now, but it seems to be coming together."

"Watch out planet Earth!" Andy cried out.

"You kill me, Andy," Otter laughed. "Now, pass that food back to us."

"Whoa. It's so perverted!" Arien exclaimed.

Tina reached for the joint.

"What is?"

"The teaching. Stupid religion has it all mixed up."

"Ho!" Andy cheered. "The kid's a wise one. Isn't that what I've been saying all along?"

"Kinda, Andy. But it's not so easy to explain what I'm seeing." The roach was back in his fingertips, almost burning them. He took the last hit before it dissolved into brown, oily paper lip and ash. "I think, maybe, Christ fights with God. They're not on the same bus at all."

"Wow, how's that?" Tina asked.

Arien was 'hearing' the Voice again, *Believe that the world is truly ignorant of where you are,* it said. *Everyone must do it for himself. Your ability to be believed is not something you should trouble yourself with. For you are Everything. To whom does Everything address itself to? – To God in his infinite mercy. This is the great secret and why it must be so.*

"You just can't come out and say it. There's no easy way to say it and keep a trip together. It's just, just that everybody has to do it for themselves."

"Otter, pass me my shoulder bag, okay?"

Otter found Andy's bag near his bedroll there and complied. Andy pulled a hard-cover sketchbook out of it and began taking notes.

"I'm so young," Arien said, feeling green and tender in this intense a light. It wasn't the first time this thought had crossed his mind but rising to the occasion, whatever it was or was going to be, called for reserves he never dreamed he had. On the other hand, he sensed there was an urgent imperative to grasp and master it lest it crush him. That side was truly terrifying. He thought of the crazy people he'd seen in his life, the ones who talked to themselves in public and made utter, raving fools of themselves and how far they had always been from his pity. It was so much easier to laugh at them.

"So, Arien, let's back up. What's Christ's beef with God? Can't say I've ever heard that."

"Andy, God's the way everything is. You can't fight that because you *are* that, you know, Dude? But, Christ fights it anyway and doesn't accept it as it is. He kicks the game board and pieces hit the floor; some of them get broken and the game is never the same again."

"Wow!" Andy exclaimed. He wrote as fast as he could.

"It's where the rubber hits the road," Otter offered.

"Right, and where the thing goes up hill, or holds still in a river when the river wants to wash it down. It's always going against the flow."

Arien was offered another chance to drive after they crossed the border into Illinois. He readily accepted and pushed on past Peru, about dead center in the northern part of the state. There, they opted to leave the freeway for the two-lane highway that would run parallel to it all the way into Chicago. Van Gogh was the lead vehicle now. It was Oak's suggestion in Iowa that that they tighten their formation, keeping each other in sight, and if night approached without a planned stop, the VW would put itself up front, leaving the evening's logistical decisions up to its more nimble occupants. This would be especially important as the caravan moved into the eastern third of the country where everything got closer together.

Arien sure liked this. It was grounding to have a practical influence beyond being keeper of Tree Family's staff. He had to think in terms of sufficient space for parking and family activities, privacy, access to water and, if possible, bathroom facilities. It made him feel awfully grown-up. He would share his opinions with Otter, Tina, Andy and Jeff, and together come to a consensus.

"Matthiessen State Park is up ahead," Arien called, seeing the sign. "Starved Rock is a few miles further." Off to his right he could see glimpses of the tree-lined Illinois River as the road surface gained or lost altitude. It was nice country. They passed open fields and grassland, tidy farms with ancient sandstone outcrops and glacial erratics vying for lines of hedgerows and patches of woodland.

"Starved Rock," Tina said. "The map shows camping there."

Arien pulled over to the side of the road and waited as the bus and step van got onto the shoulder and crept up behind. "There's a turn up ahead that heads down to the river. I'd like to scope it out."

"Go for it, Man," Otter agreed.

Tina, next to him, bobbed her head, Jeff shrugged and Andy waved his hand. Arien got out of the car and walked up to the driver's window of the bus. Willow slid it open to thrust his face out.

"Hang here while we check out the turn off. If we don't like it we can go on to the state park."

"Okay, Grove."

Arien raised his hand like a traffic cop to the folks in the step van, and then held up the open fingers of both hands. They flashed their lights.

Rad. He clambered back behind the wheel and headed for the turn.

The road went down by the river as Arien expected it would. He guessed it might terminate at the state park, but before coming to it, there was a dirt drive that passed over a cattle guard and continued down to a perfect spot by the riverside. It looked like private property. There were no buildings in sight. There was a broad, flat, grassy area that was just right for the vehicles and a clustered mix of black oak saplings and sumac appeared to offer a reasonable screen for a modest fire.

"What a nice place!" Tina exclaimed.

"Damn. Good call!" Otter praised, peering out a side window.

"He knew where to go," Jeff chimed in.

"Aw, Van Gogh's got a good nose, don't you, Van Gogh?" Arien patted the instrument panel. He stopped the little bus where he could stare out at the river. It was fairly broad from here. It reminded Arien a little of the Willamette, above Portland and the falls. The river was thickly lined with a variety of hardwoods but the clearing at the bank here provided a fine view and ready access.

Arien leaned over the steering wheel and took a deep breath of river-scented air. The late afternoon was warm and humid and his clothes stuck to his body. He gazed longingly at the water as the motor idled.

"Y'all get out, now," Jeff said. "I'll go back for the others."

"You're alright, Jeff!" Andy praised. "I don't care what they say about you."

Arien's grateful smile was apparently all Jeff needed. He hopped in eagerly after Arien got out and soon Van Gogh was working its way up to the road.

"I forgot my bathing suit," Arien said, hesitating.

"Forget it!" Andy called, stripping off his clothes.

"Dude, you just can't wait to see me naked."

"It's annoying how right you always are, Arien."

Arien caught Tina's glance. He had no doubt she knew of Andy's cruel and intractable problem. Everybody must have by now, though no one had brought it up. The signs hung out like flags on a battleship. It was likely he'd even confided with Otter, but as long as he held up, and he seemed to be doing that alright, he was left to resolve it on his own. Arien's thought was time, patience, and everybody's love would heal the pain in poor Andy's good heart.

The four of them were still in the water when the vehicles pulled in with cries of delight and squealing kids. Jeff stripped down faster than a super hero in a phone booth as he ran for a large rock that hung above the bank to cannon ball off of it. He was followed by several others, Willow, Clayboy, Aspen, Hawthorne and one of the mommies, "Cassie," for Cascara, a single-mom with her seven year-old boy, Wally. Oak had his overalls rolled up and sat at the edge, sinking his feet in. Soon, more people got in to swim. Myrtle waded in with a bottle of Dr. Bronner's and her auburn hair was shortly white with suds. Willow joined her with a bar of soap.

The current was fairly mild where they were. Arien stroked out with Tina to deeper spots. He was no Olympian, but he swam well enough and felt confident in water. He and Tina laughed, splashed, cavorted and kissed each other. And, when they finally came out of the river, and stood glistening in the golden light of a lingering late afternoon sun, he felt totally washed and refreshed and from there it was a short ride to the very edge of rapture.

He held Tina's hands and gazed into her love-lit eyes, gently swaying with the delicious puffs of air against his skin. From a corner of his awareness he felt the congregate gaze of the whole tribe upon them, but he gathered that also to himself, and smiled. "My cup runneth over," he whispered to her, taking King David's joyful words as his own.

The sky practically swirled above them when a stirring of his sex called for urgent attention. It began to swell. They were not in a private place! His exhale slowed his heart's rhythm, as he had done before and that only partly worked this time. What held him, standing confident and proud, were the blissful, loving and desirous feelings projected by the people there who were not voyeurs but rather fallen into an adoring chorus of eager devotees. They'd internalized the spark of sun caught by the silver OM hanging from his neck. They saw the perfectly beautiful, wholesome girl at his side with her firm breasts, nubile figure and long, wavy, golden hair.

And Myrtle found herself standing by a rich vine of early-flowering honeysuckle and she had the wits and time to weave a pair of crowns which she came up to set on the couple's dancing heads as they stepped and swayed in place. That got Otter to rummage in Van Gogh and when he came out he bore the water buffalo horn in one hand and the Tree Family's staff in the other, which he handed to Andy to bear. Together, they approached. Otter placed the horn's chord over Arien's head and draped it by his side as Arien inserted an arm while taking the staff from Andrew in the same motion, but never removing his eyes from Tina's. It was fluid and graceful. And then, how the murmurs went around with Oak's nearly stunning realization that today was the first day of summer!

Andy freely wept. "You are so beautiful!" He cried, and tears of joy and deep connection went around among them all, mixed with the wafting cloud of aromatic sage Hawthorne produced. And then Clayboy and Willow came to the edge of the circle with their drums while Aspen returned from the bus with her dulcimer. She picked a haunting melody out of it, evocative of a most ancient song. The girls hummed and the boys began to chant, hand-in-hand in a spontaneous, dancing circle.

"I wish Tree were here to see this!" Oak declared, his eyes brimming over.

"Oh, he's here," Myrtle told him. "He's right here with us."

And then the boy with the honeysuckle crown turned on his heel, working the staff into the earth at his feet, and lifted the horn to his lips, he took a deep breath, threw his head back and pushed out a long, searing, tenor note. He felt it vibrate his very bones.

The chanting and drumming stopped as the note flew around the area and over the river's ripple and the silence that came after lasted. Arien perceived he'd blasted open the deepest vein of love in the mountain of life. It bubbled up in his breast and shone out of him and gave everything he saw a golden-yellow cast. The greens of the foliage became greener and their scents became more pronounced, the sky's blue was deeper, the children who began to run around him and Tina giggled as they circled, like little planets, and their happy peals resonated, ever so subtly.

Arien now recalled something the Voice had said, *"...step out of there into Paradise,"* when Clayboy, among all who were present, was the first to approach. For a mere moment he stood uncertain, searching, and then breaking through his hesitation, sighing, wrapped his arms around Arien in a vice-like bear hug, as if to squeeze the very air from his lungs. Arien was sure something passed between their hearts. He could hear their beatings sync together for an instant. And then everyone came up to join in the hug, to touch him, to kiss him; to draw strength, energy, love. Arien swooned. Their need was so great, and these were the wide awake! My God! But as once before at Crater Lake, he fell into the Source and found it infinitely deep and inexhaustible.

Would you bleed for them? Arien surely heard the Voice ask him.

Must I die, now?

No. You must live!

Then my last tear, my final sweat and squirt of cum and drop of blood is theirs.

Arien didn't know what it was, but he knew it was there. It had a presence like a living person, and he apprehended it by its charisma. He heard the "Ohs!" and "Whoas!" and "Check that out!" before he saw it but he knew it was there before he looked up to take it in. It had a sound, of pattering droplets that rode on a lack of sound, an audible hush. The diminutive cloud appeared by the river, and drifted up to stop and hang suspended over the assembled people there, a foggy-white balloon with a tinge of gold on its sunny side, barely a man's length over everyone's head, and a steady mist rained down out of it, evoking the tentacles of a jelly fish. It gently cooled the heads and shoulders of the astonished witnesses. Arien had never seen anything like it or even heard of anything like this, but it was right there! It was no bigger than the compressed circle of people. It hovered there for a few precious moments. Some folks fell to their knees; others looked up at it with upraised hands and cried.

And then the cloud moved away, dissolving into the ambient air. The warmth of the afternoon refilled the space it had occupied and everyone stood there, dumfounded.

Slowly, Arien and Tina made their way through the tight group of folks to where they'd left their clothes. Everybody wanted to touch them and follow along as they passed. It was very strange, and yet Arien understood it because the energy that flowed through him was as natural as gravity. It was a rush, coming to Otter, who also had to hug him and who shook his head in amazement. "I swear, brother, I saw traces, just like on acid – I still see them when you look at me!"

"Tell me about it, Otter," Andy raved. "Man, your aura was pure gold! It was plainly there, like a –" He stopped, wiping tears from his eyes with the back of his hand.

"I'm glad I know you, too, Brother," Arien said to him. "And I love you very much." He watched as his words sank in. Andy daubed his eyes with the back of his hands.

Somebody passed Arien the cut-offs he'd worn that day, and he burst out laughing as he stepped into them.

"What's so funny, Arien Grove?" Willow asked.

"I've had to shut down the most awesome hard-on in my life, and now I can let it happen!"

The roar went all around. People doubled over in merriment and shrieks of laughter. But it was Clayboy who found the presence of mind to ask Arien if it was safe here for the drums to come out tonight.

"It's safe," he said.

Of course a fire pit was already there. It was nestled in a hollow of the gray, striated sandstone that was all over the area. There was even a stack of wood next to it. Otter told Arien that if this place were any more suited to them it would have had an ice cream concession. They were obviously squatters in an old, well-used campsite and it provided ample room for that night's party. Before it could happen though, the back doors of the step van were opened and the kitchen set up. Oak was on top of all that. He made sure a latrine trench was dug, too. It was in a sheltered area up by the barbed-wire fence that straddled the entrance. With everybody pitching in, it came together pretty quickly, except for the more constricted sleeping accommodations, the Tree Family camp hummed along much as it had in the Medicine Bow.

Dinner was black beans and rice with Tamari sauce. In spite of the protests, Arien helped serve. It wasn't all spirit of service, either. He had too much energy to sit around, and he was enjoying everyone so much this night he turned down Jeff's suggestion to take a break and go for walk up the river bank with Tina.

She was good with that, too. Tina flowed. Arien loved the way she flowed. He often thought about how lucky he was to have such rad friends but the thing that blew him away the most was the fine companion to him Tina was. It was unreal. She had no expectations, no hang-ups, and when he was busy with something or someone she found plenty else to involve herself with. But, when he wanted her, she was right there.

When the drums came out Aspen, Willow and Ben, an Asian lad, who was among several of the folks hanging with the family without an arbor name, brought out guitars. Sundew, Ben's wife, a "vanilla & chocolate" mixed-race girl, stood just behind him with a tambourine that Arien hadn't heard before.

Aspen had a beautiful guitar in the classical style with nylon strings. It had astrological inlays in mother-of-pearl. Andy was all over it, because it looked like the guitar Gandalf would have. Aspen had a lovely contralto voice to go with her instrument. She sang a variety of folk songs and there were three Arien found especially engaging. He made a mental note to ask her about them.

Willow and Ben played instrumental duets and sang a lot of Beatles tunes that the drummers and the dancers had fun with. Arien joined in with the dancing when the women and girls insisted, but it didn't take all that much insisting, and eventually he danced with nearly everyone there. He still wore the honeysuckle crown, was barefooted, and especially when the sweat-soaked T-shirt came off, appeared in the firelight every bit the prince of the woodland elves.

"That last one ground a rock in my foot." Arien hopped over and sat on a camp stool next to Tina. He was out of breath.

He heard Otter say to Jeff, "This family's smoking us out."

"That's impossible Otter."

"No, I mean, there's no way it'll last until the middle of August. It won't last 'till the middle of July."

"We do have some time to kill," Jeff said.

"Maybe I should hitch back to San Francisco for more once we get settled" he hesitated, "wherever that's going to be."

Arien was about to join in that conversation when Oak tapped him on the shoulder. "Grove," Oak said, leaning down to whisper, "there's a car at the cattle gate."

When he stood, Arien could see a glimmer of headlights through the foliage. "I'll check it out."

"No, I'll go check it out."

"Come with me, then."

"Hope it's not bulls."

"They're not. Be right back, Tina." When Otter looked up Arien gave him a sign to stay. Things had quieted down for the moment. The fire crackled, people chatted, one of the guitars gently strummed.

The two of them slipped away and ambled up to the cattle guard in the pathway of Oak's flashlight. Arien had to limp because the ball of his foot was still tender meat.

The car idled right in the opening of the fence. Arien assumed it was somebody familiar with the spot and they'd found a big party. He didn't get a troubled vibe. What there was came from Oak, who was keeping his eyes open.

Arien's brain fired a rocket as they approached. Maybe it was the shape of the vehicle. It was black in the darkness but it looked like a certain rusty station wagon. "We don't have any car parts," he said with a smirk, when the driver's window rolled down.

Harlan looked out, stupefied, from the back window. It was Sally-Ann who shrieked with excitement, inside the old Chevy, and Arien could hear Luke going, "No! No! No way!"

The kid in the driver's seat broke open a baffled smile as recognition came over him. He gawked up at the still sweaty lad with lengthening hair sticking to the nape of his neck and falling on bare shoulders, and a crazy-drooping honeysuckle crown on his head, standing still before him in the dim and reflected light.

An intoxicating rush splashed and swirled around him. Arien could only take it in.

"After you guys left, I couldn't sleep," Gary explained in a rapid, baffled tone. "I don't think any of us could."

There was a side of Arien that certainly asked how it could be possible Gary found his way here. But another side of him knew. That was the real rush. He took a deep breath to calm his galloping heart.

"Drive down and you'll see the bus, Dude. They'll be room to park behind it."

"Wow, Arien, I - I–"

"Go park it. I'll be by the fire."

Oak shone his light on the Oregon license behind the vehicle as it picked its way down the drive ahead of them. "I'm very confused. You know these people? Was that an impossible coincidence or was there a plan to meet you?"

Arien barely heard him. He drifted inside himself with a sideways, falling sensation that gathered speed like a dizzy head-rush, or peak-jumping with a parasail. It was purely an instinctive, internal, escape-reflex, a bit like pushing away from the solid face of a cliff. "Oak," Arien answered, in awe of his own reflexes, since he coasted on his last toke, which was right after dinner, and he'd had only a cigarette or two. He wondered if his disengagement was quick enough. "I may draw trouble. I don't want anybody to get hurt."

"Huh? Say, what, Brother Grove? You'll have to turn a light on. It's dark in here."

"I can't say it." He shuddered.

"Grove, are these people dangerous?"

"No. No, they're cool. They're fine. It's all good. It's just that–" Arien couldn't say it because his impulse didn't make any sense. That impulse again, was to run. But, run to draw a danger away from his friends that wasn't necessarily intended for him – or was it? He realized there was no way without them. "Oh God," he said.

Arien purposely slowed his steps, both to favor the still sore foot and to gather his thoughts. This too was contradictory. The excitement was undeniable, to see these friends who just made an improbable connection, to jump up and down and cheer and celebrate with them!

"Should I drop to my knees and pray, Oak?"

"Oh my word, lad, I'm in awe of you, that you would even ask that question."

"I don't know who to pray to." Arien stopped absently as cheers and excited squealing erupted by the fire pit. "Sometimes there's a voice in my head. But it's like another person, not like God. He's a teacher. I don't know much else. It wouldn't feel right praying to him."

Oak listened.

"But, maybe I do," he said, with a contradictory thought. He shoved his fingers in his pockets. "I died and went off to the stars once, on acid, and I think I spoke to everything. Maybe that was God. He promised me I would come home again someday."

"That sounds like God, Arien Grove."

"But I don't get this. I feel this kind-a stuff has something to do with me, and nothing like God's involved; not directly, anyway."

Oak scratched the chin on his solid, strong-man's face. "What stuff?"

"Well, like now, Dude. These people are here. I never told them where I was." Arien continued walking.

"Maybe Goddess led them to you." Arien got Oak's wink in the darkness.

"It works like music." Arien said. "I've got a sound, a vibe, a rhythm. They could hear it, but like it was in their sleep. They didn't know that, but they probably expected to catch us at the concert, anyway." Arien had a clear picture of the mechanism but was having a great deal of difficulty trying to put his sense of the connection into words. He gathered the lost feeling this man next to him projected. But then they approached the group of people tightly pressed around the fire who parted for Arien and their own version of awe was projected at him. His guests got it, too. Perhaps someone said something; maybe it was the body language or bated breath in the popping, fire-lit circle.

"Wow!" Arien exclaimed with a big wide grin. He spread his arms and one-by-one hugged the newcomers as trickles of laughter and happy energy circulated.

"Amazing synchronicity!" Andy called out.

"Yeah," Otter agreed. "Tell Arien what you told us!"

"We were just stopping for the night," Gary said, with a merry, still-flabbergasted expression.

Sally-Ann giggled. She'd given Arien a kiss when they hugged. Lanky Harlan nodded at Luke, who looked deeply moved. "It's like it's meant to be," he said. "Oh, Thank You, Jesus! It's going to be alright! I know it! I know it now!"

Later that night as the fire imploded to a heap of embers and occasional yellow-fingered flare ups and the drumming and singing died down to cozy murmurs with spearmint tea, Arien's earlier apprehension seemed distant and irrelevant. His own embers glowed.

A doobie he smoked probably helped. He tried several times to give it away but people followed each other's refusals and he smoked it all by himself.

The Trees jockeyed constantly to be near him. He watched the group from Oregon try find their way among them. Luke and Sally-Ann were the most successful. They sat on the ground behind him with satisfied smiles, coveting their tea.

Arien could feel it through the energy that they drew from him, but it wasn't all one-way. The process gave something in return. He realized how a lesser state of mind might be either pumped or sick of it, like a celebrity sweeping into a restaurant with a groupie or ducking for cover instead. What was the critical ingredient to maintaining a sense of proportion? There was no playbook. Something was beguiling on this trip that felt so natural, at a very deep level; and he was for once at a loss to struggle against it and for the first time saw serious consequences of resistance.

"It's cool," he said. "I think I get it."

Tina leaned into him, linked to his arm. "What?"

"I guess I'll buy it."

"What?"

"I just have to let the chips fall, Babe, and see where it goes. It's even scarier if I don't. Anyway, so far so good, you know?"

He wasn't sure if she did. He leaned forward, elbows on knees; face ruddy with the glow from the fire pit and an inward chuckle when Tina got up and disappeared through the cluster of folks into darkness. The odds were slim anyone would take her spot right next to him.

"Aspen," Arien called.

She looked up from her guitar. She'd been strumming it just below the conversation.

"You did some awesome songs before. There was one about a girl named Suzanne. That was so rad."

She smiled. "It's Leonard Cohen."

"Would you mind doing it again?"

"No, I don't mind. And thank you very much. Sure, I'll play it."

Arien admired her teeth. He imagined kissing her, as he knew Otter did. It was purely a daydream. She was a beautiful, talented girl.

She sang.

Otter made eye contact. He sat cross-legged on a blanket a few bodies to the left.

Arien chuckled. I like travelling with you, he mused. "This stone's a little like acid, you know?" he said to Otter.

"How so?"

"Well, you think of something, and then it's there, like all the connections bring it together, and some of them are in your head and some of them are outside, and they're all –" he searched for the right words "– just as important."

"We can talk about it."

"Just a bigger brain, I guess," Arien mused, innocently enough. And then he looked back to Aspen, to watch and listen to her. Wow. What a great song! What a rad babe!

An enthusiastic applause greeted her conclusion. Arien thought it was so beautiful.

He turned to Luke, "When did you guys leave Prineville?"

"Two days ago, and this was our second stop, Arien," the teenager reported.

"Awesome."

"You know it." He shook his head in ongoing disbelief.

"Arien, Andy told me you know a cool song," Aspen called out. Faces were on him.

"I don't play the guitar, Aspen."

"Well, how does it go?"

"I don't know the chords, sorry. What one is she talking about, Andy?"

Andy and Hawthorne had just clinked their mugs together. "You sang it in Van Gogh, man." Andy said.

"Which one?" Arien hoped to diffuse the situation.

"I don't know. It was like…"

Oh no. "That's from the Joshua Tree." People looked at one another and shrugged. "What the heck?" Arien began to sing it acappella.

He knew all the words. After the first verse, Clayboy batted out a tolerable drumbeat, and Aspen found chords to compliment it. Arien indicated where to keep drumming and playing, during the instrumental refrain. It wasn't U2 but it wasn't half-bad, either. There was genuine applause. A few people asked about it.

"Can't help you, Dudes n' Babes. They haven't hit the charts, yet…" Ever-so-briefly, Arien felt the empty space where something once given was now gone. He worked through a verse of his own in his head, 'The future is a land that's far away. Maybe I'll be there again, someday.'

"Did you say, Joshua Tree?" Clayboy asked.

"No, that's U2's CD."

"U2s sea dee? " Jeff asked. "Cool name for a band."

"Hold that thought, Jeff," Arien said with a sly grin. He drained the last of his tea and set the cup down by his feet.

"Arien," Aspen called from the other side of the circle, "You said something, 'see dee? What's that?"

"Well, Babe, in twenty years vinyls bite the dust. You'll do your tunes in a compact disk player, about this big." Arien put the tips of his index fingers and thumbs together to make a circle about six-inches across. He held it up in front of his face. "Digital technology, Dudes."

It wasn't a long trip from lost to found; maybe an instant of time, but the interim returned with his worry. I have to dodge it or it will find us.

28 — Reality is for people who cannot cope with drugs

All the would-be helpers were distracting. Arien had to dismiss them while organizing his personal stuff. There just wasn't enough for anyone to help with in his Spartan arrangement. He felt perfectly capable of doing this sort of thing for himself. He did send Myrtle off on an errand for Andy and he let Clayboy help Tina get the bedroll and one of her bags to Van Gogh. Clayboy was turning out to be a good fit. He was hanging out more with Arien and Tina, but unlike some others he managed to be unobtrusive and had a way of actually being useful, and Arien was growing fond of him. He knew they had something in common and it made Arien feel protective.

Arien was looking for where he'd set the Tree Family Staff before bed when Otter approached. He followed Arien's local wanderings and saw it before he did. "That what you're looking for?"

"Oh. Yeah, Dude. Thanks."

"I heard Oak say he wants to have a council before we take off."

"Cool. Who'll be there?"

"Everyone, I guess."

"You know what about?" He cupped his hands over the top of the staff.

"Not all of it, but some of it concerns our recent arrivals."

"I told him they're good."

"I think he buys that. It's what you didn't tell him. And I think I get that, too, Arien." He paused. "There's something else, too."

"Yeah?"

"They're looking for some direction."

"The direction is east."

"He's past that. You have to give him some credit."

"Maybe they should have thought about that stuff when I tried to give this back." He said, tamping the staff on the ground.

"Arien, that's unkind. They – we – want to get into it together. I think you know you're the one they're looking up to for answers."

Arien reached in his day bag for a cigarette. Instead of the nearly empty pack he expected to find, there was a full, unopened pack of Pall Mall reds. "Wow. Where'd these come from?"

Otter didn't respond to that. He did say, "Maybe you've noticed, more people are smoking those commercial cancer sticks, Arien, and I think it's because you do. I don't know if you saw it, but the last time we stopped at a store they carried cartons of them out."

"Dude, what do you want from me?" He batted the pack against the back of a hand and pulled the zip-tape at the top.

Otter didn't hesitate. "I want your full and undivided attention, Arien." Otter's words conveyed his most serious tone. "You may be a baby-faced kid, or whatever, but you've taken a castle built for a very strong man, whether you meant to or not. You just better think about that because real hearts and lives are at stake."

Arien felt ambushed. His temper flashed enough to redden his face, but he stifled it. He was just getting used to all the cloying attention and this was cold water. "You're a trip, Otter," he managed to say. He tapped a red out of the pack but instead of lighting it he stuck it over an ear.

The family council was well attended. Even the kids were there. Everyone joined hands first, including last night's arrivals, and they chanted an OM and then Oak asked for the staff.

"Last evening these good folks came to us," Oak began. "When they came, Arien Grove mentioned something that got me to ponder. Brother Grove," he addressed Arien, "you have turned out to be a very magnetic person." A chorus of 'Yeah!' and 'Ho!' went around the circle. "We feel it is a gift, both for you and us, but it's like the strongest drug. Tree had it. If this isn't charisma, it's something similar. But a seeker had to get to know Tree, and he grew on you while he sustained you."

A silence followed. Oak may have been ready to go on when Otter raised his hand and the staff was passed, as always leftward, until it came to him. "I think what he is saying is a strong drug can be dangerous. It's kind-a like we're all tripping and we know how good that can be, but not everybody can handle it."

"Nah," Hawthorne exclaimed. "We should put it in the water for the cities to drink." That brought some chuckles.

"No!" Andy called out. He stood next to Otter and took the staff from him. "Otter has a good point. You don't give acid to kids, right?"

"But we're not talking about kids," Myrtle protested.

"That's right," Andy said, "but we are talking about the stuff our Arien Grove does. It – it digs out archetypes, you know what I mean, Arien?" he looked over at him, "You turn me on, man. My balls are stressed." That was met with some shrieks among the women. Arien blushed and looked down. "And I see people falling over each other to please you. Where does this come from? You didn't ask us. It just happens!"

Willow raised his hand. "You do have a power," he said, when the staff came to him. "You knew this perfect place. You drew friends from two thousand miles away that landed right here. The chances are zero for that to happen by chance."

"Yes," Otter interjected. "And what else is coming?"

Murmurs circulated. "I'll never forget the cloud. He's a holy man, like Tree," somebody said.

Arien raised a finger and the staff went right to him. He held it in his familiar way, with both hands interlaced over the top, which was about level with his chin. It was so quiet the passage of a gentle breeze rustling through the leaves above them and some contentions ducks on the river fell upon their ears. He felt very solid as he gathered himself, visualizing the furiously-spinning fulcrum of will-force in the sight of his single eye. "I don't know," he began. "I'm just being. Some of this really blows me away. I don't know where it's leading but I know I'm going to Woodstock. I've always thought it was for the concert, for the mud, and the stone and the fun, but most of all for the freedom. Now, I don't know. I already feel so free – I had no idea! But, in some ways I'm not so free. You know? It's like my train is on a track, going somewhere, sure, and there's no stopping it. I can't stop it. Heck, I've been on this train since I came here. What's scary is I don't know if it's me or everything else."

"What else is scary?" Oak asked. "Please tell us."

"Oh – it gives me the creeps." Arien felt the blood run out of his lips. "Maybe I should leave you all," he continued. "It would kill me to have any of you get hurt."

How quickly the mood of the assembly changed to a hair-raising dread. Oh, he was so connected. That frightened him. And it was awful to see the anxious look on Clayboy's face. And then he remembered disengagement, that pushing-away-from-the-cliff feeling and soaring high over a treacherous chasm on his own silent wings.

"Oh my God... No!" Myrtle shouted. And other protests likewise circulated.

"What is it, Arien Grove? We can defend ourselves!" Oak shouted above it.

Arien sighed, shook his head, and shifted his weight, leaning heavily on the staff. "Helter-skelter," he whispered.

A lot of people began talking all at once.

"What is it with that?" Otter asked, sorely distressed.

"Polarities." When Arien said that, the little assembly quieted again. Everyone listened. "We aren't free from everything else." Arien searched his vocabulary to describe the space he saw. He was not used to speaking like this. He expected it wouldn't be easy.

"So, what does that mean, Arien?" Willow asked.

"Yeah, what does that have to do with us?" Jeff added.

"Everything." Arien spoke almost ruefully. "We – I – have made some waves in the ocean. I just don't know where it's going, but I think I can see the other side of me and as sweet as I become, it becomes that bitter, and I don't know how to change it or if it can be changed. It may just be the way the world is."

It may have been an intuitive gesture, but the folks in the circle joined hands. Hawthorne was ready. He pulled a matchbook and several paper twists of Tibetan rope incense out of his bag and began to step around the Tree Family circle when it was lit.

"Well," Arien continued, "I don't want to think about it and I don't want to speak of it because it might feel me and come for me and try to right its wrong."

"Hey, Arien, if it did that it might cancel itself out," Tina said, hopefully, and Arien was glad she had something to add.

"It may not matter. It's something like Andy's angel with the flaming sword. It just does what it does."

Then Oak said, "You're a green forest, Arien Grove. Are you saying there has to be a desert because there is a forest?"

"Something like that."

"Oh my. That's terrible!" Tina said. "I'd like to think we could plant more flowers and make it much more beautiful."

Arien felt her hand tighten around his. The clenching of hands went all around. It was almost painful.

"Nah, nah. There's got to be a way." Andy was adamant. "This calls for serious magic, man. We need to do our homework. There's no antithesis to the Light."

"Right on," Otter agreed. "There's got to be room for something new. The world changes with each of us, one at a time. That's the Revolution."

"Ah," Arien sighed.

"Come on, Arien," Andy responded. "Do what you did yesterday. Feed us that sweet love, man. We'll come together and join our heads and solve the problem."

"But don't you see? That's exactly what may draw evil!"

His last words caused a very creepy sensation to go around. It certainly didn't feel right to Arien. People are not supposed to feel like that. So, it was Arien who started the OM. He knew it was the right thing to do. He pitched his voice higher than the accustomed note. One by one, the others joined in with a convergence of keys.

As his heart regained some balance, Arien stopped and waited for the OM to die down. "I may be wrong. I know I'm connected to it somehow, but I may be wrong about all of us together. It should make us strong enough. I just don't know yet, but we should probably do what feels right."

"Go with your gut, man," Otter said.

Arien did. He was suddenly ashamed he'd frightened his beautiful friends and resolved not to let it happen again. If it's out to take me, he said to himself, it will just have me alone. And then he remembered something pretty cool. It was only yesterday's communion:

Would you bleed for them? Arien surely heard the Voice ask him. Must I die, now?

No. You must live!

"Ah...." The sweet swoon returned to the circle of his friends, his Grove. There was no mistaking the energy. People stood, hand in hand, and some of them cried.

"What's your prayer now, Arien?" Willow asked. "How would things be if you could have it your way?"

He smiled. "We'll need a place for us to hang until the concert."

"What about after that?" Myrtle asked.

His smile broadened. "Live for today!" Arien sang out.

Laughter went around, but Arien's eye saw him dodge another bullet.

Before the council ended it was decided to skip a stop in Chicago. Gary spoke for the recent arrivals when he said they'd expected to visit the big city, but... It was evident they were overcome by the energy among these people and around Arien. Now that they'd found it, they were not about to let it go.

On the way to the vehicles Willow approached Arien and Tina inviting them to ride with the bus. "It's our turn," he said.

"Sure, why not? I'll get my pack out of Van Gogh, first."

Clayboy was on it. "I'll get it, Arien. I know just where you put it."

Arien called after Otter, who was just up ahead, and Otter stopped to wait for him. Arien approached with the staff over his shoulders, like a yoke. He scratched the back of his neck with it. Tina stood beside him. The young man in the fringed jacket regarded him.

"Otter, I'm sorry I ragged on you before."

"Man, I've been expecting it. Most kids like you are still the center of mommy's world, or a hot jock that carries the school's ball. This is different. But you know that. To your credit it's taken this long for cracks in the skull to appear."

Arien chuckled. "Cracks in the skull?"

"Yeah, man. When your head grows too fast it cracks the skull."

That made Arien laugh like a schoolboy after a saucy joke. Tina grinned and nodded at Otter. Andy came over and stood near enough to hear.

"You said back there you were worried about summoning a demon out of your love," Otter continued.

"Maybe like that, I guess."

"Well, that demon doesn't have to come look for you, man. He's with you all the time. It's only your love and compassion and humility that keeps him in his cage."

"Wow, Otter," Andy praised. "That's good stuff!"

"Yeah, it is. You sure know how to clean my window, Dude."

"It can be a thankless job, but somebody's got-a do it, young Prince Grove." Otter put a hand on Arien's shoulder, clasped it and gently shook him. "Arien, the first rule about being a stoner is to keep your eyes wide open. You got-a do it, kid, every minute of every hour of every waking day. And don't ever forget we're here to help you."

"Otter?"

"Yeah?"

"Why?"

"Maybe I'll know the answer to that when you do."

"Otter?"

"What?"

"I love you!"

They embraced and Tina and Andy joined in, pressing their heads together in a playful and messy, four-way kiss.

While Oak managed the step van, Willow usually drove the bus. Driving it looked like a no-brainer to Arien. The big International 392 had an eight-cylinder gasoline engine, a standard, four-speed transmission and easily handled 60 miles per hour on the highway. Arien studied Willow's driving. He decided he'd ask him if he could take a turn when Chicago was behind them.

Riding the bus was a blast. Arien and Tina rode up front by the door with Clayboy behind them. After they got going, Arien kicked back with his feet on the horizontal hand rail and watched the road ahead. He munched on a wedge of bread and peanut butter Clayboy snagged for them, and nursed a cup of a grape concoction referred to as "bug juice" that was served out of a five-gallon water cooler with an aluminum shell. Willow had a small transistor radio in a black-leather case sitting on the panel box to his left; its long antenna stuck out the sliding window. It was tuned to a rock station out of Chicago. Little Eva sang, *Locomotion*. The curtain between the front and rear sections was tied back, opening the whole inside. People sang along with the radio, swapped stories, napped or read.

"Who buys the gas for us?" Arien asked Willow, realizing that he finally acknowledged the obvious. Oh, it felt so good to be a part of something and to have a role to play and to find the respect of people he admired. Only half of him attended to what Willow said as he explored his own hesitation. But wasn't this a commitment? And wasn't making a commitment a form of trust? Was it safe to trust? Did it make him less free?

"What keeps the wheels turning?" he asked, chasing his first question as if to throw Willow off the scent. There had to be an out if he wasn't sure. He was no liar, at least. Woodstock was the goal. Even to consider anything else was like a betrayal of trust to himself.

"We're not hurting. Oak told me Tree left behind seventeen hundred dollars of his own money, and nobody told you Oak's a trust orphan, huh? It's the biggest secret around that everybody knows. Then, we had a kitty with a few hundred in cash and food stamps. It should last for a while."

"Willow, what's a trust orphan?"

"Shhhhhh…," Willow hushed with a confidential wink. "It's a secret!"

"Who decides how to spend it?" Tina wanted to know.

"Tell you the truth, Tina, it used to be Tree, and Oak, too. After Oak got back with the bus he asked me to keep receipts, since Tree is gone. Major decisions that concern everybody gets everybody's attention." Willow pushed his cap back and scratched his forehead. "Everyone's expected to contribute in some way. I expect we'll find out the intentions of your friends from Oregon, if they're going to hang with us for a while or what."

"They haven't said."

"They stuck to you like flypaper last night."

"Yeah, just like everybody else." Arien realized this wasn't a modest thing for him to say, but it was true enough.

"You are rather amazing, Brother." Willow said after a moment's passing. "You're like life on cocaine with some atomic energy thrown in. I've never known anybody like you before. That cloud was wild!

It's like you dance with the elements, man. Do you even know how you do it? And you're such a pup, too."

"Tree called me that. I think I look younger than I am, though." But Arien was as blown away with that little cloud's appearance as anyone else, maybe more.

"Then, how old are you?"

"Last I checked I was seventeen."

"Wow, Man. The energy makes you timeless, in any case."

"How old are you, Willow?"

"Twenty-four. And, Tina?"

"I'm eighteen."

"Damn, you robbed the cradle, woman."

On hearing that, Arien stuck his thumb in his mouth and cried, "Wah."

"Don't let that fool you, Willow. His cradle rocks."

"Yea," Arien agreed. "Rock me Baby, rock me Baby," he said, throwing his arm around Tina's shoulders and pulling her against him. Then he turned to look behind. "How old are you, Clayboy? – Hey. Check it out, Tina! Clayboy's crashed."

"Wow. Cool station. They're playing albums." Arien had been napping against Tina, who was writing a letter on a sheet of loose-leaf paper. Willow's voice called him out of a dream. He opened an eye and both of his ears to listen to the band's amazing singer's haunting words from *This is the End.*

"Ride the snake. Morrison's so high," Willow praised.

"Ha! The blue bus is callin' us!" Arien cried out. "Driver where you takin' us?"

"Woodstock!" Willow said.

"Wow," Arien thought out loud. "I'd never listened to that song before! I wondered why he wasn't there!"

"Where?" Tina looked up from her letter. She stuck the end of the pen in her mouth.

"Morrison. He wasn't at Woodstock." Arien regarded the pen. He reached for it, but Tina pulled it away. He started to reach past her when she stuck a finger in his ribs. He giggled and jumped back, then grew more serious. "He's on the dark side."

Willow caught that and laughed. "Well, yeah. That's the whole idea!"

"The Stones weren't at Woodstock, either," Arien mused out loud, ignoring Willow's point. "This is awesome, I may be getting it!" he exclaimed, with a rush of unexpected excitement.

"What's that, Arien?" Tina asked.

"We might actually be able to make the difference." It was a significant understanding, but it made peculiar sense when he considered how, along the way, his mind had increasingly been blown in 1969. Arien had no idea how it would happen, but it was a very good guess that something would happen that could literally alter the world, and by extension, reality, itself.

"How?"

"Ha!" Arien cried. "Willow, I was at a drug re-hab class one day and we were getting fed this shit and there was a sign on the wall that said, *'Drugs are for people who cannot cope with reality.'* Ha! And my housemate, Dan Fowler – I thought the dude was a bit of a jerk, but hey, I might actually like him if he was here with us now. So, he says… Arien smiled, "He says, *'Reality is for people who cannot cope with drugs!'* Ha!"

Willow laughed hard at that. Tina did, too, yet Arien guessed neither got the reason he told the joke, and then Clayboy spoke up from the seat behind them. "There's different realities."

"Yeah, Dude! Awesome! And, when they come together we have the world. But even that's a paradox. This wizard dude in San Francisco made me think about paradoxes. Reality is a paradox, you know? It's – it's a balance of forces, light and dark, good and bad, hot and cold, but it's all a dream, too; in my head, and outside of it, and all the while it's in both places at the same time. And, it looks like there's all kinds of space between things, but it's more like a solid with everything a part of everything else. Thought changes it, and then all of it is changed." Arien stopped for breath.

"Arien?" Willow asked. "Are you tripping on something you should have shared with us?"

Arien chuckled. "Nah, not now, but I've been thinking about all that a lot lately." He hadn't realized his monologue attracted the attention of others in the bus, and they'd crept up to pack the isle behind him, listening.

"What can we do?" Myrtle inquired, dropping into the seat next to Clayboy.

"I don't know yet, but we all have a role to play; that much I feel in my bones." Arien found an ounce of hope. He guessed the danger hadn't passed, but it no longer seemed implacable. "I need to learn more. I feel so stupid." He reached for a cigarette but stopped himself.

There's no ash tray, he told himself. But all he could think about after that was lighting one up to feed the craving.

The highway rest stop lunch in Indiana invited stares even polite people couldn't resist. It did look a bit like a happening, with the bus and the van and the VW and Gary's beat-up Ford station wagon simultaneously parking, and then everybody popping out to lay down blankets on the grass for a picnic. It was as organized as any church group. The line formed behind the step van and sandwiches that had been made on the road were passed out.

"How's the bus?" Andy sauntered over from the step van with his egg salad sandwich on store-bought rye bread in one hand and a big chocolate-chip cookie in the other. Hawthorne was with him, and Otter, with Aspen and Jeff who had ridden in Van Gogh, were already there. Myrtle, Willow and Clayboy passed out camp cups with room-temperature bug juice. Clayboy was quick to get one to Arien and Tina.

"Thanks, Dude! Rad. I want to drive it."

"You already do," Otter said with a nod to Andy. "You drive all of them, Arien."

Arien grew serious. "I don't know, but I might have to before this is over."

Otter's stare invited an explanation Arien was unready to deliver. He put more of his sandwich in his mouth than he should have and took extra time to chew it up.

Tina chuckled and reached out to put a finger over his lips. He laughed because there was too much food in the way to bite her finger and some of it fell out on his shirt.

"Wow," Andy remarked, still standing and gazing from Arien to the brothers and sisters arranged laughing, eating and enjoying themselves around him. Some teenagers came over to the periphery and the boldest among them opened a conversation with Kelsey.

"Arien, I think I see the archetype! It's really fantastic."

"Rad, Dude. What is it?"

"I'll save it, Brother. I would hate to spoil it."

"By all means, don't spoil it, Andy," Otter said. "But you can tell me. Here, whisper it in my ear." So Andy knelt to Otter's ear.

"Hmmmm." Otter deliberated.

"Well? What do you think?"

"Maybe. I'll have to think about it. He could just be a warrior, or even a warlock, or he'll be a seer or a wizard, like Jamie Sun." He looked at Arien, who heard all of this and caught the drift but didn't guess it.

"Can I?" Tina pleaded.

"No. Definitely not you, My Lady."

Arien got to drive the bus in Ohio and it put him in seventh heaven. From there it was a couple of hours to a more zoned-out place that wasn't advertised by his senses. His fingers caressed the braided string wrapping the steering wheel that kept the whole bus, with its treasure of people, in the lane. He watched the swooping lights of passing cars multiply as darkness shrouded the western approach to Cleveland, and he listened to the radio drifting in and out. The station picked it up with Simon and Garfunkle looking for America. It was a suitable refrain.

Then he slipped into the rhythm of the motor; *vrum-vrum, vrum-vrum, vrum-vrum,* that mimicked the beating heart's *lub-dub, lub-dub, lub-dub,* at a good jog. I wonder if I can help it any? Arien stuck out his index finger and twirled it, clockwise to the rhythm; *vrum-vrum, vrum-vrum, vrum-vrum,* pushing slightly faster. Oh, maybe that's the wrong way! he dreamily considered, reversing his twirling finger. To Arien's astonishment, at the instant of very the first *"vrum,"* as his finger began its reverse rotation, the engine shuddered and began to lose power.

"Wha–what happened? What'd I do?" He cried, coming hyper-alert, grabbing the wheel tightly and then turning it gently to the shoulder revealed in the headlights.

Ben had been playing a folk tune at the rear of the bus that stopped in the middle of a phrase. Willow was at Arien's shoulder in no time. "It just died?"

"Yeah," Arien answered. When the big bus rolled to a stop he cranked the motor but it wouldn't catch fire. He recognized the lights of the step van in the big side mirror. It pulled up behind them. Arien caught Gary's tail lights trail away behind Van Gogh as they just kept on going.

There was a box built in to the right of the front entry where Willow fished for a flashlight. Soon Oak was there and the two of them got the hood open on one side and climbed up for access to the opening. "Stay there, Arien, and hit the key when I say," Oak instructed.

"Okay."

They fiddled up there for a bit. "Now!"

It wouldn't go.

"Try again!"

Still no go.

"It's not getting a spark," Oak said.

Arien hadn't a clue. He was no mechanic. It was disappointing to sit there in the driver's seat and not be able to move the bus. He got out to watch Oak and Willow fiddle but couldn't see much with them in the way. "He's paralyzed, "Arien said. "Check to see if his spinal chord snapped."

"Right, it's like that, ha?" Oak mumbled at the engine. "Start it again, Arien. We'll check the coil."

Arien got back in and cranked it.

"Whoa!"

"What?" Arien shouted.

"Fat spark!"

That was encouraging though the engine still wouldn't start. Then the hood was dropped and soon Oak and Willow filed up the steps to tell everyone they needed daylight to try anything else. Willow said the spark was getting to the distributor but not the plugs and that was their clue for the morning.

"I'll roll out a bed for you guys." Clayboy said.

"Thanks, Clayboy, I'll do that," Tina told him.

"Hey, you don't know the bus like we do. I'll fix you a spot."

Tina smiled at him. "You're so good to us, Clayboy!"

Arien opened his mouth to speak but made way for a rush of sights and feelings that burst uninvited into his mind. It was 'the Voice' again.

Arien, Tina and Clayboy volunteered for breakfast detail. Arien wanted to get out of the tortured bus and the best way to do that, even feeling a little haggard, was to get into something constructive. The night had been fitful, after all. Cars and trucks in the adjacent highway lane sped by mere inches away. Their roar against the exposed side of the bus came often and it frightened little Sammy, his sisters Heather, and Crystal, who were two, three and four years old, respectively. Kelsey was up all night with them. She sang softly to comfort, and they would begin to quiet, and then another monster would blast by and rattle and lurch the whole bus. It didn't help that River Blue, Ben's little boy, who was about three and a half, slept like a log on the seabed because Sammy's shrieks made up for them both.

The first thing Clayboy did was pull out the steel bar frame the bus had attached to its entry side. He draped the canvas stashed in the underside storage box over the frame that made up a private area for the poop and ash buckets and the washstand. Tree had set up this system a year ago as the traveling family grew and nights on the roadside found them away from natural screens as well as facilities. The rig was also used for a shower where a 5-gallon jerry can of hot water could be set up high enough for a siphon hose to feed the shower head. Arien was in and out of there, first, and then he made his way back to the step van, passing Willow and Oak carrying a pair of tool boxes.

There was just enough water in the holding tank above the stove to make the oatmeal and fill the coffee pot. Clayboy found a bag of raisins in the metal wall cabinet and dumped a bunch of them in a big, boiling pot. Tina liberally added brown sugar and Arien set up a pile of spoons and stacked enamel bowls on the trim, stainless-steel counter that took up two-thirds of the van's rear opening.

About the time the congregation formed for an early breakfast, Tina told Arien she saw Van Gogh pass by on the other side of the highway. "I wonder what took them so long?"

"They probably waited for daylight," he surmised, to the sound of the bus engine cranking up ahead, still most unwilling to go.

"Ho, Arien! Save any for us?"

"Yeah, Andy. Hi guys," Arien greeted. "Where's Gary and his gang?"

"They opted for breakfast at a diner. What happened?"

"The bus quit."

"Is it bad?"

"Don't know, yet. Willow and Oak are working on it."

Clayboy filled five more bowls with oatmeal and Tina passed them over the counter to Otter, Aspen, Jeff, Andy and Hawthorne.

"We need more water," Tina observed, as she put empty bowls into one of the big, round, steel pans that were used for clean up.

"Just stack 'em," Clayboy said. "They can soak later."

Arien read a puzzle in Willow's expression as he approached. The early sun put a gloss on the smudge of grease clinging to the side of his nose. "Breakfast?"

"Sure."

"So, what did you find?"

"The darnedest thing." Willow scratched an ear with a knuckle of his greasy hand. "We pulled the distributor cap and cranked it. The rotor won't turn!"

"Jesus!" Arien exclaimed, but there was no way to explain the connections in his astonishment or wave of guilt for having messed with it. He was sure now it couldn't have been a mere coincidence but that he had actually caused the thing to break! "Uh, what's the plan?"

"Well, Oak and I agree, we have to get down into the shaft or gearing. The thing is obviously broken. I just don't get it. Whoever heard of something like that happening?"

"Damn, what d' ya know?" Jeff agreed. "I've got tools. I can help," he offered.

"Well, first we need to get off the freeway," Willow said, shoveling his oats down.

"Van Gogh will have to tow it."

"OK, let's try that, Andy," Hawthorne chuckled.

"We can get everyone on ropes, Egyptian-style," Andy added, with a twinkle in his eyes.

Arien shoved his hands in his pockets, unwilling to hazard pointing a finger at anything. "Jesus!" he said again.

Oak finally ambled over to the step van. Clayboy had to scrape the bottom of the pot but it made a decent bowl of oats. He passed it to Oak who had a spoonful and thought a moment. "Rotor," he sighed.

"I suppose we'll need to call for a tow," Jeff said.

"Yes, but where to?" Oak shrugged. "We don't need a garage. We need a space to work on it and hang if we're waiting for parts."

"I'll go with you, Jeff," Arien joined, pulling himself together. "We'll get off the highway and drive around and see what we can find, first."

"The pigs will be on us shortly," Otter warned. "We have to have a plan or they'll make up one for us."

"We have a little time," Arien answered confidently.

"Yes," Oak agreed. "If they come by, we'll just tell them we're broke down and dealing with it. Meanwhile, we have to keep it together; keep it clean and sober." He set his empty bowl on the counter and wiped his lips with his sleeve. "River!" He called sharply to the little guy standing behind the bus. He stood just inches from the roadway. "You get over here! In fact, I think you should get inside, now." He briskly strode over to the little fellow and scooped him up with an arm full of giggles and with the boy akimbo in his arm, Oak called out, "Jeff! Before you drive off, we'll load up that van of yours with some water cans to get us through."

"Got it, Oak."

"I'll do the invisibility spell," Andy said.

"Just make it so the tow truck can find the bus," Otter provided, with a pointing finger.

Van Gogh probed a dead-end road that had seen better days. Its shoulders lay naked in the daylight, shameless and wanting. On one side, rusty train tracks lead from broken old structures framing shattered windows, broad and tall, with bare red brick, their sparkling remnants scattering like emeralds through tufts of grass in the fossil beds of rusted iron gears and hulking, forlorn shapes of a bygone era. On the other were leaning chain-link fences that struck out ahead like a drunken night's pathway home. They surrounded nothing but wounded open spaces, with scabbed patches of dark-stained earth and cracked concrete slabs.

"The telephone must be in Pennsylvania," Jeff said, unconsciously letting up on the gas.

"What did they make here?" Tina wondered from the back.

"Your Dad's America," Otter mused.

"I love that." Andy said.

"No, don't slow down, Jeff. Not yet."

"Alright, Arien, it's your call."

Arien indulged a deep drag on a Pall Mall but blew most of the smoke over his forearm, which hung out the sliding window. It was a delicious drag, like smoking used to be before it became a habit. It was his first since yesterday. Heck, it was hard to pass up when wanted. The irritation in his throat almost felt welcome. He gurgled up a little wad of spit and shot it cleanly out of the van.

"It's pretty neat," Andy declared.

"What's neat?" Arien responded, when no one else did.

"We're all together again, just us."

"Yeah, consider me reminded. We skipped out on Clayboy. He asked me if he could come."

"Did you say no?"

"No, I said, sure, but I think he was cleaning up the kitchen when we took off." Arien felt a little guilty. He liked Clayboy and the lad's attention, but the momentum was to get going and Arien hadn't wanted to interrupt that with a pause to wait for anyone.

The air was close and humid and carried an industrial smell that vaguely reminded Arien of the emissions from the paper mill in Oregon, on the Columbia River's Vancouver side. The odor blended with the lurid landscape, bringing out russet colors of broken industry with the backdrop of a billowing white mountain of thunderhead, fanning-out its top in a vivid-blue sky. Then the chain-link fence gave way to fall over on its side as if it had been struck and run over. It was right in front of a yawning Quonset hut that looked like the airplane hangar that got lost on the way to the tarmac.

"Stop!" Arien ordered, pointing. "Let's check it out."

"Jesus, Arien!" Andy marveled. "You did it again! Moses, leading us to the Promised Land!"

"Let's consider him a shaman who knows where the game is." Otter considered. "As I recall, Moses never made it to the Promised Land."

"I don't even see a 'no trespassing' sign," Jeff praised.

But Andy saw the faded sign in the yard on a square of weathered plywood. It faced the sky still attached to the fence with muddy tire tracks across it. Andy kicked it, and then Arien stepped over to grab an edge. Together they yanked it up in silent agreement and flipped it over on its face. "What sign?" Otter, watching, asked.

"We still need a telephone," Jeff noted, looking into the building. Except for a long oil-stained plywood table on one side framed with two-by-fours, it was a big empty space, large enough to pull the bus all the way in.

"We'll go past the exit on the way back," Arien suggested, "where we could have turned left. I saw a sign there for a gas station further on. We could fill the water cans while we're at it."

"Think we'll be left alone here?" Jeff asked.

"It's a dead-end, and there's no traffic," Otter replied.

Andy walked to the back of the building where a sign on the door to a small room announced, 'Boy's Room.' He went in there a moment and then came out to say the water was shut off.

"Is there a potty?"

"Yes, Jeff, but there's no water."

"We can flush it with our jerry cans," Arien said, considering the resources in their caravan. "It's mega hot city in here but it will hide us and keep us out of the rain." As if on queue, a flash of brilliant light overpowered the sunshine in the building's opening. A rumble from the spreading white thunderhead rattled the structure's faded gray steel skin.

"What a hoot," Andy cheered. "Downtown Cleveland is barely a few miles from here but we might as well be in Manitoba."

Arien sat in Van Gogh's door sill with Andy. He hit on the doobie and passed it. He felt pretty ripped. This was the second one in succession. His exhale hung over them in the muggy, stinky air. Both Van Gogh and the step van were parked on the north side of the Quonset, blocking them from the road. They'd driven the step van in first so outside activity could be confined to this side and access to the man-door in the middle of the north wall of the building would keep people going to and from the building out of site. Then, Gary's car parked and that was followed by Van Gogh. With the bus tucked in the bay, the clan was basically invisible.

Arien felt outwardly secure at least. Inside, he was troubled. With their forward momentum halted there was nothing for him to do except catch up with himself. He watched as Clayboy approached. The lad came forward and stood uncertainly.

"Hey, Dude. Where ya been?"

Clayboy looked from Arien to Andy. He couldn't get it out.

"I'm sorry," Arien said. "We didn't mean to leave without you. It was time to go. But thanks for helping out after breakfast. You're a rad dude."

Clayboy's eyes brightened. He leaned in and reached to give Arien a hug. It caught Arien by surprise.

"Dude," Arien said. He smiled faintly over Clayboy's shoulder. The boy clutched him so tightly Arien had to stand to make it feel right. Wow, the kid needed it.

"I love you," Clayboy whispered.

"Thanks, little Brother. That's so rad."

Andy, watching, drew a long toke. He staunched a run in the doobie with a wet finger and passed it to the misty-eyed boy who finally let go of Arien. "Here, Boy. I got the sickness, too," he said sympathetically.

"You have it worse," Arien said.

"Probably. Clayboy didn't kiss you."

Clayboy cocked his head. Arien could see his wheels turning. Then the boy grinned.

"Oh, you think it's funny?" Andy asked.

"You should, too," Arien gently defended.

The boy accepted the roach, tweezing it in his fingers. He took a deep hit that made him cough.

Jeff came over with Willow from the bay. "We've got the purple imp," Willow announced.

Arien inspected the thing in Jeff's upturned hands. The shaft was shorn clean through down near the base, before the gearing. He shook his head ruefully at the two of them. "I'm sorry. It was an accident," he earnestly said, even if it felt more like an ignorant mistake. What blew him away was the sense that there was still so much about the world he didn't know. He thought it was a miracle he could feed himself without gagging.

"Sure enough." Jeff said. "So now it's a run to see who has it. Wanna come?"

"I'll beg off, Dude. I need to chill. And, come to think of it, you do, too. What's Gary doing? Let's ask him if–" Arien's sentence was cut short when Harlan ambled over.

Harlan had a can of Coors in each hand. "What's up, Arien?" He acknowledged the others and offered Arien one of the beers.

"Thanks!" Arien held it up for Andy. "Want some?"

"Sure." He took the first slug and handed it back.

"Clayboy?"

"Yeah!" Clayboy happily took the can and had the next gulp of it. He burped and smiled and was about to hand it back when Arien motioned for him to pass it to Jeff. Harlan watched as Jeff and then Willow had some. There were two swallows of beer left when it came back. Arien was grateful it was still fairly cold.

"Harlan, you guys want to do us a favor?"

"Sure, Arien, what can we do?"

"Take this, will ya?" Arien indicated the broken rotor shaft Jeff still held. "It's for the bus. I'd be obliged if you and Gary can find the part in Cleveland. Be sure and get some money from Oak, okay?" Arien looked to Willow for confirmation.

"Oh, yeah, Oak has the money for it."

"Well, sure, Arien." Harlan was about to have a draught of his beer but shifted awkwardly on his feet. He offered the can to Arien who smiled and waved his finger around at everybody. "Oh, right. Here, man!" Willow stood closest to him so he passed Willow the drink.

"I was prepared to go," Jeff said, watching Harlan troop away without his beer.

"I want you here. And Clayboy, please ask Otter to come here and get Oak and find Tina, wherever she is." Arien set the first beer can down when the second was given to him. He took that last swallow, not sure if he actually liked it, but he craved a bigger buzz than the doobie had to offer.

"What's up, Arien?"

"Oh, and I think Hawthorne should be here, too, and anybody else that gets into the Tree's business."

Clayboy turned proudly on his heel and disappeared into the side door of the Quonset. Arien reached into the van to retrieve the staff.

It took a while to come together. Gary needed a pad and pencil to take all the orders for people when he was in town. Arien touched base with him, too. He said to let Luke and Sally-Ann stay behind, to represent him and Harlan, and he wanted a pack of Pall Mall reds and a Hershey bar.

When everyone assembled in the late afternoon, they formed a circle out there in the yard, just beyond the vehicles. Arien actually opened with the OM. He set the staff to his left and grasped it as Tina did, to her right, and everyone joined hands from them. Luke and Sally-Ann were there standing freshly attentive; transfixed in the group. They all looked to Arien awaiting his words.

"Some of you know I've had a teacher in my head. It's weird. He laughed to himself. It felt so awkward to be saying this.

"What's his name?" Hawthorne asked.

"He's Mexican, maybe, with a name that's like, Cypriano. When I finally asked him, I'm sure that's what he said. Anyway, he spoke to me again last night." Arien stopped. He looked into the faces of the Tree People. He could hear the traffic from the highway in the distance, sounding a bit like the Pacific off of Land's End. The shadows stretched before a cinematic sun that just broke under the horizon's wall of receding thunderclouds. A light, damp breeze began to play in his hair. People waited patiently for Arien to go on.

"I don't understand everything he said, but I don't think it's meant just for me and our Stand. Cypriano told me I'll find my way around the circle. I'll hold the staff. I'll know the way. I can't argue so far." There were murmurs of agreement. "Now, this is what I don't get: 'In the east is red, like the morning sky where the sun rises, and the south is yellow, when the sun is high, burning bright, and in the west it is white, where it sets into the sea, and the north is black, where it is midnight.' He said to bring this to my people and see if it speaks to them." Arien shuffled his feet. He shrugged. "Rad. I didn't forget what he said!"

"It's a medicine wheel," Andy exclaimed.

"Yes," Hawthorne agreed.

Oak nodded, introspectively. He watched as Arien rested his arms, one over the other, on the staff.

"It's like the Magic Circle," Andy went on. Only, the colors are different, but the sense is the same."

"How does that go?"

"Well, Arien, the east is blue, the air element. The south is red, for fire. The west is white, for water and the north's green, for earth."

"The actual elements are in the same places," Hawthorne considered.

"We'd have to ask Arien's Cypriano." Aspen suggested. "But it sounds like that to me."

In a curious way, it crossed Arien's mind he could have been making it all up, except he hadn't known about any of this stuff before.

"Oh yeah," Tina added.

"So, what's the point?" Arien couldn't help but ask.

"The wheel is the Way, Brother," Otter explained. "It's the Wheel of Life."

"Exactly," Andy agreed. "But it has a ritual significance. It's mythic."

Arien wasn't playing dumb. He knew he was learning things. Here, he gathered anew the threads of his experience and through the lens of his inner remembrance, he saw deeply into the great tapestry of his connection. Whoa! "On that last night with Tree, Tree told me not to fight it," he cryptically admitted. His eyes welled up. "Maybe I could still slide in some of that Woodstock mud."

In that moment Arien looked so sad, Tina raised his hand to her heart. "Sure, Arien. Why not, Babe?"

Jeff, on the other side, and those nearby stood silently waiting.

"This is so beautiful!" Oak cried. "Tree is here!"

"Yes he is!" The words went around the whole group of them, "Tree's here!" "Tree is here!"

After nightfall and a thick, kale and navy bean soup with lots of garlic and hot rolls out of the oven, a few kerosene lamps were set out to the rear of the bay and they laid a bunch of wool Army blankets on the concrete floor. Oak had one particularly beautiful, antique brass lamp with a round wick and glass panes that he placed in the middle, and folks arranged themselves in a circle to face it. A faint, spicy incense graced the air to commingle with the skunky smoke Otter rolled. And then Ben broke out his guitar and Willow joined in while Aspen strummed her dulcimer.

Arien beamed in the golden light of the lamp and the mellow embrace of the Quonset, utterly transformed from a stark, empty shell by lamplight and an animated, loving company. He'd never been to summer camp but this had to be like some magic carpet version of that. Cross-legged on his blanket, he leaned his shoulder into Tina and faced her with a smoldering doobie stuck backwards between his lips. She nodded and kissed him gently while he blasted the shotgun into her lungs. She fell back laughing and coughing up a cloud of stony smoke.

"I love your dimples when you laugh, Babe."

Andy reached for the doobie when Arien took it out of his mouth. "This place is amazing!"

"It's totally rad."

Oak crept up. "You think the guys in town are okay? We kept some dinner out for them," he said.

"They got lost."

"You think so, Arien?"

"Yeah, they're panicked but they're good." That was easy. And he wondered how he could know it for sure.

"Damn. Well, how will they find their way back?"

"By not trying too hard," Arien answered.

Andy shook his head in admiration. "That's still a kid," he reverently observed.

"Tell me about it," Oak agreed, moving to sit down. Arien and Clayboy had to make room for him. As usual it was tight. Everybody wanted to sit next to Arien and this evening was no exception. Arien's radiant demeanor had a dreamily magnetic quality that animated the space. This fed and in turn, was fed by Ben and Willow's guitar jam as it grew into an energetic and melodic duet contained with a very determined dulcimer. Its rhythms cleverly fit what might have been the usual role for percussion. It intruded in a way that delighted Arien. He found himself first hearing it and then watching Aspen play it, and then seeing himself watching Aspen as she played.

She kept her hair short. It framed the strong lines of her patrician jaw, and the rake of her neck, and her inclination to the instrument in an unusual way Arien found very attractive. He mouthed the word, Wow, when their eyes met, and that chased a heady rush because her glance rode over the music and joined with his, and there were no blocks to her soul.

Arien looked away. He felt others' eyes on him and he may have spilled a little innocence into the moment. Oh God! It made him dare to turn up the heat so bad he could taste it. He covered it with a brave smile and then laughed to himself.

He looked at Tina.

"What?"

He leaned close to her ear. "Wish I had a rubber skull."

Arien played that wish again soon after. He'd pissed in the Quonset's commode and before he could tuck it away an exquisite, randy rush washed over with the vengeance of a seismic wave. A primeval moan carried his swoon. On the other side of the door was the music and the people and a certain lady whom he understood how insane it was to dwell upon, and this was much worse, and easily as pointless as asking someone not to imagine a moose. Well, this creature found itself crashing, snapping and stomping onto the shores of his Pleistocene undergrowth. It was headlong. It was crazy, and his inordinately insistent erection craved immediate attention.

He bit his lip, hard. This is sooooooo bogus! An image of the struggle came to mind, like legs that would run being mired waist-deep in snow or an impossible struggle of an insect's delicate wings plastered by a raindrop to the face of a leaf. He even found a fleeting second to review his contest with "God" and the backdrop of the world; the way things actually were as opposed to convention and still, he could marvel how often it failed to meet his own righteous expectations.

"Oh, Tina, I love you!" Arien moaned to the dancing wisp of flame from a votive candle that was set to the side of the sink. "Oh, Otter! I'm so sorry!" He dissolved into a picture of Aspen, her face, her lips, the angle of her neck and it felt way too good not to simply give in to it.

Arien felt dissonant when he came back out on the floor. He worked his way around the edge of the room to the man door and went outside. It didn't seem enough to have simply gratified himself with a misbegotten image like stolen art on his wall. It grated against the inside of his pants with the smart taunt of residual wetness. He felt trapped and incomplete. It made him want to do it again, but to make it real!

The music receded as Arien stepped out into the night. The tortured field beyond the glowing Quonset was quiet and empty but for the silent witnesses of a few stars valiant enough to twinkle through Cleveland's ruddy industrial nimbus. He opted for Van Gogh's familiar comforts and was surprised to discover someone was there ahead of him.

"Aspen?" he whispered, truly expecting it to be her and taken by how quickly his longing rekindled to – gasp - another throbbing insistence.

"Arien? No. It's me."

Arien was sorely confused. As he braced himself for some kind of confrontation, the owner of the voice fell into place with a gentle follow-up,

"It's me, it's…"

"Oh, Andy!" Arien sighed. "Oh, gosh, Andy, Andy–" It must have been something in his voice but Andy was right there and they unexpectedly embraced and Arien felt Andy recognize this passion in his pants. Andy froze, but then embraced him so much tighter, closer.

"Andy," Arien whispered in Andy's ear, "Do it again. Do it again, Dude. Suck it. Suck it, please, Brother. Take me before I do something really stupid."

"Oh Brother!" Andy wailed, pulling his shirt and the drawstring pants he was wearing off and falling to his knees. He sobbed while fumbling, first with the button and then a balky zipper. And then he took it into his face and Arien pumped him with a fury on the border of rage as his jeans fell around his knees.

Andy wouldn't quit with the release of that first, furious hot jet, and he took it from Arien again and again and again, throwing him down on his back and pinning him there and by the time Arien fought to disengage, he was too weak to stop it. By the eighth time he literally saw Andy's silhouette through a blood-red lens. He huffed and panted for air as it seemed the very life in him would be sucked away. "Stop! Stop! Stop!" Arien gasped, trying to push that determined head away while his body jerked, pulsed and shuddered. But Andy, sweating like rain, his long, wavy hair slickly matted to the sides of his head, neck and shoulders, forced Arien to give up one more before he did.

The lad lay completely still among soft, dizzy waves that pulsed against the limits of his human form, as he peered through the scarlet light show in his eyeballs. His breaths were slow and deep. He swore, but it was more an exhale than a word.

Andy sniffed and blew out his nose and Arien felt some misty droplets spray across his tummy. "You can stop crying now," Arien croaked.

"A r i e n," Andy drew out the word like the title of a blessed psalm. "I am in Heaven!" He crooned. "Jesus! That was the most beautiful thing that ever, ever happened. Oh, God, I can't believe it! You are such a stud! Nine times! You came nine times!"

Arien hadn't the strength to laugh. It felt like one time to him, one continuous, rolling orgasm, with peaks and valleys, and he wondered at Andy's stamina, to keep going like that, and to be able to go after, sustain, and so artfully elicit such a response. "You're amazing," he awarded. He was truly impressed.

"Really, Arien? Oh, wow, wow."

What happened next truly blew Arien away. He knew she was there before she said anything. He'd felt her presence and was so exposed he could only bless the darkness, hold his breath and wait. He heard the faint sound of hollow wood and the subtle vibration of sympathetic strings as the instrument glanced against something on its way to rest. Andy must have been holding his breath. It was like he'd merged with the darkest of the shadows.

"Is this a bad time?"

"Actually, uh, it's probably perfect," Arien admitted.

Aspen sat on the threshold of Van Gogh's side doors and set a hand down on a damp, naked foreleg. Arien could feel her tenuous grasp grow accustomed to her surprise. She patted it first and then rested her hand there.

"Uh, Andy, do you have a doobie?"

There was a pause that filled the darkness and the darkest shadows in it.

"No, Arien, but I'll go get you one."

Arien surely detected a distant note in the intensity of Andy's reply.

"Awesome, Dude."

Andy swept himself out in a mere minute, picking up a dropped sandal with his clothes under his arm.

"It smells funny in here."

"It could use some incense."

"No it's not bad, though; kind of musky, like a locker room – or, I could say it smells like hot boys."

"It's not far from the truth." Arien was so zoned he found it difficult to pronounce the words. It was as if he were talking in his sleep. But in any case, he'd rejected denial as an option. Though he didn't want to move a muscle, he sat up, mainly to keep awake, and he realized it was about all he could do. As he moved, Aspen's hand slid down his foreleg to rest around an ankle. It was so fluid and sensual. Nor did it ask too much of him, but it certainly felt right.

"You play so beautiful, and I really love your voice."

"Thank you so much!" She sounded genuinely pleased.

He rocked his head back, unsure what else to say. Truth be told, Arien was (literally) blown-out, exhausted and spent. He chuckled to himself, feeling like the village idiot. His foremost objective was sleep.

Then, Aspen impulsively leaned in to kiss him. Arien rallied when their lips met. His naked body was so damp and clammy and this must have intrigued her because she pressed herself into him and allowed her hands to join around him, pulling him closer, and the feeling in his loins was something between a dull pain and a link into his body with a chain to his basin's stopper. Arien sighed, collapsed into her, and passed into a blissful sleep.

30 — "Be still. Listen to them. Feel them."

Arien awoke to a reality check. Tina was sitting next to him in her nightshirt, reading a paperback by the mid-morning light. She gazed down at him when he blinked and rubbed his eyes. He nodded and she smiled. He looked up at the ceiling but his gaze didn't stop there. He wondered what she knew and how he should feel about it, sifting through a range of emotional detritus that pressed upon his tent like the blizzard of a long night. Andy, Andy! What have you done? Should I hate you or be glad you interfered?

"I need a shower." He threw the blanket off, proving his point with musty-dankness.

"It's set up," Tina said, though Arien knew it was.

"Where's the towel?"

"Hanging over the door." She pointed it out.

Arien grabbed it, wrapped it around his waist and set off toward the bus. He could feel her eyes behind him on his back. Now, he was ashamed but then felt anger for being ashamed. That's bogus. I'm just being me. I'm just doing my thing!

He tossed the towel over the folding chair by the entry and stepped into the shelter. Arien wet himself down. The water was a little cold but it was refreshing. The stainless soap dish had a fresh bar of Ivory. No sooner had he gotten it wet than it slipped from his grasp and fell between the slats of the wood palate he stood on. "Damn it."

"That you in there, Arien?"

Why did this have to be him, now? "Yeah, Otter."

"What's happening in there?"

"I dropped the soap." His fully extended hand could touch the bar but there wasn't room to hold it and pull it out. Arien wanted to cuss again but stifled it.

Otter pulled the sheet at the entry aside and stepped in with Arien. He wore a towel around his waist and, of all things, he was holding the staff!

Arien gawked incredulously at it. "What are you doing with that?"

"We're rescuing the soap, Arien. Put your hand down there and grab it." Otter pointed at Arien's feet, he pushed the end of the staff between the slats and with a quick motion got under the bar and flipped it up.

Arien laughed excitedly, in spite of himself. He caught the slippery bar with both hands, then it flipped up like a fish but he caught it and cupped it surely before it got away again. He grinned a little sheepishly.

Then the staff unexpectedly whooshed back down, smacking a big toe smartly on the way.

"Ow, ow, fuck! Bitch! What the fuck, Otter?" Arien shouted.

"Now," Otter said evenly, "if you drop the ball like your soap, you may not have anybody around to help you pick it up."

Arien stood stunned under the spray of water. A sharp, throbbing pain reached up past the knee. Arien's toenail was ringed in bright red. Otter leaned the Tree Family staff in the corner of the screen before leaving. Arien reached for it now to keep himself from keeling over and maybe to thwack after Otter with it. His stomach felt queasy. "Damn it! Bitch!"

He ignored a few people that followed him back to the van. Tina was still there. She watched him with concern, limping with the staff and when she saw the bloody toe, scrambled through baggage for the first aid kit. He sat on the threshold, leaning against the jam with his pulsing foot out in front. Tina sat down there alongside and set his foot onto her lap.

"Ow! Damn it!

"Aw, Grovey," she crooned, presently squeezing some jelly stuff out of a tube and wrapping gauze around the toe, linking it carefully to the adjacent one. "I wish we had some ice. How did you do this? Did Otter have anything to do with it? He came for that staff right after you left!"

"Tina, I have something to tell you," he said, gritting his teeth.

Tina locked her eyes with his. "Arien, you don't have to tell me anything I don't already know."

"How's that, Babe?"

"Well," she said, taking hold of the staff, "Otter said he needed this to fix another crack in you skull and I remembered something you said to me last night. You must have gotten it then. Or, maybe it was after you left."

"Ha. Well, damn. That never happened!"

"Oh, something must have happened." She laid the staff across her lap where she sat. She actually began to laugh. "I thought he was going to crack you in the head with it!" Her sudden merriment was incongruous. She was the same loving, cheerful Tina.

"Andy loves me too much," Arien said with a sigh.

"He loves you, no doubt. But you know, my Dad always said, there's a reason for everything." She looked out at the broken yard and into the distance, turning the staff over in her lap. "I don't believe good people do bad things."

"Oh, Babe, no way. Good people do fucked-up shit all the time."

"Well, you might see it that way, but maybe that's just what they need to do or, maybe it's the role they have to play."

"Whoa, what are you smokin', Babe?" Arien couldn't believe Tina was saying this stuff. He began to feel dizzy as he often did when he lost his bearings. First, Otter scratched his heart like a raging hell cat and now – Who is this girl? "And what's this about roles?"

Tina regarded him patiently. "You're not the only freak around here, Arien," she intoned. "I've done acid, too. I think things make sense. We have a destiny. Our lives are already in God's mind and may have been since the beginning."

Arien said, "Wow. You're strikin' hot, Tina. You make me so proud." He pulled a red out of the pack that was lying with his clothes and winced with a pain stabbing deeper than his toe.

"What is it, Clayboy?"

Clayboy had come up and was shifting awkwardly. He reached into his pocket and handed a matchbook to Arien. Arien lit his smoke and took a deep drag at it.

"Otter wants to know you won't try to kill him if he comes to make peace."

"Ass hole," Arien said under his breath, but he cracked a sorry smile when he saw the grin Tina wore.

Arien took a deep breath when people began to materialize around Van Gogh. He might have expected everyone to be caught up in the drama but it was interesting to actually see. There were lots of long faces, worried glances. He wondered if he should make himself appear angrier than he was, to strengthen his case as it were, but the painful truth was he had been deeply hurt. He looked up grimly, and with his toe still throbbing when Otter came forward, wearing a fresh T-shirt and cut-offs. His hair was barely dry and hung with a dark gloss on his shoulders.

Jeff stood to one side, Andy on the other. Oak and Willow, who came right up front, and Aspen, Hawthorne, Ben, Cassie, Myrtle, and everyone else was there, too. Clayboy sat on the threshold next to Arien and Tina, which was noticed.

Arien watched as Otter flashed the peace sign, like a military salute.

"Before you say anything, Arien, I'm sorry I drew blood. The staff got heavy in my hands."

People shook their heads and shuffled. There were murmurs off to the side.

"Dude, why did you hurt me? I love you, Otter. I would never hurt you. What the fuck did I do to you?"

"Your head swelled." Otter looked right into him.

"You tell me what I did wrong. If I did something wrong I'll fix it!" Arien flicked ash off his cigarette. Soon they were lighting up all over the place. Even Clayboy scoped Arien's pack and reached to serve himself one.

"Really, Otter. You went too far to make a point. You have to let people do their thing," Andy said.

Otter's gaze held steady. "Arien, do you know where you are?"

"Yeah, we're outside of Cleveland."

"Think again. And Andy should know that, if anybody does, and when he wakes up and gets it he'll stop talking stupid."

Andy was about to protest but Jeff put a hand on his shoulder. "Wait," he said.

"Brother," Otter continued, "you're growing so fast I've had a hard time keepin' up, but I've been doing my damnedest. It's really important you get this, what one person does and what you do are two different things." Otter let that settle and then drove on. "I'll even risk our friendship to keep you awake. And, it would break my heart but – Otherwise, the people who love you, Arien, will get burned real bad."

"Oh my God, Otter!" Andy scoffed.

"And you, Andy, you cut him way too much slack! If you're just happy to bask in his glory, you'll get stuffed like a rubber and find yourself under the tires on Lover's Lane."

Andy looked shocked.

"Now, Arien, I apologize for making you bleed. I'm really sorry about that. But you owe me something, too."

Arien was getting exasperated. "Otter, you're a bully, and I don't need a Dad. My Dad died in Viet Nam. Why should I apologize to you?"

Otter groaned. He began to look defeated. He turned to walk away.

"Otter, Otter, wait!"

He continued to walk away.

"Otter, alright, I'm sorry I kissed her! Is that it? Is that what you want?"

There were more murmurs and chatter from the witnesses.

When Otter turned around, his expression was changed. It said something else. Arien spun wheels to read it. Otter came back and hunkered down, like an umpire, with hands on his knees to be at eye-level. "It's not the fact that you kissed her," he whispered. "I'm more okay with that than you realize. Everybody wants to kiss you and would jump at your invitation, and that's just an inch from a sense of entitlement and, and Arien, do you think you can handle it when so many people, a lot older and wiser than you are, haven't been able to? You're no rock star, man. You're more than that."

Then Otter stood up, ramrod straight. "And it's not really an apology I need. That's the wrong word, Little Brother. It's something else. I hope you figure it out, because I'll be going if you don't." When he walked away Jeff accompanied him.

Arien's heart now was numb as his toe. He looked down at the ground, where the pebbles and sparse weeds and a few rusty lengths of rebar, half-buried in the dirt, blended into an unfocused play of dull tone and washed-out color. He acutely felt the eyes of the family and interpreted their sympathy but in the high court of his own internal review, he found himself wanting. "Damn it," he cursed to himself.

"That was harsh." It was Andy, who now stood near.

Tina regarded him with a neutral expression and when Andy began, "I'm sorry, Tina, if I–"

She cut him off with a wave of her hand. "You have a heartfelt role to play," she said. "Here," she added passing the staff up to him. "Feel this, it really is heavy."

"Wow! Heavy!" Andy agreed.

Clayboy moved around into the van to sit, cross-legged, very close behind Arien. He put a hand on Arien's shoulder and leaned his forehead against it, like a little kid would do to sooth his Daddy or an older brother in pain. Arien could sense the boy's heart, as he had once before, and he easily apprehended the profound sympathy of emotion between them that called him, as if from a very great distance. Oh, he cried inside, this is way older and much bigger than I am!

Arien looked up at Andy and Tina. "No," he admitted. "God damn, I get it. I get it. It wasn't harsh enough!"

A very tenuous thread links us. It was the Voice, the voice of Cypriano.

How did it happen?

You tuned in.

Is it–?

Yes, like a radio.

What can you tell me?
Will you live for them?
Yes, I said I would. I said I —
Cypriano interrupted: *Be still. Listen to them. Feel them.*

Arien found Otter behind the Quonset in the shade where people had placed cushions and pillows to hang out, read, sew or play with the kids. Jeff was there, and Otter studied a little yellow book. He looked up without expression when Arien came near. Those who were nearby continued to do whatever they were about but obviously with ears cocked.

"What are you reading, Otter?" Arien opened.

"The Dhammapada. I'm reading the 'Canto of Affection'."

"Is it anything like Andy's 'Gita'?"

"They're both spiritual epics. The Dhammapada is the words of the Buddha. Here, I just read, *Whoso is perfect in virtue and insight for vision, is established in the Dhamma, has realized the truths and fulfils his own duties, him do folk hold dear.*"

"Rad, Brother. That's a lot to live up to."

"For most men, it's the work of a lifetime, Arien."

"I don't know if I have that much time."

They were silent for a moment. Chortling came from the direction of kids who stacked bits of broken brick with a blue-plastic bucket and a little toy shovel. Willow's transistor radio was tuned to a station playing '50s rock and roll. Otter slipped a doobie out of the jacket lying next to him. He lit it with a stick match and quickly passed it to Arien for the power hit.

"How's the toe?" Jeff asked.

"I think if I cut it off it wouldn't hurt as much." He passed the smoke back to Otter.

"God, I'm sorry, Arien. I just wanted to scare you. I never intended to hit you so hard with it." Otter had a certain twinkle in his eye. It appeared to be both sincere and playful.

"You're off the hook, Otter. Andy and Tina both agree. The staff really is heavier than it used to be."

Cheers went up to the sound of a car's arrival. "That will be Gary and Harlan," Jeff observed. He stood up to go. "Thanks, Arien!" He applauded, with apparent, heartfelt relief.

"Nah, Dude." Arien shook his head. "I should be thanking you, and Otter, too. Thank you, Otter, you bitch, for splitting my toe open."

Otter broke a wide smile over his most sagacious nod.

"'Cause I know now it's much better to limp into the Light than run on the Dark Side without you."

Otter joined his hands in a prayerful gesture and bowed his head slightly. "You're most welcome, O worthy One."

31 — Treachery is everywhere, but especially hides within

"Oh! Sooooo awesome!" Arien cried out when the sign reading, "Welcome to New York, the Empire State" chugged by. Laughter and hurrahs filled the crowded little van that came straight from Cleveland on I-90, south of the very big lake, and crossed a corner of Pennsylvania, and then turned onto SR-17 into the great state that hosted a most legendary concert. There was a moment Arien actually felt like a kid, free as the wind.

Tina was driving. Finally, before leaving Ohio she blasted the boys for hogging the wheel. It was the first time Arien saw her temper flashed at people and he found himself loving it. "You're so cute when you're pissed!" he'd said, and everyone concurred, making her feel even more aggravated, and they knew when it came down to submission or else. She wore righteous pride as their exultations subsided. "We made it, guys!"

"Here, it's not distance but time we have to cross," Arien mused, considering the open weeks that still lay ahead.

"And how should we cross the time?" Jeff drawled. He sounded more Texas just now.

"Maybe we could go to summer camp." The idea lit Arien up. Summer camp would be a perfect way to do the summer!

"I went to camp when I was a kid," Jeff noted. "I hated it. There was a bully there, and he hassled me 'till I cried to go home."

"Aw, poor baby," Tina comforted, staring at the road ahead.

"Let's look for a store," Otter said. "We need a bag or two of ice."

"What for, Otter?"

"It's a surprise."

"I think I lived in a castle in a past life," Arien volunteered. They had just toasted their noble pasts. Andy was laughing and chiding people for typical answers like a king of France or pharaoh of Egypt. "Most people were serfs, soldiers or sorry bastards who lived mean, grubby little lives," he insisted.

Arien felt a bit guilty indulging in Otter's 'surprise.' He held the little Dixie cup of bubbly with due consideration. He thought, what are Otter's criteria for sharing? Or, something along those lines, because anyone riding in the station wagon, the bus and the step van were shit out of luck. Of course three vehicles followed Van Gogh to the little gas station store for the ice; it seemed indulgent, even though everyone appeared to appreciate the stop but the hapless proprietor, who must have believed his restroom key was lost forever. Some shuffling added Aspen and Clayboy to Van Gogh's passengers.

Aspen turned out to be a good idea. Arien was nervous at first, but he got over it. On one level he was still working on Otter's 'lesson' and on another, some latent, unresolved irritation. He admitted to himself he probably didn't see the whole picture, but also wondered if he could have been taken advantage of because, after all, he was only seventeen and Otter was twenty-five.

But Aspen made a connection that was open and honest and as inviting as ever. Maybe what was so exciting about her was she was closer to Otter's age than his. She was mature, so lovely, so exotic and accomplished. Her singing and technical virtuosity with both guitar and dulcimer was fantastic. He wondered why she didn't make records. Come-on! I'm a hot kid! He sorely yearned to know what fucking her would be like – and, he hoped not to show that to Tina.

I'm more okay with it than you realize, Otter had said. Did he mean that? And, what exactly was the hair that weighed the difference, the divide of rightness and what was natural and good, from – what was it Otter called it – a sense of entitlement? It was, after all, about self indulgence, wasn't it? Arien thought so because it was when he grasped that and owned it, as it were, that the energy changed and what could easily have caused a painful schism ended at a new level of mutual understanding.

It had been a very public airing, too. Arien could see how proper resolution to a sticky problem was at least as important to do as whatever it was he had that dazzled people. Perhaps the craziest realization of all was Arien had never known his mind to be capable of contending with this kind of stuff! Talk about swelling a head! It was the polar opposite of a vicious circle, a source of inestimable pride with a valve stem in its ear.

Arien made it a point to formulate a very careful question to ask Cypriano, What is the greatest danger? He was impressed with the resonant reply that came and without delay: *Treachery is everywhere, but especially hides within.*

Tina seemed relaxed enough. She'd chatted with Aspen as naturally as anyone else. Arien didn't see it as a competition. Maybe that's why Tina didn't behave as if it were, but still. Arien had no desire to know the limits of her tolerance.

Clayboy was clearly so happy to be riding in Van Gogh, among the Stand and with Arien. Arien's heart swelled with pride to look at this kid who was surely the best little brother a fellow could hope to find along a road. Now the lad was a little tipsy. His grin was stuck and he giggled easily.

After the ice stop, Jeff held the wheel again. He balanced his cup between fingers on the edge. He'd been fairly quiet. He tended to be anyway, but now more so. He looked ahead at the highway and seemed to be elsewhere.

And then there was Andy. He certainly wasn't ashamed of what he did. On the contrary, he had this cat that ate the canary air about him. It was annoying. But he made up for it with his obvious affection that was courageous to Arien, because it was genuine and it was true and yes, flattering.

Andy laughed again, "So, let's see, you lived in a castle – then you probably were the old crone that swept the kitchen."

"No, stupid, I was the king! Damn, Otter, this is good!" Arien drained his cup and held it out for more.

"Alright then, another round," Otter agreed. He fished into the ice of the open cooler and hauled out another pretty bottle. Arien never had champagne before and quickly warmed to its seductions. He watched Otter peel foil away from the top, untwist the restraining wire and set his thumbs under the cork. POP! They winced as the cork shot the ceiling and ricocheted to thud among them on the quilt-covered mattress. Otter deftly caught belching foam in his cup. Seven refills almost drained the bottle. He set it down between his legs and raised his drink. "To New York State and to Woodstock!" he declared.

And all joined, "To New York State and to Woodstock!"

Jeff called a gas stop on 17, the state route pulling along the Allegany River and the railroad tracks that trace their way of least resistance between forested foothills and gradually, the higher range that graciously shares its name with the river. It was a pretty country of quaint, old farm houses and small clusters of brick and granite that wore their Nineteenth-and-turn-of-the-Twentieth-Century storefronts in shades of faded 'Empire' and a few roadside, touristy Indian motifs.

"They call these molehills mountains," Andy pointed out the window.

"A dude could skate 'em," Arien said absently. "Catch some air."

Jeff guided the van over the bridge from Steamburg and turned at the Mobil sign that came up on the right. The little two-bay station was a white-painted wood-frame structure with big, multi-pane windows on a gray granite footing. It had a metal roof and an overhanging drive-through supported with square white, clabbered columns. The man at the pump had bronze skin and jet black hair.

"Hear the Legend of the Admen, Ere they conquered all creation!" Aspen declared. "In the Prophylactic forest, on the shores of Coca Cola, dwelt the Moxies in their wigwams – Old Sapolio, the chieftain, Pebico, the grizzled prophet, And the warriors young and eager…" I don't remember the next verse. I'm all mixed up." She giggled.

"What is that?" Otter nudged her.

"Oh it's a fun poem my Mom read to me when I was a kid, a spoof of 'Song of Hiawatha' I think."

"This is the country, I imagine," Andy said.

"Are there Indians here?" Clayboy asked, perking out of a drowse.

And then Andy said something that stopped the action, "The only good Indian–" he didn't finish the sentence. He dangled it out like a plank off the side of a brigantine. But Arien could see no one wanted to step on it.

"Oh, I know what you're goin' to say," Jeff guessed.

"–Is it, setting the charges at Mt. Rushmore?"

"Clever, Andy," Otter applauded.

Arien was pleased to get the joke but that couldn't totally explain why he was relieved. While the bus was gassing up and Van Gogh waited in the parking area near the water and air station, he had an urge to move on ahead of the group to check things out. He had a feeling about this area. He needed to be a little further up the road, free of the clutter of everybody.

Jeff was checking the tires when Arien came to stand by, barely keeping the lid on his urge to scoot. "You dudes need to stay here or park where you can for a while."

"Van Gogh?" Jeff wrinkled his brow.

"Everybody."

"Why, Arien?"

"I don't know, but I don't think I'll be gone long."

Arien felt a little foolish, walking so fast to the road. That power-walk made his sore toenail complain. It rubbed against the top of his Keds in such a way, he thought, that he could actually lose it. Fuckin' Otter! Shortly, Arien was at the road and felt a few pairs of eyes at his back, simply wondering, and then become rather surprised which turned to alarm when he stuck out his thumb and the very first vehicle to approach, an old, dingy white International pickup, stopped and scooped him up.

"Where are you going, Sonny?" The man at the wheel kindly asked as Arien pulled the door shut behind him. He looked like he could have been a farmer, in a plaid shirt, jeans and dirt boots. He was lean and appeared to be middle-aged. His hair was gray. He wore a VFW cap.

Arien was still for a moment, both to catch his breath and gather a few thoughts. The truck was up to 60 miles an hour in no time and the inside of the cab provided a new perspective on the world. He looked out at the road ahead, a fascinating country of lush green and wavy grasses, stands of hardwoods between a smattering of old, wood-frame houses and here and there a sliver of lazy Allegany winding smoothly through the hardwoods along its banks and occasionally cut by the rail lines that drove their way east and west. Behind all was the backdrop of forested mountain rumps that tumbled away north, east and south. He was so excited to be here.

"The town up ahead will do it."

"Salamanca?"

"Right on."

"You're not from around here."

"Oregon – uh, San Francisco."

"Oh, I was in Oregon, once. It was back during the war. Nice place. Rains a lot, though. Trees get real tall. Did you know the Japs actually landed some bombs in there?"

"No, Dude." Arien pulled the Reds out of the pocket of his T-shirt and offered the man one.

He accepted. "Thanks," he said. "Well, they did. Didn't do much, though. Landed in the woods. Started some fires. True. You didn't know that?" He dug a Zippo out of his pocket, clicked the lid back and lit Arien's cigarette first.

"What brings you to Salamanca? You have to be barely out of school, huh?"

Other than driving through, Arien really didn't know the answer to the first question. "Barely," he owned.

"Have you been here long?"

"We just got here today." Arien blew his smoke out the open window. The passing wind whipped his hair. He rolled the glass up half-way.

"Oh, 'we,' huh? So, you're staying back there?"

"Well, no, Dude, we're headed through, eventually. We're going to Woodstock but we have over a month to burn."

"I don't follow you, Son. You have a job coming up, school?"

"Nah," Arien laughed. "The concert, Man.

"Well, I don't know anything about that."

"You will." Arien chuckled to himself.

"Alright, okay." The driver scratched his forehead with his thumb, bringing the ash-end of his cigarette close enough to his hat brim that it knocked the ember off and dropped it in his lap. The subsequent distraction caused the pickup to veer into the oncoming lane. There wasn't time to think. Arien grabbed at the wheel with his left hand and yanked it to the right. They came so close to an oncoming car Arien inwardly braced for the hit.

"Ha!" The man laughed. "That was close enough to magnetize the fender!"

Arien suppressed his scowl. The driver seemed entirely too blasé.

"Hmmmmmmmm, the man mused. So you want to know why I am going to town today?"

"Oh, yes, I've been waiting all my life."

"To meet somebody."

"Oh." The person Arien might have preferred to name was "Bozo."

"And, the funny thing is, I don't know who it is. But I'm growing suspicious. He has a sense of humor, my friend does. We were in the war together. He was so brave, but he never lost his sense of humor! After the war he went back to the reservation at Sells and I returned here. He called me – and he hasn't called for years – the other day, he called me, and he told me I have to pick somebody up in Salamanca. So, I said, 'Cypriano, who is this person?' and he said, 'I will know who it is because he will save my life!' Ahhahahahaha!" He laughed merrily to himself.

Arien smiled in spite of his nerves. This wasn't a bad person. His vibe was really pretty cool. The name, Cypriano, shot a rocket, too, but gathering clouds of confusion and self-doubt swallowed it. He wondered now if maybe he should have blown his silly impulse off and not left everybody in the lurch. He totally rejected one nagging possibility as too unlikely.

The driver worked his way into town, west, around road construction and over a green, steel bridge spanning the river to a right-angle main street where old brick and wood-frame structures clustered together in what to Arien appeared very 'Old World.' There were some things about it that reminded him of San Francisco, and parts of Portland, which used more wood and stucco than brick and granite, but reflected a similar age and style in the older neighborhoods. The pickup came to rest at the curb in front of a tobacco store with a large wooden Indian out front. The sign said, "Bedell's Wholesale."

"Well, Son, this is my first stop. Will this do it for you?"

"Oh, uh yeah. Thanks, Dude."

The man sat indecisively. "Then, indulge me, Sonny. Wait here while I go inside."

"Uh, what for?"

"Because nobody's out front. Either he's inside, or he's already sitting in my truck."

"Does Cypriano even know what I look like?" Arien asked Ellison Black Snake. They stood on the bank of a perfectly lovely creek running along a grove of ancient sugar maples, maybe a quarter-mile from where the pickup was parked. Arien noted how his train so often stopped at places like this and how right it seemed to be. The dark brown trunks sustained a majestic canopy above them that sang into the currents of humid air percolating through a strong, young-summer's bright-green leaves. Arien was grateful for the rest. His toenail throbbed inside the sneaker. He guessed it oozed because it felt damp and sticky.

Ellison had been fairly quiet up until now. It was a little unsettling but the vibe was not ungracious. In his mind, Arien reviewed their time together since leaving the tobacco store. Ellison had just gotten enigmatically back into the pickup and pulled away from the curb without saying or revealing anything, other than the pensive way he'd grasped the handle off the steering column and engaged first gear, and the idea did cross Arien's mind that maybe he was being kidnapped.

When they arrived at a big wooden house in town, Ellison conferred with a young man there and then they were back in his pickup, headed someplace else. It did offer a curious contrast to Ellison's initial, easy intercourse, to wait for half an hour before volunteering his name, which confirmed his origins, and now that Arien was assumed to be a guest, to pass long moments in pregnant silence. Arien was tempted again and again to speak but he held it back. Maybe the man was testing him. Arien was determined to prioritize the veritable riot of his competing thoughts and questions.

"I think he would be surprised," Ellison finally answered. "He must know that you are young but young near you looks old."

"I'm older than I seem," Arien defended.

Ellison studied him. He chucked to himself. "When my boy was a baby he was older than you."

Arien didn't answer that. He wished he had a comeback but couldn't think of anything other than a response to, 'your mother's so fat that-' and it patently didn't apply.

"So, how many people are you traveling with?"

"About twenty five."

"Ohhhhhhh, Cypriano, you owe me big-time!" Ellison said, squeezing the words between his lips in a fervent oath. He scratched his forehead as he did in the pickup, but now without a cigarette to entrap him. "Save my life!" He squealed, and laughed. "My friend and brother has yet to understand that I don't get even, I get ahead!" He confided this to Arien with a mischievous twinkle.

"I pity the dude," Arien said, catching on. "But you must have done something very bad to him, huh?"

Ellison's guilty expression was endearing and his easy laughter, infectious. Arien liked this dude.

It seemed they were barely over a creek and out of town when Ellison stopped the pickup in a field off the end of a dead-end road that had gone over two sets of railroad tracks, the first, running more to the south and the second predominately eastward. The drive seemed like it should have ended somewhere. Whatever it was had been cleaned up. Arien got out of the truck and looked around, waiting for the man to say something.

"The Zawatski farm was here. The house and barn used to be back there." Ellison waved his hand. "They want to put the freeway here. I'd rather they didn't."

Then, Ellison led him down an overgrown trail through creek-side woods. Arien kept up as best he could, favoring his foot and unable to mask a slight limp. The trees allowed each other enough space for last-year's leaves to carpet the open ground in shades of earth and tan, and then opened out into a swampy glen where little frogs leapt invisibly into still pools of water, and hide in impenetrable clumps of cattail rushes as footsteps approached them. Arien stooped to check out a monster turtle shell, white as an egg, with its carapace still attached. It was right by the trail at the foot of a big, broad rock that seemed out of place.

It must have been here a long time! The shell was easily as big as his forearm. Ellison stopped and waited patiently while the teenager inspected it, turning it over in his hands, running his hand over the rough, patterned surface on top and imagining the awesome creature it must have been. Then something called him back to the rock. It was very big. It pointed up out of the ground at a low angle but the peculiar thing about it was the hollows and channels in its surface. These didn't appear to be natural.

"Rock Eddy," Ellison said. "It's been here longer than that shell."

Arien clambered up on top to kneel over, feeling it with his hands.

"Spear points were honed in those channels, and corn ground in the bowls with a stone, right here, eight-thousand years before Columbus!"

Arien said, "Wow, awesome!" He set both hands flat on the cool surface of the thing and something of the enormity of time and the long-ages of the first inhabitants pressed upon him with the enormity of Rock Eddy. This was suddenly the most special place he had ever been, right up there with Old Rock and the fireball. "Wow," he said again.

Ellison made no effort to hurry him and they lingered there as long as it took his guest to absorb its silent message.

Arien wanted to give it something. There was nothing of value in his pockets, so when he climbed off of the rock he picked up the turtle shell, placed it on the edge, and slowly turned away.

There were clusters of wild huckleberry nearby and a rhododendron that had much smaller leaves than its western cousin. Arien touched them as he moved past.

With sharpening senses, Arien stopped again, apprehending the proximity of another creature's body. It was a young buck sporting velvety, adolescent horns. It was perfectly still. It was off to the side, barely twenty feet away. The critter's deep whistle, when it knew it was discovered, sounded like leaking air from a broken organ pipe. But it stood its ground. Arien's delighted smile was observed by his elder companion.

Continuing, they moved through a zone of noisy blue jays that raised a ruckus with a quadraphonic intensity, monopolizing the air. "I'm sorry you feel that way," Arien told them, forgetting the man with him for a moment and goofing on the birds. One of them jazzed back at him but Arien said "Ah, baloney," and when he laughed all their complaining stopped, returning the space to muffled sounds of the creek and the shuffle of dead leaves under their feet.

At length, their way wound to where the creek running at their right joined the Allegany River. "This is where Great Valley Creek gives its life to the O'hee'yo." Ellison said. "Once upon a time, there were the long-houses of our people near here."

Arien knew it was time to acknowledge what was happening. "This is a special place," he said. "We're all obliged."

"Well, it's no summer camp. Sorry, I wasn't able to provide that. But, a field for your jamboree it is and it's only a couple of miles to town."

Arien smiled inwardly. No summer camp! Ha!

"Come, walk with me back to the truck. I have some business to attend to so you can wait there at the end of the road for your friends."

Arien hung about by the old, rutted drive to greet everyone when they arrived. It seemed like forever. Now he paced. He smoked two cigarettes in a row and then had to laugh at himself. He recalled what Cypriano said, *Be still. Listen to them. Feel them.*

Arien fell into a moment where he considered what he would say to Cypriano now. The bridge between that past and this moment was again, as he'd seen so clearly while tripping, a quality of his sense of the solidity of space, or whatever it was between the things in it. This wasn't explored with words but rather a pure kind of awareness. It didn't matter if it were a thought or an object. Thoughts were, no doubt, more subtle, but they were still things and related to the same forces or laws that governed all things. He felt so connected!

But it's easier to do this for other people than it is to do it for me, he wanted to say. And that led to another consideration. He sighed, foreseeing a Herculean struggle to have to master himself, a person he knew as an emotional astronaut strapped to a yoyo, quick to anger, open to rapture, horny as a buck, addicted to fortune, susceptible to flattery, to review just a few of them, and that hardly considered the skull he wore in a size too small.

It's not that I don't believe you, he said within. It just may be asking too much of me.

No, to be master of yourself is a misleading goal. It is far better to surrender to yourself. Trust him.

"Wow," Arien said out loud. He broke into a smile. Here's where one God takes on all the others. And, he knew he could be grateful for their services instead of having to fight them. How bogus that would be!

Cypriano didn't speak to that but Arien was sure of his approval.

Arien studied the terrain. Tall grass filled a wide-open area where there would be plenty of room to park and spread-out. They would need the tarps and tents. He knew the Tree Family probably had enough from the camp at Medicine Bow packed on top of the bus, but two or three more would get him and Tina some privacy and provide a shelter for Gary's carload. He scoped a site for the latrine in a stand of maple and beech just north of where he stood. It was quiet. The creek, the river and circling trees would provide a good buffer. Thanks, Cypriano!

The sound of vehicles and especially the whine of the bus broke Arien's reverie. A car he hadn't seen before led the skirting cloud of dust and the crunch under tires and fenders. Arien waved the peace sign at the vehicles, with faces pressed to their windows, passing him and circling to a stop. He watched as Tina wagged a finger while she flashed that grin of hers at him. I can't help it, he shrugged.

Oohs and Ows, and Wows tumbled out with the people as they came to stand in the tall grass and look about. Gradually, everyone drifted over by Arien while he and Tina briefly embraced. They watched as the young man Ellison spoke with earlier drew up to introduce himself. "Thomas," he said simply, holding out his hand.

Arien grasped it firmly. "Arien Grove," he replied. Then he looked into the eyes of his friends, his Sisters and Brothers, and he said, "I think we'll need a few more tents. The latrine can be up there. The Creek is that way," he pointed to the north of where they stood, "and the river's over there," indicating the opposite direction. Town is just a couple of miles away. That's pretty convenient, huh?"

"My God, Arien, this is unbelievable!" Andy gushed.

"Well, it's not a summer camp." Arien said with a straight face. And then he winked at Thomas. "But it should suit us just fine."

The new encampment came together in a series of modular stages over the next few days. Cassie, with her little boy, Wally, stayed planted in the back of the bus, leaving the middle section to serve as an evening salon and day-center for the mommies and kids that Cassie kept in order. Ben and his wife, Sundew, along with Kelsey, Sammy, Heather and Crystal's Mom, pulled a tarp tightly over the bus' top rack to keep it cooler inside during the day. Nobody wanted the children getting near the water unless, as Oak successfully argued, they were supervised with multiple adults, so the bus had to be kept comfortable for use at any time.

Almost everyone else set up tarps and tents in the nearby woods. The natural canopy provided daytime shade from summer's sun, but it was closer to the creek. As there was a problem with mosquitoes there around dusk and the first hour or two afterwards, campers generally congregated at that time around the fire pit. It was constructed in the field with a circle of rocks within a stone's throw from where the vehicles were parked.

Arien enjoyed helping with that. He and Clayboy found the perfect flat rock for the ubiquitous coffee pot and the two of them worked up a sweat pushing, dragging and rolling it from the edge of the field.

"Clayboy, where are you from?" Arien asked at a rest to catch their breath.

"Sacramento." He stared blankly at the rock.

"How long since you were home?

"Maybe two years." Clayboy looked up at Arien, sharpened his focus and set his jaw in a defiant grin.

"Wow, awesome, Dude. Jeeze. What happened?"

"I ran away."

"Where did you go?"

"The Haight." Clayboy's grin broadened. "Summer of love, Dude."

Arien was impressed. "How did you do it?" This kid had to be pretty young when he threw himself into that.

"Wasn't easy. I had to keep duckin' for cover. Pigs scooped me once but I escaped from 'em. They left the barn door open and they couldn't catch me." His grin traveled from one side of his face to the other before fading. His eyes seemed to be rummaging inside among his trove of memories.

"Do you think anybody's looking for you?"

"I'm not who I used to be, Arien. I'm Clayboy. They don't know who to look for anymore."

After fitting the rock into the fire ring, Arien and Clayboy went out with a wood-gathering party. "Dead branches, sticks on the ground only," he instructed, but the idea was originally Oak's. He'd said to Arien, "We're guests here, right? So, we don't want to tear it up, and our fires should be mostly small ones, to conserve wood."

Gary, Harlan, Luke and Sally-Ann made the first run to town on the morning of the second day. They'd taken orders for people, a couple of letters to mail, and a list of food supplies. When they returned they had good things to say about Salamanca. They also brought back a nice present for Arien and Tina.

Arien and Clayboy worked their way out on the trail with an armload of firewood when Arien caught Gary and friends fussing with a rather big, light-green canvas tent piled in a rectangular heap. The site was ample and level and had a view of the creek through an opening in the trees. Harlan was driving stakes in the corners with a hatchet while Gary waited, holding its eight-foot center pole.

"Hi, Arien!" Sally-Ann called. She had an instruction leaflet in her hands.

"Yo, Sally-Ann. Is that your house?"

"No, Arien. This one's yours," she said.

Luke chased that with, "That's right, Arien." He upended a small duffel bag and a few more stakes dropped out to clank together on the ground. "It's from the Outdoor Store, in Salamanca."

"Aw, guys–" Arien's 'you shouldn't have' grimace was followed by dropping his bundle of broken branches and sticks. He stood in the middle of them like a man condemned to burn.

"Man, you have to take it," Luke said seriously. "You and Tina need your space."

"That's right," Sally-Ann followed. "We wanted to get you two something and this seemed like the perfect thing."

"Wow," Arien exclaimed. He was pretty blown-away. This was major. He guessed it had to be an expensive tent.

Sally-Ann stepped over and gave him a hug. "Think of it as a 'Thank You' from us, and especially Luke."

"But what for?"

"That's right," Luke agreed, gathering four slim poles, about six-feet high and setting one down at each corner. "Thanks, for maybe saving my life! I'd be headed to Nam if you hadn't come along."

"And probably the rest of us, too," Gary added.

Arien's reaction to that surprised everyone, including himself. As the wide dam of bitterness he'd carried forever began to break, tears spilled over his eyelids and he couldn't hold them back.

"Knock, knock!" Otter called, later that afternoon. He stood under the attached awning that hung over the entry of the big umbrella tent. It was held up in front with six-foot poles. As Arien waved, Otter zipped open the wide screen door, stepped inside and zipped it up behind him. "Here's a pair of sandals for you." They were the brown leather type, open in front and they had a buckle on the sides.

Arien was resting inside in a pair of boxer shorts. He leaned against his bedroll with one bare foot pulled up close and the other straight out in front of him.

"Whose are they?"

"No matter, Arien. Let's see the damage."

Arien indicated a very soiled gauze bandage.

"Take it off."

It made him wince. It pulled a little. But, it felt better to have it off and his toe exposed to the air. The gauze carried a faint, spoiled meat odor. "Yuck," he said. "Thing's been in my sneakers all day. It doesn't fit with socks."

"Wow, that's quite a reminder," Otter said. It had a nasty appearance in black and purple under the loose nail and the adjacent flesh was a shade of red. "Shall I kiss the boo boo?" He tenderly took hold of Arien's foot and began raising it.

Arien smirked, bit his lower lip in a defiant gesture, yanked it away and flashed Otter his middle finger. "You can kiss my ass."

"That's the spirit," Otter told him. He sat cross-legged on the bare canvas floor facing Arien. The sounds of campers drifted up to them, voices from other sites and beyond, the rustle of air in the branches overhead, a ding of the step van's bell. The back of the tent had a big, screened window that was zipped open and a breeze moved freely through the space.

"Cool digs, man."

"Really. It's from Luke, Sally-Ann, Gary and Harlan."

"I know. Neat people. They must have picked up two of them. They're still setting the other one up over there." He waved at a direction. "I finally met Ellison Black Snake today. He stopped in briefly at the fire pit and chatted with me and Andy and met Oak and Willow, too."

"What do you think?"

"He's amazing. He's really helping us! I asked him why and he told me it was a favor for a friend."

"Yeah, a friend who's telepathic." Arien slipped one and then the other foot into the sandals. He said 'Thank You' with his eyes and Otter nodded. "Funny thing is," Arien continued, "He talks to Ellison on the telephone and me, in my head."

"How does that work? You haven't said much about it."

"Like a radio, I guess, tuned to the same vibe."

"Where is he?"

"Ellison mentioned a place that sounded like, 'Sells'. I don't know it."

"You didn't ask?"

"No." Arien couldn't explain why. It was certainly something he was curious about. An image came to mind – "Window," he said simply. "A very small window."

"Huh?" Otter's furrowed eyebrows pleaded more.

"Only so much can go through at a time," Arien said. He smiled shyly.

Otter forced air through his nose. "You're getting kind-a Zen, you know? Andy's sure you're the Once and Future –- Oops, he asked me not to tell you – but if you want to know what I think, you may be like a reincarnated Zen master."

Arien shook his head. "What's Zen like?"

"The teaching is like how you said what you just told me. You have to stretch your brain or meditate to get around it. It's heavy."

Arien laughed. "If I stretch my brain too much won't it crack my skull?"

"That's different, Brother Grove."

Arien watched through the front window as Clayboy worked his way up the trail hefting a rather large item.

"Ha! And, I'd better get the difference, too, huh? Or, you'll cripple me and they'll have to carry me around in a chair."

"Problem is I think they would."

Clayboy struggled on until he stood panting before Arien's tent. The big item was a dark-blue and white, short-knapped carpet rolled up with a rope. "There were two of these in the bus," Clayboy explained. "This one's yours." He zipped open the front door and set it down there at the front, then proceeded to roll it out, stopping at the center pole. Otter obliged Clayboy by lifting the bottom of the pole aside enough to continue rolling the carpet out. Arien had to get out of the way and move his and Tina's bedding, duffels and day packs. The carpet covered the eight-foot square tent floor almost perfectly.

"Wow, Thanks, Dude. This kid's awesome," he said to Otter as he stretched-out on top of it.

Clayboy smiled proudly and plunked himself down with them. He was still catching his breath.

"He loves to be useful," Arien praised. "That's Clayboy's drug."

Otter began to tap-out a rhythm with his fingers on the pole along side of him. "Oh, I almost forgot. Ellison said some people from the reservation want to meet you."

"That's cool. When?"

The way to the river was a very old path, worn smooth by generations of foot traffic. It wove a way of least resistance according to the contours of rock, tree and elevation, until opening where the two streams came together and then westward, up the north shore of the Allegany, or O'HEE'O as the Seneca pronounced it, along with the flow. Arien had been thinking of a hike up that way and decided to bring the staff along. With him and Tina was a little entourage of the folks from Oregon along with Clayboy and Andy. They stood now at the edge, where water pulsed between the spaces of foliage, deadfall, rocks and feet, to the uneven beat of a rippling current.

Arien could see tadpoles in the shallow water. They scattered when he set the staff he'd used to favor his tender-toed stride down here, plunging it a few inches deep, when he looked up and saw four men standing by the bristling branches of a pussy-willow about fifty feet away. They appeared to confer but Arien came aware they were watching him, even as his friends remained oblivious of their presence. As everyone else left clothes on the shore and eased into the river with a spontaneous decision to get wet, he nonchalantly meandered along the shoreline, as if he were himself unaware of the others, and then stood erect with the staff planted firmly by his side and locked eyes with them. He nodded slightly and waited.

Truth be told, Arien had no idea what the men would do. The thought crossed his mind that maybe they didn't, either. But, they came over to him directly. Arien set his hands over the staff, feeling the cool stone on top of it under his palm.

"So, you are the medicine boy Ellison is talking about," one of them opened, eyeing the Tree Family staff with evident curiosity. The speaker had long, white hair. It was tied behind his back in a pony tail. The other three were middle-aged, graying, two also with pony tails and one, a stout fellow, was cut jarhead short.

"I'm Arien Grove." Arien's demeanor was friendly but he wondered at this introduction. Uncertain, he was relieved when Andy, who was out of the river, pulled his shorts on and walked over to stand dripping alongside.

"Is it true you lead this group?" The old man directly asked. He stared now at Arien's headband that Andy gave to him only that morning before breakfast. The headband was an unusual, large white bandana with a set of four, royal-blue, seven-pointed stars near the middle of each corner. Andy had folded it so only one star was visible at the center of Arien's forehead before tying it off for him. "The Hopi People in Arizona have a legend of the Blue Star Kachina," Andy told him then, and this struck Arien very deeply because of the awful association with that name. He guessed that if Andy had actually known Blue Star he might have thought it too awkward a gift, especially with Otter, Jeff and Tina. But Andy explained the legend of the White Brother who walks in the Way and it seemed acceptable to him and he liked how he looked wearing it, seeing his reflection in one of the step van's side-view mirrors.

"Well, I —"

"Yes, he does. He really does," Andy sincerely answered.

The men quietly assessed Andy, well into his 20s, with the uneven pink scar of a bullet hole at the edge of his pectoral and then looked back to the younger lad, standing squarely with the staff. The man with the short hair said, "He wears the Blue Star."

"But that isn't from our story," another, who wore carpenter-style overalls, countered as if the conversation were private. He stood with his hands in his pockets alongside the old man.

"This is from the record-keepers," the short-haired man said.

"How long do you think to stay?" The first one asked Arien.

"This month, mostly," Arien answered, growing uncomfortable with the interrogation.

Andy added, "We're guests of Ellison Black Snake and he told us we could be here."

"Right now Ellison is the keeper but you must understand this place only came back to us recently and it is not nor will it ever be your property. Is that understood?"

"Oh, yeah, Dude," Arien said, a little defensively. "We're just chillin'."

"And we don't want any trouble brought here." The man in overalls added.

"There won't be any trouble, mister," Andy assured them.

Arien's urge was to tell these people where to go but thought better of it, having no idea who they were.

Without saying anything further, the four visitors turned away to walk further up the path where they disappeared around a bend.

"We may have met the hostiles," Andy quipped, watching after them. "Did they even tell you their names?"

33 — A method that will work

Tree Family's big canvas tarp was set out over poles staked with guy-lines, as they'd had it at Medicine Bow, but this time one edge was anchored off the back of the step van. There, Arien learned, Oak and Willow with both of his girlfriends, Laurel and Nita, had set out a series of folding horses surfaced in 1 x 12 boards to make a long dining table, three boards wide, that could accommodate everyone sitting on crates, a few benches and wooden folding chairs. The boards were tacked down to the horses with box nails to keep it all reliably together.

Supper that night was wok-fried rice with broccoli, carrots and cottage cheese melted in it. With a sprinkle of Tamari sauce, Arien thought it was delicious. By now he'd mastered chopsticks and used them exclusively, like everybody else.

"This is too perfect here," Jeff declared. He sat across the table from Arien. "I'd like to check out town." He leaned forward with his hands on the table top, as if protecting his bowl.

"It is pretty close." Cassie pointed out. "We can practically walk there."

"Yes," Myrtle agreed, "I'd like to check it out. This looks like a fun place." *Listen to them, feel them.* Arien received that with some urgency. He reached into himself. What am I supposed to do?

"Did anybody on the town run happen to see what's playing at the Seneca?" Oak asked.

"Butch Cassidy and the Sundance Kid," Gary said.

Arien liked what he was hearing and chuckled inwardly, dwelling on his former life at YPH, with its contentions and lack of any real conversation, but something was pressing. What could it be?

"Hey there, Sisters n' Brothers," He suddenly called out, and everyone looked at him. "Andy, you said something when we were back in Illinois. You said we needed to do our homework, or some magic, or whatever. What did you mean?"

"Oh, that. You were scaring me, man. I was thinking we needed to focus our power to shield us, or defend ourselves if we had to."

"Ah." Arien digested this. "Well, I think you're onto something. But it's more than that."

"Ho!" Oak pronounced, with a proud smile across his ruddy face. He passed the Tamari to Nita. "Our forest needs rain, our garden needs tending. Arien, I was hoping not to have to bring it up because you have to own it, just like Tree did, and I'm thinking, Praise Be! You really do!" Oak's expression was joyous.

Arien appreciated having his finger on some pulse, as yet unnamed, and here it lay on that table in front of him as sure as his bowl of dinner. In a way, he found it by marshalling courage to take his blinders off and follow the trail where it led. Feel them. But he was getting a little push from behind, too. "Oh God, Oak, I'm not ready." Arien's expression practically pleaded. "I don't know anything about this stuff."

"You just have to let yourself be, Arien," Hawthorne said.

"Yes," Andy chirped. "You *are* this stuff!" He beamed.

"And, don't worry, Arien, we can attend to the details," Willow assured him.

Hawthorne and Clayboy collected bowls from people who were finished with dinner.

"I'm confused," Sally-Ann admitted. "What exactly are you talking about?" Luke sat beside her and Gary and Harlan were on that bench, too. Harlan shrugged.

"That's a very good question," Andy said. "And, I believe it begins with our circle and our ability to focus the energy. I may know how to formalize that and what Arien's Cypriano said about it, so that's a good place to begin."

"Is this about the 'Wheel of Life, Andy?" Kelsey inquired.

"Yes, basically; it's the magick circle."

"We've got to keep it clean," Otter suggested. "Crowley, the Golden Dawn–" He spoke to the table, as if confiding his reservations. "There's so much crap in there."

"How right you are, Otter. The alchemists called it dross, the waste-product in the purification process."

"A circle is a circle, what do we need all this for?" Arien asked. He squeezed Tina's hand next to him. She hadn't said anything but Arien got her vibe, right there with him.

"That's another good question, so I'll say now that whatever we do we'll make sure we know what it's for." Andy promised.

"I like it," Arien said, rapping the table with his chopsticks. It made a hollow sound that carried. "Wait. Cypriano just said–" Arien searched for the words to describe the sense of it. "Conditions for medicine must be made. We need to believe and have faith in each other." Then, Arien broke into a running translation for the first time, "I suggest a circle in which all join hands, to regulate egos. An opening prayer to the highest of beings, the 'Mother and Father of All Things', where the purpose of a gathering is clearly spoken, a light in the center may be lit to symbolize that Mind of our Creator, 'In this thread to which we tune in – or tune – ourselves."

"Wow," Andy remarked. "That's high, Arien. "Let's say that again. Let's make it pretty. "To the Highest? Right? To the Highest and deepest Mother and Father? No, One, uh huh, One, – let's see, deepest, highest–"

"Subtle?" Oak suggested.

Listen to them. "Yeah," Arien applauded. "Good!" And then in an aside to Tina, "This is so bitchin' rad."

"– To the Highest and Subtle One within, why not like that?" Andy went on.

"May we attune–" Willow offered, feeling his way in.

"Focus!" Oak declared. "May we focus ourselves in You, a – a"

"A pathway to the beginning," Hawthorne tried.

"A thread?" Arien suggested.

"Right, it's like a thread," Otter joined. "A thread that we tune in to."

"Only alive," Tina said, excitedly.

"Yes, it lives," Arien agreed. "It's a living thread and it goes all the way back to the beginning!" Arien was rapt in the wash of his new understanding of what it was all about. His head swooned in a pleasantly intoxicated way. He played with his bowl now, turning it with the tips of his fingers.

"Right on, that's good," Hawthorne applauded.

"Okay, good, let's see," Andy said whirling his hands around his head like a conductor. "To the highest and subtle One within, may we focus ourselves in you, a living thread to which our circle attunes!"

"Our harmony: Let's recognize what we have to do there." It was Aspen. "Like singing together," she declared. "We will harmonize."

"– A living thread to which our harmony attunes." Andy finished. "I need my notebook, we've got to write this down!"

"Great start!" Arien applauded. "Now Cypriano's on the directions. This is what he's said before, "In the east is red, like the morning sky when the sun is rising, and the south is yellow, where the sun is highest, and in the west it is white, where it sets into the sea, and the north is black, like at midnight.'

"Well, Arien, I don't know that," Andy said, struggling. "The east, in the magick circle, is blue. That's the air element. The south is red, for fire. The west is white, for water and the north green, for earth. And, I'll go one further, the east gets a sword, the south a rod, or a staff, the west is the cup and the north is a pentacle."

That's not what you said, Arien probed in his mind.

Listen to them.

But that's not what you said.

Listen. You must find the way together.

"Arien? Arien are you with us?"

"Oh, yeah, Andy. I'm good. I don't get it, but it's all good. I think Cypriano is trying to tell me it will all work out, somehow. Here now," he said, asserting himself, "Cypriano is saying, every quarter has its prayer. We'll find them. And now I have this. Oh wow, somebody write this down."

"Got it, Arien." Andy said, standing up to look for his day pack. It was right by him, hanging off the back of his folding chair. He pulled his notebook out of it.

Arien repeated aloud what ran before his mind's eye: "We speak of a psychic fire that needs to be kindled in process." He lingered on those last two words. "The fire powers the engine that moves the work. If this can be done in chanting or song, fine, you should try it. What has been suggested is a method that will work. We bother to say so because it's really important that the method does work." Arien followed that with a "Wow," in his own words, and there were not a few nods of agreement among them.

As evening wore on toward 9 pm and the long shadows of day's end stretched under the tarp, Oak got up and went off. He soon returned with his beautiful brass lamp which he sat in the center of the table where Andy wrote as quickly as his fountain pen would part with its ink. The lamp cast a woodsy, rosy glow in a circle around it. To Arien, it seemed to project the way his heart sang. Aspen was right. He sensed a marvelous resonance with everyone and their working together.

The parents had been the first to go, to put their children to bed, and then a few early birds, but a representative core remained until the wee morning hours. The air, sweet and flowery, blending with the smell of incense, tobacco and kerosene, drew the luscious summer night around them with a pulsing rhythm of insistent crickets, and a twinkling sprinkle of fireflies, and then a haunting whistle before the rolling rumbling, muffled clatter of the Erie-Lackawanna, which coursed the track nearest to their camp.

In the ensuing hush, broken when a whippoorwill called from somewhere in the woods, Otter produced the night's last pair of pre-rolled doobies and sent them off in opposite directions. And, Myrtle served spearmint tea in her fine, picture-glazed teapot.

Oak stood to stretch his big frame. "Well," he praised. "We have a nice container for our gatherings, our yearnings and our heart-songs." He took a light toke on the doobie as it came to him.

Arien noted he rarely saw Oak smoke weed. He didn't smoke anything for that matter. He was nearly always sober-minded and on task, whatever it happened to be. This guy rocks, Arien mused, watching Oak's exception prove the rule.

"Oh yes," Andy agreed. "It has a proper opening, middle and an end. I'd say it's so crap-free, Otter, it's almost revolutionary for a magick service."

"Downright neutral," Otter assented with a smile. "I could imagine a Christian, a Hindu, a Jew and a witch all being good with it."

"Yes," Hawthorne added, "and there's nothing any serious person would object to."

"You'd be surprised," Oak chuckled, and a few others did, too.

"I love the prayers of the quarters," Tina lauded, clasping her hands. "Where did you get that stuff, Andy?"

"I have to give Yogananda some credit. He wrote some lovely elemental praises. I thought our invocations should be like that. Actually, I borrowed a lot of it from him."

"It's gear!" Tina went on. "And Jeff, you got me when you came up with that perfect opening!"

Jeff sipped at the rim of his teacup. They were using the metal camp cups from the step van. The rim was hot and he barely touched it with his lips as he blew over the top. "Well, that's the way the Bible opens," he said shyly, not looking at anybody. "It made sense to me."

"In the beginning was the Word! I love it!" Andy exulted. "And the Word was with God. Even though I haven't the slightest idea what anybody reading a Bible actually means by the name, God, this is perfect!" He nabbed a couple of quick tokes from the dying roach and passed it to Tina.

"Oh, c'mon, Andy. You of all people should know exactly what they mean," Tina protested. She set the roach on the table.

"Well, let me phrase it this way, what I might know and what they claim to know is probably not the same thing."

"The crickets stopped." It was Clayboy, who sat over in a corner. He'd listened all through the discussion and honing of the ritual without speaking until now.

"Probably the passing of the hour," Andy declared. "Has anyone else noticed how the passing hours of a magical work seem to be measured with changes like that?"

"Rad, Andy. I wondered about it." It seemed pretty obvious to Arien now, especially when it was pointed out. He recalled noting a certain bird song earlier, and then an owl when it hooted, out in the woods. Still later there was a gust of steady wind and then, further on, a perceptible cooling of the ambient temperature. The timing did appear to be intuitively synchronistic, though more like the accent of a movement in a musical piece, than an actual hour, but he didn't own the words. It referenced his experiences of the rhythm of knowing, like when to pull over and camp for the night. He drew a crumpled pack of Reds out of his pocket and fished in it.

"You out?" Ben asked. "I have some."

Arien thought for a moment. "Thanks," he said, "but no thanks. I think I already smoked my last one. They nag me all day and they're starting to taste like shit."

"We're not done yet." Arien and Tina drifted in a beautiful, deeply varnished wooden canoe out near the center of Red House Lake. He had no idea where it came from but he and Tina were told that today it was their canoe, and he was too eager to be out in it to make an argument. Now, Arien squinted over the surface of the pocket of crisp, clear water that was littered with their lazy regatta. Like bean pods on the surface of a tropical garden pond, a number of the Tree Family floated, faces shining in the double-dose of reflected sun, voices animated with echoes in the carriage of a light, balmy breeze, and ka-chunk of oarlocks from the aluminum rowboats.

"What's not done, Arien?" Tina relaxed on the slats, with her back against the curved gunnel at the bow and her feet stretched-out under her cane seat. She looked up at him, deep in thought, with the paddle resting over his knees.

"This circle thing; something Otter said last night stuck in my head: 'I could imagine a Christian, a Hindu, a Jew and a witch all being happy with it.'"

"I know what he means. It's so simple," Tina agreed.

"OK, but what gets them there in the first place?"

"Well, I think he means it would fit anybody's trip."

"But what would get them all to be there at once?"

"A major disaster?" Tina laughed.

Arien smiled. "Damn, I want a cigarette so bad I could taste it."

"Smoke another joint."

Arien chuckled. "I'll have a lid-a-day habit," he said.

"Aw."

"Don't 'aw' me. It's all good. I'm just goin' to tough it out."

"Atta boy!"

Arien took a deep, smokeless breath. "So, besides a disaster, what would get them there?"

"You could invite them."

"Consider them invited already. It's on their answering machine. They got the fax, Babe. What will make them come?"

"Did I ever tell you, you were cute but spooky?"

"Yeah, Tina. You probably did. What's that about?"

"The things you say. 'Got the facts?' What facts?"

Arien grinned. "So, you're not helping much. What will get them to come?" He stared at the paddle in his lap, stood it up on the floor and twirled it this way and that between his knees.

"They have to want to come."

"Damn, I wish I could get it. I feel so stupid sometimes."

"Well, maybe you're not listening."

"Yeah, Babe, I'm listening. How do you get them to want to come?"

Andy and Hawthorne were in one of the dinghies. Their approach was a bit fast and Hawthorne had to row backwards quickly to keep from hitting the canoe. Their wake rocked it enough to get Arien's attention but not throw him off the question. "Okay, Dudes, I have a problem."

"Speak, o' sage, that we may solve it." Andy answered ponderously from the stern.

"How do you get a Christian, a Hindu, a Jew and a witch to want to come to the circle we worked on last night?" Arien reached with his paddle to bridge the two crafts. Hawthorne grabbed and held onto the other end.

"You offer to buy the beer?"

"The Christian doesn't drink."

"Oh, God, Arien." Andy shrugged at Hawthorne who returned the gesture. "You're talking Bible-beater? Why even invite them? You're asking to be disappointed."

"What makes people want to do things?" Arien's question revealed some impatience.

"They have to?" Hawthorne offered.

"That's something. What else?"

"Do you know the answer to this?"

"No, Andy, but I really want to."

"I asked you because I had a professor who never said anything but questions in class. He just asked questions and wouldn't stop until somebody gave him what he wanted to hear."

"That's not me."

"They have to, they want to–" Tina rattled off. "I don't know," she continued. "They just want to sell their thing, you know?"

"Yes, she's right, Arien. That's all they want to do," Andy agreed. "That's why they only talk to each other, or likely new prospects, maybe."

"Hmmmm…" Arien considered it. "I feel like that's getting close, 'sell their thing.' Maybe, if they were invited to prove their thing they would want to come."

"But you just hit the wall, Arien. You can't prove religion. It's not science."

"I'm not really inviting anyone either, you know. I just want to create the space where–"

"Wow, man," Hawthorne exclaimed. "That's high. I think I get it."

Arien felt a jolt of adrenaline. "Do you, Hawthorne? Oh, that'd be rad."

"Oh, hey," Andy followed. "You're really working on the sacred space, aren't you?"

"Yeah, Dude. I'm sure that's what Cypriano meant by 'magical conditions.' He said, 'magical conditions must be made.' If it works for you and me it has to work for everybody the same; it has to work for *us*, you see? If we can really prove anything to each other we've done it, and if we can't, it can't be done and it's all bullshit."

Tina wore a beautiful smile. "I'm not sure I get it but I get it," she said.

"Nah, the truth is out there but it doesn't change anything. People just hear what they want to hear and do what they want to do," Andy sighed.

Arien vigorously shook his head in the negative. "That shit doesn't matter. It's confusing, anyway, right? What matters is the truth is there and people who want to can find it. We have to prove it. We have to invite ourselves and we'll want to come because we have something to prove. It means everything!"

"Well, then it really doesn't matter if these people show up or not," Hawthorne speculated. "What matters is if they did, it would work."

"I think so. Cypriano told me, 'the medicine has a purpose and we know what it is.' For my purpose, everyone feels important in the circle, like it matters."

Tina jumped in. "That means to me that they have to feel welcome, and, and–"

"Needed, wanted, like we're all hanging on what they've come to say." Arien finished the sentence, drawing out those last words with a satisfied smile.

"Then we need a preamble to capture that idea."

"I suppose so, Andy, but you'll have to tell me what a preamble is, first, and then maybe you can make us one."

Tina laughed, calling out, "Do we have any volunteers?"

"You can let go of the paddle now," Arien said to Hawthorne, "and thanks for the help, Dudes!"

Tina looked surprised when Arien abruptly announced he wanted to head back to shore. She got back up on the seat and stuck her paddle in the water as he swept their craft around and forward, steering with his blade in a direct line to the boathouse. "Are you going to miss your flight?" she asked.

Arien couldn't explain the impulse but he was getting used to following his intuition. The practice hadn't failed him yet and he was very pleased with its growing list of self-evident results. "Yes," he said, flatly. Tina would have to bear with him once more.

As they approached the dark brown clapboard building Arien already knew the person standing on the dock in front was Ellison. Though Ellison had been by the camp once afterwards, meeting Otter, Oak and Willow, Arien hadn't seen him since the first time they'd met.

"Is that–?"

"Yep, that's my plane," Arien said with a wink. He jumped out of the canoe to steady it at the shoreline. When Tina was out, they pulled it up out of the water. "How is it?" Ellison asked, pointing down at Arien's black and purple toe.

"Nail's coming off. The water's helping, I think."

"That's good. And, who is this pretty lady?"

"This is Tina. Meet Ellison, Babe." They shook hands.

"Pleased to meet you," Tina said. "I love the story of how Arien met you."

Ellison nodded with a rueful smile, "His mentor back there in Arizona owes me big time. There's one trickster that will get his!" They all smiled at this.

"Since I last saw you I met some of the people in your party."

"Yes, Otter told me. Thanks for your help."

"That Otter fellow, he's very strong. He watches through the night. You must listen to what he says."

"I suppose he does." Arien nodded and lent a quick glance to Tina, who focused back at him.

"There's another thing." Ellison paused to connect. "Some of the Elders in the longhouse are not so sure I am doing the best thing here. They feel, maybe, you won't be right for what I told them you will do. For one thing, you are not Iroquois. You're a White man, and you're very young, at that."

Tell him he will be there.

Arien grimaced. His train was moving very fast to the next station. He was so close and had no sense of having a vote in the direction he rode. *What is it? Everybody seems to know but me.*

Tell him.

Ellison calmly waited.

"Cypriano said to tell you, you will be there."

"Well, that makes two of us, then, Arien Grove," the man said, taking it in. "I'll give the others that and they should feel better."

Ellison pointed out over the lake to a pair of Canada geese landing on the water. They'd come from opposite directions and came to rest on the surface at the same moment, their outstretched wings almost touching as they passed each other, their subtle wakes rippled with the dark reflections of tall evergreens standing on the island behind them.

34 — It's like sex; you do it when you're ready

Salamanca rolled well enough with the Tree Family invasion. It was just big enough to swallow them and offer plenty to do. The lure of the busy, industrial town wove its spell over everybody, so by the fifth day in the area only Kelsey and her three kids hadn't spent any time there. She was all ready to go with some of the others on everyone's run to the lake the day before when little Sammy came down with a bug. Now, with a widely anticipated trip to Fentier Village, an "Old West" amusement park, Myrtle approached Van Gogh's window to tell Jeff, Kelsey would beg-off today as well. "I think Sammy has a fever," she said.

"That explains the delay," Jeff responded, loud enough for his passengers to hear. He followed with an "I thank-y," nodded, and engaged the clutch.

Arien watched as Gary's loaded station wagon also began to roll. "Finally!" He sighed, revealing his bemused smile to Tina. "I wonder how she was going to fit in that car, anyhow?"

"Kids on laps," Tina said.

"Oh."

Freight cars rumbled by on the Chesapeake & Ohio line as the two vehicles approached their second set of tracks. When Van Gogh came to rest Arien focused on the strobing intervals of rail-singing, clattering, whirring wheels the boxcars paraded in a horizontally cascading, up-beat rhythm right in front of him. It appeared so explosively energized and controlled. It hypnotized. He drifted, hang-gliding again, as it were, over the chasm in his most observant mode, where his sense of immanence and presence was strongest and he apprehended the Other, as he had once in his journey to the stars. It wasn't Cypriano, but he was there too, among them in an equally observant and meditative state. He thought he could hear an actual drum beat.

Arien was deeply still. The rolling cars were not louder than the oncoming roar of the Cosmic Ocean but merged within it. He was not afraid. That would have felt very out of place. Pride-of-being more properly summed it up, and great glory and joy. Joy gurgled and tickled up from the deepest currents in his well. It overflowed his eyes on their rim of gladness. He gathered his journey and secured his sense of mission and drew the mass of yearnings, the unspoken promises and dreams and private pleasures of his youth and those of his generation existent in the Living Body, as it were.

"Woodstock: you have no idea!" Arien pronounced with a fervent whisper. In his mind's eye was this mass of humanity, self-aware in its own creative vision and promise, a fair sampling of a great and powerful nation's future splayed out over the soft, green surface of a natural amphitheater in a wondrous, unconditional tide of love and the shared taste of a hive's sweetest honey and – faithfully - making do with so little, in playful anticipation and he laughed inwardly, understanding perfectly why it could not have happened without the rain and still be real! The blessing of the rain: the washing of the people and the earth and sacrifice of the grass beneath their concentrated, thrashing, multitude of feet and the gift of the divas and the spirits of the woods and the lakes and rivers and clouds.

Vaguely, he felt the tips of Tina's fingers touch the wetness on his cheeks and his presence of mind reconstituted itself. And again, Arien understood the force of his attractive power. The gush of energy flowed out of him and veritably splashed over the faces inside little Van Gogh.

"Oh my God, Arien!" Andy exclaimed from behind.

Tina radiantly stared out through the windshield, indefinitely into the expanded view and unbroken splash of light suddenly opened by the train's passing and then just as suddenly obscured in an enveloping, closing mist that effected to frost the glass. She took his arm in hers and pressed it close to her body.

Arien could feel their tandem hearts and the lick of love between them and knew certainly she was there with it, too.

Yet still Van Gogh sat idling. Jeff couldn't bring himself either to turn on the wiper or shift it into first. The folks stuffed in back, Otter, Aspen, Clayboy, Andy, and Hawthorne had fallen into a reverent silence.

Gary's car behind them began to roll forward but stopped when Van Gogh failed to move. Arien heard one of its doors open but no one got out. They went still and waited. The waiting went on for nearly ten minutes but to Arien it was a mere instant. And then it came to him the next move was up to him so he focused back into the moment and glanced at Jeff.

The wiper revealed a perfectly clear day and was quickly turned off. Jeff willfully engaged the clutch and their conveyance lurched forward on the rump over the tracks and soon they could accelerate on the bridge spanning Great Valley Creek to Wildwood Avenue, and the short run from there, slicing an edge of the city and crossing the river to their destination.

Arien considered their destination. Was an amusement park the right place to be, now? He wrestled with it. The name was proclaimed below the lowest of the site's three mountain terraces like hillside high school letters on steroids: "FENTIER VILLAGE, Salamanca, N.Y.," impossible not to notice. It had been off to the left on their way yesterday up the hill to Allegany State Park, where it commanded a great view of the city. A few in their party wanted to check it out then, but Arien was ready for the lake. Today, he felt the same, only more so. He worried about feeding a crowd who wouldn't know him. But, a lot of the folks were along and they all started out expecting to visit Fentier Village, so he didn't object when Jeff braked to make the left into the parking lot.

Maybe if we walk fast I can lose myself in the crowd, Arien thought, attempting an unrealistic pace to the ticket window. The entourage out of both vehicles sensed his discomfort. They instinctively pulled together to surround him, but moved in a palpable bubble of manic energy so there were a lot of curious stares.

"Can you dig this?"

"I don't know, Otter," Andy replied, fussing with the strap of his shoulder bag.

"Contact high, again." Jeff observed.

"I feel like we're in a fish bowl," Tina added. She held Arien's hand like the wind would carry him away.

Willow asked, "Did you guy's drop?"

Arien said, "No," catching Oak's glance harboring a similar question.

It was frustrating. On one level he was feeling spunky and giddy which left little room for paranoia and he needed to lose himself in play. The rub was the manner of play suggested and how it conflicted with the proposals of his surroundings.

Oak beat the group to the ticket window and stood there counting people. He presented something of a study in his faded overalls and the frayed, dingy white T-shirt he wore, pulling a roll of bills out of a pocket to pay for everyone, like he was Daddy, fresh from the job. Gary offered money but Oak refused. Arien and Tina stood by holding hands. He heard Myrtle confide to Aspen, "The little cloud hung around Van Gogh like an aura! Did you see that?"

"Of course," she said. "How couldn't we?"

Everybody bunched up to get on the same cable car, including a group of teen-agers from town and a family of tourists, so it took a minute for people to sort themselves out. While this was happening, one of the kids came to stand near to Arien and he said, "Are you guys headed for Woodstock?"

The words were electric. It was the first direct reference to the festival from outside of their group. "Yeah," Arien responded, surprised. "How do you know about that?"

"Oh, it was in the paper the other day; big AquArien Expo at Wallkill. A friend of mine who works for Newberry's said they're hiring all kinds to help set it up."

Arien, jolted by the news, was at a loss for words. His glance bounced off the kid's impenetrable aviator shades to his friends standing around him.

Not yet. It was Cypriano; though it wasn't like he was there listening just then in Arien's head, but rather as if he'd set a 'pre-recorded' snare for such an instance. The picture attending those two words was clear: *All in good time.*

"Arien, this is perfect!" Andy declared. "We should go for it!" His voice reflected the excitement hitting everyone in earshot.

"Not yet," Arien heard himself say, against a struggle in his heart that would have had them running there right now.

"I'm going soon as I can," the boy in the sun glasses added, before Willow squeezed in front of him.

A couple of young children on the cable car approached Arien just to smile and bounce off his knees. Their mother was Seneca. Arien was seeing the indigenous people everywhere he hadn't noticed them before. He guessed his connection with Ellison was responsible. Without having to say anything, Ellison was being a teacher by helping to further open Arien's eyes.

She nodded and Arien thought he recognized her. It was odd how that happened, a total stranger he couldn't possibly have seen before pleaded in his memory for a name.

The kids took to Tina as well, again in a familiar way. Maybe it was the energy she shared with him.

When the cars stopped to empty passengers at the busy main street both Arien and Tina had to guide the children back to their mother when they began to follow. Again, Arien's party clustered around him. It felt awkward. 'I'm good," he said, looking around at them. "I'll be okay. Go have some fun." As they walked, first Oak and then Willow broke away but not before checking with Arien, who encouraged them, waving his hands. He relaxed into a pleasant awareness of general good-feeling among the visitors there, where he could lose himself among them, shifting his presence, as it were, and most of the others in their group likewise began to scatter. When Andy lingered, Otter grabbed at his shoulder to pull him along while Jeff pushed him from behind and Andy, rolling his eyes, gave in.

Then Arien spied Ellison with Thomas at a corner of the Red Garter Playhouse, a two-story board building with vertical log battens, a rococo Western façade above it and some wagon wheels out front.

Arien greeted them with a curious smile just as a flurry of gunfire erupted further down toward the other end of the village. Many of the people on the street naturally gravitated in that direction, much as they do at the zoo when the lions roar.

"They're having a shoot-out down that way and the Indians are still dying," Ellison said with a wink.

Arien laughed, remembering how he shot Indians when he was a little boy. He really liked this guy.

Tina greeted Ellison and Thomas with a nod as did Clayboy, who ignored the general encouragement to let go and assumed a place beside Arien and Tina, instead.

There was a sudden distraction with shouting on the street. Some fellows dressed as cowboys materialized and began to shoot at one another. It was theatrical and fun. One of them was shooting from the balcony overhead until he shuddered with hits and fell over the railing down onto the road.

"Ouch!" Tina laughed.

The guy opened one eye and winked at her.

Ellison's glance met Arien's with a bemused smile. "C'mon," he said. "It might be safer inside. I'll buy you all a root beer."

"It may be safer, but it's louder, too!" Tina quipped. The five pretty dancers in brightly-colored dresses and wild bonnets on stage were throwing their legs in the air in time with a lively show tune. Arien hunkered over the table, leaning into Tina to hear her while watching frosty mugs of root beer slide down the bar. Ellison caught them one-by-one, and weaving his fingers into the handles, brought them over to their table, a round wooden one with an unobstructed view of the stage.

Clayboy wore a big, toothy grin. Someone in the room had passed him the better part of a smoldering cigar that he gripped in his fist like a handle next to his face.

Thomas laughed. "You're too young to smoke!"

"Not really, I know how!" Clayboy belted back.

Ellison sat himself in the chair on Arien's other side. He still wore that VFW cap. "I've read about your big festival, now. Wallkill is giving them a hard time. It may not happen," he opened, cradling his mug.

Arien searched through his muddle of particulars. "Yasgur's Farm, is that in Wallkill?"

Ellison shrugged.

"It can't be there, but it's going to happen."

Tina slid her mug the short distance it was from his and clinked them together. Clayboy puffed on the cigar. Its pungent smoke wafted over the table. Thomas, watching him, smirked. On stage, the girls sang to the top of their lungs, "Ou la la, ou la ou la, ou la la..." They kicked this way and that, throwing their dresses up like rocking anemones.

Hawthorne, wandering in, saw Arien and came over to take the remaining chair at the table. He sat quietly, acknowledging with his eyes and folding his arms together.

"Is everybody having fun?" Tina asked him. She shouted to be heard.

"Most of them went for the train ride around the mountain. I wasn't quick enough."

Arien signaled with his root beer. Hawthorne nodded and Arien shot it past Tina. He raised it in thanks and helped himself to a good slurp of it. His lips said, "Andy's looking for you."

Ellison whispered in Thomas' ear, passing him a dollar bill. He seemed to study the table's interactions as Thomas obliged; pushing back his chair, he headed for the bar.

The rain fell in buckets on the tent. Tina had just moved a few items away from the wall where a little puddle was gathering from some seepage along a seam. Arien was stretched out on their sleeping bags, his head raised against a rolled-up army poncho. The air had been thick and humid. With the rain came a luxurious gush of cooler air that smelled like the woods.

"This is rad," he said, waving the sheet of paper he was studying by the light of a kerosene lamp dangling from the ceiling. "I think Andy did a great job with the preamble."

"Read it to me, Arien." She sat down next to him.

"I want to get going so bad. Did you hear that kid today? They're hiring people to help set up Woodstock! How rad does it get?"

"Well, what are we waiting for?"

He rattled the paper in his hand. "Don't know for sure but I think it's this stuff. We're putting it together. It takes time."

"Read it."

There was a flash of lightning and then a clap of thunder Arien felt shudder through his body. "Whoa. Radical bang, Babe!"

"Maybe we should go to the bus," Tina suggested with a worried look. The rain battered even harder now, forcing the finest of invisible misty spray between the mesh of sheltering fabric.

"Nah, it's cool. I like this. It's so cool." He did, and the drop in temperature felt perfectly wonderful.

"Read the preamble then."

"What? Too loud. What?"

Tina snapped her hand for the paper but Arien whipped it away by a whisker and she fell over on top of him. He started to tickle her and then it became a laughing tussle that ended with a beautiful, passionate kiss between them. He loved the way her hair fell around his head and seemed to swallow him. He loved the way it smelled. He loved the whisk of her eyelids mingling with his own, and the press of her nose against his and the quiver of her lip and her dancing tongue.

"He never did read it to me," she said to Myrtle at breakfast.

"I don't read out loud that good," he admitted. The oatmeal needed something. It wasn't very interesting.

Oak was up, pushing against the sagging tarp to run the water off. It was a lot cooler this morning than the previous day and the rain might have considered stopping after the evening's thundershower but obviously had changed its mind. It was a soft rain at this point but the areas where people congregated were already getting muddy.

"Do we have any cream cheese?"

"We might, Arien," Myrtle answered. "I'll go look."

"No, Myrtle. Forget it."

"Did you like it?" Andy called from a few seats away.

Arien knew what he meant. "It's awesome, Dude. Why don't you read it to all of us?"

Arien started to fish the folded paper out of his pocket but Andy waved his hand. "Keep your copy," he said. "I have it here in my notebook."

Arien banged his spoon against his camp cup. Everyone fell silent. "Andy's got the preamble for the circle. He's gonna read it. Shush."

He hadn't seen Myrtle get up and slip away but he watched her step down from the van and approach with an opened package of cream cheese. "Myrtle!" he moaned.

"Shush!" It was Crystal.

Arien shrunk back, covering his mouth, and there were giggles from the kids.

"Shush!" Crystal's sister, Heather added.

Andy fiddled a little with the catches to the flap of his shoulder bag and then turned pages in his notebook, first one way and then the other, looking for his place. Arien thought Andy was probably stoned. But then Andy began to read in a most earnest tone of voice, "The Preamble for the Tree Family's World Peace Circle." He let that sink in and then went on. "We believe there is One Life, the Mother and Father of All, and to know that and to explain it has been the revelation of the prophets and saints of all time and places and has been, is and shall be essentially the same. It is primarily the different perspectives of time, place and historical situation that orders the various religious traditions. All the great prophets, initiates and seers, if they were to sit in the Circle together, which is essentially what they do, could commune with One Life, the Mother and Father of All Things, in perfect understanding, mutual agreement and in peace."

Everyone fell so quiet a falling leaf would have split the air.

Oak was the first to comment. "We were talking the other day, Andrew, and you made some heat about it not being possible to change anything." (That brought Arien to remember their conversation at Red House Lake, "the truth…doesn't change anything. People just hear what they want to hear and do what they want to do") – "Do you still believe that?"

Andy thought about it a moment. "Uh, yes," he said.

"Then why do you bother?"

"Because it changes me."

"Then tell me how that doesn't change the world?" Otter asked, with a hint of frustration.

Arien spooned a dollop of cream cheese out of the foil package and dropped it into his oats. "I don't know," he said. "But we're making this item, like some kind of basket; to hold something we can't see but we all know is real. It's like sex; you do it when you're ready. It's going to work because, because, well, I think I trust myself. (Did I just say that?) But I have to admit, I don't even know what it does."

"I have an idea," Aspen said, wiping her lips on a folded bandana. "It seems perfectly obvious to me; it's all about bringing people together and creating harmony."

Arien smiled at Aspen and then looked down at his bowl, thinking, Hot, that babe is so sizzling hot. He couldn't believe how his mind ran in circles like this, chasing its proverbial tail. A big toe had practically exploded in the minefield down that road. It only recently began to feel normal, though the new nail had a ways to grow, and the very harmony Aspen spoke of was nearly destroyed as well. It still amazed him he hadn't totally lost it and run Otter off then, and thought, how lucky was that? It would have been like junking a fast car because the brakes worked. And Tina? At this point she was so much a part of who he was and her body had to be the most comfortable and satisfying thing in the world. He was at peace with her. And yet, who he was included a real and insistently squeaky part that still saw and felt and yearned for more. Oh! It was maddening! If he could trust himself in these other matters, surely there had to be a way? He remembered hearing about Mormons, once. They had a religion that allowed a man more than one wife.

I wish I had someone to talk to about this.

There is.

Oh, yeah! Of course. But Arien had a sense Cypriano might tell him something he didn't want to hear.

Listen.

What?

Listen to them. Feel them.

"Are you finished, Arien?"

"What?"

"Can I take your bowl?"

"Oh. Yeah, Clayboy. Go for it."

"So what did I miss?" Andy asked. "Hawthorne said you ran into Ellison yesterday."

Arien was sitting at the table in the mess area, poking through a stack of books that Willow put there after breakfast. Willow and Oak played chess on the other end.

"You sure you want to do that?" Oak politely asked. A light rain pelted the tarp. The sound of clanking pots came from the step van along with a wholesome aroma of baking bread blending easily in the humidity.

"Ellison talked about Native stuff."

"Wow.

"It was hard to hear him," Arien reported, "so I listened harder. It was noisy in there. I don't know how it got started. And–" he laughed, "Clayboy got an upset stomach!"

"Oh, you!" Willow growled.

Oak chuckled while he removed a piece from the board.

"What did he say?"

Arien absently selected a hardcover, drawn to its title, "*Hero with a Thousand Face.s*" "Well, for one thing, there's that dam on the river. It happened just a few years ago. The Seneca were dead-set against it. He said, Kennedy promised he would fight it when he was running for President, but when he got elected he signed the bill. They were pretty mad. A lot of people had to move from their houses. They took it to the Supreme Court and lost."

"So? That shit happens all the time."

"Well, it's not supposed to happen," Arien explained, recalling the gist of Ellison's story. "He said a treaty with a sovereign nation is supposed to have the force of the Constitution. The treaty was made with George Washington. It guaranteed the reservation to be off limits to the Whites."

"Oh!" Andy chided, "Just over there is a big town full of White People. What about that? What are they doing here?"

"That's different, Andy. The tribe owns the City of Salamanca."

"For real?"

"Real. The leases will be up in the 90s sometime. Maybe they'll raise the rent." He chuckled. "Funny, huh?"

"Wow. Think about it; it's too bad the whole country isn't set up like that. After all, this was their country to begin with."

"I don't know if I heard it right, Andy, but I think he said someday they'll have it all back, anyway."

"Salamanca?"

"No, not just Salamanca, he meant the whole country, too!"

"Oh, Willow! Geeze!" Oak bellowed.

"I'm sorry, my friend, but she's mine, again!"

"Oh, that's far-out," Andy said, regarding the book in Arien's hand. He took it and opened to the preface. "Here," he pointed, and read, "As we are told in the Vedas, Truth is one, the sages speak of it by many names."

"Wow. Cool. It's like what you said in your preamble. Should I read it?"

"I don't know if it's your speed, Arien. You may be too busy proving it."

Arien wanted to read it (I am too busy proving what?) though reading for him was a trial. Books – especially tomes like this one – were full of things he didn't get described with words he didn't know. But he took it back to his tent, holding it close to keep the rain off. Maybe I can beat it into my head, he thought. Tina was there along with Laurel and Cassie, with little Wally. Wally was intrigued with the Tree Family Staff. He didn't look up when Arien stepped in, but continued feeling it, tracing its undulating lines with his fingers. "Mommy, this feels good," he reported.

"You should put it down, honey."

"It's alright," Tina said.

"Hi, Arien!"

"Yo, Babes." He stood there uncertain. He hadn't expected company. Laurel's eyes were ringed and red. "What's up?"

"Nita's passed her period," Tina said.

"Wow," Arien pondered. "Does Willow know?" The shower outside grew heavier. He would have gone back out if it weren't for that.

"Yes," Laurel sniffed.

Arien was unsure what to say. He sat down cross-legged on the carpet. It was so dingy in there all of a sudden he thought he'd light the kerosene lamp hanging over everybody's head. Tina was on the same wavelength. She handed him a matchbook.

The little yellow light did provide a spot of cheer in the green canvas gloom. When Arien sat down again Wally came over to be next to him, dragging the staff along behind.

"Oh, what should I do?" Laurel sniffed, to no one in particular. She sat in a worn, but appealing flowery cotton dress, between Cassie and Tina. Her choker was typical of Kelsey's craftsmanship, which emphasized brightly-colored, small beads in a narrow macramé fashion, worked with fine natural fiber string. This particular version, a twisting knot pattern with three small but intricate trade beads first worn by Willow, was then seen on both Laurel and Nita at about the same time. It seemed everybody had one. Arien wore his Kelsey Choker today, too. It had five red center beads, for the sign of Aries' ruling planet, bordered by two white ones. Tina's was basically opposite, having seven white, for Venus, Taurus' ruling planet, and two flanking red beads.

Arien had to ask, "What does Willow want to do?"

"He wants Nita to have it." Laurel was choking up. "I told her to watch out. She hasn't been taking the pills I got for her. She doesn't believe in them. Well I think it's the best compromise, but no; not Nita." Tina wrapped an arm around her. Cassie placed a hand on her knee.

Arien's wheels turned. *She's feeling left out.* Wally offered the staff to Arien, who set it across his lap.

"I suppose I'll be moving on," Laurel declared with a sigh. "I just can't handle this anymore."

"You don't have to go anywhere, this is your home," Cassie assured her.

"That's not big enough. I would see him every day. I have to make a break." Her expression went blank.

"Say, Babe," Arien appealed, faced with either making an investment or going back out in the rain. "I see your point, but hang with us to Woodstock. It's just a little longer. Be a sister for them in the meantime; be a friend, okay? You can do that, huh? Then, soon we'll see all kinds of people and there'll be tons of stuff to get into and, you'll see, everything will be cool." Tina's approving smile made him glad he'd said that.

Arien's words seemed to stir Laurel's funk. Her attention focused to everyone. She nodded. "Do you have anything to smoke?" she asked.

"Yep, check this out!" Arien reached into his back pocket for a thin, glossy, tan-colored tube made from a cut section of bamboo. It had a soft wood stopper that looked like a large tooth, attached with a bit of fine metal chain.

"Wow," said Tina. "Where'd you get that?"

"Cool, huh?" He opened it over the cover of Joseph Campbell's seminal work and spilled-out a little pile of ready-clipped Mary Jane that only had a few speckled, glossy seeds in it. The papers were in the pocket of his T-shirt. "Ben Franklin's, in town."

"That's from the five and dime store?" Cassie asked.

"Exactly," Arien laughed. "Sally-Ann said she found them in with ladies' knickknacks. They're made in Japan. She told me she bought all of them.

"Did the pot come from Ben Franklin's, too?" Tina giggled.

"Speaking of," he went on, grinning, "Otter's already found a dealer in town."

"That's good," Tina responded. "It's too late to be hitching back to San Francisco for more weed."

"Right, I heard him say that." Arien was beginning to master rolling a good joint. He only felt he needed to work on his speed. He folded and licked the yellow Zigzag paper, drew it out with opposing fingers, dusted it with herb and wrapped it up. He struck a book match, took a half puff to be sure it would go, and passed it to Laurel.

Laurel watched him with some intensity. She accepted it with grateful eyes.

It happened again the following day; another young man he met on the proverbial street asked Arien if he was going to Woodstock. Tina, with Kelsey and Clayboy planned to be occupied with a day of tie-dying bed sheets and T-shirts. Jeff, Otter and Aspen had taken Van Gogh to visit a friend of Aspen's down in Butler, just north of Pittsburg, Pennsylvania, and Andy was spending the day at the library and left early to catch the city bus, so Arien decided he'd go on a supply run to town with Oak and Myrtle, Gary, driving his rusty Ford, and Luke, who decided to come along at the last minute. The others had just gone outside while Oak and Arien stood by the check-out counter at Economy Drug. Arien clutched a family-size package of band aids, some rubbing alcohol and a bottle of aspirins when a young fellow behind them popped the question after catching his eye.

"Pretty soon," Arien admitted with unanticipated stress. It was growing harder to justify the delay and that vied with a rising excitement over its palpitating proximity. He regarded the straight-looking fellow with his preppie-style haircut and collared sport shirt. They were about the same age. "You're not?"

"No, uh, right, not."

Arien couldn't read that. It wasn't like the lad summarily shot it down or would not be open to going or he probably wouldn't have asked the question to begin with. Arien stacked the stuff in his hands on the counter along with other items Oak carried, for the checker to tally. Her hands slithered professionally over the register keys while the prices popped up in its little glass window and the tape chattered out.

"I'm Arien." Arien saluted him with a casual wave off the forehead. It was spontaneous and came without association, but the other's eyes widened in some kind of connection.

"Greg," he traded. Then he said, "You know, huh?"

Do I? Arien considered. "When do you go?" he ventured, uncomfortable with his own assumption and the attending feelings hovering in Greg's personal space.

"I'm off to boot camp tomorrow."

Oak turned with the paper sack in his arm, and stuffing change in a pocket of his overalls he said, "I'll be right outside."

"OK, Oak. Be right there. Can I buy you a pop, Greg?"

"Wow, uh, no. Thanks. Thanks a lot, though."

"Well, come, hang with us today."

"Oh, Man. Thanks, but there's still few things I have to do. I'm headed to Newberry's, next, for some, for some–"

"It's cool, Dude," he said, but his thinking ran, *Oh God, how sad is that? I want you to go to Woodstock! You really need to go to Woodstock!*

Outside, Luke asked Arien if anything was wrong. Arien said, "No," but there was. He couldn't explain it. It wasn't fair. In fact, it was awful and horrible and tragic. It reminded him of the pain he'd carried through his childhood, though he didn't own this particular distress by himself, but rather shared it with this strange, wild country in one of its deep, wrenching moments. Damn it! I feel like such a snook, anymore; this weepy, crappy, girly shit. What do I know? I hate it. I hate it.

Listen to them. Feel them.

I can't do this!

We're way past that now.

"C'mon. It's lunchtime," Oak said. "I hear the diner's pretty good."

"It is," Luke said. "We ate there the other day."

"Then let's do Texas Hot," Myrtle suggested. It was all their party needed. They shifted direction and walked across Main when the light at the green-painted steel bridge and Wildwood Avenue changed.

"Don't tell Willow we had dogs for lunch," Oak admonished with a wink.

"And, don't you tell Otter." Arien traded, but he watched that kid, Greg, behind them, lost in thought, on his way to Newberry's.

"What is it with that guy?" Luke asked.

"He's going to the war."

"Oh."

"Yeah, Luke, exactly."

The big beefy dogs were real good, loaded with onions and plenty of mustard and great hot sauce on a bun right out of the steam table. They washed it down with Rolling Rock beer. Arien was delighted by that little touch. Oak suggested with a twirl of his fingers Arien sit facing the window so the proprietor wouldn't yank the bottle if he saw Arien's face, framed as it was now with his blue star headband, wavy, sandy hair drifting to his shoulders, and with the Kelsey choker and silver OM, to render a perfect blend of underage boy and angel. Oak paid for them all and carried two bottles in the fingers of one hand, and set one of them down for Arien. Even though the drinking age in New York was eighteen, Arien understood he couldn't withstand a challenge. But, there wasn't any and soon he was downing the beer and if it was noticed it was ignored.

"I have a question, Arien," Oak said before they were done. He pushed a straggling onion between his lips and chased it with a slug of his beer. "What's Ellison's role with us?"

"He's going to be there."

"Well, we've gone over this thing and we've honed it and it's beautiful, but Ellison hasn't been a part of that."

"He knows about it."

Oak scratched his chin. "Where will he sit? We have an invocation for each quarter. What's he going to do?"

"I don't know, but I get this much, Oak, the circle will be open to the people who need to be there."

"Something's missing," Oak mused.

Arien caught a look between Gary and Luke that said, respectfully, they missed it all. "The beer's great," Gary said. "If it were much colder it'd be solid. Anyone want another?"

"This is too rad," Arien said. He nodded affirmatively, draining the bottle and relaxing into the brew's low-intensity rush.

Myrtle gave Gary a perky smile and both Luke and Oak agreed as well.

Arien watched as Gary made his way past some other customers to the round beer case, and snickered when the owner carded him. "I don't know, Oak," he resumed, rolling the empty bottle between his hands, "I don't think anything's missing. We just can't see it, but I think Cypriano can, and Ellison, too. Oh, Thomas told me they're having a barbeque somewhere up in the park on Saturday, with family and friends from the tribe, and we're all invited. We'll need to bring something to share."

"Man, this is rad!" Clayboy declared with a smarmy grin at Arien, wiping his lips on a bare forearm. The better part of a barbequed chicken leg dangled off the tips of his fingers. He sat on the end of the bench where he'd squeezed in at Arien's picnic table, precariously balancing his paper plate by the edge.

"The dead stuff always gets good marks," Otter declaimed. He smiled wanly over the potato salad, a pile of greens, three-bean salad and raw vegetable bits in front him.

Arien had been nibbling all morning while he and Tina helped Willow, Laurel and Sundew turn out bread and berry pies from the step van's oven, so his appetite was on hold at the moment. He did accept a cup of tapioca from Janie Redeye, a kindly middle-aged woman in a light blue cotton dress and beaded felt vest that was open in front. Her pudding was excellent, like quality vanilla ice cream with tapioca pearls might be if it could be served at room temperature without melting.

It turned out to be quite the gathering. Several native families besides Black Snake, such as Redeye, Shongo, Jimerson and Half Town were represented so, with all the Tree People, there were close to sixty picnickers at the site. The adults were warm and friendly, especially after the Trees formed into a circle and Hawthorne paraphrased their new circle's invocation, blessing the gathering as a statement of gratitude to the "Mother and Father of All Things… for the gift of ourselves and our new friends among the Seneca." All the while he'd held a smoldering smudge stick of wild sage. One of the locals responded by quickly unwrapping a broad drum, probably intended for later. He began to beat a steady rhythm out in a taught, deep tone that had everyone silently standing in accord with it. Some of the older women lightly swayed or tapped their hips and some of the men bobbed their heads. It was simple and gracious and Arien was deeply impressed both with the beautiful, easy connection among the folks at this happening and his amazing perspective as a part of it; how radically his world and his outlook had changed from that of the boy he used to think he was, and the impossibly limited options that other lad had been capable of seeing.

"Yeah, Clayboy, it's out-a sight!" Arien agreed.

Andy looked at him over a fork laden with potato salad, dipping it in a salute.

"Keep that up and you'll be talking like the hippies," Jeff warned with a wink.

The two groups basically sat by themselves to eat but the native kids were curious enough afterwards to hang around the Tree folks and some had questions about their origins, their road trip, the up-coming festival at Woodstock, and about Arien. Many of them had long hair and wore a choker here and there and it didn't seem like there was much difference among them.

"So the concert is free? I heard they're selling tickets for six dollars a day," a young teen-age boy in a black T-shirt and blue jeans said. He stood behind Arien with a small group of friends that drifted over.

Arien had a slug off his second can of Schlitz to wash down the last spoon of tapioca. The beer and pudding made for a strange combination. "But if you go it will be free," he corrected.

"Believe it, he knows," Tina assured them, though they looked like they didn't quite believe it.

Arien watched as a big, swallow-tail butterfly fluttered erratically over to hover for a moment above the table. It made him think of a line from that number by Joni (*What's her name?*) about Woodstock he'd heard in a future time that by now, with every passing day, grew more fantastic and remote, and were it not for the occasional incidents of current events, lyric fragments and cultural instigations, Arien might have indulged a little self-doubt.

But everything was making Arien think about Woodstock lately. And, when Aspen, Willow and Ben produced their guitars they opened a set with "We Shall Overcome," perhaps as a conscious effort to connect with native people's issues – which was well received – and he was sure he'd recognized another hit from the movie. In any event, the "Keepers of the Western Door," the title Ellison had told Arien his people proudly carried, appeared pleased and a few drums that were produced by some of the people underlined the melody with a reasonably conventional rhythm. There was a drummer that especially attracted Arien's attention, a woman among them, who was old enough to be his grandmother. She tapped-out a unique, complimentary sound in counter-point to the rhythm. She was very good.

When the song came to an end however, the drumming continued and gradually altered to an aboriginal pulse. Some of the people sang along with it in paradoxical cadences both unfamiliar and timeless to the Western ear, to blend into the surrounding forest and some of the deepest places of genetic recollection in the souls of the listeners.

Arien was sure he heard modulations and breaks in the rhythms he'd never noticed or considered before and it came to him that it was not rote and repetitive drumming he heard, but an articulation of the mysterious place where nature and human experience come together. The rich awareness washed through him, speaking through the beating of drums, heavy with a subtle yet fulfilling substance of gratification, worthy pride, and as a bulwark of confidence like a deposit of bullion to his account, and yet infinitely more precious than anything real bullion could possibly obtain. It was clearly a part of him and who he was and he could appreciate how that justified the new and amazing proportions of his life.

When it got dark Coleman lanterns came out. Many among the Seneca families said their goodbyes and drove away, but those who remained set up folding chairs and pulled benches in to join the Trees in an intimate ring around a blazing campfire Thomas and some of the young fellows built-up and fed. Ellison said a prayer by the fire in a quiet voice Arien couldn't make out from where he sat, but he was excited to see Ellison wearing a small fur cap with a single feather attached to it.

Arien nudged Tina, when Ellison sprinkled flakes from his fingers into the fire. The unassuming little cap suddenly seemed magnificent, its evocative feather appearing to come alive in the firelight.

Ellison sat down in a deck chair next to Arien when his prayer ended. Thomas brought him a cold can of beer. Carefully Ellison opened it with a little folding can opener on his key chain. Arien had seen these before at Andy & Bax, the Army surplus store in Portland. Ellison made a small cut on the edge of one side and then a longer one on the other, which he bent in with his thumb against an edge of the opener.

The evening breeze was erratic and the musicians had to move occasionally to get out of the smoke. Aspen, Ben and Willow, with the addition of a teenage Seneca girl, introduced as Emily Half Town, played popular folk tunes participants could sing-along with. A few of Emily's, she announced, were by Buffy St. Marie. In their breaks, the native lads with the drums beat out ancient songs that easily resonated among the Tree Family.

"There's someone waiting to meet you," Ellison said without looking at Arien.

"I'm ready. Where is he?" Arien had just made eye contact with Otter, who was a few feet away, along with Jeff and Andy. Arien's dismissive expression begged another question from his friend.

"She's ready now, too. I see she's put down her drum." Ellison stood with a motion for Arien to follow and together they made their way around the fire circle and the others there to a picnic table set back beyond a stretch of darkness. The table was covered with a red-and-white checkered oil cloth, starkly illuminated in the brilliant halo of a Coleman lantern. The woman drummer sat there by two other ladies with coffee cups before them and a stack of used paper plates at one end. They all smiled as Ellison with Arien approached.

"Mother Shongo, this is Arien, who is keeper of his young family's staff."

Arien focused on her eyes. They seemed to him bigger and deeper than they could possibly be, as if the night sky, itself, was somehow locked in them. He'd been drinking beer but hadn't smoked pot at all today, and he wondered at the visual anomaly.

Ellison introduced the other women as Alice and Wendy. They were all well into their middle age, which to Arien was as distant as a school board. They were reserved, but carried a familiar quality, happening a lot lately, and though Arien was comfortable with that feeling it always caused him to marvel.

"My compliments to Cypriano," Mother Shongo opened.

Arien nodded, assuming Ellison must have told her about that, but this was the first time he'd ever heard an outsider repeat the name of the voice in his head.

"So, the big fuss in the Catskills is what's brought you through our Western Door, eh?"

Arien grinned. "Yeah," he agreed.

"What do you bring there?"

Arien wasn't sure how to answer that. He almost deferred the first thing that sprang to mind, but with no worthy alternative in the queue, reluctantly gave it a voice, "We bring a circle for unity and peace." It still felt so awkward to say that to someone, especially an older woman he'd never met who was born a thousand miles from his generation.

"Then yours is a gift for the ages," she said with a smile, both to Arien and the others, who nodded in affirmation. "Tell me, young son, how well, then, do you know the Great Mystery?"

"There's a rad song the Beatles do," he thoughtfully answered, "about the love within you and without you. It's like that."

"Ho!" Her smile broadened. "This one's a gem, Ellison." The others agreed, smiling at Arien and one-another. "What place do you call home, Arien?"

It had grown quiet. Arien could hear Aspen's singing from the fire circle and she'd undoubtedly captivated her audience. He wished he were over there just then. He hesitated. "Uh, Portland, uh, but really here, with the Trees."

"Hum, yes, I see," Mother Shongo said. "That's good. Now, I'm sorry to keep you from the others, but please sit down because there are some things we need to discuss and we don't have much time." She patted the bench along side of her and Arien sat down on the end while Ellison went around to the other side of the table. "Would you like a cup of coffee?"

"No thanks."

Mother Shongo smiled patiently. She was a diminutive woman, this time with eyes Arien saw as sharp as spears. Her double-braided hair was mostly grey with streaks of white. She wore a necklace of brightly-colored beads that hung in several strands on a blouse of crushed green velvet. She projected considerable strength and dignity, which Arien got, and his presence was finally bound to her with a sudden and genuine curiosity.

"Arien," the elder woman continued, "You probably have some idea of the forces arrayed against you, yes?"

"I do," he nodded emphatically, like she'd opened a door being pushed by a bear from the other side. "It scares me sometimes."

"Yes," she agreed, resting an elbow on the table and her cheekbone against her knuckles. "Tell me, have you ever been struck by lightning?"

Arien felt a chill at the back of his neck as he grasped for a connection. His mind raced – lightning, lightning… "No." But he really wasn't sure.

"Hmmmm," the woman mused. "It's simple, but complicated, too. You know? I feel this about you. The lightning wants to try you again. It had some experience and knows the way you can be taken."

Arien searched himself for the storm but he couldn't find any. Yet something about this woman's words resonated and he suddenly felt so vulnerable. He grasped his hands together on the table top. He actually began to tremble.

"Hmmmm," Mother Shongo mused again. "Stay connected, son. Reach and hold it. Relax. Breathe easy. You're safe here. I'm sure I can tell you that. And for what is to come, as long as you can be connected to the Mystery, the life that is within you and without you, the oneness of all things, it will be as the life ring is to the man on a sinking ship."

Arien was silent for a moment, contemplating this woman's words. Then, he had to ask her, "Is the lightning my enemy?"

"No son, but it can be its weapon."

"What am I supposed to do?" It was an honest question. Her choice of the possessive adjective, 'its,' struck a chord. He'd always thought of his terror as a force and not merely a person.

"Ah," she said, flipping her hand back, away from her face, "strategy changes with your choices, young man. I don't have infinite advice for anyone, but a few generalities may offer some guidance. There's much, by example, to be learned from the opposites that you see. They can be the stone and flint in your hands."

The word, paradox,' came to mind. So far, Arien followed this.

"Always find the high ground," Mother Shongo continued. "Be as wise as you can. Allow the time to know the wisdom in your soul to seep into your mind. Be as honest with yourself and with others as you can be. Look in the mirror of your life and declare that you know the truth!"

Arien said, "Wow," under his breath. This lady was a trip!

"Be consistent," she said next. "Be like the rock that everybody can be at peace knowing what it is. And then, don't forget respect; respect for yourself and all others, your brothers and your sisters, your friends, and the little creatures that are just pieces of the Great Mystery and that includes you."

She leaned forward, lowering her voice, "Then it will be right to use your power, to free your gifts, and when they come home, and they will come home, like birds that have flown away for the winter, you will welcome them with joy and gratitude in your heart."

Arien laughed, not with disrespect but excitement. It was a strange feeling, like a sudden rush of energy.

And the woman smiled back at him. "You are beautiful," she said. "You are a butterfly and no longer a worm." She placed her hands on her lap and Arien knew their meeting had ended.

"Who is she?" He wondered on his way with Ellison back towards the fire, his friends and his family.

"Mother Shongo is one of the Wisdom Keepers of the Onodowahgeh," Ellison explained. "She speaks with the river of voices that go back to the beginning of time, and you know, young fellow, it is now as it has always been; the true way will always come to you through the spoken word. This is the greatest gift of the Creator, so that you will know that he is still with us, always."

Andy was quite visibly moved when Arien Grove told his Stand about the meeting with old Mother Shongo. He'd held back the whole story until now. It was this threat of lightning that worried him. He'd wanted to understand it, first, but couldn't, and the pressure to tell them was great. Previously, packing up the camp in Salamanca totally kidnapped everyone's attention, sweeping them along with such energy everything was folded up, tied-down and ready to roll in just over a day. Woodstock! Woodstock! Arien was getting drunk with the prospect. "I wish I came with you to meet her, but–" Andy finally said.

"We weren't invited," Otter reminded, finishing the thought.

It seemed Otter could always suck Arien in. "Well, Ellison just got up and took me over there and–"

'It's okay," Tina assured, smoothing it out expressively with her hands. "We are not important."

"I'm glad I wasn't there," Jeff pronounced, smirking over the wheel.

"Ohhhhhh–" Arien groaned, and even Clayboy, on the seat next to him, giggled.

"For a seer, you sure are easy," Andy chirped, but Arien knew the previous flash of emotion had been real as rocks.

When Arien turned around his eyes briefly connected with Aspen's. She sat with her back to the rear compartment, squeezed in between Otter and Tina. Her denim skirt was short and it seemed to exaggerate her shapely legs, stretched out in front of her. He tried to look one way or the other to face forward again but locked his eyes along the length of her instead, to finally disengage at her bare feet. Ouch! He felt like he was jammed in a can with Prince Albert. This is not easy.

Tina didn't seem to give it any energy.

And what said the glimmer from Otter? He couldn't be sure. He stared at the road ahead. Van Gogh was the lead car again. Arien briefly wished it were bigger, not as big as the bus, but large enough to include Oak, Willow, Hawthorne, and maybe even Luke and Sally-Ann, from among the Oregon folks. As it was, Van Gogh felt very small to be really going anywhere with the two extra people. Some of their stuff was now on top, secured by a clever system of straps Jeff devised to clamp onto the rain channels. Arien mused on the van

Youth Promise had – or would one day have; the one a much older
Andy will drive with a bunch of other kids to a trail by a beautiful
waterfall in the Columbia Gorge. That was a ten-passenger Dodge van.
It was very cool. It would be just about perfect.

Clayboy wasn't a large fellow but his little victory, to sit up front
next to Arien, put the gearshift between his knees. It usually worked
better with Tina there. But Arien could feel Clayboy's happiness. It
wasn't all that different from the doggie that's most content to be right
alongside.

"Elmira up ahead," Jeff announced. "That's 'bout half-way there,
huh?"

"Oh Rad!" Arien fished the Standard Oil map of the Northeastern
United States out of the shelf and folded it out. Neither Bethel nor
White Lake was even shown, but Thomas had pointed it out on the
New York State map in Ellison's pickup before Arien and his party
departed; it would be on 17B just up from Monticello. "We'll take 97
down from Hancock." He pointed at it and held it up and Clayboy took
it and indicated the spot for Jeff to see.

"Right on," Jeff said. "We'll be pushing it to make it that far
today."

August 15th was still over two weeks away. Arien knew that, but it
didn't matter. He just wanted to be there. The last few days had been
an excruciating test. Oh, he was fine when the Trees performed their
circle ritual from its "alpha" to "omega" for the first time. In fact, it
had been more than fine. Ellison was there that evening and he'd worn
his Seneca cap, with the eagle feather on top. The flakes he'd sprinkled
from between his fingers in blessing were of native tobacco that came,
he said, all the way from South Carolina by way of a Tuscarora friend
who regularly visited there.

"There's some people we haven't met who will be here with us,"
Ellison said, waving his hand around the circle where the Trees all
stood. "They don't know it yet," he added, to nobody in particular.
His smile was enigmatic.

Arien remembered saying, "Sure." He got it right away, like the
kid who'd solved the Rubix cube in twenty moves, a coming together
in a natural way, easy as falling and feeling so very, indisputably right,
and yet he was totally blown away. It was mind-boggling. "It's a
crazy miracle!" He'd exclaimed, and people around the circle said,
"Yeah!" and "Right on!" Though he didn't expect them to know what
was going on, really, anymore than he did. He was just following the
scent, and it was getting so totally exciting.

He recalled when it still felt like a straight-jacket, holding him down on a gurney with wheels in tracks, all laid in one sure-fire direction, regardless of what he - he thought - he wanted to do. He laughed to himself and in the corner of his eye caught Clayboy studying him.

It was hot, and humid as rain. When Van Gogh slowed down for the traffic in Elmira, Arien could smell the kid's sweat and warm, animal body right there, but it was earthy-sweet and salty, and not unpleasant. Clayboy was barefoot and his feet came together around the base of the gearshift. He wore cut-offs. His knee pressed against Arien's leg but Arien was confident there was nothing Gay about it. It didn't feel the same as it would have if it were Andy. In fact, Andy was going out of his way to avoid being close like that anymore, probably because it could make him perfectly crazy. Maybe he'd given Andy too much and his expectations were always in the watchtower. Whatever. Arien was thinking Andy had been doing well these days. He'd learned some trick to get high off his yearning. With Clayboy, it was more like a little brother thing. His heart felt pure and strong and he was devoted to a fault.

Tina's face materialized in the space over shoulders. She put her elbows on the seat-top, pushing them against boy and boy younger. "What's up?"

Clayboy smiled shyly.

"Elmira," Arien said.

"We should be through it, soon," Jeff assured, but he was braking for a red light.

"Why are you going so slow?" Otter asked. "It's stifling back here."

"Red light."

"No, you were going slow."

"Pig behind us. I didn't want to worry you, but you asked."

"How long?"

Arien turned around and could make out the red bubble through the rear-view window. He kissed Tina before facing forward again.

"A few blocks," Jeff said, staring straight ahead.

Andy intoned, "Ommm Sri Ram, jai Ram jai jai Ram,"

Rad, Arien thought.

"Ommmmm Sri Ram, jai Ram jai jai Ram."

The light changed and they were moving again.

"Worked like a charm," Jeff announced. "They just turned at the corner behind us."

"So, Arien, what about the lightning? What did you say to her?"

"Nothing, Andy. I don't think–" But maybe. There was a persistent yapping in his head. Lightning, lightning.

"Wait a minute, Man," Otter said. "There was something Blue Star told us when we met you, remember?"

"Oh right," Jeff laughed. "'He was really smoking!'"

"'Like he was on fire!'" Tina added.

Arien was stymied. He wasn't sure he actually remembered that or if it only seemed like it because that's what they recalled about that night. For him it was fuzzy. There was an accident. The car hit the pole. "My jacket was ruined," he offered.

Tina's voice was close to his ear. "I still have your T-shirt. It wasn't."

"Oh, wow, yeah. You haven't worn it for a while."

"I'll wear it to bed tonight." Her smile was right there.

Arien gently pinched her cheek. "You're a cutie," he told her.

Tina managed to nip his ear when he turned away. "Ow, Bitch!" He cried out, swatting at her, but Tina had the advantage and she grabbed it, with a hunk of his hair in her fist, yanking his head back. He flailed helplessly.

"Do you give?"

Arien tried and failed one more time to get free of her. "Clayboy! Help me!"

"No way," Clayboy scoffed, pushing into Jeff, who had to steady the wheel.

"Do you give?"

"She's killing him!" Andy remarked.

"She's a tigress," Otter agreed.

"She's got a great approach," Aspen said with admiration.

"Ow, ow!"

"Give?"

"Yes, yeah, fuck yeah! I give, I give!"

But Tina wouldn't let go. "Put your hands on your lap," she demanded. When he complied she hung over him to plant a wet kiss on his Adam's apple.

"Ohhhhhh," Arien groaned, but not from pain or humiliation. "I want you right now," he whispered.

"Hold that thought," she whispered back,

About twenty-two miles east of Binghamton, the largest city along their route through New York, SR-17 turns south-east into the canyon of the Delaware River. This is where the rolling western foothills of the Catskills begin to press upon the road, where the hardwood forest arbors over it in sections of deep green and begins to rise into leafy, vertical walls on either shoulder, and white-sided farm houses older than the Civil War can review the spare traffic like benches at a bowling lane. This is where the Tree Family finally pulled off the road for a break and a bite to eat. They were at one of those unmarked rest stops with picnic tables by the river that come up now and then. A car load of kids was already there and they gawked at the little caravan of micro-and-macro bus, station wagon and step van that jockeyed to park in a small area without hemming in the car that was there first.

It felt good to get out and stretch and attempt to relieve the sticky clinging of the seat of his pants and shirt stuck to his back. Arien fixed a gaze on the water.

"It looks like we can get into the river from here," Willow observed. Nita was beside him and it was obvious they were becoming a couple to be taken seriously. Nita still didn't look pregnant but she seemed different in small ways that added up to an air of confidence and maturity that Arien hadn't taken in before. He noticed both she and Willow wore their Kelsey chokers but happened to see Laurel, who walked toward the water with Cassie, did not.

Laurel seemed to be hanging in there though Arien understood it was difficult for her. It was like she'd lost her lover and best friend in one fell swoop. He guessed it didn't have to be that way, but her ongoing reaction to Nita's pregnancy was taken as an insurmountable slight. She still hadn't found a way to cope with it. He found his strengthening sense of empathy an annoyance. Who gives a damn? But, he couldn't help it. He could feel it in the Trees, like a tiny splinter, even if he didn't want to be bothered.

Willow and Nita continued to a short trail down to the river bank, which was in plain sight.

"Otter."

"What's up, Arien?"

"Come here a minute, will ya? And you, too, Oak!"

Otter and Aspen were holding hands. Arien could see himself clasping her other one. That was another source of irritation.

"Dudes," he opened, when they were close enough, "You guys have a way about stuff that I don't. It's Laurel, you know? She's on a – bum trip." Arien heard himself say that, choosing words from among his peers.

"Yes, she is," Oak agreed.

Otter grimaced. "I thought she would ditch us in Salamanca."

"I asked her to hang with us 'till we got to Woodstock. Well, she's hanging, alright."

"By her neck and twisting in the wind," Aspen commented dryly to nods of agreement.

"Right."

Sammy ran over and tapped Arien on his hip. "Can we go in the water?"

"Ask your Momma."

Out of the corner of his eye, Arien could see Laurel head down to the river. Something wasn't right, but he already knew that.

"I'm thinking there'll be something for her to do when we get to Bethel," Oak suggested.

"That's what I said to her." Then Arien added, "How 'bout a hit of acid and some sweet music?"

"Not one of your better ideas, Arien," Otter wagged. "You know me, Man, I love the stuff, but–"

Arien waved his hand dismissively. But he barely did that when a veritable psychic-tsunami of sensations assaulted him from out of the proverbial blue. It was like that vision of another friend's last moments, only with a different menace. Here, clearly a lack of air, unable to breathe, a wrenching rush of terror wrapped in sheets of sorrow and regret such as he could never have imagined possible, with a futile grasping for the shimmering light. He had to struggle through it with sheer force of will in the face of a gathering darkness, a burning black fire, consuming an appalling, gagging stab of certain asphyxiation and immolating awareness, itself, in a dunning blanket of sleep. It went by really fast! He grimaced horribly as a hoarse, guttural, bellowing-animal shriek exploded through his lips in a dear-life fight for disengagement from this furious assailant. His primal utterance caused those standing around to jump back in surprise and horror!

"My God, Arien! What-the-FUCK?" Otter cried at full volume. He rushed forward and grabbed Arien's shoulders to shake him and intensely stare into his eyes.

Arien felt his own breath plunge into his lungs. Rallying, he hollered, "Quick! The river! There's no time to – oh, God! It's too late! Too late!" But he bolted away as fast as his legs could bear in the direction of a scream and shouts that now came up from the river. Arien looked in time to see Willow running furiously, splashing, slipping and sliding along the wooded bank, followed by others who frantically called out after the current, "Laurel! Laurel!" And they were soon out of sight behind foliage.

Everybody ran after the commotion. Nita, stricken, hollered, "It doesn't look that deep!" As Arien hurried by, Cassie cried out, "It happened so quick! We were right here!"

Arien was on the scene pretty fast and was among those who plunged forward at a full run into the river to grab a young woman floating in a shallow eddy like a rag doll, her light-brown hair flowing out around her on the surface of the water in a mock illustration of undulating solar radiance. He gasped for wind as he and Willow and then Oak, pulled Laurel to the edge and then lifted her onto the shore.

Soon everybody, it seemed, was standing around in a prevailing glare of white-faced disbelief, including the carload of kids that greeted them on arrival.

Oak sprung over Laurel's inert frame and rolled her on her side and began to pound at her back with the flat of his hand.

"Wait!" Willow cried out, and with tears running down his cheeks, he bent over her, awkwardly, to blow air into her mouth.

Arien reeled with a banged-in-the-head faintness. It was as if all his energy was sucking away and he collapsed down cross-legged, barely in control, to blankly stare into Laurel's expressionless face. He watched it regularly contort with Willow at an awkward angle huffing deeply between her lips.

Arien swooned further and fell back, only to be caught and steadied by Andy, who had come up by him, along with Tina and Clayboy.

It would have felt good to cry but he couldn't. He looked at Otter who was kneeling by him, gazing into his face. Otter reached out to touch the side of his head, as if to assure him but also to assure himself. "You were there, weren't you, Arien? You were with her!"

Jeff, along with Sally-Ann, very distressed, came forward to say, "Gary went to call for help."

"Right," Jeff added. "The Ford's faster than Van Gogh." His shoes were wet. The press of the crowding on shore had forced him to step into the river.

"She's gone," Arien said blinking.

"Oh no," Andy hissed under his breath, just behind Arien. "Now the pigs will be coming." And Arien saw Otter connect with that.

Then Arien let go. He simply blanked right out.

The "Temple Circle of Mother Earth"

Otter knelt down to feel Arien's forehead. He stuck a slim doobie between barely cooperating lips. "Smoke this," he insisted. "How long have you been awake?" He flipped the top of the Zippo and as it clicked back it came to life. It was something new. He'd flipped the lid back and got the thing lit in the same motion. It takes twice for everyone else.

Arien heard the question but was more fixed on the lighter and Otter's little trick. How did he do that? He felt movement. Van Gogh jostled and skipped over the road. It lurched this way and that in the twilight between a running curtain of trees.

"Hit it!" Otter ordered.

Arien sucked the smoke into his mouth and inhaled it almost as an afterthought, as in, What do I do with it, now? Oh.

Otter left it dangling in Arien's mouth, but before clicking the lid closed held the flame up to look into Arien's eyes.

He was dimly aware of the others. The smoke expanded in his chest and a cough came up out of there that blew out of his face along with the doob, which landed in his lap. He could feel the ember burn the skin just up from his knee. It was distant. He analyzed it.

"Jesus, Arien!" That was Andy. He reached the same time as Tina and their hands collided in the effort to pick it up. There was a faint smell like burnt hair.

Arien calmly sat back against the cushions. His arms hadn't moved at all. He was dazed and numb as a hammered finger and were connection one of ten options, he would have picked the other nine. Where are we going? The effect of the smoke tingled in his lungs and a burning sensation lingered in his throat. He coughed more.

"You're scaring me, Arien," Otter said.

Tina poured water from their canteen into a tin cup. She raised it to Arien's lips and he took a sip, examining her features in the fading light. What a rad babe.

"How far should we go?" Jeff asked from up front.

Otter answered, "Pull off when we get to 17B. That ought to be far enough."

"Then what?"

"I don't know. Maybe Arien knows. Let's give him a little while and then we'll ask him."

Arien, disengaging, fell back into sleep.

When he awoke his kerosene lamp was lit and hanging from a rear corner hook in the head-liner. The side doors were open but Van Gogh's curtains were drawn. Folks were crowded around him in there munching. He could smell the tuna. Jeff, who was nearest, held an open can, plucking out a chunk of fish flesh with chopsticks. Tina downed a cracker, Andy was digging into his shoulder pack and Otter sliced raw broccoli on the wood board. Both Clayboy and Aspen were looking at Arien. Then all of them did.

"Dudes, where are we? What's going on?" His vocal chords felt weak and the words sounded flat, but he was in there and the relief among them was palpable.

"We had to get you away, Arien, just to be safe."

Arien thought for a moment when the crest of an ominous rush poured over him like a freak wave. In his memory there was chanting in a foreign language – Asian? Native American? It had to be the latter. Ah. He could see it now.

"I was dreaming," he said. "Awesome. But maybe it wasn't a dream." He smiled weakly. An oppressive weight was being held back, barely. Nobody spoke. They listened.

"I'm givin' 'er all she's got, Captain!" he reported with a brave tone of voice.

"Scotty!" Andy said, hearing the First Engineer of the Star Ship, Enterprise, to amused recognition among them.

"She cannah take much more o' this," Arien added, and he was telling the truth. If it hadn't been for Cypriano... He shuddered. He'd sensed the alarm in his mentor and the great effort Cypriano had taken on his behalf. They were by a hot little fire in the center of a wide, round, ocotillo corral set out among scrub islands in a barren, dusty plain. Arien saw a crouching, middle-aged, bony man, with hair pulled back from a dusky, lined face. Lances leaned against the pole-rack there with feathers dangling, and a shield sporting the painted image of a stick-man in the middle of a maze. The drumming was steady and strong, its reverberations fading into the next beat with the effect of a continuous note underlying a really ancient song. It coaxed him. It tickled his will.

Arien's detached analysis went something like, If only this thing I do had a volume control. It's either on or off. He was grateful for the intense love and concern he was feeling from these people with him now in Van Gogh. They provided a reason to struggle against the hollow, but easy, half-life it was to succumb to such a wrenching, soul-gutting, vicarious death experience. Once had been terrifying, twice was nearly enough to kick him, stupefied and numb, out of his box. It brought it all back. It threatened to overwhelm him completely.

Bravely, he smiled.

"Arien," Otter implored, "Tell us what we need to do to help you."

Arien didn't have an answer but rapped-out the next best thing, "Smack, Dude. Speedballs, downers, a bag of blow, PCP, a gallon of tequila, a bottle of aspirins and a box of sleeping pills." His eyes welled up. He drove his fingers back into his hair.

Tina crawled over on all fours. She kissed him. She came alongside and hugged him.

"Fuckin' awesome, I'm still alive!" He uttered with a deep sigh.

He was back in Salamanca, on the Saturday night before the barbeque with the Seneca. They was at Pauline's, on State Street, within a decent walking distance of the camp at the site of Zawatski's old farm. The place was jammed, between the town's own revelers; it seemed of all ages, and the addition of a good contingent of the Trees, who were warmly welcomed. Surely it was their energy, with its disarming hippie charm encouraging eager and positive curiosity among the kids and party people of the town. Yes, these were outsiders, but they were young and hip, engaging and into a good time and their money was good enough.

The band had stopped playing and everyone was riveted to the big, portable television with rabbit ears on a shelf in a corner of the bar. If it were any quieter at that moment, the thick, eye-stinging curls of cigarette smoke might have been heard rubbing together while settling through the air.

The announcer said, "Neil A. Armstrong, stepping out now–"

Then the first man to set foot on the surface of the moon said, "One small step for man, one giant step for mankind."

Arien saw it once in a documentary. But this was the real thing! The static over the airwaves from the moon smoothly enhanced everyone's spellbound focus in this happening night spot on planet Earth, and that with an emotional equation of world-wide wonder, awe, pride, patriotism – for surely, America was now everywhere, and all could mutually identify in a fleeting glimpse, so rare and beautiful, of the sublime possibilities inherent in the most historic of moments.

Arien could apprehend the billion sets of eyes glued to this one scene on the TV. Somebody said it was like when Kennedy had been shot, only it was wonderful. How totally awesome an experience to be here, to feel the people around me being so together!

But there was that other side, too. Oh, to die like she did! She gave up, and then it was too late!

Everyone dies.

I tried to help her!

You did what you could with what you had.

If I hadn't asked her to stay…

You don't know that. Remember Mother Shongo's words.

"It says 'Yasgur' on the gable of that barn over there," Andy said.

Jeff was asking him, "Hurd. Hurd Road, Arien. Do you know anything about it?"

Arien was solidly into his thoughts. He was barely aware of the excitement in the car with him.

"Arien! I think we're here, Babe!" Tina was animated. "Check it out!" She looked at him, pleading for him to get with it. Van Gogh turned through an opening in a hedgerow where a big, wildly painted school bus was parked. Some tents were set up. Arien knew they were early but that was the plan all along. They were here. He was really here! He was wrung-out and cried-out, but if he hadn't been he might have cried for joy.

"Where are the others?" he asked, grasping the rest of the circumstance.

"They'll be here," Otter said.

"Why? Why aren't we together now? We need to be together! I shouldn't have left them!" Arien tried to stand in the shifting vehicle.

"It's okay, Arien. Listen!" Otter restrained him with a steady hand.

Listen to them. Hear them.

"They'll be here," Otter repeated strongly. "We thought it would be best to get out of there. Oak and Willow caught up with us. They said to assure you they would handle it. Think, man! The police, Arien. The police were coming. Andy didn't want to talk to them. You were in no position to take questions. Your ID may have been good enough in that ding-bat food stamp office, but maybe not for the New York State Police."

Arien settled back down. That engagement took a lot of energy. He drifted off.

He awakened to a dingle of sharp musical notes. It came from Clayboy, sitting cross-legged in Van Gogh with him, engrossed with a thumb harp. He gently bobbed as he singled-out a tune, *Ding, ding, ding-ding, ding, ding, ding, ding, ding, ding-ding,* intently twanging-out the opening notes of "Lucy in the Sky with Diamonds."

The kid's good, Arien mused, watching him. When Clayboy noticed he was being observed he stopped playing and modestly smiled.

"Where is everybody?"

"Oh, everywhere. Tina's with the step van, down the road a bit. They're doin' lunch for the carpenters today."

Arien was more rested and suddenly was aware of a gnawing in his belly that took a moment to recognize as ravenous hunger. "Oh God, I'm famished!" he exclaimed. Suspecting Clayboy of acting on it he said, "Let's go take a walk, Dude, see what's going on, and grab a bite of it, too."

He was a little bemused by the extent of his zone-out, because the scene outside surprised and delighted. All around was the most beautiful country of rolling green fields, sparkling in the summer-hazed sunlight. They were in a small clearing that had apparently been smoothed-over by a bulldozer, which was parked in a corner. Rolls of chain-link fencing were stacked nearby. The Trees' bus was there, with its awning draped out where Cassie, Kelsey and some of the kids Arien knew and some new ones he didn't were coloring on big sheets of plain white paper.

"Hi, Arien!" Kelsey called. Cassie waved, along with some of the kids.

Nearby trees were already festooned with bolts of colored cloth and under them in grassy spaces were more tents. People were coming and going. The sounds of hammering and an abrasive whine of power saws could be heard now and then where most of the activity appeared to be, along with the rumble of heavy vehicles chased with light trails of dust on the dirt road. An electric guitar could be heard in the thick woods beyond that. It didn't look like a place to find an electrical outlet.

Arien stood where the road crested for a better all-around view. There had to be hundreds of people swarming over the site.

A hawk circled lazily, high overhead. Arien could make out the low towers on the edges of a broad, grassy bowl and the rather large ones that were closer, where he recognized the still-happening stage. There was plenty of activity there, lots of rat-tat-tat, folks humping lumber and plywood.

"Awesome!" he cried out, laughing, finally blowing out of the remnants of his dark cloud like a fighter jet. "God, Clayboy! Do you realize what's happening here? Holy shit! This is so way radical, Dude!"

The step van was a short way further on, with its table set up as a serving area. A contingent of dusty, sweaty freaks scooped up a scrambled eggs and fried potato brunch. Some hung there and wolfed it right where they stood. There were a lot of people Arien didn't recognize, though an inordinate number of them seemed familiar to him. This felt so crazy but not in a bad way. He could tell some of them had to be tripping. Amazing. They were actually being useful and goofing on it, too. A few Tree family folks looked up and waved, scanning his demeanor to see how he was doing.

At the van, Arien was deeply relieved to see Oak stooping over the range. He clambered in and Oak dropped his spatula in the broad pan he'd been working to embrace Arien with a bear hug.

"It's good to have you back, Grove!"

"I never wanted to leave, Oak!" Arien said, returning the warm greeting. The stolid fellow's embrace was good and comforting.

"How you doing, Grovey?" Tina asked. She entered from the forward cabinet with a sack of potatoes in both hands.

"I'm cool," he said.

She set the potatoes down on the narrow counter and smiled at him. "What happened with Laurel?"

"Willow called her folks in San Diego," Oak reported. "They flew out to Albany, rented a car and drove down to see where she died."

"Whoa. I must have been out of it."

"A couple of days, Arien," Tina said. "But you were never alone."

"Thanks!" he said, to her and Clayboy, who appeared relieved and happy.

"We want to do a memorial for her, here in Bethel. We were hoping you could join us."

"Let's do it, Oak."

The memorial for Laurel was held that very night and Tree and even Blue Star were remembered as well. It was the first time the Trees convened their magic circle in Bethel. It was a good trial run. A bunch of folks from the work crews attended. Though lights had been set up to illuminate the stage area for some sound wire lay-out after dusk, the main construction effort quieted. Many of the people who happened to be leaving for the day drifted over to the adjoining field on the other side of Hurd Road to see what was going on. Hawthorne was working out the placement of the quarters according to his compass. Arien overheard a few from the fence crew wondering about the likelihood tomorrow of their day's effort being the way they'd left it. There had been some vandalism that morning. A carpenter held a big Rockwell circular saw and a roll of extension chord. He stood by a dude who offered him a bottle of beer. "Look at this," he said to his buddy. "It's a twist-off top!"

Arien thought what happened next was pretty rad. When the Trees came together to hold hands in a circle and invoke the "Temple Circle of Mother Earth," which Andy pronounced as a humble prayer, most of the onlookers came over and joined in with the OM. A bunch of hippies were making a circle! The carpenters had to stand up their beers in the grass.

Andy continued, "In the beginning was the Word, and the Word was with God, and the Word was God," he said, not breaking his concentration, but winking at Arien, too. It was endearing. It brought back some of the conversations on spiritual matters they'd had along the way together. "In this Word was Life and the Life is our Light and the Light Shines in the Darkness and the Darkness comprehends it not."

Oak struck a match and lit his beautiful brass lamp. This he placed in the center.

"Mother and Father of all things!" Oak declared. "We come together in unity, for together we are One with You, and One with Life and One in the Light, so we may Listen and Feel and Know."

Next, Hawthorn, lighting a tight bundle of sage, intoned, "To the highest, Most Subtle One Within, May we focus in You, a Living Thread to which our Harmony attunes."

It brought Arien back to the discussion they'd had, early on in Salamanca. Who was he to say? It was all so new to him, but he repeated something there Cypriano said about a psychic process that is kindled, like some kind of engine, that – what did he say? ... *leverage open the door to the celestial ship of the Gods.* Such a beautiful way to say it! Sure they were high, but they got it and it begged the question, did they need to be high to get it or could they get there by simply knowing about it?

Arien was up next. He would speak first from the east, and for Aries in the Zodiac. He was by a blue pennant on a sapling pole they'd stuck in the ground, for the color of the Air and he stood with the Tree Family's staff to say, "Breath of Life! We come upon the Wind and the song that rides there!" And then, for the first time in public, he raised the water buffalo horn Jamie Sun gave him in San Francisco and blew out a clear, tenor note. It had been a while since he'd done that. The crisp sound had a marvelous effect as it rolled away over the fields and deeply into the trees. Some of the hippies smiled blissfully or sighed. And everyone heard the squawking crows in the woods beyond them in a nice touch of synchronicity.

In their early discussions Arien objected to this next thing, but Andy had insisted Arien should do the clockwise perambulation, or "undertake the journey of the sun around the circle of the year" as he explained it, and say all the invocations in their proper order. "You must," he'd said. "Who else is there?" And Arien had to give in because everyone agreed that it was true.

More people would have pressed in but the circle didn't expand for them further than the placement of those four pennants, which were planted at opposing points of the compass on an axis of about sixteen feet, or "four multiples of four," which Andy taught was the number of the ruling authority, who is Sky Father. So others who drifted over spontaneously formed an outer ring to watch or add their energy.

Arien recalled his amazement at how much Andy knew about this stuff. It was clear he stood for a genuine tradition he evidently hadn't made up. He'd used a strange word, "Hermetic," which Arien could recall because it had something to do with the god, Hermes. Arien's memory was pretty good, even if his education left gaps. He recalled Andy citing sources from dudes called Transcendentalists and there was a Great White Brotherhood that had a temple in the Andes, it was said. They were a magical order that may have been around hundreds of years. And he retained names like Madame Blavatsky (how spooky was that?), Alice Bailey and Manly P. Hall. Willow had some of their books. And Andy knew about white magicians, whose color was about the kind of magic they did, not their race. There was a guy named Levi and another called Regardie, and writers, (Diane, was it?) Fortune and Herman Hesse, Andy had spoken of. Arien wondered if he'd ever get to reading any of their stuff. Probably not.

It was time to continue around the circle and recite the other invocations. He marveled how simple it was. He always thought magic was supposed to be complicated and impossible for an ordinary dude to understand. Andy had assured him it didn't have to be that way. A lot had been complicated on purpose for a few reasons. One, in the old days, was to hide it from the Church, another was probably just to make some people more special than everybody else.

This was pretty heady for Arien. He could never have articulated it to Andy's level, but he got it, and that only proved Andy's point!

"Father of Elements!" Arien declared, stepping southward where Ben stood, and planting the staff by the red pennant. "We look to your source in the Sun, from where all Life is quickened, and to the subtle Fire of Transformation that is crowned in our Knowing!" A small fire ring had been placed here and now Hawthorne lit the stack of split wood and small logs in it. There were over sixty people checking out the happening now and still more were on the way – though gathering darkness kept it to those who were closer than might otherwise have responded, and yet it remained quiet enough for everyone to hear.

Tina sat at the base of the white pennant to the west. There was a small ceramic bowl of water in the grass in front of her that was taken from Filippini's Pond. Earlier in the day Andy and Hawthorne consecrated it in a small ceremony. They used ash from the fire pit at Medicine Bow, and sea salt from an old-lady friend of Hawthorne's who had been with Gandhi, on his march to the sea in India. Arien planted the staff right by it and recited, "Ocean of Consciousness, reflected in Life's Waters! Your endless waves break upon our awareness. In your stillness our Mystery is reflected and your living currents know the depths of all Being." The weird thing was the fat raindrops that began to splat down through the dingy darkness just as he completed the invocation.

"Ha!" Arien exulted with a delighted smile. If asked, he could never have explained how such a thing was possible yet on another level, it was becoming a given. One of the late-night discussions in Salamanca asked this question and attempts to answer it at first fell flat. Some expressed the popular belief that the performer was simply doing magic, in effect, making it happen, and that was that. Arien thought Andy came closest by a more obtuse pronouncement that "The essence of magic is timing." Andy, in his most brain-teasing language, had further declared that, "Magic defies science because it is no more repeatable than any day we have lived, the circumstances are always different, but its results may both confirm and measure its truth and effectiveness." He'd read it right out of his notes. Now, there were a few "Wows" and "Whoas" from the attentive crowd but the Trees mostly smiled at one-another in the practically predictable wonder of this whole project.

There were shuffles and movement with the threat of a deluge. The drips were large and ominous, but they remained far apart and for the moment at least, no one was getting wet.

At last, Arien stepped to the northern quadrant where the green pennant was planted, to pronounce between the drops, "Mother Earth! Our destiny unravels on your surface. Within your system of birth and growth, decline and death we know the Life within and without us that comes down from the beginning and continues to the end of time."

Sundew, sat here. Arien wondered about her. By and large, he saw very little of her. She spent her time with Ben, of course, and often the kids and moms, but she rarely approached Arien or had much to say to him. But he got a steady vibe from her that said she was there, and satisfied, and busy, and she didn't need nor desire the rush others sought in Arien's usual hemisphere. He liked that about her and now he appreciated all the more her presence in the north. She held a dunbek drum set between her knees and beat it, 1-2-3-4, 1-2-3-4, 1-2-3-4...

Andy said, "Arien will take the staff and plant it in the center by the lamp," which Arien did, along with a strange tingling sensation that seemed to cling to it. The staff usually felt strange to handle anyway, and Arien had mentioned this to Oak before, but now there was another quality about it. He couldn't be sure what it was, but his own connectedness, as if kindling another, extra sense, appeared to manifest the focus of energy in their space. He made a note to mention this to Oak and probably Andy. Then, after a moment's stillness, he took the staff and returned to sit by the blue pennant where he began his circling. He could still feel the subtle vibrating in the staff when he stood there with it.

"This is the time we reserve for a brief title to what we bring here, where everyone is invited to share it with everyone else," Andy explained, "but tonight we remember three of our friends.

'Laurel,' Leslie Delato, was born in southern California on February 28th, 1945, and passed on just four days ago, while we were on our way here, and–"

Arien had a terrible nightmare. Blue Star drowned and died with a dark secret and now Arien was the only person left who knew what it was. The contorted face was smeared in blood. It was an incongruous image but it dogged him. When they pulled Blue Star from the water Arien was told he could be saved with a breath of air, but he refused to make contact with his friend's bloody lips. He awoke with the guilt and shame of allowing Blue Star to die.

His cries awakened Tina. Her hands found his face in the darkness and became still when the tips of her fingers found his lips. She snuggled closer to him.

"I don't know what will happen if I have to go through something like that again," he whispered. "I've never been so beat up in my life!"

"What does Cypriano say?"

"I think he's sweatin' it."

"Did you ask him?"

"No, but he knows."

She pushed herself up on her elbow. "He can't protect you?"

A stream of images and feelings pulsed through Arien's mind in the usual way but something seemed to be lost in the transmission. Or, had it? Maybe the deficit was in the receiving. He had to ponder it. "It's way out there," Arien said. "I don't understand."

Step back from your fear. You are safe now.

Arien understood that well enough.

Cypriano tried again.

"Oh no!"

"What Arien?"

"No, no, no!"

"Tell me?"

"Oh. God, I don't know how to... Balance, I'm... it's... like a balance of things. I've opened something up and I can't just pick and choose. I get it all. Cypriano can't protect me from my own connection. I just have to buck up and keep my balance!

"And yeah, he did help. He may have saved me from getting wasted but it took a lot out of him."

"Oh, Arien, what's going on?"

"I don't know but I keep coming to a blank, this – It's dark out and the ground is pure white and it doesn't make any sense. I can't see past it and it's real close and getting closer. Jesus, Tina, it's creeping me out."

Worry and the uneasy residue of his dream receded the next day after downing a stack of step van buckwheat pancakes with peanut butter and maple syrup lavished over the top. Arien was there early because he hadn't slept at all after his troubling dream and it improved his outlook to lose himself behind the stove with Tina, Clayboy and Myrtle, who were manning breakfast. They wound-up serving a lot more pancakes than expected as new people were arriving like a rising flood. It was apparent that many of them were neither volunteers nor on Woodstock Ventures' payroll, but were coming to set up campsites and otherwise hang out. Some of these brought little or nothing along and they just followed their noses to the morning line. It made Arien smile to see them. He knew they were merely the advance spray of the breaker of the wave before the ocean of people who were coming. Those around him could sense it, too. This one would be something truly new and the excitement and anticipation was pervasive.

The Trees had been getting into volunteer projects at the bustling site so most vanished shortly afterwards. Nita once attended nursing school, so she and Willow went off to assist with setting up a medical tent they laid-out the previous day with a doctor from Monticello. Jeff joined up with an electrical crew on one of the towers. Otter, very much in his element, informed Arien business opportunities abounded and he was prepared to take full advantage of the fact. Both Kelsey and Cassie would manage day care today at the bus. Ben and Sundew were sticking around for lunch detail. Oak, Harlan and Gary joined into the stage projects. Arien overheard Oak mention the rotating stage that was designed to facilitate band set-ups between acts. He complained that nobody listened when he suggested a better way to attach the wheels, but it wasn't his project, anyway; he just wanted to help out and he would try to stay out from underfoot in the process. Luke and Sally-Ann, along with Hawthorne joined the trail crews who were clearing passages under trees between vendor kiosks, information stands, camp sites, play zones and entertainment venues that were going up all over the area. Various sites and trails were given cool names, such as "Shroom Hill" and "Groovy Way," and tons of signs had to be painted, too. It seemed pretty chaotic because opening day was bearing down like a runaway log truck, but it was obvious how much fun and so little sleep most people were having.

Andy found his way to the van in time to help with clean up, and afterwards the five of them struck out on a hike to take it all in. They were soon on the dirt track that ran behind the stage and between it and the clearing and woods bordering Flippini's Pond. Oak was already well engaged there, up on the wooden catwalk that ran overhead like a super-size Hot Wheels overpass connecting the stage with the field behind it. A fellow on the ground passed him a two-by-four. Oak managed to take it and wave at Arien at the same time.

A wooden wall was going up under it on their right. Arien and his party had to allow a flat bed truck to get by them to park there and a Ryder rental truck came right behind it. Then a bare-chested fellow in a leather vest with a mop of very curly hair framing his baby face ripped up on a BSA motorcycle. He stopped in front of Arien and his party to set his foot down and look up at the construction.

"Rad! I know you!" Arien blurted out.

The guy on the bike turned to see who said that. He raised an eyebrow. "Oh?"

"Well, actually, we haven't met, but I saw you in the movie!" Arien was delighted to be talking to someone he remembered from the movie. He grinned from ear to ear. Tina, Myrtle, Clayboy and Andy merely stood there.

"What movie is that?" the young man asked with a curious smile. He revved his motor slightly. "Did you see the Miami Pop?"

Arien realized his error. "Uh, yeah," he lied, "but you're going to make a flick about Woodstock, aren't you?"

"Yes, hope to. It's in the works."

'Rad, Dude," he praised. "I'm Arien."

"Michael," the guy on the BSA said, accepting Arien's hand.

"Michael!" A man on the overhead walkway called, "Can you come up here a minute?"

Michael waved up at him and revved his motor. "Well, uh, Arien, duty calls."

"Go for it, Dude. There's a ton of it."

"Right you are," Michael agreed with a nod. He gunned the motor and the bike rolled off toward the field where the long ramp came down to meet the ground.

"Who was that?" Andy asked.

"He's the boss." Arien watched until Michael got off of the bike at the entrance to the ramp.

"He seems young," Myrtle observed.

"He does, but you'll see him in the movie. I promise."

They walked further up the road to where a large field opened up on the left. A few cars were parking along the road there and tents were going up in it. Already, there was a trace of anarchy in the atmosphere with most new arrivals appearing to figure it out on their own.

"Wow, Arien," Andy remarked, "You've been talking about Woodstock all along, but it's a trip to see it happening. And, the thing's still days away!"

"This is nothing. You wait!" Arien grinned over a corona of giddiness. He shied from sinking deeper from there. He knew the unnamable haunting of his journey was below it someplace. "I should stay clear," he barely said.

"What's that, Babe?" Tina asked.

Arien exhaled heavily, as if he were winded. "I'll be high as a kite with the contact high when this thing gets going. I won't need to add anything."

"Otter would recommend more acid," Andy replied with a twinkle in his eye.

"I vote for that!" Clayboy cheered.

They walked for a long while, circling around, back through the woods on their right that ultimately bordered the big bowl-shaped field of dreams. There was a lot of activity here and they ran into Luke and Sally-Ann with an armload of Christmas lights.

"Look what we got into!" Sally-Ann greeted.

"Whose bright idea was that?" Andy asked.

Luke rolled his eyes. "I take full responsibility," he admitted. Then he said, "Say, Guys, there's going to be a band playing at a set up to entertain the troops. It's back behind where the Tree's bus is parked. Let's head over after dinner and see what they got."

"Sure," Arien agreed to general assent among them, and surprised himself in the meantime by nearly taking a hit of a cigarette Clayboy lit and nonchalantly offered up. "What am I doing?" he asked out loud. "No, Clayboy. Thanks, damn it."

"Who's the band?" Myrtle inquired.

"Quill," Luke answered. "I never heard of them."

"Neither have I," Arien concurred.

Myrtle said, "I have. They're an East Coast band. They're good!"

They were good. It was a great party, too. Several hundred volunteers, Woodstock Ventures employees in their cool guitar-and-dove T-shirts, and early arrivals were there and there was lots of dancing and pure fun. Arien especially liked a percussion riff Quill performed that seemed to turn into a free-for-all of open-ended drumming by everybody who could find something to beat on. The band had thrown out some maracas and a few tambourines to get it going, and soon the crowd produced dunbeks and a large Celtic and some Native American hand-held drums, cow bells, didgeridoos, tin cans, spoons, glass jugs, and even pots and pans. It was crazy, infectious fun that had everybody dancing and shouting along in unison and it went on for a very long while.

Arien got himself fairly ripped on a jug of wine he shared with Otter, along with some of the precious Panama Red Otter measured out on the rare occasion. The joint was as slim as a swizzle stick and was gone in one tour around the Stand, which included Aspen and Clayboy, who were there at that moment. But, it had the intended effect read in Otter's merry glance, like an extra shot of adrenaline with a euphoric, heady rush. Arien had to keep wiping the sweat out of his eyes. Tina, likewise, stroked at the hair sticking to her face to free her sight and her smile and determination to keep up with him.

It was a warm and humid evening, visible in the fluttering insect, hazy glow of naked bulbs strung out around the low stage. And Arien gathered the pulsing rhythms deep in his body, to feel it in his gonads and interpret his exaggerated steps and flailing arms with the abandon of all the hippies around him. Even so, he marveled how he could be so incredibly happy and at home and in love with the moment and himself in it with all that remained unresolved, and he realized it was in spite of all that he gave himself totally to the physical, cathartic experience. I'm at Woodstock! I'm at Woodstock! Oh, wow, I can't believe it, but I'm really, really, really here! And, opening day was still nearly a *week* away!

Jeff, Otter and Aspen had set up Arien and Tina's tent in the woods, not far from the bus and Van Gogh, and Jeff stayed there while Arien was 'out of it' and crashing in Van Gogh. The morning after the party with Quill, Arien was invited to make the switch and with just a trace of a hangover he agreed. Clayboy helped move their stuff and afterwards, having been up all night, retired to a pup tent he reported finding in a duffle he found in the road. Arien was pleased to see it right next door. Clayboy was unabashedly devoted and if he was not seen by Arien's side it was usually because he was off on some errand. Then, there were usually others hanging with him, too. Andy was very often seen with Arien, and Otter, Jeff, and Tina, of course, besides an assorted number of Tree People. As a matter of simple observation, outsiders had already taken notice of the young man with a seemingly permanent retinue and rumors were beginning to circulate about who he might be. On that basis when Jeff wondered when and how Ellison would find them, Andy smiled knowingly and eloquently said, "A highway to this tent would hardly make it easier for Ellison." And, Arien readily agreed.

Indeed the tent was now adorned with a standard. A stout, straight pole stood before it with a section lashed near the top, like a yardarm on a tall ship's mast, and a bolt of white duck cloth with the broad silhouette of a green tree painted on it was draped over the arms like the shawl of Saint Peter. Arien thought it was "Awesome," and wondering who made it was told it was, of course, Kelsey's idea. Standards like this were beginning to crop up at various places and it was real cool to see the Trees had one, too.

Settled in, Arien relaxed on top of his bedroll while Tina organized her baggage when feet shuffled outside.

"Hello in there!"

"Come in, Andy."

Andy entered and folded his legs on the blue and white carpet. He wore a silk Hawaiian shirt hanging out over a pair of shorts that were short enough when he was standing to effect only legs there.

Those short shorts – even though I have a pair: the one '60s style I can't get used to, Arien mused to himself. Oh, but bell bottoms are pretty sorry, too. "What's up Dude?"

Andy let out a brief laugh. He reached in the pocket of his shirt and pulled out a loose joint. "Got a match?"

"Got 'em," Tina said. "They're here – they're here –" She dug in one of her packs, then another, to produce a book of them.

Andy handed it over for her to light. "Well, Arien, Tina told me you've had a scary vision. I thought we should talk about it."

"Maybe I'm not ready." Arien stared up at the ceiling.

"What's holding it up?"

"I don't know what it means. I don't even know if it's real."

"It probably is, Man. Maybe we can help. You know, two heads are better than one, as long as they're not both yours."

"That would make you a freak," Tina chimed.

"I already am." He took the joint from her and toking up, passed it back to Andy.

"What does Cypriano say?"

Arien felt the THC rush come over him, though it wasn't an "up" this time. It had more of a leaden effect pot sometimes has, tasting off and inviting a headache. "He hasn't brought it up, yet. Maybe he doesn't know– I think he's betting on the circle."

"Yes, I'd say it's a given we'll do the circle when the festival's happening. All roads lead to there."

"I agree," he said, passing on the doobie with a wave of his hand when Tina took a hit and held it out again. "I wish we were closer to Salamanca. I'd like to talk to Mother Shongo again."

"We could, if that's what you need to do." The joint went out and Andy set it down on his lap.

"Nah, we're here now and everybody's gotten into it. The roads will turn into free parking in a few more days, anyway, and we might not be able to get back in here."

"Wow. Do you think so, Arien?" Tina asked.

"I know so."

40 — … it's calling me, too!

Arien picked his way through the dense, humid air and the leafy smell of woods and trampled grass and wet, churned soil and endless perspiring bodies, clustered in defiance of the previous evening's showers, to absorb the mesmerizing scene. What can I offer this? The press of people with faces like flowers, thousands and thousands of blooms on the hillside, like a living carpet, spreading out in all directions, so dense a delight and deep, and aware of itself and its ineffable joy and fellow-feeling, as liberty of the hearts' most earnest yearnings, such as knowing why, and how, and to what end, forever and ever with every throbbing fiber of one's being in concert with every fiber of every others', as in the humming of the bees, and the chorus of the birds, and crescendo of the crickets and grinding, ratcheting cicadas, and the swirling butterflies, and now the people, too, have come, in a way locked deep in the racial memory of a – sadly - rare time in the long history of our race, such as now, when true freedom, O God, True Freedom is manifest, and felt and tasted, and how a thing of sterling love it is, that any pure metal or precious jewel or rare fur or polished wood or gadget or widget can be weighed against it and be found utterly wanting, and hollow, and empty, and imprisoning in an infinite, demonically ingenious number of ways, and how, if it does not feed the people and make them whole and give them life— Everything flows from that! Arien realized. A consciousness like this could, and would, really heal the world! Everything else is so awfully small and stupid!

Arien saw himself in the nearest eyes. It was akin to beaming back at himself as he picked his way, this way and that, around people in front of the stage who basically hadn't moved in two days. One fellow looked so hungry. Arien reached into the net bag Tina filled for him in the morning and worked out an orange and some almonds and dates and gave them to the guy, who laughed with gratitude and delight.

A lovely barefoot, face-painted girl about his age with a reddish tint to her hair stood on a muddy blanket with a few other people. Something about her besides her bare breasts and short skirt locked Arien's eyes. He needed to step by her to continue around the stage but he halted there and regarded her. She looked awfully familiar but that was becoming such a common occurrence now, he was beginning to accept it as the new normal, so he chalked it up to that.

She returned his wondering, curious smile. "Hi," she said. "What's happening, Man?"

He laughed. "Uh, Woodstock Ventures is putting on this little show for a few people." *God, where have I seen this babe before?*

"It's groovy," she deadpanned, and then catching the quirky way he looked at her, she unselfconsciously asked him his name.

"Arien."

"Oh! I *love* it! That's such a groovy name." She stuck an index finger under a lip, studying him. "Are you an Ares?"

"Uh huh, March 22nd."

"How do you spell it?"

"A-R-I-E-N."

"Cool. Tell you what, Arien, if I ever have a baby boy, I'll call him that."

"Wow. That's so rad. And every time you call his name it will help you remember Woodstock," he said.

"Remember what?" She giggled.

Arien had an urgent impulse to get her name but the next band had barely been introduced while he was focused on this babe and already their streaming, hypnotic organ riff and exceedingly catchy rhythm was throwing a net over the throng and hauling them all into musical history.

And that's when he began to come on to the button tea. "No, Otter! No, I don't need it!" he'd protested, his wary smile reflecting how comical Otter appeared, offering up this mason jar of dark liquid with all kinds of pulpy, fleshy stuff floating in it, and a spare scent of orange peel and jasmine.

"Yes, ya do, Arien!" Otter laughed between a silly, pleading expression that was another piece of his charming repertoire. There were times on the road when even Arien had to dismiss a hamburger stand along the roadside for that look; that think-of-the-animals, pleading – yet somehow commanding – look. And now, how could Arien resist when Otter reminded him, "I've carried them all this time, since that day at Zadkiel's when I got them just for you!"

The tea was sweetened with maple syrup that barely disguised its repulsive taste and it wanted to come back up only a short while after it was down. Arien thought he was supposed to keep it. He didn't know, so when it finally had its way it nearly blew out of him horizontal, just missing his friend. But he felt better after that, and he grew a little heady and dizzy too, but not in a bad way, and he smiled – or was it, smirked – at Otter and struck off on his own into the thick mass of muddy defiance patiently facing the stage, like a vast army of resistance to the foibles of weather. Nothing – not yesterday's showers nor mud or the lack of food and a dry place to lay was going to sully the fun! Nothing – not the brown acid, not the broken glass underfoot, nor the increasing whiff of excrement and vomit or lack of sleep or private, easy place to piss would dampen their courage to overcome these piddley inconveniences and simply enjoy the music, trip-out, get laid, and goof on one-another! How beautiful is that?

So he'd struck off towards the high stage with its set of iconic towers, apologizing, sending word to Tina who was making "stone soup" with the Hog Farm, and Clayboy, wherever he was, and excusing himself in a modern-dance-like progression into the wilderness of unpredictable, animated flesh where it didn't look like anyone could possibly blaze a trail. But he was getting higher and he moved with the vibes like water over and around rocks in the bed of a stream. It was not unlike the blind hike with Tree to the pinnacle of rock in the wilderness of Medicine Bow. And it carried him right smack into this pretty, topless girl! God, where have I seen her before?

"Oh, awesome!" he cried, recognizing the sound blasting out from the stage. "It's fucking Santana!" And he began to dance where he stood – not that there was any room to do that anywhere else – and the sweet, mysterious girl danced with him and it felt so good he could hardly believe it.

He held it dearly in his head, reeling it out like the movie: Hugh Romney, the Hog Farm dude, "...What we have in mind is breakfast in bed for four hundred thousand," and old man Yasgur, he was so cool! "...a half a million kids...can get together and have three days of fun and music...and I God Bless You for it!" And Quill; Arien was impressed to hear them in the early afternoon. He didn't remember them from the movie but experienced some kinship already, having seen the band up close. And he loved yelling, FUCK with all his might back at Country Joe. That was so rad! He'd opened wide and let it all out. Take THAT, Berkeley, for your stupid fence, and THAT, killers, for your lack of mercy, and THAT, senseless, Dad-eating War, and THAT, Civilized World, because I am FREE! Oh, YES! I am F R E E EEEEEEEEEEE !

"Arien, you're too cool!" She shouted with familiar glee, as the band drove their crisp fusion relentlessly, thrillingly on into rhythm, transcendent percussion, ecstatic, surfing vocals, and glowing colors in the faces of panting, dancing people, with hair and limbs flying in exuberance and joy, tossing it back to the stage and catching it again with every bow of Carlos' guitar, erupting congas and phenomenal charging drum sticks, like kids with a beach ball. That dude, Santana, he has to be tripping! I know he's high!

And Arien knew he knew her! Where? Where?

Maybe it was a past life? That was gaining credibility. It explained a lot. Tina tended to support the idea and for many of the Trees it was a given. Andy wasn't so sure. The other night, with a glowing fire, a cup of tea and Aspen strumming her dulcimer, Andy said, "I think it's all out there in the 'mind-stuff' that makes the Universe. When you tune in, it's like you vibrate with it, just like all the strings in a harp vibrate when you pluck one of them. The historical connection is already there in the experience of the race, like the countryside in the background." Andy ruled whenever he pontificated like this. The Trees regarded him a wise elder, even though he was younger than Oak, and it was reported that he crept away to cry from time to time.

And what did the Swami say yesterday? – How rad to see this guy! He was the guy in the movie! He was the very dude Andy talked about before (And it was so bitchin' to catch it with Andy)! He remembered something Satchidananda said about sound, sound and music: "...It is the sound that controls the whole universe..."

His thoughts were holding it all, feeding-out fragments – the great, expansive heart of Richie Havens, the swami's ineffable joy, Sweetwater's cool mix, Bert Sommer's galvanizing rendition of "America," and all along a progression of the Mind of the crowd that they were part of something new and special and hosting a flame they'd ignited that was available to anyone and everyone forevermore! He blended now with that Mind, in glances across the glittering sea of eyes, to meet it at points of geometric patterns on a pastel, breathing, multi-colored, undulating pillow, occasionally orchestrated from the stage like a gargantuan, amorphous marionette, and at other times, especially between sets, subdued and reflecting upon the wonder of itself.

"Arien! I love you!" she called through a slide of notes blasting out over their heads, blowing him a kiss and winking to her friends who were up dancing on the blanket with them.

Arien fell to watching the tight roll of her breasts move with her lithe body. He didn't feel like a lecher, either, but an admirer of beauty who has found something dear to relate to. A similar light was in her eyes. What is she thinking? This babe is so rad. Where do I know her from? Damn! He had a crazy urge to show her his birthmark. Why that?

Oh, damn it, but a force began to pull at him, subtle at first, like the little hand of a child on Daddy's pant leg, or the receding lap of a gentle wave, before the next and the one after that. He ignored it at first and for as long as he could, until it was stronger, more urgent, a turning tide that would hurry the gentle waves away to pull the great mass of water out beyond exposed mussels, marooned starfish and slithering slugs. A loud fantasy to find some way to nestle his face among those nubile boobs and smell her and know her and take his rest there was now countered with another, insistent tugging, as if his every cell were made of iron and some powerful, scrap yard magnet was inexorably focused on removing him from where he danced, wondered and longed.

"I gotta go," he said.

"What?"

It was harder to say it the second time. "I gotta go!"

"You're going to split?" She wore an incredulous look that fell heavily upon him.

It was something he couldn't explain but he knew with every fiber of his experience and ever-growing respect for whatever worthy gifts he'd come to know. He was well-past resistance, like a soldier who hears the bugle and accepts his commitment and his fate. But, it would be an understatement to say it merely hurt.

"I'll be back!" he promised, and he locked up the hopeful nod she returned, and began to beat himself up as soon as moving away, Why didn't I kiss her? Why did I only touch her hand? Why–"

What do you want from me, you Bitch? Why couldn't this wait? But it was worse than a bodily urge that would not accept any further delay, like the *now* that told him to turn off the road to find that perfect place to park. He tried to wrap his mind around it. It was something big! Maybe it was the peyote tea talking. Maybe it was just something big. Is this your doing, Cypriano?

No, Arien, it's calling me, too!

It took a long time to make his way to the road where an incredible jam-up of empty cars were packed in so tight with people trying to move along, through, over and around them a bee could hardly have flown between. A broken line of helicopters landed and took off from the field behind the stage and the procession of delivered notables disappeared to the stockade of trailers and tents or paraded uncertainly on the wooden gangway like a march to their execution. There was no going that way, and though Woodstock had already been declared a "free concert" this was one passage to remain blocked and unassailable, like the mighty keep of an otherwise fallen citadel. Arien cleaved to the shoulder of the road where it rose and afforded another jaw-dropping vista of the vast throng among the detritus of its transportation, its accumulating litter, and the distant sprinkling of tents, buses and pavilions extending out everywhere through a patchwork of rolling fields and woods, as far as the furthest horizon.

Whatever lingering irritation remained was soothed with a rising anticipation, borne on bare feet that seemed to float over the ground in the all-encompassing bubble of Otter's powerful tea. Colors stood out the most. They were intensely sharp and seemed brighter than the surrounding light. The pink of cheeks and knees, the radiant sheen to everyone's hair, their little banners, flags and headbands, the sparkle of their beads, the glow of the canopy of trees all delighted the eye in a living, moving, Impressionist canvas, and everyone made their way through this milieu knowing and not knowing, to greater or lesser degree the Mind of them All which surely contained them and allowed among them for Arien to find his way to his tent.

He laughed to himself, realizing he had no idea where he was going yet now he was here, and there on their bedroll was the Tree Family staff and that amazing horn in the blue velvet bag. They laid there like two people waiting. Where is everybody? "We're here!" He answered for them, aloud, chuckling to himself, because he was thinking of Tina and Clayboy and the rest of the Stand and all of the Trees, not the two "souls" on the sleeping bag. He gathered them up and stepped outside in the waning light of a highly memorable day.

Now what? He waited uncertainly for some directional tug but there was nothing. He was impatient. Maybe I'll go back and find that girl! Still, there was nothing. So he said it out loud, "I'll go back and find her!" And again, nothing answered, but he knew in his heart that the horn and the staff were not for bringing there. Reluctantly, almost fitfully, Arien sat down on the wooden folding chair in front of the tent and waited.

"Why do you cry, Arien?" It was the voice of Ellison Black Snake. Arien looked up through his blurry eyes to see the Seneca man regarding him with young Thomas at his side. Thomas carried a leather satchel over his shoulder. He said nothing.

"I know who she is!" Arien pitifully sobbed, with the staff between his knees and flanking a side of his head. He leaned into it, wrapping an arm around it and cradling the horn on his lap. He was sitting there when it came to him like a bullet between the eyes and he couldn't hold back the flood of grief and irony and even a strange, begrudging sense of wonder that overwhelmed him the moment he knew. When he got it he wailed like a baby, as if Nanna and Momma's tragic date with a drunken automobile happened all over again, mindless of the people moving around and through the camp. None of them were Trees or anyone he knew, and they likely assumed he was having a bad trip and didn't intervene.

"Who?" Ellison asked.

"My Mom, Ellison! I saw my Mom! That was my MOM!" Tears splashed from his face with an emphatic gesture. He couldn't believe any force in the Universe would have had the nerve, the presumption, the utter, unmitigated gall to tear him away from the young Maggie Austin. But, it had!

Ellison hung there, attempting to take it in. It was obvious there were some things Ellison didn't know about. Both he and Thomas settled into a patient waiting for Arien to compose himself and perhaps elaborate on the matter.

Gradually, Arien began to appreciate that Force, with unmitigated gall, had led him to Maggie in the first place! He allowed the tremulous wave of relief and gratitude and towering mountain of awe that only awaited his invitation.

"I'm sorry, Ellison," Arien said, sucking air, wiping his eyes with the back of his fingers and spitting out a glob of phlegm. "I'll find her again," he resolutely announced, holding forth a new personal mission in all four ventricles like a slippery jewel.

And then he felt that tug! It pulled him to his feet. He was still high as a kite, but he was in control again and he imagined his crying was behind him for good.

When Arien began to walk, Ellison smiled at Thomas, who nodded in return with obvious relief. Arien heard that as certainly as if it were plainly said. Had they invested everything in a blubbering fool? What kind of cosmic joke could that be? Yet were it not for them, Arien imagined, he might have plunged back into the thick of it in a determined frenzy to find her. He would do that later, he would, and he'd be damned if he'd let anything stop him! How awesome can it be? I never knew she was at Woodstock!

They made their way down one of the well-prepared paths through woods with craft booths and empty or shuddered food and drink stands that had been sucked dry in the very first hours and couldn't be restocked over impassable roads. Already, an early contingent of helicopters with a beat and chop and aerial concussion Arien vaguely recalled from the riots in Berkeley hovered above the arching trees. He wondered about that sound, knowing full-well Woodstock in the movie was unmolested by the National Guard.

"Here!" Arien said, dodging left and right, like he really knew where they were going, but he followed his inner nose and it led him deeper through the crowded woods over a busy trail to the rear of Filippini's Pond, where people stood around in the muggy air just looking at the water, and on to a crowded hill that had an excellent point of vantage.

Arien felt like he'd floated the whole way, battling imaginary monsters in a shamanic quest painted by 'Mescalito,' patently altering the world. They were one-dimensional creatures, dancing symbols in a deeply personal dreamscape, with bright colors and hybrid bodies like satyrs and mythic beasts. I am past that; I am so way beyond that!" He called out as he vanquished them with a wave of the staff, one after another. And all the while he strode on, oblivious of the collection that gathered behind Ellison, Thomas and himself, Andrew, Hawthorne, Clayboy, Tina, with a bowl and a canteen, Otter, Aspen, Jeff, Oak, with his big brass oil lamp, Willow, Nita, Kelsey, hauling four rolled-up pennants over her shoulder, Myrtle, Ben, Sundew, Luke, Sally-Ann, Harlan, and Gary. Arien had the presence of mind to wonder: Where did they come from? Who's watching the kids?

The little procession halted at a clearing with an odd acoustical anomaly that enabled them to hear the next band and something of the multitude's oceanic pealing, as if captured in a seashell. It was almost dark now and the last hopping-bluesy numbers of the group that was up there were coming to a close.

Gary smiled. "Canned Heat," he said.

"Yes," Tina agreed.

Rad babe, Arien thought with admiration. She sure knows her tunes!

"How's your high?" Otter asked with the full, rounded, resonant words of a fellow-tripper. A flicker of smile acknowledged the acutely charged physical tension between them.

"You wouldn't believe who I saw!" Arien whispered to him as the circle came together.

"I might. Was it Bob Dylan? There's a rumor going around that–"

Arien giggled, but the moment snapped him back. He could feel the potent brew sweating through his pores, squeezing another rush in a declining but still pulsing train of them. He could follow the sinews of his legs and tendons of his feet making contact with the ground, like the trunk of a tree drawing energy and life from there and his hands tingled with the cool force gathering to the staff. This is so fucking cool!

Steady yourself, lad.

Oh, Cypriano, if you only knew!

I know, White Brother. But this weekend you did show me what even I haven't imagined before.

Dude, I saw it all in the movie!

And so you've foretold.

"Now let us dedicate our gathering of the Temple Circle of Mother Earth!" Andy called out and he began an OM everyone picked up. As their OM rose up into the surrounding trees Kelsey made her way around, vigorously attempting to plant the pennant poles in the ground. None of them stood. But the obstacle was easily overcome. Each nearest took hold of the pennant and simply held it there, like a standard bearer. The effect was unintended, but lent it a noble dignity.

In his circle of expanding awareness, bouncing from the highs among the Tree People and perceptibly dense electricity of the vibe in rural Bethel, Arien opened his eyes connecting with others who had simply joined in. He was almost startled to see an elder Black woman who smiled at him. Where did she come from? She held a rather large African drum under her arm, supported with a shoulder strap, and was just setting it down on the grass before her to mingle her fingers among theirs. Not far from her, was a young girl who couldn't have been a day older than Clayboy. Indeed, she stood beside him as he curiously regarded her.

What happened next was unexpected. As the Trees went to their respective places the new participants stood in place ahead of them before the pennants of Earth, where the Black woman came to be, and Water, which was taken by the girl. They faced Ellison, at Air, and Ben, who occupied Fire. Ellison brought a smile that put most everyone at ease, but Arien was unsure and feeling protective. His eyes met Andy's and they agreed.

"Excuse, me," Andy said, but fell silent as Elison raised an open hand.

"All is as it should be!" Ellison declared with words of bedrock certainty.

The Black woman who stood to the north, in the Earth Quadrant, looked about her for reassurance. The cast to her body said, "Don't I belong here?" And Arien easily detected the inner grin of his ephemeral mentor. "It's cool," his gesture assured with a wave and a nod.

He looked at the White girl in the West, and Ben in the South and it tickled his brain. Ben is Chinese –

The young girl pushed back her hair and folded her hands as Tina bent over to place the little ceramic bowl before her and fill it with the cloudy water in a mason jar. Then she stood beside her, into the quadrant.

Arien marveled at how this thing worked itself out and came together with the blowing of his horn for the second time in a sacred circle and the opening invocations he'd pronounced at Laurel, Blue Star and Tree's memorial. And when Ben lit all of the incense sticks Hawthorne presently supplied him, and stuck them in the ground, the import fell upon Arien with a swoon. "Hey, Andy," he called out. "Check out the colors!"

To which Thomas said, "Oh, see! All of the races are represented in the circle!"

E'e-Toy! We have waited so long for this moment!

Arien repeated that sentence for everyone. "Cypriano said that," he self-consciously explained, unsure if he'd rightly heard that strange word.

"Ho!" Ellison acclaimed with upraised hands.

Then, behind a communal sigh and an ensuing deep and reverential silence, there rolled the opening notes of the next band to play at Woodstock.

"Blood of the Sun," Willow said. Everyone heard their opening scream. "It's Mountain. They're heavy!"

Now, it was Ellison who appeared to weep, though with an utterly joyful countenance. "This is something new in the world," he pronounced, blowing a small pile of Carolina tobacco off the open palm of his hand. "We bear witness to a prophecy of long ages, kept by our desert Brothers, the Record Keepers, the Tohono O'Odham, and coloring the circle for five thousand years! Five thousand years!" he repeated, for effect. "It has finally come to be!" And he was evidently in awe of his own words.

Arien keenly sensed Cypriano's beaming pride, and it centered him fully for the first time since his stunning realization of a certain girl's mysterious identity. He stepped forward from where he'd come to rest after his perambulation, to plant the staff by Oak's brass lamp.

How he marveled at the tangible accumulation of force energizing this thing in his hand! The blatant, eye-popping, sensual power crept up his arm, like a wet glove with an infusion of waves as if from bone-penetrating, concert-speaker sound and it should have been audible. Oh, but it was! He could hear it now! It was a high-pitched tone, very faint, radiating outward in a steady wavelength and was soon heard by everyone as they focused on Arien's evident astonishment. And in the distance was the heavy music of the band, blasting out a deeply serious interpretation of Rock, to mix with this subtle but penetrating, beautiful, soaring, soulful key emanating clearly, but so softly from the center of their circle.

Holding onto the pommel of the staff with both hands now, Arien initiated an OM, taken up by all of the others, in an earnest attempt to match the faint note they could barely hear. He felt his voice blend first with Ellison's and then Andy's, followed gradually by all of the others. It was underlined with a low beat of the big drum the visiting woman had brought. It was a perfect moment!

A fine mist began to fall around everyone. It would have been impossible to tell if it was anywhere else on the site other than here in this place, but it blanketed them in the close darkness as they focused on the note. Arien concentrated fully, with the peculiar clarity of the mythic drug in his system to supplant his earlier experience in waves of colors and their emotional fields, the often fantastic coincidences of life, or the journey of his soul through the city of worldly traps. But its still viable infusion came to a new place, much as a life may reflect upon the bodily-clock and experience-altered perspectives of youth, adulthood, maturity and old age, though compressed within the particular symbology of intense experience! And the notes of the assembled celebrants met above their heads to collide, as it were, in the space over their heads, refracting off the mist and fine droplets of water to reveal a mutually perceptible image!

What is that?

"Check it out!" Kelsey cried.

The image faded as their OM trailed. Oh, but the inspiration was powerful to follow it again with a robust heart-song for the wonder of this thing! The next OM was louder and more sustained, and the edifice was clear and sharp. Arien could barely believe his eyes, compounded with the innate appreciation of shared experience. There was no other way to processes it than accept the illusion, at least, they were inside of a cathedral! But that was only the beginning. In the course of wavering, and catching their breath and going at it again in longer salvos, the master stroke of the phenomenon was for it to reverberate with the echo of their voices!

"We're inside of it!" Tina exclaimed with awe – and everyone heard her words reflected in their surroundings.

"Sacred architecture!" Andy reverently said.

As if welded to the pommel of the Tree Family staff, Arien spun on his feet to drink it in, the magnificent, shimmering rose window and a set of four ancillary lights, the soaring columns, spreading arches high in the dome, the shadowed alcoves and passages of its great hall and naves – it was all about them! As it dissolved with a lessening of volume, what seemed to stick were the lines. They shimmered in fine silvery strands in a majestic lattice of interlacing complexity and how it blended with the fractals of the mind and then their minds together, and how that interlocked with the branches of the trees and the patterns in the skin and the ways of the rivers, streams and capillaries, and faces of the rocks, and spreading branches to the tiny leaves and their veins and on, to the infinitude of the majesty of Creation!

How easy this is! Arien thought, raising the staff like a magister, spreading his arms, understanding full well the irony of his process. What it had taken to get him here had not been easy. He roamed with thoughts appraising people coming together in churches and building a place reflecting and expressing their inner state, with a bottle shy of a six-pack, without a clue of the expanded consciousness that reveals all the most deeply held secrets of the race. My body is a key and it fits this lock perfectly!

But, is there a plan for us? Are we an experiment?

As we are made whole, we are pieces of the whole, the healthy cells of the Living Body, and we are invited to partake in the ongoing process of creation.

Cypriano, you are so wise.

You have drawn it out of me, Little Brother. I thank you for allowing my voice.

"As we are made whole, we are pieces of the whole, the healthy cells of the Living Body, and are invited to take part in the ongoing process of creation." Arien recited. "Cypriano said that."

"Tell that road-runner bird we hear him!" Ellison joyously ordered.

How sweet that was! It made Arien laugh. He clearly understood the balance, the equanimity and proportion necessary to a successful magical experience. If they had been too serious (Heaven forbid!) the vessel would be brittle and could crack! He wasn't getting it out of any book but by the irrefutable test of his own experience and his normal intelligence here engaged with a classic event in expanded consciousness and its enhanced perceptivity. Sure, it was an illusion, but it was a real illusion, easily as real, and likely more real than the illusion of the world as he had experienced it in his normal, waking life!

The next OM was a spontaneous outpouring of wonder and joy. Again, the great cathedral appeared around them. Something invited Arien to drop his eyes from the ceiling, when to his amazement was a most marvelous setting before him. Everyone was there! They stood around what appeared to be a massive slab of marble! It was perfectly round. The colors were clearly laid out, bisected by runners in a cross of deepest purple, and this was equally bisected with another set of runners, indicating the circle's cross-quarters. The cardinal points were faced by the four officiates of each quarter, Black Mother, Red Father, Yellow Son and White Daughter, with each of the four elemental colors, Green, Blue, Red and White rotating away, leftward. Arien's placement was roughly between the cross-quarter point of the Fire Element, the sacred Son, and the cardinal point of Water, which was occupied by the virgin Daughter. He didn't quite get it. For that matter, Tina's placement was about a third of the way around from him. He was thinking it should be either by his side or at least opposite him. He looked at Andy, who soberly returned the stare.

Andy knew. "You mark where we are in the year, Arien, like the sacred kings of ancient times," he explained, his voice echoing down from the gothic ceiling high over their heads.

Ellison began a chant. It was low at first and as everyone listened the image of the magnificent structure around them faded and morphed into sparkling fragments of light in the mist, to reform in delicate silvery threads, to lines and arcs, proscribing an exceedingly complex structural design. It brought an elaborate snowflake to mind; only a three-dimensional version that surrounded everyone in a bubble of fine beams of shimmering light. The light beams brightened as Ellison's chant grew louder. It was even manifested below them! It was all around them! They appeared to be floating in it!

In his memory Arien heard the words of Cypriano, *We have leveraged open the door to the celestial ship of the Gods.*

Where shall we take it?

Arien, do you not remember your 'first lesson', these many weeks gone by?

Arien struggled to imagine what Cypriano was getting at. This was all so much to absorb and understand, much less put to use! But it was the inclination to a 'use' that jogged his memory. "Oh!" Arien cried out to the variously stunned and speechless witnesses. "Some of you may remember, back when we were on the road, I told you something Cypriano said to me, 'The medicine has a purpose and the wise one knows what it is."

"You're way ahead of me, Arien," Otter said.

"We have to learn what this thing can do before we decide what to do with it!" Andy exclaimed.

The delicate structure seemed to absorb their words, spoken within it. The nearest beams glowed, pulsing, and diminishing with an outward wave as if touched by every single syllable, like a light board on a music console, but with a far subtler and responsive interface. It felt so good inside! It was peaceful, protective, loving.

Implications cascaded through Arien's mind as he quickened to the reality of the structure. Surely, it was a fabulous machine! He sensed the others grasped it now, too, and there would be much to ponder, and discuss and attempt to understand.

"Mother and Father of All Things," Andy declared, taking his queue from the energy in the moment, and reciting the words to close the circle,

"We Thank You for the gift of each other and for our Sacred Time together, an Arc of our Covenant, a repository of our Keys of Transformation. May we become a living embodiment of Light and purpose in the darkness of this world, and may our works always have your Blessing!"

Gradually, the shimmering image faded and as it did a brightness began to penetrate into their awareness and the Trees and serendipitous guests were further amazed by the light of day, a humid morning, gray skies and the body-piercing base notes of Jefferson Airplane, *"One pill makes you larger and one pill makes you small and the ones that mother gives you..."*

Making his way back to camp was a strange readjustment. Initially, Arien was pretty 'blissed-out' as the expression would have it. To be sure the feeling was shared and the others clung to him, making it difficult to navigate the trail. He was also tired, hungry, felt a bit grungy and pestered by thoughts of Maggie Austin. Might I have lain with her? Oh my God!

"We were transported to the morning!" Willow exclaimed in his ear.

"It was like that!" Oak agreed nearby.

"Ya have to wonder where else we could have gone." Jeff added.

The urge to find Maggie, to see her again, was overpowering. He would call her name and she would remember him. It was so awesome! They'd connected! They'd really connected! I'll find her!

Thomas pressed in. "Will we do it again?" he asked.

Arien wondered about that question. With Ellison, his eyes on fire, right there it seemed like a no-brainer. "I expect so, yeah," he replied with a dreamy smile, but it was a little beyond where he was at. He was barefoot and had to watch where he stepped. The long hours and peyote trip had taken a good portion of his energy. As with most people here, he was working on the better part of the last forty-eight hours and it exposed his limits. His joints moved with an unaccustomed dryness. He was thirsty. He needed a shower.

We must be a sight, his whole troop of people making their way through littered woods with damp, hanging wood smoke, and folks everywhere rolled up like larvae in blankets and bulky sleeping bags, laying on ponchos and sheets of plastic. There were much more of them than rich kids in vehicles or tents. So many had come unprepared! Arien recalled Tina's definition of a rich hippie and it put a grin over his weariness.

The air was so thick he could almost feel the percussion of conversation in the woods and smell the people there, the oatmeal and wafting Mary Jane and the pond before it came into view and even now, this early in the morning, people were staring at the water or meditating by the shore, but no one was in it. What's with this? In the movie the lake has naked hippies! It had a swampy smell along this section of shore. The bottom looked mucky but the water appeared clear. Later, he thought. It will feel so good!

Arien never intended to stop. Reaching camp, he and Tina went straight for the tent and in the time it took to lay the staff in a corner of the floor, and hang the horn in its velvet bag on the center pole, Tina was sprawled-out on the bedding, fast asleep. "Oh, Babe," he cooed, bending over to kiss her, and that felt so good, and it was even better to snuggle with her for only a moment and, whoops! He was a goner.

The thunder woke him up.
"Oh shit!"
But Tina didn't hear that. He shook her and it was like shaking a talking doll with low batteries. Ripping a leaf of paper from a notepad, Arien scribbled, *I'll check back later got something to tell you so rad you my babe luv you so much Arien.* He set it down next to her, pulled the good Army poncho by the door over his head and stepped barefoot out into the rain.

Arien's nose was assaulted with air saturated in a carnival assortment of odors and muffled sounds. If he could smell bodies in the morning it was a blatant assault in the afternoon, and the wood smoke was steamy and the conversation more subdued as folks everywhere sought vainly for a dry place to be. As he walked ankle-deep in mud, Arien began to feel guilty for the protection of his excellent poncho, though it did feel moist against his bare chest where natural perspiration had no outlet. He was relieved to see a young mommy cradle a child in her arms, uselessly attempting to ward off the wet under a gradually soaking blanket. "Here!" he said, pulling the poncho off to give her. "Keep that baby, dry!"

"Thanks, Brother! It's little help from my friends!" She beamed, allowing Arien to assist her with putting it on.

"Aw, did I miss him?"

"Yeah, sorry," she empathized. "Cocker's set finished in the nick of time, too!"

The rain on his body was a shock. It was chilling, which was likely exaggerated with the abbreviated rest, although he felt awake and energized enough by the reality of this whole crazy thing. Arien resolved not to let sleep overtake him again. No way! Hereafter, he'd run on the molecular residue of the fumes of his last few drops and when that was exhausted he'd chase down some of that "medicine" for Jane or Charley, that was advertised in those public service announcements from the stage between sets.

That brought up an idea; maybe he could get an announcement on the PA!

He took several deep breaths and relaxed into the chill, to be with it. It tickled down his back, seeping inside the hem of his shorts, inviting all of himself to be drenched, like opening the wicket of your goat stockade to the siege of the Mongol army. He glistened back at everyone else around him, and most of them were likewise surrendering to the inevitable, bucking it up and soldiering on.

The air reported with the sputtering sound system admonishing people in the strongest possible terms to get off of the towers or risk electrocution. A vague flag rose up in his mind about this as the sky briefly flashed, throwing a deep rumble in timely support of the warning. Mother Shongo, I'll be fine. I'm here for a reason!

Approaching the broad amphitheater was a hoot, a study in washed-out color and the redoubling of many multiples of stubborn pride and stoic defiance. Nothing, nothing is going to spoil this! Not the rain, or —

"Please! Please get down from the towers!" Please, People, please stay away from the towers!"

God! It's raining cats and dogs!

And then the PA popped, sputtered and said, "Arien? Arien! Would a boy named Arien please come to the south corner of the stage? The girl who danced with you yesterday wants to see you again!"

Oh Jesus! How his heart raced, banging in his chest like a canary whose little cage was tipping off the table. But even in haste, Arien couldn't resist a run at the slide. Awesome! There it was, just like in the movie he'd seen up there in 1988 or '89! And plainly its course was in the right direction! The receiving line of soggy, muddy, giddy kids opened to let him run at it and with flailing legs out front he ripped into the chocolate slurry with a terrific silky-gooey splash. "Yea!" He exulted, flying prone with outstretched arms to land in a dancing ensemble of laughing feet and hands to help him up. Oh! What a rush! How awesome! But, he denied himself another go. Maggie waited. He wouldn't make her wait!

Arien was covered in the stuff. He literally wore glistening, soupy Woodstock all over his body. Would she even recognize him? Oh wow. He turned his face up to the sky so the blessed rain would wash his face.

Some of the drowned kids looked so cold but many wore the enigmatic grin that could have been taken from Mona Lisa, herself. He slid past them with nods, smiles and a toke of somebody's damp, smoldering doobie, and had to squeeze past a soggy sleeping bag with four legs, and a corner of plastic, and he nearly lost footing on a slimy section of cardboard.

Arien, slow down.

Not now, please!

Arien!

No, not now! What's the problem? Maggie's waiting for me! He wondered at this impertinent intrusion. Their connection had never gone that way before! It never required even hearing advice contrary to his needs, and this was a needy thing, like the shining towers of El Dorado would have been, with its flags all snapping in the wind, had Coronado actually laid his eyes on them.

"Cool OM, Man!" A fellow said, pointing at the Sanskrit letter glinting against Arien's streaking mud-splattered chest.

"Thanks, Dude! He hurried around the corner of the stage's ten-foot stockade and no-man's land of pulpy muck and the moving or milling traffic before the packed bowl of souls. There were legions that gladly replaced anyone leaving, to jockey for a closer spot and many more waiting certainly for the downpour to let up and bring back the music. And then Arien saw her! She was looking the other way, maybe mulling over a decision to let him go.

He saw the dark curtain of another heavy wave of rain and the flash in its corona as he broke into a slipping-sliding run.

Arien, Stop!

A man above him warned, "Hey, Man! Not that way!"

"Lalalalalalalalalalalalalala!" He defiantly hollered as his foot hit a hard, round thing like a snake, buried in the mud when the hairs of his body bristled – and he felt every single one of them. And then there was an incredible, ringing white flash, silence, distance, a gray nowhere, and drifting, drifting. A far off light.

Epilogue:

Arien lay exposed in an open space. It was dark and terribly cold. He tried to lift his head but it spun in some incremental proportion to the inches he could raise it, until it whirled like the nexus of awesome forces he had known, only this time his thought and will, thoroughly stunned and disabled, rode the dense, gray hurricane of furious rotation until it crashed him smack into that inner plane. He smelled an odor like ozone; that snap of an electric spark. His ears screeched like locked wheels on steel rails. His stomach heaved.

First, the side of his face and then, as his awareness took stock of this improbability, a forearm, the length of his torso, and then hips and legs sizzled with the stabbing-cold, ice-crusted snow. It was snow! He spastically shivered. A sound emitted from him that was somewhere between a cry and a groan. He drew himself into a ball, focusing with everything he had inside to stay conscious.

Tune in, get connected. He felt himself merge into an infinite emptiness and knew the darkness and apprehended the lay of a glistening rise with the pale glow of outdoor lighting just beyond the crest, a naked woodlot at the border, a wood post-and-rail fence along a road, and on the other side, dim light from the window of a house. Then Arien felt the life in a zigzag-gamboling, close-to-the-snow, sniffing-snuffing, hairy creature, whining as the distance between them closed. And then it was on him, panting and yapping. It licked his ear and wagged its tail excitedly.

With a tremendous effort Arien rocked onto his muddy shorts, taking hold of this big, friendly dog and pulled it to himself, like a drowning man. He hugged it close and it squirmed and panted and licked Arien's nose and lips in a method guaranteed to achieve release. The dog's breath smelled earthy and moist and its clash with air hazed the definition of nostrils, dark, thin lips, pale, rosy tongue and snow-white teeth in a fine, frozen mist.

This timely angel began barking, not at Arien but with him. It was so close to him, so loud, Arien's ears recoiled with a searing ring and he instinctively covered them with his stinging, freezing-wet hands. But the brief shot of insulation, that little bit of body warmth and ebullient doggie had been enough. He could let go and merge with the cold, itself, and let his consciousness fade fearlessly into the dynamic solidity of the landscape.

When Arien next awoke it was in somebody's bed. He felt comfortable and clean in full-length pajamas and soft blankets pressing over him. He knew it wasn't a hospital. It was too quiet and dark, with barely enough light to see. The muffled sound of icy pings and shifting air pressure against the storm window drew his attention to the outside twilight. The sides of the outer window frame were rounded, crystalline-white. This isn't August! It's way too cold. This isn't Woodstock!

A horrible, desperate feeling came over him. "Mother and Father of All Things," he keened aloud. His anguished voice filled the room and then died as gust-driven, icy snow-pellets pattered like grains of sand against the glass. But then Arien heard steps and a shuffle from the doorway. It opened with a wedge of brighter light from the hall to frame the silhouette of a man – a stooped, humble old man.

He was mostly bald, with thinning gray hair clinging to the sides of his head. His eyes were sharp. They looked familiar. Who is this dude? Where have I seen those eyes? Jesus! Tears ran down the aged, topographic face!

"Arien, Arien!" the old man cried. He came over and sat on the side of the bed as Arien sat up, scooting away against the backboard. "What a marvelous thing! Oh my God, you're so beautiful! You're still the same, you are still the same!"

Now Arien started to cry. "Oh shit!" He sobbed. "Where's Tina?"

"I'm so sorry, Arien. She couldn't wait."

As the enormity of his loss took hold, Arien was emotionally catapulted to the deepest hollow of lonely places known to our species and only the hand of the old man over his and a chant, distant at first, but then nearer and dearer, kept him from being swept away in the cascading implosion of grief, utter despair and bereft desolation.

"Ohhhhhhhmmmmmmm. Ohhhmm, Shri Ram, jai Ram! Jai jai Ram! Ohhhmm, Shri Ram, jai Ram! Jai jai Ram!"

"Ohhhhhhh," Arien sighed, feeling the most tenuous thread dangle from the opening to the pit so far above him. His bitterness tainted in whimsy, "I have a Brother who could be my grandfather," he said. Tell me, Andy, when is this?"

"It's December, twenty-twelve, Arien. You're just in time."

www.ingramcontent.com/pod-product-compliance
Lightning Source LLC
Chambersburg PA
CBHW051443260626

47162CB00001B/231